AF588368

ALL THE LIVES SHE LIVED

Nathalie Abi-Ezzi

THE BOOK SOCIAL

The Book Social, 51 Gower Street, London, WC1E 6HJ
info@legendtimesgroup.co.uk | www.thebooksocial.co.uk

Contents © Nathalie Abi-Ezzi 2026
The right of the above author to be identified as the author of this work has been asserted in accordance with the Copyright, Designs and Patents Act 1988. British Library Cataloguing in Publication Data available.

Print ISBN 978-1-91829-1-841
Ebook ISBN 978-1-91829-1-858
Set in Times.
Cover design by Dania K – cestdania.com

All characters, other than those clearly in the public domain, and place names, other than those well-established such as towns and cities, are fictitious and any resemblance is purely coincidental.

All rights reserved. No part of this publication may be reproduced, stored in or introduced into a retrieval system, or transmitted, in any form, or by any means electronic, mechanical, photocopying, recording or otherwise, without the prior permission of the publisher. Any person who commits any unauthorised act in relation to this publication may be liable to criminal prosecution and civil claims for damages.

‘Immensely enjoyable and beautifully written, *All the Lives She Lived* is a fascinating evocation of a woman’s experience in two very different places, and shot through with the tensions of trying to come to terms with the ever-present past that we carry with us, no matter how far we travel.’

Elisabeth Gifford, author of *The Mischief Makers*

‘An atmospheric and affecting novel, beautifully capturing the constraint, repression and dreams of possibility facing Doris in her life in England and then in Baghdad.’

Jane Johnson, author of *Secrets of the Bees*

‘*All the Lives She Lived* paints a vibrant picture of how we misunderstand ourselves and others, and how good intentions can lead us in the wrong direction. Gorgeously immersive and richly detailed, with characters you can root for and despair over all at once.’

Gráinne Murphy, author of *Greener*

‘Tender, moving, and at times shocking, this book is a masterclass on family and the importance of love. It gripped me immediately and refused to let go until I’d devoured every last page.’

Awais Khan, author of *No Honour*

‘Richly atmospheric and emotionally resonant, *All the Lives She Lived* is a compelling novel about identity, belonging and the many selves we carry through life. Nathalie Abi-Ezzi writes with grace, insight and compassion, creating an unforgettable heroine whose story lingers long after the final page.’

Kevin McManus, author of *The Light at Evening*

Nathalie Abi-Ezzi was born and grew up in Lebanon during the civil war. She moved to London, where she completed her PhD and began to write fiction. She is the author of two novels, *A Girl Made of Dust* and *Paper Sparrows*, as well as a collection of poetry, *Needle Around Her Neck*. Her work has been recognised by the LiBeraturpreis, the Desmond Elliot Prize, the Waverton Good Read Award, the Author's Club Best First Novel Award, and the IMPAC Dublin Award.

For my siblings.

ALL THE LIVES SHE LIVED

CHAPTER 1

Better Cloth

Harborne, 1938

'Be out, be out, please be out.' Doris inches the key into the lock. In the hall she slips off her wet things and creeps into the kitchen in stockinged feet.

But upstairs, a floorboard creaks. Nan has spent the better part of the last fortnight lying down with the curtains closed and a damp cloth across her forehead. When she does emerge, it's only to do essential chores and mutter darkly to herself; or, if she crosses paths with Doris, to stop and heave a long, aggrieved sigh.

Well, Doris certainly won't go upstairs yet. She hefts the basket onto the table. Although the packages are nastily damp, she'll unpack the shopping instead of leaving it for Nan the way she usually does. After all, Nan will need to be sweetened up by Saturday.

Rain streams down the window, making the room wobble and waver. The marrowbone's soggy in its wrapper, but Doris will never have to handle one again, nor hear that stupid bell jangle above the butcher's door. Earlier, she walked down the north side of Harborne High Street as far as Serpentine Road, then came back along the south side past the bakers and ironmongers, the post office and the Green Man pub – her farewell to Harborne, even if Harborne was too stupid to notice. As she received her change at the greengrocers, she bestowed her kindest smile on Mr Briggs, in spite of the fact that he's a perfect fool to be stuck there among carrots and potatoes for the rest of his days.

Now there's only one thing left in the bottom of the basket: a brown paper parcel. Her parcel. Beneath the outer wrapping is a layer of tissue paper, and beneath that are two chemises, one pink and the other mint green; shiny, slippery things that she grows warm just thinking about. Miss Ibbs sold them to her. Miss Ibbs who was once engaged to a boy who never made it back from the Great War and has become as fat and dowdy as you like. Doris swears that no matter what happens, she'll never let herself go like that. Nor will she waste her life serving people in a shop. She's cut from better cloth than that!

Miss Ibbs explained that even though the chemises are made of artificial silk, they're still good quality. 'Good' doesn't mean genuine, of course, but as far as Doris is concerned, the fabric looks and feels just like real silk, so is practically the same thing.

It's still raining. In the garden, dandelions have forced their way out of cracks in the paving and sprung up here and there in the grass. Summer has arrived so slyly that Doris hasn't noticed, but then again she's had more important matters on her mind.

The house has fallen silent, and holding the parcel to her chest, she tiptoes up the staircase. Nan must be resting again so there'll be no need to lie about what she's bought herself. But at the top of the stairs she stops.

'What are *you* smiling about?' Nan's standing by the open trunk in Doris' room.

Doris hadn't realised she *was* smiling. 'Nothing.' The truth is she was thinking about Leon. He's taken up residence in her head, where he pops up along with almost every other thought she has. Leon who's more handsome than any other man in Harborne. She crosses the landing, moving the parcel to her other hand, out of Nan's eyeline. 'I did the shopping,' she says, but Nan doesn't bat an eyelid. 'And I put it all away.'

Is she even listening?

'I could clean the kitchen later too if you like.'

Nan swallows audibly, then turns back to the trunk. 'I don't suppose the crockery'll make it there in one piece.' She has gifted Doris the good china that was passed down to Nan by her mother.

'Oh, it will, I'm sure it will. I've wrapped it in tea towels, and blankets as well, see, to be on the safe side.' The trunk's going to be collected tomorrow and shipped ahead, but Doris has the feeling she's forgotten something. Her summer and winter clothes are packed, and a sketchpad, her box of paints and a few packets of flower seeds, but that can't possibly be all she'll need.

'You've got enough linen at any rate,' says Nan, who doesn't know what things will be available in such a godforsaken place and so has packed enough bedclothes, tablecloths and tea towels for a family of six.

'Yes. Thank you.'

Doris goes to the wardrobe, but Nan has spotted the parcel. 'What have you got there?'

How scandalised she'd be if she found out! 'Oh, just some new stockings.'

With no reason to disbelieve her, Nan returns to her previous train of thought. 'What sort of food do they have there anyway?'

'I'm not sure.'

'Why, doesn't he tell you things like that?'

Doris laughs. 'That's not the sort of thing we talk about, is it? Food. He's a university graduate.'

'So? Doesn't his sort still need to eat?'

Doris starts to say something back then stops. She mustn't argue. Instead she opens the wardrobe. Only one thing is hanging there: the dress she'll wear this Saturday, an eau-de-Nil satin-silk that cost her a fortune even in the sale. She lays her parcel gently on the wardrobe floor.

'Do they have eggs?' asks Nan. 'Are there chickens out there? And what about milk? Will there be bread?'

Doris slams the wardrobe door shut, setting all the empty hangers clinking and clanking.

'My poor head!' Nan puts her hands to her temples.

'It's a perfectly civilised country, I've told you already.'

Silence.

'It is. It's looked up to by its neighbours; people travel there from all over.' This is one of the things Leon has told her, but she hopes Nan won't ask for details. 'They've probably got nicer things to eat than we have.' Remembering Saturday, she lightens her tone. 'And you're not putting eggs in with my clothes!'

But Nan doesn't smile.

Butter her up. Smooth the way. 'Not that I'll be unpacking any of this. His family's got servants, you know.'

Nan's ears prick up. 'Servants?'

'That's right.'

'Oh.' Nan looks impressed. 'Oh, do they.' She was once in service herself, a parlourmaid in a fancy house where she met Grandad, who was a coachman. 'You never told me that.'

'Well, they do.'

They stand gazing into the trunk as though it were an open pit. 'It'll be the high life for you then,' says Nan. The engagement's been a sore point from the very start, and the cause of long, deafening silences between them. A few weeks ago, Nan placed a jar of dried flowers (zinnias, love-in-a-mist, larkspur, lavender, all blooms robust enough to survive drying) in Doris' room, but now Doris notices that the jar has been moved to the windowsill on the landing. Another of Nan's ways of punishing her, of trying to make her feel guilty when it's Nan herself who ought to feel guilty, for God's sake!

But never mind about that. All Doris has to worry about now is Nan not making a scene in front of Leon. 'When Leon comes over... that is, when he comes to pick me up...'

Nan presses her lips into a line and starts to take deep breaths, like a volcano about to erupt. Which it does. She hurries over and takes hold of Doris' arm. 'You're making a mistake, love. You can still call it off, it's not too late.'

Doris' first instinct is to give in and wipe the slate clean. Perhaps then things can go back to the way they once were between the two of them – not loving exactly, but with pockets of tenderness – back when she was a little girl. But the temptation lasts no longer than a second. She shakes Nan off. 'Don't be absurd, I don't *want* to call it off. Why should I?'

'But you can't marry him! For heaven's sake, Dot, not a man like him!'

She knows exactly what Nan means by that. A foreigner, and not one from Europe either, which would be bad enough. But she couldn't care less because soon she'll be beyond Nan's control. She's sick to death of recriminations, of Harborne and 45 Nursery Road. Of the narrowness of her bed, the narrowness of her life.

'You have to promise me one thing,' she says. 'On Saturday, promise not to say anything.'

A line appears between Nan's eyebrows. 'What on earth do you mean?'

Must she spell it out? 'I don't want you saying anything… you know, about *them*.'

Thoughts flit behind Nan's face, then settle. Her forehead smooths out. 'I see. It's like that, is it.'

'No. I'll tell him in my own good time, that's all.' A plain, fat lie.

'I see.'

Doris has one more weapon. 'So if you want to see me again, you won't bring it up.'

Nan bends, apparently to tuck a stray corner of tablecloth into the trunk, although Doris suspects it's really to hide her face. 'All right, I won't say a word. Not a word unless I'm spoken to. Does that suit you?'

Doris' shoulders relax. Yes, that suits her just fine. So long as nothing spoils the day. 'Thank you.' She thinks of the faux silk chemises wrapped up and waiting in the wardrobe, bright and unspoiled beneath their tissue paper. Her new life waiting. Because no matter what Nan might think, she and Leon are going to be the happiest people on earth.

CHAPTER 2
Saturday

Harborne, 1938

It's Saturday. *The* Saturday. She wakes up and realises that this will be the last time she wakes here. Already her bedroom has an abandoned, hollow look about it. Her trunk was roped up and sent off days ago; now only two suitcases are left, brand new and rather small, but packed and ready, the labels neatly written out and tied to the handles with string.

It's like a fairytale (apart from using the outside privy, which is as needs must) and as she dresses, her thoughts flutter, unable to settle. Who is she going to become? Once she's on the other side of married, and thousands of miles away from here, who will she be then? Somehow she can't quite imagine it.

On the landing, the door to Harry's room is, as usual these days, closed. But Doris knows exactly what she'd find if she opened it. The same maps on the wall, the same pile of books on his desk, the pebbles and pens and pencils. Under the bed, a box of Meccano and another of the comics he read as a boy; on the shelf an empty bird's egg he found and some small animal's skull. She has no intention of opening the door to Harry's room though. That door will remain firmly closed.

What, she wonders, will become of her own room once she's gone? Will it become a shrine or will Nan just use it as a place to store apples and empty jars?

Nan has made Doris her favourite breakfast of coddled

eggs, but Doris is too unsettled to eat, and besides, she doesn't want to risk dripping egg onto her new dress. Nan bit her lip when she first saw the gleaming, fluid fabric cut in at the waist then flaring out at the hem, but she's given up saying anything.

Just before ten o'clock, Leon arrives in a taxicab that's going to take them to Birmingham New Street station. Wearing a new suit and tie, and with shoes that have been polished to a shine, he looks neat as a pin. He's freshly shaven, and comb-trails are visible in his thick black hair. If only he wasn't fidgeting. It makes him look nervous, like a man having second thoughts, which is simply not the case.

He carries her bags downstairs and to the taxi. Then he, Doris and Nan stand in an awkward grouping in the tiny front garden.

'Well,' Nan says, 'one can only hope things will turn out well.' She's standing on the step, as though barring Doris from ever re-entering.

'They will,' says Doris.

Nan is most decidedly not a weeper, but now tears start to slide down her cheeks as though she's sprung a leak. 'You're never going to come back, are you?'

Although Doris doesn't cry, she's aware of a pain pressed down deep in her belly. 'Of course I am.' How silly Nan is being, how unreasonable.

'I almost forgot.' Nan goes inside and reappears with a round tin which she presses into Doris' hands. 'It's a bit of wedding cake for you.'

The tin is heavy and cold in Doris' hands. 'Oh, Nan.' The pressed-down pain threatens to bob up. She reaches an arm around Nan to hug her goodbye, but the uncharacteristic gesture is so awkward that she draws back again.

Leon steps forward. He hems a little, opening and closing his hands. 'Goodbye, Mrs Linnet.' And he leans forward and gives Nan a quick peck on the cheek.

'You'll look after her, won't you. Out there.' Nan trails off, unable to countenance what being 'out there' might entail.

'I will. I promise.'

The words, pre-empting what he'll say later today, bring the blood crashing to Doris' cheeks, and like a pendulum, her love for Nan swings over to him, a feeling so enormous it almost knocks her off her feet.

Leon is stuck for what more to say to Nan. They've only met once before, after all. Briefly, awkwardly. 'You have been very kind,' he says – which is carrying things a bit far, Doris thinks.

'Yes, well I'm sure you know what you're doing,' says Nan. Doris had pleaded with her to be civil ('pretend if you have to, I don't care') and not to talk about anything other than the day. Leon too has his instructions.

'Well,' says Doris, 'the taxicab's waiting and we don't want to miss our train.' Because it's not inconceivable that Nan will blurt out the whole story just to be spiteful.

Nan comes down off the step, and suddenly she seems small and old, just one of those women who end up living on their own. 'Goodbye then,' she says in a strangled voice.

Leon doesn't like this goodbye. He feels guilty, Doris can tell, for taking her away from her home. 'It will be difficult,' he says to Nan. 'Of course it will be difficult for Dolores to be so far away from you.'

Nan's entire body flinches. She backs away, hitting her heel on the step.

Oh God, he forgot! Doris reminded him but he went and forgot!

Nan swings round to Doris, and a cloud passes over her face. 'Dolores?'

Leon looks stricken. Doris lays a hand on his arm. 'Darling, would you be a dear and take this to the taxi?' She hands him the cake tin. 'I'll be right there.'

'Of course.' He clears his throat. 'Goodbye again.'

Doris watches him go to the taxi. When she turns back, Nan's eyes have hardened. '*Dolores?*' She shakes her head. 'Oh, Dot, how could you?'

'What does it matter? It's just a name.'

Nan raises trembling fingers to her forehead. 'How could you be so… so *wicked*?'

Something flares inside Doris. 'Don't ever call me that again!'

Nan lowers her hand, startled at this outburst.

There's a tapping coming from the back garden: a song thrush smashing a snail against a paving stone, again and again. 'Well, we'd better be off.'

'Yes. Yes perhaps it's for the best after all.'

Her grandmother's tears and objections were one thing, but this cuts deep. A curtain next door twitches as Doris turns away. Waiting for her beside the Austin cab, Leon looks nervous and devastated at the same time. He opens the door for her to get in then gets in himself. Across the road, two faces are watching from an upstairs window. Let them. Let everybody see her go.

The engine starts and the taxi pulls away. Doris doesn't look back.

'I am sorry,' says Leon. 'I forgot.'

'That's all right,' she says, although her insides are wound tight.

'Why did she get so upset?'

'I told you, she doesn't like me using that name, don't ask me why. There's a batty old woman for you.' She leans over to kiss him and stop any more questions.

New Street Station is vast and full of noise and people. Whistles are blowing and doors are being slammed. There are men in trilbies, women in toques, station masters in pillbox hats and trolley-boys in caps. On the platforms, trains hunker and grumble like monsters, spewing out so much steam that the black metal framework holding up the vaulted roof is nearly obscured.

Soon they're on the train, and with a screech it lurches forward, stutters, lurches again and they're on their way. The rest of the day (this momentous day, every second of which ought to be seared into Doris' memory) passes in a blur. She and Leon sit side by side with her hand in his as the miles stream past. Then they're at King's Cross station, where Leon buys an overpriced bouquet of flowers for her and a single pink rose for his buttonhole before another taxicab carries them to a small chapel.

Harry is waiting outside, terrifically handsome in a navy three-piece suit, with a carnation buttonhole and the biggest smile she's seen in a long time. She hugs him so tight she thinks it might leave marks.

'You look radiant,' he says.

She introduces Leon and he and Harry shake hands.

'You're a lucky man,' says Harry, and she could kiss him for saying it.

Inside, they're greeted by a vicar with a drawl and a double chin. 'No other family?' he asks, glancing behind them.

'No.' Doris puts her arm through Leon's. 'It's just us.' And Leon gets that look on his face again that says *How terrible that you have no father to give you away, no mother to weep happy tears. How terrible*. But he's already sent their details ahead, and almost before she can draw breath, it seems, they're saying their vows, a few flimsy words that will turn the tide of their lives in a different direction. A ring is put on her finger, and she is his, but more importantly he is hers, officially and forever.

During the short ceremony, Harry has been standing off to one side, but when she meets his eye, he looks pale. She goes and puts her arms around him.

'Her name,' he says in her ear. 'Her name.'

'Yes. But so what?' she whispers. 'It's not as if she needs it any longer.'

After that Harry is quiet.

In the vestry, Harry and the sexton sign their names as witnesses into the marriage register. Then the vicar copies down the details from her and Leon's passports.

'Wait.' Doris puts out a hand. 'That's a seven, not a one.'

The vicar's finger hovers above the page. 'Pardon me?'

'That says seven. My date of birth. Nineteen *seventeen*, not nineteen eleven.'

'Darling,' says Harry, but she ignores him.

Adjusting his glasses, the vicar looks again at the passport. Sure enough there's a stroke at the top of all the handwritten ones, which she's extended on the last so that it makes it look more like a seven.

'I should know when I was born!' she laughs.

'Yes. Yes of course.' Looking again, he finds that the one must indeed be a seven and amends it in the register. Harry looks shocked but they don't notice. Leon signs, then she does, and finally the vicar, and there it is, one more lie set down forever in a legal document. Well, she thinks, in for a penny, in for a pound.

After the ceremony they only stop long enough for a cup of coffee and a sandwich with Harry in a fancy tea shop, the conversation stilted between the three of them, before it's goodbye.

'When will I see you again?' Harry asks.

'I don't know,' she says. 'Soon, I hope. Very soon.'

It's difficult, almost impossible, to loosen her hold on Harry's hand. Then it's another cab to Victoria Station, where men are heaving sacks of mail onto the boat train, and she and Leon climb aboard. Once they've crossed the Channel, they'll travel across Europe by train, passing through Paris, Lausanne, Milan, Venice and Trieste (they'll avoid Germany, of course, and the newly annexed Austria), then on to Belgrade and Sofia. After arriving in Istanbul, they'll cross the Bosphorus and continue on the *Taurus Express* to Ankara, Aleppo and finally Baghdad. And there her new life will begin.

CHAPTER 3

Practically the Same Thing

London to Baghdad, 1938

The train is large and rattling, and the scream of the whistle keeps startling her. They have a Wagons-Lits compartment with seating that changes into beds for the night – beds made up with starched white sheets, pillows and blankets. There's a tiny sink too, but down the corridor is a bathroom with a toilet and a larger sink, as well as a dirty-looking bar of soap she knows she won't want to touch.

Leon takes off his hat and jacket. As he helps her off with her coat, she gets a waft of his cologne and is aware all over again of his physical presence.

'Thank you, darling.' She starts to take off her hat, a small-crowned cream affair with a net veil that comes down as far as her nose for that added touch of mystery, but the elastic band securing the hat to her head has caught in her hair.

'Let me help you.' Leon tries to ease the hat off.

'No, stop that!' Her hair's snagged, and his tugging is going to pull it out – pull out her hair that's too fine and thin as it is. 'I mean, I'll do it.'

But it's too late. Leon has already stepped back, hands held up the way men do in gangster films when there's a gun pointing at them.

She untangles her hair from the stupid hat. 'Don't look at me like that. My hair was caught and…' She tosses the hat onto the seat. 'I'm just tired, that's all.'

He lowers his hands. 'I did not mean to hurt you.'

'I know that.' She looks around for some distraction. Pinned to the wall behind the sink is a sign – *sous le lavabo se trouve une vase* – while under the sink is something that looks like a gravy boat. 'What's that? Ooh, are they going to bring us flowers?' Flowers because they're a newlywed couple. She smiles, charmed, but Leon titters.

'What is it?'

The titter turns into full-blown laughter.

'What? Did I say something wrong?'

But he can't stop. His face has turned red and tears are glinting in the corners of his eyes.

'Leon, for goodness' sake.' She's starting to feel irritated. He's laughing at her, or at least at her expense.

'Sorry.' He tries to stop. 'But it is… not a vase.'

She looks again at the sign. 'But that's what it says.' She may not understand French like him but she can certainly make out that one word.

He bursts into laughter again, and suddenly she dislikes him, because her ignorance has made her the butt of some unknown joke.

At last he stops laughing and wipes his eyes. 'It is for a toilet.'

'What?' She looks at the gravy boat. 'What on earth do you mean?' She points at the sign. 'But it says vase.'

'Yes, but it means bowl. They are suggesting that we can urinate in it.'

'No!' Not here, not in England. Although it is a French train, so anything's possible. 'I ask you!' She looks again at the gravy boat. 'Well, you're not going to catch me peeing in that!'

Leon laughs again, and this time so does she, even though that awful feeling hasn't yet entirely dissipated.

'I'm going to learn French one day, you know.' She likes the easy, well-oiled sound of French, and she will learn it one day; as she would have done already if they'd bothered teaching it at school instead of forcing her to do Domestic Science, which she'd paid no attention to.

Leon goes off to find out what time dinner is, because further down the train is a dining pullman with tablecloths and waiters ready to serve them dinner, and then tomorrow morning, breakfast. Sitting on the bed, she picks up Leon's newspaper and glances through the headlines. Britain has set a new world record for the fastest steam train at 126 miles per hour. There's more violence in Palestine, but H.M.S. *Emerald* has been sent to Haifa, and a third battalion of British troops is being dispatched from Egypt.

She turns the page. Something about Mussolini and wheat. She turns over again. There. Norma Shearer's starring in a new film called *Marie Antoinette*, and will have wonderful hair and even more wonderful dresses.

'Trouble,' Leon says when he returns.

She looks up, panicked. 'What trouble?'

He jerks his chin at the newspaper. 'Hitler.'

'Oh, him.'

'He has started to make trouble in Sudetenland now.'

She's not sure where that is but she's not about to say so. 'Oh, they'll sort him out.'

'Who will?'

'Why us of course. Great Britain.'

He sits beside her. 'Your Prime Minister does not want war. It is too risky.'

She closes the paper, folds it in half and puts it on the tiny corner table. 'Are you saying we wouldn't win?'

'I am only saying he does not want war.'

'But surely you don't think we'd lose.'

Leon shakes his head. 'I don't know.'

'Good lord!' She lets out a surprised laugh. She's appalled at his lack of faith, but then again he's not English. There at least she has the upper hand; which puts her in a good mood again. 'Let's not talk about that, darling. Not today.'

He smiles. 'You are right.' He checks his watch. 'We should go and have dinner.'

'I don't want dinner.' Earlier, she'd noticed a pretty woman getting on the train, and she doesn't want Leon's attention anywhere but on herself.

'You are not hungry?'

'Not especially, are you? We could just have some cake.'

'All right.'

'You don't mind?'

'Whatever you want, my darling.'

Whatever you want. How lucky she is.

Wrapped in wax paper and nestled inside the tin Nan gave her is a rich fruitcake. It conjures up Nan's teary face again, and that awkward embrace with the cake tin hard and unyielding between them, but she brushes the memory aside.

They don't have a knife, so she and Leon break off pieces and try not to make too much of a mess as they eat. When they're done, she stands to brush the crumbs off her dress and he catches her as the train veers round a bend. How she loves it when they touch – when their arms brush or they hold hands; when they have their arms around one another. Kissing him, as she's doing now, gives her goosepimples.

But today kissing is not enough. She wants to see his naked chest, wants to run her hands along his bare shoulders and get to know his body the way she knows her own. They've only had sex once, and it's been a long wait since then.

She kisses him with more purpose but his body tenses. 'Not here,' he mumbles as she presses her lips against his. 'Not on the train.'

She doesn't stop. 'Whyever not?'

'There are… other people… Someone might… come in.'

But she won't let him pull away. *Do* the guards have a pass key? *Would* they just barge in if they wanted to? 'I don't care.' She's waited long enough.

It arrives in her brain with a sudden clarity. Why it should, God only knows, yet it does: that if Dolores were here in her place, *she* wouldn't continue. In order to make Leon happy, *she'd* put aside her own desires, and the two of them would sit and hold hands like a pair of nitwits.

But pooh to what Dolores would have done! Doris starts to unbutton Leon's shirt. He's looking at her, at her eyes and lips. There was a time she used to mind her eyes being so large, with the whites showing beneath the pupils, but Bette Davis has eyes just like it and she's famous, so now Doris uses eyeliner to make her eyes look even bigger.

With his shirt off, Leon smells different, muskier, and she can see muscle running beneath the skin of his arms and shoulders. She's suddenly aware of the new chemise she's wearing (the mint green one, to match her dress). Will Leon notice that it's not made of real silk? Will he realise that this isn't the genuine thing?

The train lurches again and for an instant, with her new husband half naked in front of her and the walls hemming them in, she's scared – of him, of herself and their future – but as quickly as it arrived, the feeling passes. 'I love you,' she says, and she does.

'I love you too.'

She'll never tire of hearing those words. Outside, the world whooshes past, the old speeding away and the new rushing towards them. She recalls a brief conversation with her friend Gladys about sex. Gladys said it turned her stomach to have to do it with her boyfriend, but there was no avoiding it if she wanted to keep him. Leon's shoulders are warm and slightly damp, and Doris' insides flutter, but not at all in the way Gladys meant when she said stomach-churning.

She and Leon lie down. One minute she's above him looking down and then he's above her looking down. Her heart floats up to the ceiling then plummets down to the tracks. Pleasure suffuses her body until it becomes a new place, in the same way that a twig in full leaf is not the same thing as a twig in wintertime. Leon is making soft, deep noises, and now this compartment may as well be the entire universe, with the sun rising over the door handle and setting behind the sink, because everything she wants is here.

Afterwards they eat more cake, then make love again. And with each passing mile of trees, fields and downs, she leaves Doris Palmer further and further behind.

At Dover the train goes onto a large boat with railtracks in it, and from the window she watches men in boilersuits and heavy boots secure the carriages with chains before they sail. The following morning the carriages, like a toy trainset, are jolted off the boat and onto land again.

She hears French being spoken, then Italian, and marvels at the new styles of skirts and shoes, the hats worn straight or tilted at an angle, and trimmed with feathers and ribbons, with lace and bits of fluff.

It grows warmer. The air changes, and the plants, the birds. They stop at countless hotels where pageboys scamper about the place with luggage, and where there are lifts with gates that are pulled open and shut by yet more boys in caps and jackets. Among the English travellers the discussion is about the royal family, and there's talk of Hitler and Mussolini. The papers are full of it too. There are articles about the growing restrictions on Jews in Germany, who now have to report to the police to be given identification cards; about the Manifesto of Race that's just been published in Italy, and the conference in Évian-les-Bains that's ended in a stalemate because no country in Europe is willing to accept Jewish refugees. This is what she can't help picking up, but she quickly turns to the gossip pages instead to read about the rumours of an affair between Joan Crawford and Clark Gable, and to look at photos of the ticker tape parade for Howard Hughes, who has flown around the world in just three days.

She and Leon discuss how they're going to arrive in Baghdad; how she's going to meet his mother, and what a wonderful woman his mother is. But she's not sure about mothers, knows little about them.

'How long will we be staying with her?'

'Not long.'

'Yes, but how long?' The last thing she wants is to have to share him with another woman already.

'Maybe a couple of weeks. Until we can find a house of our own.'

'I hope she'll like me.'

'She will love you.' He kisses her temple, her eyebrow, the tip of her nose. And she waits for the night, when they can be properly alone in their hotel room again and undress each other piece by piece, removing one item of clothing after another until there's nothing left to be shed.

Later he'll smooth her hair back off her face and she'll go to sleep holding his hand, and wake up the next morning still holding onto it. Then she'll stand in front of the bathroom mirror with her makeup lined up on the shelf and put herself back together again, tracing eyeliner, rubbing on rouge and dabbing everything over with powder, ready for another glorious day spent in the gap between two places – neither England nor Iraq, single or married, girlfriend or wife. Not yet.

Clouds disappear. The sky grows wide and hot, and they arrive in Iraq. Here, almost all the men are as dark as Leon, and many of them darker, but none of them are as handsome. Because the railway line hasn't yet been completed, they must travel the last leg to Baghdad by car. Their driver, like everyone else they've met this last week, looks at her but talks to Leon.

She knew there would be desert. She knew it, and yet now, faced with the reality, she's entirely unprepared. Its endless nothingness terrifies her. They drive on and on with nothing visible behind them and nothing visible ahead, their driver singing to himself in Arabic and the car blowing up clouds of sand. They drape towels over the windows to keep out the sun. She has never known such heat.

On her knees she holds a map open and tries to locate

where they are, but it's impossible because apart from a single black line going straight across it, that part of the paper is entirely blank.

'What's that?' she asks Leon, pointing to the thick line.

'The petroleum pipeline.'

'What do you mean?' She looks out of the window. 'Where is it?'

'Under the sand.' He explains it to her: how after the Great War, France and Britain divided up the Ottoman Empire between them. 'They were thinking of oil,' he says. 'Britain received Iraq, and even though the rest of Palestine was under international control, they also got the port of Haifa. Now petroleum travels through the pipeline from the oil fields of Mosul and Kirkuk all the way to Haifa. In Haifa it is loaded onto ships and taken to Britain.'

'What, all of it?' She's shocked. 'All the oil?'

'No. The rest goes to Lebanon, which is under French mandate, and is put onto French ships. And now the Americans also have a quarter share.' Sand whirls up around the car. 'Each year, they pump four million tonnes of oil through the pipeline. Can you imagine this?'

No, she cannot imagine such a quantity.

'And do you know what Iraq gets out of this arrangement?'

'What?'

'Nothing.'

Even though it's not her doing, she feels guilty and turns to gaze out of the window, wishing she'd never asked.

A few times, like ships passing at sea, they encounter rundown-looking cars and lorries, and vans full of robed pilgrims on their way to Mecca. That's what Leon tells her at any rate. He points out a caravan of camels and Bedouins of the Ruwallah tribe, whoever they are, and a shimmering mirage that looks for all the world like a lake in the middle of the dusty flatness. She flaps her shirt collar for air, undoes another button and peels her back away from the seat. So hot.

So very, very hot. Leon tells her that this is where the Garden of Eden was thought to be.

'Eden!' She can't help laughing at the lunacy of such a notion.

The sun moves round behind them and she covers her head with a scarf. Leon presses a folded handkerchief to his forehead, then returns it to his breast pocket. His face is moist with sweat but he doesn't seem to mind. Then, finally, they cross the Euphrates River at Fallujah and spot the glint of the Tigris in the distance, and the forest of palms and minarets of the city on its banks.

Baghdad's skyline is strange with bulbous-domed mosques, and her heart quickens as they drive into the city. She senses a tightening of expectation in Leon too. To her there's nothing to identify one street from another, yet for him there must be that inexplicable feeling of drawing close to your beginnings, of knowing that soon you'll open one particular door and step inside a space that remembers you.

He points. 'I fell there once when I was a boy and cut my leg. But that— ' He turns to look at something that's already gone by. 'That was not here before.' Why does it surprise her that he should know this place? Yet it does. Until now, she hadn't truly comprehended that he has lived his entire life elsewhere. Then, as they turn a corner, he reaches over and grips her hand. 'We are nearly home.'

CHAPTER 4

Awd Goggie

Harborne, 1917

Jump! – one foot, two feet, one foot, two – on the hopscotch squares chalked onto the pavement. The elm tree has shed a pile of bronze leaves crisp as ginger biscuits, and when Doris gets to ten, she will win them all. Riches. A treasure beyond all imagining.

Turning around, she begins to jump back, trying to think of one of the hopscotch songs they sing at school, but all she can hear is

Doris Palmer! Doris Palmer!

Got no mother and got no father!

Settled on the low stone wall, Stanley watches her out of his green cat eyes as though he knows exactly what a bad one she is.

'Hasn't anyone ever told you it's rude to stare?' She picks up the stone and takes aim, then sees Nan coming down the road.

'Hello, love. Where's Harry?'

It's Saturday so Harry's gone to play with the Bartletts. When Doris says so, Nan grunts. Nan thinks the Bartletts are common as muck.

Tucking her stone into a nook at the foot of the elm, Doris follows Nan inside. 'Can I have something to eat?'

'You can wait till lunch.'

'But I'm hungry.'

'You'll ruin your appetite.'

She trails Nan into the kitchen. 'Just some bread and butter. Pleeease?'

'You shouldn't eat between meals,' says Nan, but cuts her a slice of bread anyway and applies a scrape of margarine.

'Can I have some sugar on it?'

'Sugar!' Nan gives her a look. Just like butter, sugar is scarcer than it was before the war. 'You're perfectly spoiled, Doris Palmer, that's what you are.' But Nan goes ahead and sprinkles some sugar onto the bread. 'Just a little to sweeten your chops. Now sit yourself down.'

She does. 'How's Mrs Hobbs?'

Mrs Hobbs has just had a baby, and Nan's taken some things over. 'Fine. The baby's fine too. Pretty little thing. Mind you, I don't know what she's thinking having another. That husband of hers ought to let her alone, that's what,' she adds in a low voice.

Doris takes another bite of her sugared bread. 'Nan?'

'Don't speak with your mouth full.'

Doris chews, swallows. 'Nan?'

'Yes.'

It's only because Nan has her back turned that Doris feels able to say it. 'Tell me again what happened to my mum and dad.'

For a moment Nan doesn't move. Then she folds the tea towel corner to corner twice and lays it down. 'I've told you before.' She checks the kettle, moves the saucepan, rubs at a speck of something on the hob with her finger. 'They're dead and gone, aren't they. Don't you remember my telling you?'

'Yes, I remember.' When she was a tot, the story was that she was a gift from the sky. She liked that. It made her think of herself as part of the weather – part of the clouds and sun and rain. Two years ago though, when she was four, she'd asked about it again, and that time Nan told her her parents died in an omnibus accident in Birmingham centre. Which was as much as to say that she wasn't made of clouds and sun and rain after all. Nor was she a gift.

'You're lucky to still have family. You can't beat blood, you know.'

Doris' parents were her flesh and blood. Whenever she thinks of them, they bear a striking resemblance to the illustration of Mr and Mrs Craven in her book *The Secret Garden;* but, as Nan would say, that's neither here nor there. She takes another bite of her bread and margarine, the sugar like grit between her teeth. 'Yes, but tell me again,' she says, 'about how they died.' She would like details. Was it a horse-drawn bus and her parents trampled underfoot? Why didn't the driver see them in time? Did it happen at night? What were they doing four miles away in Birmingham city centre without her? And how is it that there's no cemetery plot to tend to?

Nan reaches for her apron. Her hair, parted down the centre, has begun to turn grey. That, together with the straight line of buttons fastened to her throat, always makes Doris think that she's somehow made up of two different halves. And this feels true, because Nan loves her, Doris knows that: she sprinkles sugar on her bread and calls her 'love' and kisses her. But then there's another part of Nan that speaks sharply and wants Doris to be as prim and proper as a doll. It's this sharper half that, reaching round to tie her apron-strings, speaks now. 'I'm not about to go through it all again, so stop asking questions. *We've* inherited you, that's all – me and Harry and Grandad. That's the important thing, isn't it?' She comes and sweeps the crumbs off the table into her waiting hand, then drops a kiss on Doris' head.

'But I just want to know.'

'What, more questions? What have I told you about asking too many questions? If you carry on, you'll have Awd Goggie over.'

Just as it always does, Doris' spine tingles at the sound of that name.

Nan takes a large bowl from the cupboard and unties the

square of oiled linen covering it. Inside, dried fruits and nuts have been soaking in a mixture of black tea and brandy for a month, and the liquid (which ought to be all brandy, says Nan, and would be if it wasn't for the blasted Germans) has turned thick and dark. 'He's never far, you know, Awd Goggie isn't. He's always watching, and if you're bad... well he'll know about it.' Using a large metal spoon, Nan gives the soaking fruit its daily stir, the rust-coloured liquid rising and falling against the white sides of the bowl. 'He leaps up to the window and hangs there by his long nails and stares at you at night.'

Several images spring into Doris' head: strong hands, goggle eyes and a face that's been alive a very long time. Over the years Awd Goggie's grown solid and real. She knows, for example, that he has iron teeth and tangled hair; she's familiar with the way he lurches and swings across the ground, almost on all fours; and his laugh is horribly distinctive.

'Where does he live?' she asks, even though she knows the answer to that too.

Nan waves towards the garden. 'Out in the woods. Oh, you'd know him if you saw him all right.'

Doris' breathing quickens. The woods the garden backs onto, right there on the other side of the shed and the plum tree.

'But he travels around, mind. He can be here one minute and there the next.'

'But' – Doris has never ventured further than this before – 'he doesn't actually take children away, does he?'

'Only very wicked ones.'

Doris' heart is beating in a strange, lopsided way. 'What does he do with them?'

'Carries them off to his hidey-hole and gobbles them up of course.' Round and round goes the metal spoon, up and down go the raisins, swollen lumps in dark liquid. 'But *you're* not wicked, are you, love?'

Perhaps it's the smell of the brandy and black tea that makes Doris feel so peculiar.

Nan covers the bowl and puts it back into the cupboard. 'It likes to be in the dark,' she explains. The Christmas cake will be baked in the last week of November, after which it'll be fed once a week with a precious dribble of brandy. *Feeding*, that's what Nan calls it, as though it's alive.

'There, you finish off your bread and butter now.' Nan nods towards the half-slice on Doris' plate. 'Waste not, want not.'

But Doris' appetite is gone.

That afternoon, Stanley follows her up the road – or more precisely, follows the dripping she's smeared onto her fingers. The dustcart clatters past, pulled along by a large horse, but the muck-man pays her no heed because cats aren't rubbish, so she and Stanley carry on. They pass the cracked paving stone, the house with the rose-hips hanging over the wall, and the spot where you can see the steam from the brewery in Cape Hill. Depending which way the wind blows, you can either smell the hops from the brewery or chocolate from Bournville, where they're making 'chocolate for the troops'.

Doris is nearly at the allotment gates when Stanley starts to lose interest in her fingers, so she stops and allows him to lick the rest of the dripping off, his tongue raspy and warm. Then it's only a matter of picking him up and carrying him in through the gates. On the far side of the allotment, two women are busy digging and chatting but they don't see her. She follows the path round past a plot of cauliflowers netted against pigeons, and heads straight for the far end.

By the time she gets there, Stanley, his legs dangling, has grown heavy, and she's more than happy to put him down. Here, where the allotment backs onto the woods, there is no one.

'You stay there,' she orders Stanley as she pulls the swaddling cloth from her coat pocket and shakes it loose. Nan keeps it in the linen chest along with a few of her and Harry's baby clothes, a rattle and a small pair of black shoes that once belonged to Doris' mother. When Nan isn't there, Doris sometimes takes them out to examine them, puzzling over how feet that tiny could possibly have belonged to her mother. 'This was mine though,' she says as she holds up the cloth, 'so there's nothing wrong with me taking it.'

Stanley's an easy-going cat, that's what Grandad says, and certainly he doesn't arch his back and hiss like the large tabby down the road. At first he seems interested by what's being done to him and doesn't move, which is as well because the beginning of the procedure isn't easy. As the cloth rises up his body though, he begins to protest. Doris has only seen a baby being swaddled once before, but it didn't look as hard as this. That baby didn't squirm and resist and make noises. It didn't wriggle and fuss and try to bite its mother.

The light is beginning to fade, and the two women on the other side of the allotment have left. 'Stop it, Stanley! You're not being a good cat!' There's no way round it, she explained that to him as they walked here. No matter how much Awd Goggie terrifies her, she needs to see him; she *must* see this creature with large eyes and dark hair who's not like anyone else.

First, though, he must be lured out. 'Shush!' she says as Stanley lets out a yowl. 'Cats should be seen and not heard. Anyway, it's only till he comes out. I'm not really going to let him eat you, am I?' Although this isn't entirely true, for she has no intention of risking herself for the sake of a mere cat.

'There.' It takes some doing but at last Stanley's all bound up with only his face and one ear poking out. He has shrunk – looks quite small in fact, and odd. Like a grub, she thinks, a great white grub with a furry head. 'Awd Goggie'll think you're a baby.' Perhaps, his idea of time being different to people's, he'll think that it's her, a little baby abandoned all over again.

Positioning herself behind some empty crates, she waits. The large white grub makes a few rocking movements and mewling noises not unlike those of a real baby. Except for him, the allotment's quiet and empty, but she knows what's going to happen. Soon the sound and smell of fresh meat will lure Awd Goggie out. Emerging from the trees, he'll pause a moment to look round, then make straight for the bundle.

Beyond this point her plan is hazy. Perhaps she'll wave her arms and shout, as though Awd Goggie were a goose that could be shooed away. This wouldn't be wise though, and besides, he'll probably already have made a start on Stanley by then. 'You did ruin my hair ribbon,' she whispers. The length of bottle-green hemmed velvet was a birthday present from Nan, but Doris had found it clawed to shreds, and Stanley asleep by the stove, his tail twitching. '*And* you killed two baby birds last spring. *And* you're always staring.'

The white grub moves again, but she's done a good job and Stanley can't release himself. A robin lands on the crate. It cocks its head, its tiny black bead of an eye gleaming, then flies off again, and she returns to watching the trees. Their trunks are closely packed, the perfect place to hide. Does Awd Goggie come out sometimes in the gloaming when all the grown-ups are gone? She pictures him loping to the nearest bed and crouching down, bare toes splayed. He'll dig with his hands until he finds a turnip or potato, then prise it up and bite into it raw with his iron teeth – teeth designed for crushing the soft bones of children.

Stanley gives another mew. It's getting dark and Doris' legs are stiff. Why doesn't Awd Goggie come out? Yet he doesn't. He doesn't for so long that finally she stands up. 'I'm here!' she yells angrily at the trees. 'Here I am! And I'm *not* wicked, Nan said so!'

But nothing she says will make the least bit of difference, because Awd Goggie has an instinct about such things just like Stanley does – and his instinct will assure him that she is wicked, that it's inside her whether she wants it there or not.

Tears prick her eyes. 'Don't you believe me?'

But the darkening trees hold their silence.

CHAPTER 5
Grandad

Harborne, 1918

Grandad's humming in the scullery. Harry, sat on a stool in the kitchen polishing his school shoes ready for Monday, picks up the tune. 'It's a long way to Tipperary, It's a long way to go. It's a long way to Tipperary, To the sweetest girl I know…' He looks up. 'What's for dinner?'

Doris is setting the table. 'Mutton stew.'

'Is there pudding?'

She shrugs.

'Mum, is there pudding?'

Nan brushes a strand of hair off her face. 'I don't know.' Ever since Grandad got his letter last week, she's been distracted.

Harry looks disappointed.

'Maybe I'll do some custard.'

And suddenly there's Harry's sparkling smile, and everything's better. He rubs his cloth in the tub of black grease. 'I love custard,' he announces, as though this were news.

Nan gets out the tin of Bird's custard powder then looks at it as if she hasn't a clue how it appeared in her hand.

'Smells good.' Grandad comes out of the scullery with his sleeves rolled up, his thick-knuckled hands splattered with freckles that travel all the way up his forearms. Doris wrinkles her nose as he passes. The smell of dogs and horses is one she's always associated with Grandad – with his leather boots and no-nonsense ways – and it's a smell she dislikes. He takes a sip from Nan's teacup and grimaces because it's stone cold.

When Stanley sees him coming, he jumps down from Grandad's chair and dashes out of the kitchen. 'I don't know what's got into that cat,' says Grandad. 'Strange creatures, cats. There's no understanding 'em.' He holds no truck with cats. As far as he's concerned it's horses, dogs or nothing, and that's the way it's always been. He used to be a coachman in a fine house and he's still a coachman, only at a livery stables now, running people, goods and messages between Harborne and Birmingham city centre.

'Trying to shine the leather off those, Harry?'

'Almost done,' murmurs Harry, rubbing at the toe.

Grandad frowns. 'Cross your legs like a man, Harry. Like a man, not a woman.'

'William,' says Nan.

'Well, what's to become of him, eh?'

Harry uncrosses his legs altogether.

Nan puts a large pot on the table. 'Come and have your dinner, the pair of you.'

Doris lays the last fork – Grandad's – setting it at an angle and on its side. Grandad doesn't like children, at least not her and Harry, although how anyone could not like Harry is beyond her. The local women break out smiling when they see him. Their children run up to him. And why wouldn't they? Harry with his curling hair and clever brown eyes; with his smile like the sun coming out after a long day of rain; Harry who gets on with everyone. You couldn't imagine him picking a fight on a Saturday night or shouting uncouth remarks. He's the apple of Nan's eye. Yet it's her, Doris, who loves him better than anyone and always will.

Grandad looks tired as he sits down, his moustache even bigger on his face than usual. He's leaving on Tuesday, which isn't long to wait. 'So you've been at school today, have you?' It's Doris he's talking to.

'Yes.' Of course she has, it's Friday.

'What did you do?'

'Just the usual things,' says Doris. Getting through lessons. Wondering whether the other girls fall quiet when she's near because they've been talking about her or whether it's because she's simply not part of the things they discuss. But she doesn't care – they're nasty and smelly and ugly and she wouldn't be caught dead being friends with any of them.

'What about you, Harry?'

'Friday's Greek and Latin. We're looking at Horace's poems.'

But Grandad isn't interested in Greek or Latin. It was Nan, not him, who wanted Harry to go to the grammar school. Once when he was angry Grandad said that Nan had ideas above her station from working for a posh family, and perhaps he's right because Nan's had a stair carpet put in and has hung up lace curtains; and although she'll clean the rest of the house, it's Harry who has to scrub the doorstep and wash the front windows so people won't see her working. Grandad says that instead of putting on airs and graces she ought to be grateful we've got a privy of our own and don't have to share like some of our neighbours.

'I don't know where learning Latin and Greek'll get you,' Grandad says now. 'You want to get out and get a real job: work on a farm or in a factory instead of mucking about with books.'

Nan tuts. 'A factory!'

For a moment there's silence. 'If a livery stable's good enough for me, then a factory's good enough for my son. Don't forget where the money that keeps this family fed and clothed comes from.'

Pushing a piece of parsnip across her plate, Doris steers the conversation away from Harry. 'Are you going to kill a lot of Germans, Grandad?'

'Doris!' Nan isn't pleased. 'That's enough out of you.'

It was a German bomb that hit the Austin Longbridge plant last week, but according to Nan, seeing as they'd left it lit up like a ballroom, what did they expect? Apart from that though, the war's been a faraway thing.

'But is he?' Doris wants to know. Harry's told her that they (whoever 'they' are) have just raised the age of compulsory enlistment to fifty-one, and Grandad's fifty.

'No, Dot, I'm not going to kill anyone. They're not sending me to war. They don't want an old codger like me.'

He's not going to become a hero then, and return brave and kind and full of stories.

'I'm just going to see to the horses, that's all it is.'

'What horses?' Harry told her that Grandad was being sent to a camp in North Yorkshire, but he didn't say anything about horses.

'I'm going to a place called Catterick. It's a big camp, twenty-five square miles of it, and there are soldiers arriving and leaving and— '

'There are prisoners too, aren't there, Dad? Prisoners of war.'

'Don't interrupt, Harry,' says Nan.

'Yes, there are prisoners of war too. The trains go through carrying horses for the army. Thousands of them. Tens of thousands. And I've to see to them.'

'Even more horses than that come from America,' says Harry. 'I read about it. They come on ships – a thousand a day.'

Grandad's suddenly angry. 'Sent to slaughter! That's what they're doing, and what we're doing too: sending all the horses in the world to be butchered!'

'William,' says Nan.

'Well, it's true. We've had to give up half a dozen from our stables, but what do they care? When the war's over there'll be no work left for us anyway, what with the railways, and now motorcars tearing up the roads and stinking up the place. We're a dying breed, that's what we are, horses and coachmen both.'

It seems to Doris that Grandad's right: he belongs to last

century, to the Victorian era with all its trappings, and perhaps Nan with her long skirts and old-fashioned hair belongs there too.

'Now, love, don't work yourself up.'

Grandad eats another two mouthfuls, his moustache bobbing as he chews, then the fork clanks onto his plate. 'I'm going for a smoke.'

'But your dinner, love.' Nan spent an hour yesterday queueing for that bit of mutton.

But Grandad just picks up his pipe and heads into the garden.

'You're not to go and bother him, do you understand?' says Nan. 'He's to rest while he can. He's to rest without anyone upsetting him.'

Monday is washday, but Grandad needs to take clean things with him to Catterick so the following morning Nan fills the copper and feeds the week's scraps and rubbish into the fire.

Doris is helping. 'Isn't he to have a uniform?'

'Maybe when he gets there, he will.' Nan's face is wet with steam.

'When will he come back?'

'Soon enough. Now pass me the soap.' Nan pours soap flakes and Doris plunges Grandad's trousers under with the copper stick.

'A girl at school's got a brother who went off to fight, and he never—'

'Concentrate on what you're doing.' Nan's kind half has vanished like a popped bubble. 'Children should be seen and not heard.'

It's Saturday, and Grandad's been in the garden all day again. He's taken a chair, the newspaper and his pipe outside, but he isn't smoking, and the newspaper's lying folded on the damp grass. 'Oh, it's you.'

Doris stops, not knowing what to say. She's been avoiding

going to the privy all afternoon but she can't hold it in much longer.

He glances at the house. 'It's hard to breathe in there.'

It looked like rain so Nan had lit a fire and draped the wet clothes on racks, and now the house is stuffy with the smell of laundry. But Doris has a feeling that's not what Grandad means.

'You've grown,' he says, as though he hasn't seen her for ages. 'Your face has changed.' And he peers at her as though he's trying to see someone else on the other side. But perhaps it's only because she looks different to the rest of them; her hair darker and straighter, her eyes larger – cow's eyes, her teacher calls them.

'Maybe you don't look at me often enough,' she says, because he doesn't. Not directly at her face. Not for long.

'Perhaps you're right,' he agrees, to her surprise.

People are meant to like orphans, or at least feel sorry for them, yet that isn't the way things are for her. The girls at school seem neither to like nor pity her, and it's the same with Grandad. Sometimes it makes her angry, as though she's been robbed of a thing that belongs to her by right.

Grandad touches a bud on the plant beside him. Around them the evening is still as water in a glass, and perched on next door's chimney, a blackbird is singing. Grandad listens for a while, and when he speaks his voice is hoarse. 'It's all breaking into pieces, Dot. The whole world is breaking into pieces.'

It's porridge for breakfast on Tuesday, and by the end of it there are five husks lined up on the rim of her bowl and nine on Harry's. Grandad's bag is packed and waiting by the front door. He says goodbye to her first – 'Bye-bye Dotty. Be good now' – wrapping his starched-stiff arms around her. Then he kisses her head, his moustache prickling her scalp, and for a moment she wishes he wasn't leaving. 'When will you be back, Grandad?'

'Soon. I'm not going far, am I.'

Next is Nan. She hasn't stopped these last three days, washing and scrubbing and polishing the whole house as though the King himself were coming to inspect it. Now her face twitches as she forces a smile. 'We'll see you soon enough, love. Don't fall in with a bad lot, and mind yourself with the horses; they'll be half scared to death. I'll write, anyway. I'll write you twice a week.' She gives Grandad a kiss, then turns to find Harry, who's lurking near the stairs. 'Come on then.'

Grandad gives a tight smile. 'G'bye, Harry. Look after your mother and Dot while I'm away. You're the man of the house now.' The embrace between them looks awkward, and when Grandad steps back there's a strange, full expression on his face. He hoists up his bag, and when he's gone, the clock in the parlour seems to tick louder than before.

CHAPTER 6

Pretty the Pigeon

Harborne, 1918

That summer, Harry decides that he'd like to keep pigeons. He talks about fantails and racers, tumblers and Birmingham rollers. A friend of a friend has some going cheap, but apparently not cheap enough because all Harry can afford is one. He brings it home in a little cage.

Doris peers inside. 'But it's just an ordinary pigeon!' They're kneeling in the garden looking at it. She doesn't know what she expected, but not this: not a boring, grey, run-of-the-mill pigeon just like the ones you see pecking about on the streets.

'It's a homing pigeon,' says Harry. 'You know, like they use in the war.'

But she doesn't know, so he tells her.

'They take them to the front line. Then when they want to send a message home, they let them go.'

'What do you mean?'

'They carry the messages.'

She looks again at the pigeon. 'How?'

'There's a ring on their leg, and you put a little rolled-up message into a tiny tube and fix it to the ring.'

'Does it hurt them?'

'No.'

She's glad. 'What sort of messages do they bring?'

'Oh, top secret stuff like news about what's happening on

the front. Or it could be a call for help. They've saved lots of lives.' Harry knows such a lot about things, and not just Greek and Latin.

'Is that what this pigeon does then?'

'Don't know. Maybe.' Carefully, Harry opens the cage door, reaches in and takes out the bird. It must be used to being handled because it doesn't try to escape. He holds it against his body. 'Those war pigeons, they get shot at, or injured by shrapnel, but they still carry on. Sometimes they drop dead the minute they get home, they're that tired.' With his forefinger he gently strokes the bird's head, as if it too has done heroic things.

How terrible, thinks Doris, to fly and fly until you can't fly any more. To want to get home that badly. She touches the bird's wing. It feels firmer than she expected, the feathers dry and brittle. 'What are you going to call it?'

'Pretty.'

'Is it a girl?'

He shrugs. 'Don't know. It's hard to tell. The man I bought it from, he said it's a boy, but I'm calling him Pretty anyway. Although don't tell Dad that.'

'I won't.'

'D'you want to hold him?'

She isn't sure – the hard beak with its nostrils, the scaly feet and sharp claws, the red eyes – but Harry passes Pretty over. 'Just keep your hands over his wings.'

Pretty feels hinged and jointed, like a folded umbrella that'll open if she takes her hands away, but he doesn't try to escape. Instead he makes gurgling noises and pecks softly at Doris' stomach. 'He likes me!' she laughs.

Harry smiles. 'Looks like it.'

Sitting cross-legged, she takes in the details of the bird in her lap: the white ring around each eye, the green and purple sheen on his neck, the way he ruffles his feathers then settles into her hands, warm and contented.

Harry has spent the last week building a small coop on

stilts, with netting on one side. He's put straw inside, a stick for Pretty to perch on, and two little bowls filled with seed and water. Although Nan's not much taken with the idea of having a pigeon around, she's been pleased to see him working at something with his hands.

'Why's it on stilts?' asks Doris as she releases Pretty into the coop.

'Because we don't want anything to get him.'

Doris' heart stumbles. 'Oh.' She glances at the trees behind the garden and wonders if Awd Goggie's already discovered that Pretty is here.

Whenever he sees Doris or Harry coming, Pretty coos and gurgles and sidles across his perch to the netting. They replenish his seed and water and clean the coop daily, but almost instantly he messes it up again by rummaging in the seed-bowl and knocking into the water. A few days later Harry says it's time to try releasing him, so putting him in the little cage he came in, they carry him down to the end of the road and open the hatch. Pretty hesitates, his head tilting and bobbing. Then he hops out, and with a sudden startling flap of wings he takes off.

'Look, he's heading back,' says Harry. They run home to see and sure enough, Pretty has found the coop and gone in through the open door.

'He really did come back,' says Doris. She'd only half believed that Pretty would do it, yet here he is.

The next day they take him as far as the allotments, and over the following days the distance gets further and further. On Saturday they take Pretty to Cannon Hill Park. 'It's a long way,' she says. It's taken them over an hour to get there and her legs are tired. 'What if he gets lost and doesn't make it home?'

'He will. He has before,' says Harry, but there's a little crease between his eyebrows and he takes his time undoing the latch.

They watch Pretty rise up and fly off, but this time he goes up into the trees where they see some other pigeons flapping around in the branches. 'Is he there? Is he with them?' she asks but Harry can't tell.

Pretty can see them though, she thinks. He can see them standing there with the empty cage, and he can see the park and trees and the world as he's never seen it before.

After a while Harry picks up the cage. 'Come on,' and they set off home. But Pretty isn't in his coop, or even in the garden. She and Harry walk up and down the street, looking up at roofs and guttering and examining branches, but they find nothing.

On Sunday they help Nan with preparing dinner, Doris shelling peas and Harry peeling potatoes. He's good at it, deft and quick, and the shining bits of peel gather in a pile on the table. As he reaches for another potato, she notices him glance out at the empty coop, and she thinks of Pretty flapping and rising up into the sky.

'He's been gone for ages,' she says. He loved her and Harry, but as he flew off, the two of them would have grown small and insignificant. There were other pigeons in the park that gurgled and cocked their heads and looked just like he did. He must have joined them because he didn't want to be alone any longer. 'I hope he doesn't come back,' she says. 'I hope he never comes back.'

Nan's been busy twisting and laying strips of pastry crisscross over a jam tart, but she's across the kitchen in a jiffy and the slap comes so swiftly, Nan's hand drawing a crescent in the air as it swings towards her, that Doris doesn't realise what's happening. Peas scatter across the table and her left cheek sings with pain.

'Mum!' cries Harry, pushing back his chair. 'Mum!'

Doris puts her hand to her cheek. It feels hot. No one's ever smacked her before.

'Don't you *ever* let me hear you say that again.' Nan's

nostrils flare. 'Your Grandad who took you in and paid your keep even when he'd no mind to! And you sitting here saying such a thing!' Her arm rises, a finger pointing towards the stairs. 'Go to your room this instant! You're in my blackest of black books.'

Doris bumbles out of her chair.

'But Mum! She didn't mean Dad!'

'What?'

'She was talking about the pigeon. The pigeon, not Dad!'

Several different emotions fight it out on Nan's face, and then one of them wins. Doris steps back as Nan comes towards her (it's all still near: Nan's face distorted with anger, the pain springing to her cheek) but Nan isn't angry any longer. Instead she lays a hand on Doris' shoulder, a hand that's heavy and sorry, and bends to kiss her on the cheek. 'There, don't mind your silly Nan.' Which is the closest a grown-up will ever come to apologising to a child.

CHAPTER 7

The Maker of His Own Fortune

Harborne 1918–19

Food begins to appear at 45 Nursery Road. A still-hot stew or a pan of soup. A bag of apples or a bread-and-butter pudding. They're brought over by Mrs Stott who's lost two sons to the war, by Mrs Pearson who has no one to lose, and by other women in the neighbourhood. Each offering is received with the appropriate thanks, and the food doled out to Harry and Doris. Nan doesn't eat much of anything, but washes the pots and pans, bowls and plates with extra care, then washes them a second time just to be sure before drying and polishing them to a shine.

'Here, Doris, take this back to Mrs Cooper. And don't forget to thank her again.'

'Yes, Nan.'

'Properly, mind.'

Doris nods.

'And thread her needles for her before you leave, her eyesight's not what it used to be.'

Sometimes one of the women will stay to drink a cup of tea with Nan. The two will talk about everyday things – the war, food, the weather, which of their acquaintances has been seen doing what. The visitor will say a word or two about Grandad, and then when she gets up to leave will embrace Nan and shed a tear or two along with her. Is this what Nan did during her visits to other families who'd lost a loved one these last couple of years? Probably. Except now it's her who's wearing a black dress that reeks of mothballs, because Grandad has died of the Spanish flu in Catterick Camp.

Then in November news comes that the war is over, and suddenly music is blaring out of open windows and people are cheering and banging on pots. Towards the end of the year, men and boys in uniform appear walking down the road from the railway station. Nan opens the front door to watch them, and standing close to Nan, Doris watches too, but they look more like beggars than soldiers, she thinks. They're thin and dirty and they've got a lost look to them, darting looks left and right, as though they don't recognise this place.

Once they've passed, Nan shuts the door.

'Aren't they happy to be back?' Doris asks.

'Of course they are.'

'They don't look happy. They look like ghosts.'

'They'll be right enough once they've got a few square meals in them. Anyway their families'll be happy enough. They've come back at least, haven't they?'

Nan stands on tiptoe to reach Grandad's whisky bottle at the back of the cupboard, and sloshes some into a teacup. After the first sip she pauses, but she must like it because she takes another, and another. Grandad only rarely drank whisky, and Doris has never seen Nan drink it before. She's drinking it now though – in celebration perhaps. As a toast to Harborne's boys come home from the war.

Harry's settled at the kitchen table reading a library book and Doris is trying to outstare Stanley when the front door opens and Nan, who's been out settling bills, is swept in by a gust of wind. 'Whoever heard of such winds in May!'

When she comes into the kitchen, her cheeks are pink. She smooths her hair. 'What are you two up to then? Did you sweep the kitchen like I asked, Dot?' she asks, looking into the edges and corners of the room.

'Yes.'

'Good. How was school, Harry love?'

Harry glances up, on the alert. Nan doesn't usually ask about school. 'Fine.'

'Good. You know, I've been thinking…' Harry would much rather go back to reading his book, Doris can tell, but he waits for Nan to finish what she wants to say. 'Food's not getting any cheaper. And now that your dad's…' She turns away. 'Well, it's not so easy to make ends meet any longer.' On top of her usual housework, Nan has started to take in sewing, and stays up late into the night hemming and stitching other people's clothes. At the end of the week she'll count out her earnings at the kitchen table just like Grandad used to do, but it always comes up short. Nan turns to face Harry. 'What I'm saying is… well, you're going to have to get a job, love.'

Harry blinks. 'What do you mean?'

For a few moments, no one speaks.

'What sort of job?' asks Harry. 'Do you mean at the weekend?'

Nan shakes her head. 'That wouldn't be enough.'

Harry gets to his feet. 'You mean you want me to leave school?' His voice is pitched at a strange angle.

'But Harry can't leave school. He loves school!'

'Hold your tongue, Doris!' Nan goes over to Harry. 'I'm sorry, love.' She takes hold of his hand but he snatches it away.

'What sort of job could I get anyway when I haven't even finished school?'

Nan holds herself a little straighter. 'There's a job going at the grocers.'

Doris' eyes widen. 'A grocer's boy?'

'It'll do till you can find something else,' says Nan. 'We could ask at the post office. Or there's always Dad's old place; you could see if they need someone there.'

Harry shakes his head, astonished. 'I can't drive a livery cab, Mum! And I don't know anything about horses. I don't even *like* horses.' And he moves towards the back door.

‘Harry love,’ Nan calls, but the door bangs shut behind him.

Doris goes out to find him sitting on the brick step half an hour later. ‘What are you doing?’

‘Nothing.’ He breaks a twig from a bush, then snaps it into smaller and smaller pieces. There’s already a heap of tiny twig-bits at his feet. ‘What do you reckon? Will trigonometry come in handy when I’m pulling dead leaves off cabbages?’

‘Maybe Nan’ll change her mind.’

He tries to break an already tiny piece of twig in half. ‘No she won’t. Needing money’s not a thing you change your mind about.’

‘Money. Money. I hate money!’ She searches her mind for something helpful to say. ‘Maybe it’ll be better than you think.’

He lets out a sharp sound that’s not quite a laugh. ‘*Faber est suae quisque fortunae*.’

She’s heard him say things in Latin before, but he may as well be meowing. ‘What does that mean?’

‘Every man is the maker of his own fortune, that’s what it means.’ He stands and brushes down his trousers. ‘Tripe and balderdash, that’s what they teach you at school, Dot.’

She shifts from foot to foot, feeling desperate. ‘Maybe we can swap. I hate school. And I can already read and write and count.’ There doesn’t seem to be much point to any of the rest of it. Hemming squares of calico, holding your stomach in and walking with a book balanced on your head, baking (or in her case burning) scones, sitting for hours at a time while a visitor from the National Milk Publicity Council drones on about the virtue of all things dairy. The only thing at school she actually enjoys is painting on Wednesday afternoons.

Harry kisses her on the cheek. ‘You’re a sweetheart.’ Then he pulls back his shoulders, takes one deep breath and goes inside.

She stares at the closed door, hating Grandad for dying and Nan for making Harry leave school. ‘I’m not going to be poor,' she tells herself. 'I'm not, not if I can help it.' And she turns and kicks the pile of broken twigs, scattering them across Nan's swept and scrubbed flagstones.

CHAPTER 8

Passing Judgement

Baghdad, 1938

'I don't think your mother likes me.'

Leon has been looking out of the window but now he turns round. 'Of course she does.'

Doris carries on filing her nails. They've been installed in Leon's old room, which is apparently unchanged except that a second single bed has materialised. The house is arranged strangely, as apparently most are here, around a single courtyard, with living quarters downstairs and bedrooms upstairs.

'Why do you say this?'

Doris blows the dust off her nails. 'Did you see the way she looked at me?'

'When?'

'Yesterday, when we arrived.'

The woman who'd emerged from the house as the taxi pulled up wasn't dressed in Arab garb but in a plain black dress. She had greying hair, black eyebrows and not a scrap of makeup or fanciness anywhere on her, and although she's younger than Nan, her sad eyes made her look older. She grasped Leon in her arms and laughed and sobbed while they exchanged words in Armenian.

Then finally when they came apart she turned to Doris. 'Hallo, hallo.' She took Doris' hands and gave them little shakes as though trying to dislodge something, speaking words in her language that might have been a blessing or a curse. 'Do-lo-ris.' Then she planted a kiss on each of Doris' cheeks.

Doris was discomfited, but Leon was beaming, willing them to like one another. They were led into a tiled hall spread with patterned rugs. It was dim inside, with dark wooden furniture and shutters as well as curtains at the windows. The driver carried in their bags, but Leon and his mother didn't let up talking in Armenian because the woman evidently didn't speak a word of English. It was cooler inside than out, thank God, and as Doris followed, shoes clattering over the tiled floor, Leon's mother glanced down at her high heels. When she looked back up, there was judgement in her eyes.

'She is older,' says Leon now. 'Of another generation.' Yet it doesn't seem that way when Leon and his mother are together. When they're talking and laughing and Doris hasn't a clue what they're saying.

'If you say so.' The polish has begun to chip on her nails and needs to be taken off and reapplied.

'When she gets to know you, she will see. She can be a mother to you also.'

Doris' head snaps up. 'What makes you think I want a mother?'

Silhouetted against the heat-bright rectangle of window, Leon doesn't move, and for a long moment neither of them speaks.

Quickly she redirects the conversation. 'Anyway I… I thought you had servants. You said you had servants when you were growing up.'

'Yes, but that was when I was young. My father liked to show off that he was rich – that was how he was. My mother says she can manage by herself now without anyone to help.'

This seems to be true because the old woman cooks for hours on end, making all sorts of bizarre concoctions: stews of meat and plums sprinkled with cinnamon of all things, stuffed baked vegetables, strange flat bread and spiced rice and piles of other unknown grains. There are skewers of meat and a vile yoghurt to drink. 'She wants to know, do you like it?' Leon will say when each horrific new thing is placed in front of Doris, and she must lie and say yes, while his mother nods and smiles.

'Anyway,' says Leon now, running his hand through his hair, 'there is not as much money as there used to be, you know this. The business does not do so well any more. My brother is not the businessman my father was. But we discussed how life would be – that I will work; that it may be difficult at first. I did not pretend. I did not lie.'

At the mention of lies, her cheeks grow warm. 'No. No of course not, darling. No one could accuse you of that.'

'When we talked about it, in England, you did not mind.' He waits. 'Do you mind?'

'No.'

But he doesn't seem to believe her. 'Is it not enough, just me and you?'

She throws down the nail file and goes to him. She puts her arms around him and lays her cheek against his chest. 'Of course it is, darling.' He embraces her too. 'What more on earth could I possibly want?' She buries her face into him and feels the familiar surge of her body, upwards, as if she will take flight. 'I don't need anything else.'

The skirt lying on the bed catches her eye. There was a worn patch but Nan mended it so that it's barely noticeable. Nan. Nursery Road. Seas and deserts lie between them now.

Doris clings to Leon, like a castaway to a piece of driftwood. 'So long as I have you, that's all that matters.' So long as she has all of him. All of him just for herself.

On the fifth day of visitors ranged on the sofa with their smiles and assessing eyes, she can't bear it any longer. They've come to congratulate the newlyweds, but really it's only to eat, drink tea and pass judgement. Leon gave up translating a while ago, so now she just sits there in her glad rags while the visitors eye her and gabble on and on.

Among them is Leon's younger brother, who took over the family business because Leon fell out with their father. The brother's wife has a face like a horse and two children, a fat boy and a shockingly hairy girl, plaguing her. On both these counts Doris feels sorry for her, but when Doris shifts in her chair, the woman's eyes settle briefly on her stomach, and Doris realises that they're wondering whether she's pregnant yet; that they're all expecting children from her, and soon.

Leon's mother has prepared food for the guests. There are pastries stuffed with cheese, dried apricots stuffed with nuts and little cakes, stuffed of course, with dates. Doris accepts a small cake and starts to poke at it with her teaspoon, then sees that everyone else is picking the food up with their fingers. And suddenly she is aware of how little she knows: what they're eating or how to eat it, what to say or how to be understood.

Leon follows her from the room. 'What's wrong?' he asks as soon as they're in the hall.

'Nothing. Really.' Damn them all, every last one, with their dust and their heat and their squat toilets (*squat toilets!* Leon certainly didn't tell her in advance about that!). What right have they to sit there examining her like a specimen? 'I've just got a headache.'

He kisses her forehead.

'I'm going to lie down for a bit.'

But she doesn't lie down. She walks round and round the room, putting her fingers to the walls. She picks up an ashtray to test its weight, lays a towel against her cheek. It's only when she lifts an apple to sniff it that she realises she's searching for something familiar – a texture; a weight or scent. 'Like an animal,' she thinks, shocked. 'Good God!'

There's no mirror in the room, so using the windowpane, she adjusts herself, altering her bearing and expression until she locates again the woman she desires to be. More lipstick, a hat, then she exits.

'Darling?' Leon spots her passing the living room. 'You are going out?' He comes over.

'I need some fresh air.'

'I will come with you.'

The fat boy has followed and is watching them.

'No. I mean, your family's here. Besides, we went out together yesterday and the day before that. I don't need you to come with me today.'

A crease appears between his eyebrows. 'But you might get lost.'

'I won't. I *can* look after myself, you know.'

'But the heat. Soon it will be too hot to be outside.'

She glances at the visitors fanning themselves with straw fans. 'I won't be long.' And she smiles brightly at them as she leaves.

When she steps out, the heat and light are searing. She heads to Al-Rashid Street. She and Leon have been here already. It's the main thoroughfare in Baghdad, wide and unpaved and covered in dust, running parallel to the river. At one end is a clock at the top of a tall pole (a strange thing, but how else are these people to tell the time) and the buildings have pillared fronts. A truck is spraying water onto the road to settle the dust, but otherwise there's no sign of moisture. There are a few cars and *arabanas*, the horse-drawn carts that will take you here or there for a fee, driving on the left, British-style. But she doesn't take an *arabana*. Instead she heads down a side street, edging into the shade. She has no real idea where she's going. The houses have wood-latticed windows and upper storeys that overhang the lower ones – for shade, apparently. The people are no less strange than the buildings. Many of them are barefoot (even now, several days later, this still shocks her) and wrapped in swathes of material that reach to the ground, the men wearing cylindrical hats and skullcaps, or else the traditional long headcloths called *keffiyehs*. The women are wrapped up even more, mostly in dark colours, their hair and sometimes even their faces hidden from view. In this heat, she wonders how on earth they bear it, when she's being cooked alive as it is?

She walks on into the old town where the streets are narrower, in some places so narrow that when she meets someone coming the other way, they have to stand sideways to pass one another. The market is divided into areas selling different goods, and is loud with the cries of hawkers. There are men selling clay pots, and bottles, and round copper trays. There are leather goods, the smell of them turning her stomach. Elsewhere, baskets are piled high with apples and apricots and maize, while others are full of almonds and pistachios, raisins and walnuts.

She stops to take in the bright shapes and colours of the market – perhaps later she'll paint them – but someone calls to her, first in Arabic, then in other languages. 'You buy? *Vous achetez?*' She shakes her head and hurries on.

After a few moments Doris realises that she's now in the bread market, where men sit behind rows of small ovens flipping bread, the loaves piling up beside them. Further on are stalls of sesame biscuits and Turkish Delight. Then the road forks, leads to stationary, then haberdashery with bolts of cloth, then what she thinks at first are fish strung up on lines to dry, but turn out to be shoes. A cobbler with a mouthful of nails makes her think of Awd Goggie. She walks on.

Boys with large urns strapped to their backs are selling lemonade, their faces gleaming in the sun. Women balance enormous baskets of bread on their heads, and smoke rises from meat roasting on spits, throwing out yet more heat. Her nostrils burn when she breathes, and in spite of her hat, it feels as though her head is cooking. There are awnings and there's sweat, and flies in their hundreds.

She reaches a copper market, where metal flashes in the sunlight, and men hammer, a din like hell itself. Further on, heat-bleached laundry and dogs lying panting in the shade. A huddle of children playing with what look like animal bones stop their game to gawp as she passes, and she grips her handbag tighter.

Finally, she reaches the Tigris. Riverboats are moored along its shores and there's a long footbridge crossing to the far bank. Here, men are crouched fanning charcoal and grilling fish, and there's a *quffa* station with a couple of the round bowl-boats made of wicker and tar. Out on the water, she sees one going upstream loaded with watermelons, and another cram-packed with men – all standing of course, for there are no seats. She stops to listen to the slap of water and watch the river move like an enormous snake in the sun. She'd thought it would be different – this place, Leon's mother, all of it. She hadn't known exactly what to expect, but it wasn't this.

When the glare starts to give her a headache, she turns back. Near the bridge, a few birds are sheltering under bushes, beaks gaping in the heat, and a beggar is sitting with his back to a wall, an empty hand stuck out into the sun. She doesn't know why, but with the sun crashing down on her hat and shoulders, she reaches into her handbag, pulls out some money and, making sure that their fingers don't touch, hands it over.

The man looks up at her, his face scrunched up against the light, and for a moment they stare into each other's eyes as though they comprehend one another perfectly, before she realises that the man's milky eyes are blind.

Back in the house, she lies down on the bed and closes her eyes – just for a few minutes, just to get rid of the glare. But there's a knock at the door and Leon's mother comes in carrying a cold drink in a glass beaded with condensation.

'Oh,' says Doris, half sitting up. What does she want?

The old woman comes over, murmuring to herself, and touches Doris' face – gently, expertly, the way a mother might a sick child's. Then she takes Doris' hand and puts the glass, blessedly cold and wet, into it and gestures for her to drink. But Doris isn't sick. There's nothing wrong with her, not in the way the woman thinks at least.

CHAPTER 9
Slowcoach

Harborne, 1925

When Doris was a little girl of five or six, Nan would hold her hand when they went out. The grip of that hand was a firm and comforting thing, for Nan always knew where they were going, and would lead her there and back home safely. That hand was also adept at many other things. It was the hand that kneaded bread and sewed on stray buttons, that folded sheets and felt clammy foreheads, the hand whose fingertips pressed pears for ripeness and slid along the mantelpiece to check for dust. Its characteristics – the hillocks of knuckles, the oval nails and turn of its wrist – were as familiar to Doris as her own. And when Nan had her by the hand, they might pass through the eye of a storm unscathed.

Now that she's fourteen years old, Nan no longer holds Doris' hand when they're out together. Today, however, time curves back on itself. 'Come along,' Nan says, taking Doris by the hand as they set off down Nursery Road.

'I don't want to go,' blurts Doris.

'What nonsense.' Nan is all brusqueness and business, and pulls Doris along like a dog on a lead. Her palm is dry and rough from years of housework, so that her hands feel like gloves. And that's what Nan is right now: leathery, the tender part of her drawn away, for this is the way it must be if she's to achieve her mission.

Could Doris make a break for it and run off? Could she?

She tries to stop, but Nan's grip, just like the rest of her, is determined, and she almost yanks Doris' arm out of its socket.

'Please,' Doris pleads, grimacing in pain, 'I want to go home.'

But things have already been set in motion. 'It's too late for that now.' And Nan leans forward and forges ahead like a juggernaut, her fingernails digging into Doris' flesh.

Yesterday when she and Nan were in the kitchen wrapping tomatoes in brown paper so they'd keep, Nan announced that she had something to tell Doris. It was the last ever day of school, and at first Doris thought perhaps Nan had planned something special to mark the occasion – a trip to the seaside perhaps, or a show. She'd looked up with a smile, but Nan, standing across the table from her, seemed to clam up. 'It's… it's not an easy thing… to say.'

'What isn't?'

Nan wet her lips, opened her mouth and closed it again. She looked around the kitchen but couldn't locate the answer.

'What isn't, Nan?'

Nan picked up a piece of brown paper but couldn't manage to get it around the tomato. 'You see, Dot. You see, you do actually have family.'

Doris gave a little laugh. 'I know.' She has Nan and Uncle Harry (who being only six years older than her, doesn't exactly count as an uncle). And before Grandad died, she had him too. And maybe you could count Nan's cousins in Yorkshire or Grandad's brother in Sheffield, who was, if you asked Nan, a shilling short.

Nan rested her fingertips on the edge of the table to hold herself steady. And then she said the thing she had to say.

The air was sucked clean out of the house. In the garden the sunlight dimmed then shone out bright again. The kitchen jolted, or perhaps it was Doris' head that jolted without her say-so. Certainly the body sitting in the chair didn't feel like her own. Distantly, she was aware of the hard edges of the chair against her legs, but that was all. 'But… but they were run over by a bus.'

Nan glanced at the cupboard where she kept the whisky. 'Well, that's not *strictly* true.'

The kitchen rearranged itself and Doris' body started to tingle. 'But you told me they were. You said so. That's what you said! You said they were.' She couldn't understand it. 'Weren't they? Weren't they run over?'

Maybe Nan meant they weren't killed but only injured. Horribly, vilely injured – injuries that rendered them incapable of caring for Doris and meant that they had to stay in a hospital or care home forever.

Nan laid down the square of brown paper she was holding and flattened out the creases with both hands. 'No.'

The omnibus slowed. Its driver pulled on the reins, the horses rearing up, and her parents were resurrected. They weren't run over but their fate hadn't yet been decided. They were frozen, suspended, until Nan said more.

The voice that came out of Doris' mouth was shrill: 'But that's what you said!' She leaned forward, starting to rise up out of her chair and yet still sitting in it.

Nan winced. 'There wasn't a bus. There wasn't an accident. They're not dead, love, your parents.'

The information, like water on oilskin, refused to permeate. Because she was Doris Palmer, an orphan, and always had been.

'I have a mother?' The words were a thin line traveling from her to Nan.

'You do.'

'And a father?'

A long moment passed before Nan acceded, 'Yes.'

Doris' life, all fourteen years of it, turned to jelly.

'You see' – Nan lifted her hands, pressed them into her cheeks then took them away again – 'when Susan got into trouble and wasn't married…'

'Trouble?' Doris had heard that word before. It was getting

into trouble that had made a girl on the other side of Bartley Green drown herself last year.

'Your grandfather... well I've never known him so upset before or since. He cried from shame – he did – and wouldn't speak to her after that. Said she wasn't living under his roof any longer and could sort it out herself.' Nan swayed, then dragged the nearest chair over and sat down. 'We weren't allowed to see her after that, me and Harry weren't. Grandad wouldn't even have her name spoken in the house. There was no point telling you, was there? What would have been the point?'

It was like reading a book that had too much information in it. Or like Harry speaking Latin. Yes, that was what it was like. 'But why aren't I with them?'

Nan's eyes were cast down. Her words came slowly. 'Your mother was only young, only eighteen, and so you came here. Not even your grandfather could turn a baby away, could he, and it was only meant to be for a bit. But what with one thing and another...' Nan looked up. 'You did go back one time.'

'I did?'

'You won't remember, you must only have been two or three years old. You went back, but then you stopped eating.' Nan's face softened. 'The doctor said you were pining to come home, that's what he said; so back you came.'

Nan's almost dragging her. 'Come on, slowcoach.'

But this is not slow, it's fast, lightning fast. When Nan said that they were going to see her parents, Doris had imagined a journey, bags to be packed and preparations to be made, then buses and trains to be caught, but as it is they've set off on foot.

'Where do they live?' she pants as they near Bournbrook.

'Oh, the back of beyond, that's where.'

'The back—?'

'I'm joking, love, it's only Selly Oak. Come on now, not much further.'

But Doris yanks her hand free. Tears are rising. 'I don't want to go!'

A sheen of sweat glistens on Nan's temples. Her chest is heaving. 'What on earth do you mean, you don't want to go?' A terrier's head appears in the window of the house they've stopped in front of. It yaps and barks at them, its head jolting up and down, but Nan takes no notice. 'They're your flesh and blood.'

Doris scrabbles around for an excuse. 'Maybe we should write first. That way they'll be expecting us. Otherwise it might be a shock.'

'She knows we're coming, love. I told her.' The terrier's still barking. A circle of spit-flecked mist has formed on the windowpane in front of it. 'So.' Nan adjusts the handbag on her arm. 'Let's get a move on.'

When they finally stop, Nan allows herself a moment to settle. 'Here we are.'

Doris wipes her damp palm on her dress. Her mouth is dry, and the blood is pounding in her ears like two unmoored hearts. Here she is at last – fourteen years too late, but she's here. This, then, is what The Back of Beyond looks like. There's no front garden, only a potted rosebush under the window and a single step up to the front door.

'There, love, don't worry.' Nan leans down to give Doris a kiss. 'It'll be all right.'

Perhaps she's right. Perhaps it will be fine. After all, isn't this the piece that's always been missing from Doris' life? Inside this end-of-terrace are her father and mother, ravaged with regret at the years they've lost with her. Her mother will be first to come forward. Tearfully she'll embrace Doris – yes, that's the first thing she'll do – and the space inside her arms will be warm and soft and smell of fresh bread. Then it'll be her father's turn, and he, trying not to cry, will press Doris so close she'll be able to feel his heart beating.

Beneath the potted rosebush is a scatter of dark pink

petals. Looking at the front window, Doris notices smeared handprints on the glass, as though someone has been trying to get out.

'Right. You be on your best behaviour now. Let them see what a good girl you are.'

CHAPTER 10

Fish

Baghdad, 1938

Leon has found a job teaching mathematics at the Jewish school. He loves it too. 'The children's faces when they understand it; when they solve a problem,' he says, beaming. It's been two weeks since he started there, but today being Saturday and his day off, they're all to eat a nice lunch together. Doris, Leon and his mother are standing in what they call a kitchen, and on the table is a large fish wrapped in paper, a seam of silver just visible.

'What?' says Doris.

'She wants to show you how to cook it,' he says again. 'It must be cooked today. It will not stay fresh, you see.'

She knows. She's seen fishermen selling them still alive down by the Tigris, where they'll cook them for you butterflied over charcoal.

She looks around the so-called kitchen. Low down near the floor, there are some kerosene-fuelled rings. There's also a stand made of stone and plaster on which you can stand a pot over wood and coal, and a large clay contraption where they somehow bake their bread. There's a chopping board and knives and pots and pans. But there's no oven, and no stove as she knows it.

The old woman says something incomprehensible, looking at Doris and patting the fish.

'She says a wife must know how to cook,' says Leon. 'But… well, she will teach you.'

Doris' hackles rise and she gives a sharp laugh. 'Teach me!' Lying in bed each morning, she listens to the clatter from the kitchen as the old woman prepares their strange breakfast of eggs scrambled with tomatoes and sharp white cheese, which the three of them eat before he goes to work. 'I should think I know how to cook a fish, for heaven's sake!'

Leon looks at her a moment too long. Then he turns to his mother, his hand moving to her shoulder, his voice soothing.

'It will need to be…' The word eludes him. 'The inside will have to come out. And the… um, the *skin*?'

'The scales, you mean.'

'Scales, yes. They will have to come off.'

He waits. He's expecting her to give in, she supposes, but she won't. 'Yes of course, it'll need to be gutted and scaled. What do you take me for?'

'If… if you need anything… There are things in the cellar.'

'Yes.' Downstairs is a storeroom filled with hessian sacks of grains and flour and sugar, and drums of oil. On the shelves stand earthenware pots and large jars of pickles, preserved fruits and goodness knows what else. But what any of those could have to do with a fish she can't imagine.

She waits for them to leave. She'd wanted to spend the morning with Leon, talking, laughing, kissing. They had discussed the fact that he'd have to work, but somehow she hadn't understood that it would be like this; that he would be away from her for the entire day, five days a week.

In the silent kitchen, she stands gazing down at the parcel. When she pulls back the paper, the fish is lying on its side gaping up at her. She has no idea what sort of fish it is. Putting out a finger, she touches it. It's cold and firm, its scales like armour plating, and an unblinking eye surveys her.

She swallows. She will not be defeated by a dead fish! Or by Leon's mother for that matter. The fish shimmers as she picks it up, silver body bending so the tail hangs down. It is heavier, more solid than she expected. The eye continues to stare, but when she turns it over, the other is just as accusing.

The tail and the fin are scratchy and brittle. Wanting to put off the gutting, she decides to scale the thing first, so finds a sharp knife and starts to swipe down the fish's body in the reverse direction, just as she's seen it done at the fishmonger's back in Harborne. Scales fly upwards and outwards like baby fingernails, a glinting shower of them falling around her. But at last it's done – shabbily, but done – and the fish lies naked on its paper.

She guts it as quickly as she can and shoves it in a pan. Once she's managed to light a cooking ring, she puts a lid on it and waits for it to cook. Almost all the cooking back home was done by Nan, the result being that Doris knows how to make Welsh rarebit, omelette, chutney, fruit cake and nothing else.

She can hear Nan's voice during one of their many arguments: 'Does your bloke know what he's getting? Does he know that you've been waited on hand and foot? When a dress needs taking in, it gets done for you, and when you fancy upside-down cake, then that's what you get, isn't it?' And as she walked away, Nan's voice had risen, neighbours be damned. 'Does he know that you lie in on a Saturday while the housework does itself?'

Because she forgot to add any oil, the fish is burnt. Leon's mother produces bread and salad but it makes no difference, the thing is inedible.

They pick at it in silence. Leon eats a little, but she can see that every forkful is a punishment. 'I'm sorry,' she says.

'It tastes fine,' says Leon, then a few moments later, 'Anyway it is too hot to eat.'

His mother says something, and there's a brief exchange. Leon is terse and looks edgy.

'What's she saying?'

He swallows. 'She was asking about your family, your life in England. She wants to know more about you, that is all.'

Doris reaches for her pack of cigarettes but doesn't take one out, just turns the packet over and over. Her hands still smell. She scrubbed and scrubbed them, but the scent lingers like a lie. 'And what did you tell her?'

'I told her that you are a wonderful, loving woman, Dolores. And that you have left everything behind to come here.'

His mother says something else, glancing at Doris, at her nails and eyeliner and neckline, as she speaks to her son. Leon responds, on the defensive. How strange it is to hear him talking this third language – not the English he speaks with her, nor the Arabic he spoke to porters, drivers, food-sellers and hoteliers when they were travelling here, but something else again. It transforms him, makes him sound like someone else. How astonishing, she suddenly thinks, that she married a man without first having heard him speak in his mother tongue.

The old woman has more to say. Doris lights a cigarette and inhales deeply. Oh, she can just imagine the things the old bat's saying. *What made you marry this foreign woman who can't even cook a meal? An orphan without parents to teach or guide her. And come to that, what made her leave her life behind and come all the way out here? And twenty-one? Tsch! Don't you have eyes in your head?* What if his mother and Nan were to meet and somehow be able to communicate? They'd sit down for a cup of afternoon tea and by the time they'd finished gossiping about Doris, it would be bedtime.

When silence falls, Leon turns to her. 'Don't be upset.'

'I'm not.' She stubs out her cigarette, corkscrewing it into her plate. 'Are you quarrelling about the lunch?' That wretched, wretched fish.

Leon rolls up one sleeve as far as the elbow, then the other. He wears looser shirts here, and open-toed slippers on bare feet.

'I told you she doesn't like me,' says Doris.

'It is not that.'

'Oh? What then?'

She sees him struggling to phrase it.

'Go on.'

'She says… she says that in the West, they do not know how to bring up their children.'

Doris pushes back her chair, stands and picks up her plate. 'We need our own house.'

'I know. I will find one soon, I promise. Since my father died, my mother finds everything difficult. She is alone. She gets upset.'

It occurs to Doris then that their quarrel must have been coloured by the past: by Leon's long absence, by his fraught relationship with his father and the months the old woman spent looking after her dying husband. All these things will have been hovering in the air as they talked. 'Well, I can't help it if she's alone. We've got to find a house.' If she knew how to go about it in this city, she'd find one herself. 'It won't wait any longer.'

Leon nods once, heavily, as if in acknowledgement of defeat.

His mother is watching them, and while Doris might need a translation of her words, she understands perfectly what her eyes are saying. They're saying that she's unimpressed with this new wife. That Doris is not a woman she would have chosen for her son.

As soon as Leon leaves the room to wash his hands, she stands up. 'I couldn't care less what you think,' she says to his mother. 'You're old and ignorant and you don't know a thing about me. But *he* loves me. That's right, he's mad about me, so who gives a hoot what you think?' And she turns and carries her plate across the courtyard to the kitchen.

Her knife and fork jump as she slams the plate down. She catches sight of a fish scale stuck to the kitchen wall, and another on the floor. She thought she'd managed to clean them all up but evidently not. With grim satisfaction, she imagines how the old woman will continue to come across a scale here and there over the coming weeks, each a reminder of this meal. Yes, they'll pop up unbidden, the way memories do, when you least expect them.

CHAPTER 11

The Back of Beyond

Harborne, 1925

'Right. You be on your best behaviour now. Let them see what a good girl you are.' Nan smooths back her hair, goes up the step and raps on the door.

Doris can't move. She's got a mother? A father? Nan told her there are brothers and sisters too. It occurs to her now that she's spent her entire life, and not just the last forty minutes, travelling to this spot.

'It'll be all right,' says Nan, softening. 'I promise it will.'

There's a thud of hurrying feet inside, and Doris is overcome by unbearable curiosity and also a strong impulse to turn and run.

The door swings opens. 'Granma!' A boy with a none-too-clean face and coarse, sand-coloured hair is standing there, and Nan – *her* Nan – is bending down to give him a kiss.

'Hello, Bobby.'

This must be one of her brothers, even though he doesn't look a bit like her. He leans to peer round Nan. 'Is that her?'

'That's her.' Nan beckons her in. 'Come on, love.'

As though in a dream, Doris mounts the step and edges in past the boy.

'Susan?' calls Nan.

Doris follows her in. She treads cautiously, as though the floorboards might turn to quicksand beneath her. There are no lace curtains or stair carpets here. The single picture hanging from the picture rail is crooked, and the wallpaper's grubby, especially at child height. It's probably as well, she thinks, that the floorboards are painted black.

A smell of baking is coming from the kitchen at the end of the hall. There are children's voices, the scrape of a chair across a floor, the clunk of a kettle being set on the hob.

Doris sticks close to Nan. 'There you are,' Nan says to someone as she enters the kitchen. And it's like the finale of a magic trick because here she is – ta da! – Doris' mother.

The woman who must be Susan is standing at the cooker in front of a tray of scorched biscuits, and two children are clinging to her legs like anchors.

Nan goes and gives Susan a peck on the cheek, but there's no embracing. 'And here's Doris,' says Nan, turning to give her an encouraging smile.

Susan peers at Doris, curious but wary, as though Doris might spontaneously burst into flames. She doesn't come over and hug her, although that may be because of the two girls clamped to her legs, whining and straining upwards like rising water. The older of the two, who is perhaps five, tugs at Susan's skirt. 'Biscuits. I want biscuits.'

'Good heavens!' Nan picks up the smaller one, a toddler who's fallen into a sitting position and started to wail. 'Now then Ruthie, what's all this crying for?'

But Ruthie only cries louder and extends her arms towards her mother.

With a sigh, Susan takes her from Nan and instantly the crying stops. Ruthie straddles her mother's hip, settling into the spot.

'So,' Susan smiles, 'you're Doris.'

Doris nods.

'I wouldn't have guessed.'

Nan plonks her handbag down on a chair. 'Yes, well.'

'Look at you.' The woman scans Doris up and down, taking in her suede shoes, the pleats in her skirt and the velvet ribbon in her hair. 'How smart you look!' There are no such things in this house – no comfortable armchair or flowered cushion, no dog curled up beneath the table or wireless playing a popular tune. There's only a large table with an assortment of chairs crammed around it. A spoon has been dropped – or thrown – onto the floor, and the hob needs a good scrub.

'Aren't you going to say hello, Lilian?' Nan says to the girl still holding onto Susan's skirt, and releasing Lilian's fingers, she draws her over for a kiss.

There's another boy standing with Bobby in the doorway now.

'What are you loitering there for?' says Nan, and when they come in, the new boy receives a kiss on the cheek like Lilian. Nan's done this before, realises Doris, her face growing hot; she's kissed these strange children left, right and centre, while Doris herself knew nothing about it.

And there are even more of them because an older girl comes downstairs carrying a baby. 'Hello, my angel.' Nan's face opens into a genuine smile and she hugs the girl, pressing a kiss onto her hair. 'And Reg.' She pinches the bald baby's cheek. 'Here's Granma to see you.'

Angel? Nan's *angel*?

'And this is Doris,' says Nan.

Doris and the girl stand face to face. 'Hello,' says the girl.

This one, older than the others, is thin with long hair, but Doris can't take her eyes off her. She has the loveliest smile she's ever seen, and a serenity Doris has never come across before. 'Hello.'

'There's a lot of us, en't there? Do you know who everyone is?'

Doris shakes her head.

'Right, I'll do it in order, oldest to youngest. So I'm Dolores and I'm twelve.'

When she says 'Dolores', at first Doris thinks that she's said 'Doris', only stumbled over it. But it's not Doris' name. This girl who's so capably carrying a baby, and who brought such a look to Nan's face, is two years younger than Doris.

Doris was born first but it seems she wasn't good enough because her parents gave her away. Then they had Dolores and gave her a strikingly similar name – as though she were a better, improved version. It makes Doris think of the way that sometimes when she draws a picture and it doesn't turn out as she wanted, she scratches it out and starts over again. Dolores must have turned out fine though because they kept her, and now she has everything that ought to have been Doris': brothers and sisters and parents. And love. Here she is soaking up all the love that was meant for *her*, for *Doris*.

Dolores turns to the staring boys. 'That's Bobby, he's ten. And Michael's eight. Then it's Lilian, who's five. Ruthie's just turned two – haven't you, Ruthie?'

From her position on Susan's hip, Ruthie nods, her thumb in her mouth.

'And this here's Reg.' The baby gnaws on his own knuckles so that his gums squeak.

Will Doris remember them all? There are so many of them!

Lilian frowns. Her hair has a tinge of red in it, and her face is freckled. 'Are you really our sister?'

The kitchen quietens.

'Of course she is,' says Nan.

Susan blinks back to life. 'I told you, didn't I? I explained it.'

What did she tell them? Doris would love to know.

'Doris has been here before,' says Nan. 'She visited when she was a tot and Dolores had just been born.'

'So we've already met!' says Dolores. 'Do you remember it?'

But Doris doesn't.

'Where's Jim?' asks Nan. 'Didn't you tell him we were coming?'

Jim. That'll be her father then. She's been wondering why he isn't here.

'I did, but he had to go to work. They're laying football and hockey pitches down in Rowheath for Mr Cadbury. It's extra pay on Saturdays, but he said he'd be back in time for your visit.'

And that reminds Lilian again: 'I want biscuits!'

Bobby goes to take one. 'Can we?'

But Susan slaps his hand away. 'Don't pick. Let me at least get them on a plate first.' She puts Ruthie on the floor, and before the child can break into a howl, pushes a biscuit into her hand.

The kettle's boiled and Susan pours hot water into a teapot while Nan opens a cupboard and takes out cups and saucers. 'Where are those other cups? The new ones?'

'Children broke 'em,' says Susan.

'You need new china.'

'I need a lot of things.'

Doris presses her hip into the corner of the table. That at least is hard and real.

Soon there's bread, butter and jam out as well as biscuits. Susan glances at a small clock. 'Jim's late.'

The boys, perhaps deciding that Doris isn't that interesting after all, wander off with their food, but the rest of them sit down, Doris next to Nan, and Dolores and Susan, each with a child on her lap, opposite.

Susan pours tea into a mug for Doris just as if she were in a tea shop. 'Here you go. Sorry about the biscuits; they've caught a bit.'

'They look nice,' Doris says.

'Well, just help yourself.'

Doris takes one, but she doesn't want biscuits, or bread and butter. She wants a mother who'll read to her in bed, who'll ask her questions about herself and bake her a cake on her birthday. Sneaking little peeks so as not to be rude, she gathers the details of Susan: the wide face and brown hair, the solid shoulders and eyebrows the same shape as Harry's. She looks tired; there are dark circles beneath her eyes and a tension in her face like elastic that's been pulled to breaking-point.

'And how've you been, love?' Nan asks Dolores.

'I lost a tooth last week.' And Dolores opens her mouth to show Nan. 'I think it's the last one though. I've got all my grown-up teeth now.'

'So you have.'

'Did you have all your teeth when you were my age, Doris?' asks Dolores.

'Yes.'

'Reg is getting a new tooth too. He doesn't like it though, do you, Reggie?'

'You could do with some meat putting on your bones,' Nan says to Dolores, glancing at the overdone biscuits. 'Maybe I'll take you to the fish and chip shop.'

'Ooh, I love fish and chips!'

Lilian slides off Susan's lap. 'Tell us about yourself then,' Susan says to Doris.

Doris freezes. What can she talk about? Would Susan want to hear about school? Except that's done with now of course. Or how she skinned her knee slipping on ice last winter?

Susan's waiting, as though Doris is a suspect apple that she's turning over, examining and pressing to work out whether it'll be any good to eat. The words catch in Doris' throat, but Nan answers for her. 'She's a good girl. Did well at school and behaves herself at home. Don't you, Dot?'

Doris nods. None of this feels real. They're all actors in some strange play, and in a moment the curtain will fall and they'll go back to their real lives. She takes a bite of bread and butter but it sticks to the roof of her mouth. There's a chip on the handle of her mug, and she passes her thumb over it, back and forth, back and forth, a tiny soothing roughness in the porcelain.

'There's jam if you like,' says Susan.

A little shock flickers through her then as she recognises Nan's home-made jam, the label with Nan's handwriting on it: *Plum Jam, Autumn '24*. The vanishing jams and chutneys, scones and cakes. The sausage rolls Nan said she was taking to one of her charitable meetings. There was the church committee too, the women's social improvement association, the knitting circle. But… is this where Nan came all those times she was meant to be somewhere else? Doris wants to get up and run through the little hall and out of the front door, and not stop until she finds a place where she can think.

Nan takes a bite of biscuit, grimaces and washes it quickly down with tea. 'You never were one for baking.'

Doris gapes, but Susan doesn't respond.

'I'm home!' A man's voice. The front door bangs shut and a pit opens in Doris' stomach. It's Susan's husband. Her father. That's where she gets her surname from: Palmer like him, not Linnet like Nan and Grandad and Harry.

'Hello, love.' Susan smiles as he enters the kitchen.

'Jim,' says Nan primly.

Jim's hands and face are dusty. There's a smudge of dirt on one cheek.

Reg waves his arms in excitement. 'Hello, Dad,' beams Dolores.

'Hello, Doll. Quite the crowd in here.'

'Yes.' Dolores is glowing with excitement. 'Nan brought Doris! And she and I have met before, even though neither of us remembers.'

Jim's blue eyes settle on her. 'So. You're Doris, are you?'

Nan lays a hand on Doris' and gives it a squeeze. 'Yes,' says Doris, her voice coming out odd.

'And I'm Jim, Susan's husband.'

Doris blinks.

'I'll just go and wash up.' He passes through into the scullery, and there's the sound of water running into the sink. When he comes back out, his hands are clean and his face pink where he's towelled it dry. He takes Reg, throws him up in the air and catches him so he squeals with laughter. Then he kisses Dolores. Doris half expects him to come to her next but he doesn't. 'So,' he says, 'your Nan treats you well, does she?'

The question catches her by surprise. 'Y-yes, of course.'

He turns to Nan. 'You've turned out a duchess! No expense spared, eh?'

Nan sits up straighter. 'That's right.'

There's a pocket of silence, and Susan reaches for a clean mug and pours out some tea. 'Here you go, love. It's still hot.'

Jim takes a seat as Susan butters more bread.

'Yes,' says Nan, as if answering an unspoken question, 'Doris is a good girl. She's finished with school now too, and got no work yet – so she can mind the children for you, Susan.'

Doris starts. Mind the children? What, *these* children?

'Yes,' cries Dolores. 'You can come and spend time here, with us! I'll show you everything, and we'll become best friends.'

'That's right.' Nan turns to Doris. 'You'd like that, wouldn't you?'

Doris is sweating slightly, but Nan is glaring so she nods.

'That's all right, isn't it, Jim,' says Susan, 'if she can mind the children sometimes?'

Chewing, Jim considers. 'If it helps you, it is.' He jerks his chin at the uneaten biscuit on Doris' plate. 'Aren't you going to finish your tea then? Children eat what's put in front of them here.'

Quickly Doris picks it up and eats. Then they wait for Jim to finish. Dolores amuses Reg by hanging a teaspoon off her nose and pulling faces, but Nan and Susan have run out of things to say, or at any rate things they can say in front of Doris.

'Right then,' says Nan as soon as Jim's done eating, 'we'd best be off.' And she picks up her handbag.

Jim leans back in his chair. 'Ta-ra then.'

Dolores leans over to touch Doris' arm. 'When'll you come back?' That thin hand on her arm. That girl – half angel, half girl – wanting to be her friend.

'I don't know.'

'Soon enough,' says Nan. 'Bye now, love.'

Susan stands. 'Bye, Doris.' And there they are, a nice neat little family group.

'Goodbye, Mrs...' She flushes. 'Er... Mum.'

Never has a word felt so wrong in her mouth. And almost imperceptibly, Susan flinches.

She collapses, stunned, at the foot of her bed. Nan doesn't follow her up. The house makes faint sounds around her: the curtains chafe in a breeze from the open window, the water pipes knock, a bird scratches on the roof. She feels as though she's been dropped from a great height or knocked on the head, and she can't comprehend it, not any of it. Her parents – those people she met this afternoon, who are so utterly unlike what she'd imagined them to be. And brothers and sisters! She'd never even imagined those. How could they be her family? She's more familiar with the dustman and milkman than she is with any of them.

And her father. Those comments about Nan treating her too well, and the expression on his face when he looked at her clothes. Doesn't he want her to be treated well and have nice things? Perhaps he doesn't. He didn't hug her or kiss her or even smile at her.

Susan hadn't hugged or kissed her either, but then again she *was* weighed down with children. She'd smiled at Doris though, and been nice about how smart she looked, and poured her tea for her, so although that part wasn't the way Doris had imagined, it hadn't been so terrible either. Except she can still see Susan's face when they said goodbye, and can't untangle the complication behind her mother's eyes: a mixture of longing and something else – something almost like hate.

But no, she must be wrong about that. And now, now she's expected to go back and look after those children!

She scowls at the wall between her room and Harry's. He must have come in late last night because she didn't hear him come in; and he'd gone out early this morning before she was even awake.

An hour or so later she hears the front door open and close, and Harry's tread in the hall. She hears him exchange words with Nan in the kitchen, their voices tight and clipped, then his footsteps come up the stairs – slowly, hesitantly – and stop outside her door. For a while there's no knock, and a knot of emotion builds in her: she wants him to come in, but for the first time in her life she also wants him to stay away.

At last though the knock comes, a light tapping on the other side of the door, and the door opens – not the way Harry usually knocks and comes in at all – and there he is. But his hair is uncombed, and he looks as if he's had even less sleep than her. 'Can I come in?'

Since when has he ever asked?

She doesn't move. Something is building in her. The inside of her mouth is hot.

Harry comes in and closes the door. He shifts awkwardly, and she's suddenly aware that he's up there and she's down here on the floor, and she's about to stand when he comes and sits on the corner of her bed. 'I...' He bites his lip, lowers his eyes. 'I don't know what to say.'

The thing that's been building in her explodes and she lunges at him, knocking him off the bed. They fall to the floor. Harry tries to sit up, but scrabbling onto her knees, she thumps him. 'You knew!' Nan lied to her too of course, but that's grown-ups and grown-ups have laws of their own. 'You knew and you didn't tell me!' Her nails catch him on the neck.

He grabs her wrists, fending her off. 'I wanted to. I did!'

Again, she tries to hit him, but here it is, another gap between them: she's a girl of fourteen and he a man of twenty, and that, right now, is the widest distance in the world. 'You bloody well knew and you didn't bloody even bloody tell me!' She's crying hot tears now, and there's so much to cry about. All those Palmers, and Nan and Harry, and the way her own life has been kept from her. The person she thought she was has been swept away, and now she's nobody.

That's what they used to call her at school: a nobody. They said she was a foundling no one wanted, and that Nan got saddled with her. She'd always assumed they were just being mean, but now it seems there was truth in their taunts – the same truth that made Nan's friends look at her oddly, not at all the way they looked at Harry.

She and Harry are both kneeling, and he's holding her wrists together, her hands palm to palm as though she were praying. 'I wanted to tell you. I wanted to!'

'Let go of me!'

'… but Dad said if I ever breathed a word about Sue, he'd turf me out.'

Sue! It's a shock to hear him refer to Susan; to understand that Harry, who she believed was hers, in fact belongs to the whole horde of them. Because Susan is his sister, and her children are his nephews and nieces.

'Mum made me swear on the Bible,' Harry says.

One time, an occasion that still looms dark and terrifying in Doris' memory, Nan made her swear on the Bible too. The hefty black book with its dry cover and gilt lettering was taken down from its place on the shelf and Nan made Doris lay her hand on it. Nan held that hand down while Doris swore never to steal money from Nan's purse again, even though it had only been tuppence. And pinned there between Nan and God, Doris had known with certainty that she'd be smitten with a bolt of lightning and sent promptly to a hot and sizzling hell if she even so much as touched Nan's handbag again.

'But that was years ago!' she says.

Harry's hands are clasped around hers. 'I know. But that's just the point, isn't it? I didn't know any better. And time passed and it got too late to say anything. Then when I wanted to, I couldn't. I mean, how do you tell someone something like that?'

Yanking her hands away, she sits back on her heels. Now

she begins to understand. Not talking about Susan became the normal thing to do, and as time went by it would have become less and less possible to say anything.

'I'm sorry, Dot. I'm really, really sorry. About everything. All of it.'

She breathes in, breathes out. What is there to say to that?

'Did Mum tell you what happened?'

'I don't know.' She doesn't know anything any more.

'Dad and Sue had a massive bust-up. I don't exactly remember it, I was only little, but I know it happened. She left, and then you arrived, and after that no one talked about her. I mean not a single word, just as if she'd never existed. Me and Mum weren't allowed to see her, but Mum went in secret. She took me along a couple of times and made me swear not to tell. Then when you were three or so, Mum and Dad argued. Mum said you belonged with Sue, and she took you back. But you stopped eating and they got scared you'd die, so back you came, all skin and bone. And I was so happy. Me and Mum fed you all sorts of delicious things. Dad didn't say a word about any of it. But then after he died, there was no need to pussyfoot around any more and that was when I wanted to tell you, only…'

'Why didn't you then?' she says, her voice raspy with held-back tears.

'We argued about it, me and Mum, but she said it was her business and she'd tell you in her own good time. Which I suppose is now.'

'And what if she hadn't? What if she hadn't told me?'

She waits for an answer, but none comes. What an excellent liar Nan has turned out to be. She's managed to run the two halves of her life quite efficiently while holding them entirely apart, each out of sight of the other.

Doris' doll Maud has fallen off the bed. Harry picks her up, smooths her hair and straightens her dress. It reminds Doris of the times they used to plait Maud's hair and 'prettify' her. But they aren't children any longer.

They sit quietly for a while. Doris can hear Nan riddling the stove. 'She looks like you,' she says.

'Who does?'

'Susan.' There was something about the eyes. The nose too.

'Yes, well she is my sister.'

Yes, that's what happens with family: they look like each other.

'Don't start crying again.' Harry shuffles over and puts his arms around her. 'Poor Dotty. Poor little sweetheart.'

She presses her face into Harry's shoulder as more tears arrive, and he rubs her back.

Eventually her sobs grow further apart and the world flattens out again. Harry's shoulder is damp, and as she draws away she notes that the smell of him has changed, and the shape of his face. He's taller than he used to be, and his skin and voice are different; and all of this scares her because she wants the Harry she knew to be there forever.

'They're nice people, Dot. You'll get to like them.'

They sit in silence again. Doris feels diluted, one crumb among many.

'You don't hate me, do you?' Harry asks softly.

On the bed between them, Maud lies staring up at the ceiling as though nothing's changed. 'I don't know.' He lied to her. Betrayed her. All these years.

He tucks her hair behind her ear. 'It's always been you and me. I love you more than anyone, Dotty, don't you know that?'

And her heart melts.

CHAPTER 12

Hide and Seek

Harborne, 1925

Susan uncovers the mangle and wheels it away from the back wall and out into the small paved yard. No grass here, no plants or trees. She looks worn out and pale, as if she too, like the washing, has been boiled, washed in carbolic and blued.

'Are you going to mangle the shirts?' Nan asked Susan when she dropped Doris off.

'Maybe,' Susan replied.

'Best take off the buttons then.'

'I have mangled shirts before, you know, Mum.'

'All right, no need to get touchy. I was just asking.'

'You're always just asking.'

Nan bristled. 'I will not be spoken to like that, Susan. Not after all I've done for you.' Facing one another, it had seemed to Doris that they were still talking, only silently, and for the first time she noted the similarity between them: the set of their shoulders, the line of their noses. Then Nan left.

The sheets have to be folded thin enough to feed through the mangle, and while Doris feeds them in, Susan turns the handle, water dripping from the heavy cylinders into the tin bath beneath. 'Mind your fingers,' Susan says, and her saying it makes Doris feel happy, as if every little part of her is precious.

When the sheets are done, Susan stops to turn the screw,

widening the gap between the rollers for a thick pair of overalls. 'It's nice to have you here to help.'

It's the first time they've been alone together. 'I like to help you,' Doris says. She hates washday at home, and if at all possible avoids helping Nan with the laundry. But now, here, it's different. As they work, she wants to tell Susan things – all the little details of her life. She wants to tell her about Harry and Nan and school. About the game she used to play every night at bedtime in which Maud was sent careering off a cliff or plunging into the ocean. *Lost*, she called it, but the game always had to end with Maud being found and claimed, then restored to her rightful place in her mummy Doris' arms. But instead of telling Susan any of this, Doris only says 'We don't have this much laundry at home.'

'No, not with just the three of you.' Susan folds the overalls and lays them in a basket. There are only smaller items – towels and socks, short trousers and linens – left to feed through the mangle now. And the shirts. 'He came to see me, you know, before he left that last time.'

Doris looks up. 'Who did?'

'Dad. Your grandad, I mean.'

'He came here?'

Susan nods. 'I hadn't seen him in years, not since—' She turns the handle as Doris feeds through some socks. Then she stops. 'I couldn't believe it. It was like seeing a ghost. He drank a cup of tea and… and he said he was sorry. And you know, I think he was. I think he was sorry.' She looks at Doris and bites her lip. 'I'm sorry too.'

Doris' insides give a great lurch.

'I'm sorry I couldn't keep you.'

There are sounds from the street – someone calling, a window banging shut – but they seem far away. Now it will happen. Susan will grab her and hug her, and hold on as if she'll never let her go. She'll tell her how much she wishes she'd kept her.

Doris swallows. 'Why couldn't you?'

Susan looks surprised at such a question. 'Oh, I just couldn't, don't you see? I couldn't.' She bends to pick up a fallen sock, and all the bright possibilities shrink and vanish.

No, Doris doesn't see, not really. It seems all too clear to Susan, just as it does to Nan, but she doesn't see at all. All she sees is her mother and the pile of mangled washing and a tin bath full of cold water.

Susan turns to get more laundry, then stops and turns back, as if there's something she's forgotten to say. 'It wasn't your fault, you know. I mean, it wasn't anything you did.'

Doris' throat constricts. Until this moment, it had never occurred to her that it *could* have been her fault.

Susan shakes out a shirt. 'What do you think? Shall we risk mangling the buttons?'

Bobby, Michael, Lilian and Ruthie swarm out into the yard. One of them has found a kitten, and it's here, mewling as it's passed from one set of hands to the next. They beg Susan to keep it.

'Please, Mum,' says Bobby.

'Oh, I'll do anything,' says Lilian.

Reg, who's been napping upstairs, starts to cry. 'See what you've done with all this racket?' tuts Susan, then turns to Doris. 'Can you fetch him down?'

Doris pegs up the sock she's holding then heads inside. She follows the sound upstairs and into one of the bedrooms, where Reg is wailing in a cot, trying but failing to pull himself up onto his feet. But Dolores has got there before her.

'Oh, what's the matter, Reggie? It's all right. I'm here, en't I? Here I am.' She reaches into the cot, and the moment he's in her arms, he quietens. 'Look, Reg, who's this? It's Doris.'

'Your mum asked me to come up,' Doris says awkwardly. This must be Jim and Susan's room, she realises, glancing round, and the other two bedrooms must be shared between the children.

It feels as though she has no right to be here. In this room.

In this house. This whole month she's been waiting for that elusive moment to arrive; the one where she slots into her new family. Then all the wrongness will dissipate, just as it does in *The Secret Garden*, where the neglected garden springs to life, and Colin can suddenly walk, and Mary metamorphoses into a kind, friendly girl. And of course, with the return of Colin's father, they become a real family.

But Dolores' attention is on the baby. 'What a fusspot you are, Reggie. Did you miss me?'

Reg smiles a gummy smile.

'Give me a kiss then.' Dolores brings her cheek to his mouth. 'That's it. And Doris – give her a kiss too.' Turning Reg around, she holds him up to Doris' cheek.

His mouth is warm and leaves a wet patch that Doris quickly wipes away.

'Doris and Dolores,' says Dolores. 'They're almost the same.'

Similar but not the same.

'You need changing, don't you?' says Dolores, sniffing Reg's bottom. 'Here' – she plops Reg in Doris' arms – 'I won't be a sec.'

Doris has never held a baby before. Reg in his cotton dress is compact and heavy and warm, but she can smell what's in his nappy, and averts her face. He kicks, bouncing himself in her arms, and she tightens her grip, afraid of dropping him.

Immediately his face crumples and he begins to wail. 'Don't,' she says. 'She's coming back. She won't be a second.'

Drool slips down his chin but she can't bear to wipe it away.

'Here I am,' calls Dolores from the stairwell, and she appears carrying a bowl of water. Putting it down on the floor, she reaches under the bed for a pile of rags and a towel that she spreads out on the bed. 'Lie him here.'

Judging by the stains, the towel has been used for this purpose before.

'Don't you like babies?' asks Dolores as Doris lays him down.

'I don't know. I haven't had anything to do with them before.'

'Haven't you changed a nappy before then?'

'No.'

Dolores nods towards Reg. 'Go on then.'

'What?'

'You do it. Undo that pin there. Go on – that's it.'

But when, with pinching fingers, Doris peels back the cloth, the mess underneath makes her shrink back.

Dolores hands her a wet rag. 'You've got to clean him quick, before he rolls over.'

'No. No I can't.'

Dolores laughs. 'Move over then, cowardy custard.' And settling on her knees, she wipes and dips and wipes again with an efficiency that makes it hard to believe she's two years younger than Doris.

Doris tries not to look.

'Was that mean of me?' says Dolores. 'All right it *was* mean. I'm sorry. But you ought to know how to change a nappy.'

'Why? Maybe I won't have babies.'

'Course you will, why wouldn't you? I know I'm going to.' Dolores pats Reg dry with the end of the towel. 'There. You're my little sweetheart, en't you?' She blows raspberries on Reg's bare tummy and he laughs, pumping his arms and legs, his tiny willy jiggling.

Who did this for me, Doris wonders? Who cleaned me and changed my nappy cloth? Did Susan do it, or was it only ever Nan? She can't imagine Nan cooing and fussing this way, and certainly not blowing raspberries on her naked stomach!

'Did you know about me?'

Dolores stops blowing raspberries and looks at Doris over her shoulder. 'No. Not until Mum told us last week.'

The same time as Nan told her then. 'What… what did she tell you?'

'That we had a sister. And that you'd been living with Grandma all this time.'

Reg has caught hold of the edge of the towel, stuffed it into his mouth and is babbling happily to himself. 'Did she tell you anything else?'

'Like what?'

Won't someone tell her what she wants to know? 'Did she tell you how come I live with Nan?'

'No. We're not meant to ask about things like that – grown-up things.' With her nose, Dolores nuzzles the folds in Reg's neck till he giggles, then wraps a fresh nappy around him.

'I didn't know about you either,' says Doris.

'I know. It's nice having brothers and sisters though, en't it?'

'Yes,' Doris lies.

'And now you've got a mum and dad too.'

Has she? It doesn't feel that way.

'Although now I'm not the oldest one any more. And I liked being the oldest.'

'Sorry.' Doris was born first; she can do nothing about that. Still, it wasn't long before Dolores came along and took her place. Does Dolores have such thoughts too? Does she see Doris as the first, misshapen version of *her*? Is that why she's always so nice to her? Out of pity?

Dolores shrugs. 'Oh, I don't really mind.' Standing, she hoists Reg up. 'Do you think you're going to come and live with us now?'

'No!' Doris looks down at the dirty nappy, the water bowl full of stinking rags. 'I mean, Nan hasn't said so.'

Half an hour later the kitten's gone, and Bobby and Lilian are playing a noisy game of marbles in the hall, while Ruthie, singing loudly, is pushing an ancient toy pram with a white porcelain handle up and down, banging into the walls as she goes. There's no doll inside, but then they don't need dolls in a house like this one, where there are real babies to tend to.

'Mind Ruthie doesn't swallow a marble again,' calls Susan from the yard.

'We will!' Bobby shouts back.

The front door is open, and outside, Michael has slung a rope over the crossbar of a lamppost and is running and flying around it.

Doris presses herself against the wall as Ruthie bowls past, running over her toes. She's meant to be minding them – some of them, or all of them, she isn't sure. What she is sure of is that she doesn't know the first thing about minding children. But so far, no one seems to have noticed.

Would they want her to live here? Would Nan and Harry?

She looks outside again, half expecting to see Jim coming home from work. Susan has already put the dinner on, and Doris will be able to leave soon. Michael stops swinging around the lamppost. Perhaps he'll ask her to join him and have a go. She imagines gripping the rope in both hands and running; feels her feet lifting clear off the ground.

She smiles, and Michael lets go of the rope, gives his nose a pick and heads over. 'Come in here,' he says, jabbing his thumb towards the parlour, 'and we can play something.'

'All right.'

As soon as she goes in, he pushes the door shut. This parlour's smaller than the one at home. The wallpaper's thickly patterned with flowers, and there's a table and chairs against one wall. A row of Reg's nappies is draped on the fireguard to dry, and on the mantelpiece above are brass figurines that, if they fell, might knock a child unconscious. Even with so many living in the house, it's clear that this room hardly ever gets used. 'Weddings, funerals, high days and holidays,' Nan sometimes says, 'that's the only times most people use their parlour.' The parlour at 45 Nursery Road is used daily and always has been.

'What do you want to play?' she asks Michael. 'Have you got dominoes? Or checkers?'

'No. But we could play hide and seek.'

'What, in here?' She looks around. 'But there's nowhere to hide.'

'There is. I know somewhere.' The very corners of his mouth turn up. 'Close your eyes and count to ten.'

She nods – 'All right' – and closes her eyes. She counts quickly but when she opens her eyes again, he's gone. She can see under the table, and the door is still closed.

She turns round.

'Arrrr!' Michael springs up at her from below, arms raised, and with a cry she falls back. He must have been crouched right behind her, and now he's laughing.

'That's not funny,' she says, getting to her feet.

'Yes it is. Look at your face!'

She presses her back against the wall. She'd like to slap him but she mustn't. She must be polite and proper and behave herself, just as Nan's constantly telling her to.

'Your face,' says Michael again, but his laughter peters out. He tips his head to one side. 'Are you sure you're our sister?'

Beneath her fingers, the lacquered wallpaper is hard as a shell. 'That's what Nan said.'

Michael's blue eyes are fixed on her. 'Why'd Mum and Dad give you away then?' He jerks his chin at her. 'What did you do to make 'em not want you?'

Her heart expands and contracts painfully.

'And what have you come back now for anyway? We don't need you to mind us. We don't need anyone to mind us. And we don't want you here.'

Her lips start to tremble. Then she blinks. 'What are you doing?' Because he is unbuttoning his fly, putting in his hand, taking out his willy. He is taking aim.

She cries out as the stream of piss hits her skirt. It dribbles warm down her shins and splatters onto her shoes. Then, as suddenly as it began, the arc of it shrinks back. A final drip and, without a word, Michael tucks his willy back into his trousers and does up his fly.

Stepping carefully over the puddle he's made, he opens the door. 'Muuuuum, Doris has wet herself!'

Bobby and Lilian appear and gawp, wide-eyed. Lilian covers her mouth and titters.

Jim walks in through the open front door. 'What's going on here then?'

Michael backs away down the hall, pointing back at Doris. 'She wet herself.'

Jim stops outside the parlour. He looks down at Doris' skirt, her shoes. He looks at the floorboards and his face twists in anger.

'It wasn't me,' she gulps.

Susan appears with Reg in her arms. Her mouth drops open as she takes in the scene. 'What's happened?'

Doris' face burns.

'What's happened is, The Duchess has pissed in my bloody parlour!'

Reg's fat hand opens and closes around Susan's thumb. Reg who's always safe in somebody's arms. Who can touch Susan whenever he likes, who can cry and wail and spray her with food and she won't mind. 'Doris? Are you all right, love?'

With tears pricking at her eyes, she rushes past Jim, past Ruthie's abandoned toy pram and out of the front door. Scattered around the rose bush, the fallen petals look like severed tongues, and behind her the house hums and vibrates with dislike, glad to have finally forced her out.

The front door has been left on the latch. The smell of Nan's fruitcake fills the hall, and here's Nan coming out of the kitchen wiping her hands on her apron. As soon as she sees Doris, her expression changes.

'Dot? What on earth's happened? Are you hurt?' Her gaze slides downwards. 'What happened to your dress?'

'I-it wasn't me,' Doris blurts as fresh tears start to flow.

Nan comes and puts her arms around her. 'Of course it wasn't, love. I know you'd never do anything bad.'

'It w-was Michael. H-he peed on me.'

Nan cries out. 'Michael! I'm going to horsewhip that boy. Nasty creature!'

'It's a-a mistake,' sobs Doris. 'A-all of it. They're n-not my family.' She shakes her head, her cheek chafing against Nan's blouse.

'Shhh.' Nan presses Doris' shoulders together, as if she might fall apart otherwise. 'There now. Shh.'

Doris left The Back of Beyond and no one called her back, because no one wanted her there in the first place. 'I'm not theirs. I'm not!'

'All right, love.' Nan holds her close. Nan who looks after her. Who lied to her, yes, but who loves her nonetheless.

Thoughts swarm around, darting in and out of her head like bees around a hive. Michael taking out his willy. The stream of yellow coming at her, running warm down her legs and into her shoes. The expression on Jim's face. Reg's fingers clasped around Susan's thumb. The soft heaviness of him. *I'm sorry I couldn't keep you. I just couldn't.* Dolores blowing raspberries on Reg's tummy. The bowl of dirty water and shit-covered rags. *What did you do to make 'em not want you?*

'That's enough now.' Nan's tone is verging on exasperated. 'That'll do.'

But she can't stop crying. 'I don't want to go back there. Not ever.'

'Shh.' Nan pats her back, and slowly Doris' crying eases off. Her breathing turns juddery. 'That's it. There. Now you go and get yourself changed, and then we'll have some tea and cake. How's that?'

She's had a wash and put on clean clothes. The fire's lit and Nan's pouring boiling water into the teapot. The fruitcake, still warm from the oven, is on the kitchen table, and so are cups and plates from Nan's good set – the china painted with flowers and vines that belonged to Nan's mother and that usually stays safe in the dresser.

'That's better.' Nan smiles, touching Doris' hair. Her hair that's darker than Susan's, and far darker than Jim's. 'Cake?'

Doris nods. Her eyes are swollen from crying. Her cow's eyes, large as Mary Pickford's and Theda Bara's, not small and blue like those of her sisters and brothers.

Nan cuts a slice of cake and slides the plate across to Doris. Then she cuts herself a slice. The smell of it is wrapped around the kitchen, warm and comforting as the crackle of the fire in the stove. How strange that all houses aren't like this one, quiet and orderly, with open spaces you can move across, and the flicker of leaves cast on the kitchen wall by the setting sun.

'Where's Harry?' she asks.

'Oh, out somewhere. Who knows where he goes these days? He doesn't tell me who his friends are and I've given up asking.'

Doris is glad he isn't here to witness her humiliation.

'I just wish he'd find a nice girl to bring home,' says Nan.

Harry's had two girlfriends, but neither of them lasted long enough to be introduced.

Two cups of tea are poured out, and after a moment's hesitation Nan fetches the whisky bottle. 'It's Grandad's birthday today, you know.'

'Is it?'

Nan pours some whisky into her cup. 'Just a drop to mark the occasion.' Doris has never seen it drunk with tea before; Nan sometimes has some in a glass in the evenings, but Nan ought to know. 'I can't believe that Michael. Disgusting, disgraceful behaviour. That he would think to do such a thing! Now tell me, how did it happen?'

Haltingly, Doris tells her. Then they sit in silence.

'Nan?'

Nan sips her tea. 'Yes.'

'I don't want to go back there. I don't have to, do I?'

Nan takes another sip, then sets her cup back on its saucer. She takes a while before she answers. 'No, love, not if you don't want to.'

Doris' body softens and her jaw relaxes. She doesn't have to go back there. She feels like crying with relief, except she's got no tears left.

'But what about Susan? Don't you want to see her again?'

Doris considers. Susan is surrounded by her children. She's got her new baby. 'Not really. Although…' She sees Susan's tired face again, and the way that, as she turned the mangle, she kept blowing at a stray wisp of hair. 'Does she still need someone to help her?'

Nan sniffs. 'She's made her bed so now she's got to lie in it. All those children on his wage! Why he can't just behave himself, I don't know.'

Doris would like to ask Nan to explain this, but knows when to keep quiet. She drinks some more tea and eats some cake. Nan's on her second cup of tea and whisky when Doris speaks again. '*You* want me, don't you? *You* won't give me away?'

'What? Of course I won't, love. Now eat up, there's a good girl.'

Gathering a large bit of cake onto her fork, Doris does, and nothing has ever tasted so delicious. Dried fruit bursts into sweetness beside the little hardnesses of walnut. She carries another forkful to her mouth. The fire ticks, and a log crumples into ash. She's warm and clean and safe, and she will stay here forever.

'That's it,' says Nan. 'You're better than the lot of them. And don't you forget it.'

CHAPTER 13

Dance

Baghdad, 1938

The HMV model 102 has been wound up. A needle has been put in, the speed set and one of the new records she ordered placed on the turntable. Leon is humming along as she twirls, laughing, round and round in his arms. Although the song is called 'Sing Sing Sing', there's no singing in it, only Benny Goodman's band making the most glorious sound and setting a beat so fast she can barely keep up.

Leon swings her round. The window flashes in and out of sight, the wall of the building across the street, the top of a palm tree, and she's laughing, hopping and skipping and jiggling to the music that's playing on and on until she thinks it will never stop, doesn't want it to ever stop, because here are Leon's hands in hers and no one to tell them they mustn't or give them looks; because this is their house, yes their very own house, theirs theirs theirs, with no old women to tut and mutter behind your back. Here they are, their shoulders, knees, elbows, waists, necks, twisting and bending, filling the space that's theirs, and she is euphoric with it.

The house is small, but who cares? She wouldn't care if they were in a tent so long as she has Leon. Just like his mother's house, this one is built around a courtyard for privacy from the street, and for coolness. The ceilings are high, with vents that carry the warm air up through the building. Upstairs is a covered sort of balcony that juts out over the street, meshed so you can see out but people can't see in. The facilities, naturally, are primitive. There's a kitchen with a tap at one end and a fire at the other, and a funny clay oven that she hasn't the slightest clue how to use. The toilet is as far away as it's possible to be, all the way across the courtyard next to the fuel room. She hates having to go to the bathroom at night when she can't see if there are scorpions or spiders. Leon says to wake him, that he'll go with her, but she can't bring herself when he's so fast asleep.

On the day they moved in, she'd stopped outside the front door and looked up. 'What on earth's that?'

A slipper was nailed to the lintel.

'It's for good luck,' said Leon. 'To keep away the evil eye.' And she'd laughed because it sounded like something Nan might do.

Now she's unpacked Nan's linen, and gone to the market to buy all sorts of things: plates and cutlery and towels. She searched high and low to find rugs that weren't too gaudy, and got a few other decorative bits and bobs as well. It turns out that she's good at haggling. When she gets time, she might paint some pictures to hang up on the walls too.

One thing she doesn't doubt is that Leon will look after her out here. He's checked the entire house over: the septic pit, the kitchen tap, the great clunky electric ceiling fan that stirs hot air around the room. He's made sure there's more than enough fuel. And now, when he's not at work, he prowls around the place looking for things that need fixing. He has a list of them pinned up, and everything on the list has now been crossed through. He's sanded down the warped doorframe so that the door opens and closes smoothly; he's put up hooks for her to hang her dressing gown on; and in the basement, which is the coolest room in the house and the place to escape to when it gets unbearably hot, he's managed to make things even cooler. Right up against the windows, there are cactuses growing out in the courtyard, and Leon has fashioned a net to hold them all pressed together into a low wall. Then he's run a waterpipe with holes in it along the top so that water drips slowly down, and the air passing into the room comes in cold.

For now, he's done everything he can think of to improve the house. The fixer of broken things, she calls him, which he likes. He wants to take the HMV apart to see how it works but she's forbidden him to. No one is going to tinker with her record player.

When Leon slows down, she doesn't let him stop, but makes him carry on until the song is finally, finally done. Then they collapse on the divan, laughing and gulping in deep breaths. Beneath her bare feet the tiled floor is cool, and the room is thrumming – or is it her blood beating in her ears, her breath roaring in and out of her lungs? Somewhere outside, a dog barks a staccato bark as though repeating the music.

Leon lies back on the cushions, smiling and happy, and suddenly she wants him – not tonight, but now. Getting to her feet, she grabs his hands and leans backwards to force him up, and once he's standing, she pulls him after her to their new bedroom.

He's hers, and she wants to absorb every detail of him. With their faces close together, she examines the way his eyelids grow heavy when she touches him like this, here, or here; the way his pupils enlarge, turning his eyes blacker. She lays her hands on the chest that's so surprisingly broad, as though it houses more than one heart; examines his nipples and shoulder blades, his belly button and, on the other side, the bowl-like dip in his lower back. She draws her fingers across his skin and stops to press them into his flesh. She loves him, that's what she wants to say, except that it doesn't seem apt to say so now, because whoever thought that love and sex were one and the same thing got it entirely wrong.

She finds him standing on the small verandah. He slips his arm around her waist. 'Can you smell the desert?'

She nods. It smells of hot bricks and resin and dust.

‘Look.’ He points up at a sky thick with stars. ‘There. Do you see it? The Little Bear.’ His finger scans across the sky. ‘And the Swan.’ It dips. ‘And Venus.’

She leans back against him, and it’s like the game of trust they used to play at school where you had to fall backwards into another girl’s arms. She gazes up, her vision filled with stars. She is falling backwards, and knows that Leon will catch her.

CHAPTER 14

Woman in Gold

Harborne, 1925

'Where?'

'You heard me.' Nan busies herself dusting the skirting boards. 'If you're not going to help Susan any longer, then you've got to get a job. It's one or the other.'

'But a butcher's!' she wails. 'That's just demeaning.'

'Yes, well beggars can't be choosers.'

'We're not beggars.'

'Nor do we want to be.'

'But a butcher's shop, Nan.' Doris closes her eyes for a moment as if that will shut it out. 'Anyway that's boy's work. Whoever heard of a butcher's girl?'

Nan carries on dusting until she's worked her way around the entire room. 'It's seven shillings a week – nine if you last a month – *and* free cuts of meat. That's not to be sniffed at. Times are hard; there are enough people laid off and touting round for work. You ought to be grateful.'

Perhaps, but she'd still have preferred a position in a bakery or a haberdashery shop, where she and Nan had asked but found nothing. She can see too that Nan doesn't like it either – Annie Linnet's granddaughter working in a butcher's shop! – but with things as they are right now in the country, the free meat they'll get is compensation enough.

'I've shopped at Bill's for donkey's years, so it's about

time he did a little something in return. And in a year or so's time, you can find something else, can't you.'

Doris scuffs her feet in the sawdust, trying to make herself understand that she's really here. Various cuts of meat lie on silver trays inside the counter. She thinks of the soft hides and wool and feathers they once had. They felt hot in summer and got wet in the rain; they made their own particular noises and gave birth to little versions of themselves. Yet here they are, opened up and on display.

Bill comes in from the back room. He's a large man with a broad stance and thinning hair. 'And what're you standing there doing? Didn't I ask you to chop that up?'

Quickly she picks up the knife. 'I was just about to do it.'

Bill sighs. 'That's what I get for doing a favour,' he mutters.

The beef is unexpectedly squashy. Doris has never handled raw meat before and doesn't like the feel of it, nor the sensation of the knife cutting through, the pressure she has to exert to make this happen. So as she chops, she concentrates on other things: the curls of sawdust around her shoes, the tune Bill's humming, her schoolfriends (although 'friends' isn't quite the right word). Emily, quiet and jumpy, would be a lamb, whereas Ruby with her fat cheeks and set-back shoulders is more like a pig. Hilda might be a cow, she's kind and friendly enough – and cows are friendly, aren't they? Lumbering and slow, but friendly.

Bill's watching her. 'Squeamish, are we?'

'No.'

He grunts, unconvinced.

When customers come in, she watches the way he serves them, wrapping their meat in greased paper and handing it over with a smile and a few words. By afternoon she's handling money, putting it in the till and counting back the change. In the lull between customers, she gazes out at the street. There's not much traffic, only now and then a motorcar, a bicycle or the odd milk cart, so she watches the people instead;

examines their clothes and shoes, studies the way they move, and wonders at the secrets they carry.

Two months after leaving school, she's become familiar with a new routine. They open at eight and close at half past five, or four o'clock on a Saturday. She gets Sundays off but has to be in early on Monday to scrub the floor. Blocks of ice get delivered in the morning, and she has to hack pieces off whenever they need some in the shop, or when customers ask for some to take home. At the end of each day, there's a large pool of water in the back room that has to be mopped up.

Some of these things Bill can't do any longer. He'll brings up his hands and, with a grimace, open and close them. They're all swollen around the joints and knuckles. 'Blasted rheumatism,' he says, but he shows her how to cut meat properly, how to truss a piece of beef or pork loin, and how to make good sausages. When he comes back from the slaughterhouse, she helps him unload, but he'll do the heavy work – 'Mind out, you need some heft for this bit, love' – like lifting a great side of pork, its skin scalded and shaved, and carrying it into the back room. There, he'll set to work chopping the side into the pieces that'll end up in the counter or dressing the window. As he works, he likes to talk about his boy: how the little chap's starting to walk now, and what he likes to eat, and the latest thing he's done that Bill finds funny but she doesn't see as anything special. She smiles anyway though because she likes Bill and feels sorry for his poor hands.

The paraphernalia of the job has become familiar too: the hooks and knives and cleaver and block, the stained cloths, the wax paper and string to wrap meat into parcels with, the bucket she fills with water to sluice down the block and floor, and the sheet of flypaper attached to a light fixture above the counter that's covered in dead or dying flies. Then there's Bill's red-streaked apron, and the saw that always hangs at his waist; on his face the tiny broken blood-vessels that make him resemble the meat he handles.

Twice a week, on Tuesdays and Fridays, she makes deliveries on a bicycle, and this is her favourite part of the week, with the wind in her face and the screech of brakes when she gets to where she's going. The rest she wouldn't exactly call fun. The shop is on the shady side of the street so they don't have to have an awning like the shops over the road, but even so, the meat releases its own distinct smell of blood and metal. She dislikes that smell. It sticks to her fingers and sinks into her hair. And she's surrounded by all its varied nuances. The smell of a kidney, say, is different to that of a heart (which Bill tells her is delicious stuffed with herbs). Lungs are mostly sold to feed cats, but liver is popular, especially when it's fresh. And then there's pluck hung up with a bowl underneath to catch the blood. And tripe, which is the worst.

'What's it today?' asks Nan when she gets in on Saturday.

'Leg of mutton.'

'Good old Bill,' says Harry, who's just come in from work himself, looking dapper in tie and collar pin, button-on suspenders and cap-toe Oxfords, his hair oiled and combed flat.

'Yes, I'll make spiced mutton for tomorrow's lunch,' says Nan.

Doris kicks off her shoes. She never has much appetite for the things she brings home; she's seen their ears and lips and dead eyes, and watched them being sawn into pieces. Once when she accompanied Bill as far as the slaughterhouse, she even saw some of those animals alive. Bill wouldn't let her inside, but the outside of the place was enough, and she wondered at the men who could do such a job day in day out. 'Sends them a bit barmy,' Bill admitted to her.

She lays out her wages on the table beside the mutton, and

Nan counts it out, giving her back a penny in every shilling. 'Who came in today then?'

Doris knows what Nan is really asking. 'Mrs Clarke bought some fillet of steak.'

Nan's eyebrows rise. 'Oh, did she now.'

'And Hilda came in.'

'Your friend from school?'

'Yes.'

'What did she buy then?'

'Lamb shank and drumsticks.' Doris pulls out a chair and drops into it. She's been on her feet all day.

'Poor Dotty, you look done in,' says Harry. 'Are you too tired for the pictures?'

She beams. 'I'm not tired.' She hasn't been out with Harry for ages.

'My treat. They're showing *Cobra*.'

'Oh. I don't like snakes.'

He laughs. 'There aren't any snakes in it, silly.'

'How do you know?'

'Because I've already seen it. But I'd like to watch it again.'

'All right then.'

'The pictures,' Nan humphs. 'All those women dressed in next to nothing, doing God knows what with goodness knows who.'

'Oh, Mum, don't be so old-fashioned.' Harry looks at his watch. 'We've got an hour,' he tells her.

'What about dinner?' asks Nan.

'Oh, we'll be fine with a bit of bread and cheese, won't we, Dot? But let's have a dance before we go.'

'Harry,' pleads Nan. 'Not dancing. Not in the house…'

'We won't break anything, promise, Mum.' They hurry into the parlour and Harry shuts the door, gets down on his hands and knees and starts to roll up the rug. 'I'll teach you how to dance the shimmy.'

'The shimmy!' Even without knowing what it was, she's certain that Nan would be scandalised.

'Don't you want to learn it?'

Of course she does. The shimmy sounds daring and forbidden and fun.

'Then be a sweetheart and wind up the gramophone.'

After the war, the entire world started to dance. Now there are dances practically every day of the week, except that Nan only approves of church dances. And they, according to Harry, are not the dances you wanted to go to. They play nothing but old-fashioned pieces like waltzes and lancers and quadrilles, and the vicar sits at the door like a guard dog as you come in, then patrols the hall to make sure no one's hands are anywhere they shouldn't be. Certainly a church dance isn't where you'd be practising the shimmy!

With the rug out of the way and the photograph of Grandad laid face down on the mantel, they begin. It's difficult, and Doris can neither move quite the way she should nor do it fast enough, but she doesn't care. The two of them shake and quiver and jiggle, and Harry looks so good dancing fast that way, with his feet tapping and lifting, and yet so funny, that she laughs and laughs till the blood is singing in her body.

At last they stop so that Harry can have a cigarette. 'That's better,' he says, exhaling a waft of smoke through his mouth and nostrils. Since getting a job as a clerk for a menswear outfitter, he can afford to buy his cigarettes ready-rolled, and a pewter case for them to live in too. 'How is old Hilda anyway?'

'Oh, fine. She's got a new brother. There was no one in the shop but us and she told me all about it – what a shock it was when she woke up one morning to find a baby there.'

'Didn't she know her mother was expecting?'

'No.' Hilda wasn't the sort to question things. 'I asked how the baby'd come out of her mother's stomach but she didn't know.' As Doris wrapped up the lamb shank, she and Hilda had speculated about the possibilities. Had the doctor cut it out? Perhaps, but then how could her mother have been up and doing laundry by ten o'clock the same morning? However the baby had appeared, it must be the same way Reg came out of Susan. Although she doesn't want to think about Susan, nor any of that lot. 'Maybe it came out of her belly button. Do you think that's it?'

Harry bursts out laughing. 'Don't you know where a baby comes out from?'

She feels her face redden. 'No.' She wishes she knew everything that Harry, with his cigarettes and his knowledge of risqué dances, knows.

He leans over to whisper it in her ear.

'It does not!'

'All right, don't believe me then. You can always ask Mum.'

Ask Nan? They both know that Nan would sooner die than talk of such things.

'It does though,' he says, taking another drag of his cigarette. 'It does come out of there. Poor Dot, there's so much you don't know.'

'Is there? What else don't I know? Is it... is it all that disgusting?'

'Yes, but don't you worry, you'll learn about it soon enough.' He grinds his cigarette out in the ashtray. 'Right.' He opens the sash window to let in some air, then crosses to the gramophone and starts to wind it up again. 'Ready for another?'

'Yes, I'm ready.'

'Good. Then let's have a go at the Tiger Rag.'

She's wearing her best dress (not a drop waist, sadly, but it has got a pleat in it) and the grey suede shoes that she's outgrown but are the only spare pair she has. Harry's paid for the more expensive seats in the gallery, and takes her arm as they go up the stairs. Settling into the seat, she tries to memorise everything – the velvet upholstery, the large screen flickering to life, the feeling of Harry sitting in the dark beside her.

He was right too about there not being any snakes in the

film. There's Valentino, handsome and dark-haired, whom she knows from the posters, but no snakes of any sort. The story's not particularly exciting – he falls in love with a secretary – but there is another woman who gets Doris' attention; a woman with black hair adorned with a circlet of golden laurel leaves, and who has gumption as well as looks. And her dress! There are no colours in the picture, of course, but Doris is certain that the dress is gold-coloured.

'Wasn't she beautiful?' she sighs as the lights come back up.

'Who?'

'The woman in that dress, with the leaves in her hair. I want to be just like her when I'm older.'

Harry laughs as he gets up. 'You did notice the part where she died in the fire, didn't you?'

'Yes, why?'

'Because that's what happens to women of that sort.'

CHAPTER 15
War

Baghdad, 1939

'She probably thinks I've been spending too much.' She and Leon are facing each other from opposite sides of their small living room. 'But it's our house, and I want it to be beautiful.' The old woman has just left. While she was here, she walked about slowly, as though the house were a pitching ship, or as though Doris might have set traps for her in every room; and when she saw the new wall-hangings and pictures, the new vases and ornaments, there was a disapproving tightening of lips. 'Anyway, I'm working now so it's my money too.'

Leon has got her a position teaching English at the same school, and although she loathes and detests it, and can't imagine how one can possibly teach a child a new language, she hasn't told him so.

'We're not poor, are we?' she says.

'No, not poor. But not rich.' Leon rubs his cheek the way he does when he's thinking. 'My mother has had a hard life. Beautiful things are not important to her.' His gaze drops to the new rug, its woven pattern repeating itself all the way from his feet to hers.

His mother may have had her struggles, but Doris isn't exactly living the high life. For a start, school begins at seven-thirty. Cooler or not, seven-thirty is seven-thirty! And those girls. Because she teaches only girls, just as Leon teaches only boys. And at first she did try to teach them. She talked and wrote words on the blackboard and had them repeat things again and again and again. But it was futile; they still weren't able to answer simple questions or communicate in English. And so she handed out crayons she'd found and now they mainly doodle and draw. There's a clock in the room, and time certainly passes slowly. Now and then one or two girls will break out laughing, and she has a suspicion they're making fun of her so she makes the whole class copy 'It is rude to laugh out in an English lesson' a hundred times over.

'When my father was sick,' Leon is saying, 'my mother looked after him all day and all night. I could not bear to see him that way.' It seems the old man constantly compared his sons, a comparison from which Leon rarely emerged favourably. But the disagreements between Leon and his father were suspended when the old man got ill, and when he died they remained unresolved. 'Did you know she carried me on her back?'

At first Doris thinks this must be a bad translation from Armenian or Arabic.

'Across the desert.' Leon gazes at invisible scenes in the rug. 'The Armenians were massacred, you know. They were forced to march naked into the desert with no food and no water. And this was not the worst thing. My parents escaped, but they would never speak of the things they saw.'

Doris shivers. She doesn't like to think of death.

'I cannot understand how she did it,' says Leon. 'I was only three, I have no memory of it, but she carried me over the mountains and across the desert.'

Doris can't imagine that, but she can imagine a time when Leon belonged to his mother body and soul, when he clung to her neck because in all that nothingness, she was the most familiar thing. How unlucky he is to have had such a start, and yet how lucky too, she thinks, to know his mother would do that for him: suffer, die even.

But he isn't his mother's any longer. She goes and puts her arms around him, and for a while they stand in silence.

She can make out the jolt of his heart, safe behind its cage of blood and bone.

At last he speaks. 'We should have more people to visit us.'

'What?' She pulls away. 'Who?'

'Our friends.'

'Your friends, you mean.'

He shrugs. Once he explained how he wanted to be able to choose his own wife rather than have one pressed on him by the close-knit Armenian community here in Baghdad. Now, though, he seems to want to be part of that community, and shoehorn her into it too, no less. 'They can be your friends too,' he says.

'I don't even speak their language!'

'They speak English.'

'Yes, a word or two...' She's been to their houses with Leon, and watched them all eat and talk and play cards.

'You could learn Arabic. Or Armenian. I can teach you.'

'No. I couldn't learn a language like that in a million years.' Nor does she want to. French, when she comes round to it, will be hard enough.

'We should have people over,' he says again more firmly. 'It would be good for you.'

'What do you mean, for me?'

He rubs his cheek again. 'It would be good for you to have friends here. To make a home.'

The small distance between them wobbles and wavers. 'I have a home. Here, with you.' Isn't this her home? She feels tears rising. In Europe a war has begun – England at war! she can scarcely believe it, and with a shaking hand has written half a dozen letters home – but now that war has slithered its way across an entire continent and slipped quietly into her house. She swallows down the lump in her throat. 'Anyway, we haven't enough room.' This is true, even Leon can't deny that the house is tiny.

'But *jan*—'

'Don't call me that,' she says. He's told her that it means

'dear' in Armenian, but she still doesn't like it. 'It sounds as if you're calling me by someone else's name.'

'But you are my dear.' He comes and kisses her on the nose. 'A precious thing. And it is not about space. Friends do not need space.'

She turns and crosses the room. 'I'm tired, I don't want to talk about it any more.' She goes into the kitchen for some water. After that she'll lie down.

He follows her. 'Dolores.' At the sink he puts a hand on her shoulder and turns her round. 'Dolores, please.'

But she doesn't want to argue any more; doesn't want them to disagree, their words leaving little nicks and cuts. So she tells him. She'd have preferred to tell him later, at a different time or on a different day, when the mood wasn't fraught. But she tells him now. 'I'm going to have a baby.'

For a moment she isn't sure whether she has spoken the words out loud. A baby. Their baby. Not a friend, or a member of his family, but someone who'll belong only to them. The thought makes her throat dry.

'You are?' Leon blinks. 'You are?'

She nods. It means that at some point she'll have to give up her job – thank goodness. 'Are you pleased? You are pleased, aren't you?'

And just like that, the tension in the room dissolves and he is kissing her, his warm face pressed so close against her own that she can feel him smiling.

CHAPTER 16

D Is for Dolores

Harborne, 1927

'Oh no, Nan!' she says when Nan asks if she can take some things over to Susan's.

But there's no arguing with Nan. 'Stop your mithering and get ready,' she orders, putting a loaf of bread, some ginger cake and a jar of piccalilli into the shopping basket.

'Do I have to?'

'You do.'

'But… aren't you coming?' Since that awful day more than two years ago, Doris has only stopped by at The Back of Beyond once, when Ruthie scalded herself and the doctor had to be called. That time Nan had been with her, and they hadn't stayed longer than half an hour.

'I've got mending to do and the dinner to prepare. Then there's the mattresses still need turning. But Harry'll go with you, won't you Harry.' She presses down some of Doris' outgrown clothes into the top of the bag. 'I hope you never think of having that many little ones, either of you.'

'Uncle Harry!' Ruthie hurls herself at him.

'Hello, hello, hello!' Harry lifts her up. 'Aren't you getting to be a big girl. Heavy as a sack of spuds.'

He carries Ruthie into the kitchen, where Susan and Dolores are clearing dinner things off the table and Jim's stuffing his pipe with tobacco. The house smells of steak and kidney pie and boiled cabbage.

'Doris!' Dolores comes and gives Doris a tight hug. 'You've grown.' She stands shoulder to shoulder with her. 'Look, you're even taller than me.'

'Only a teeny bit,' says Doris.

'All right?' says Jim.

'All right?' says Harry back.

Dolores goes back to clearing the table, and Doris hangs back as Susan gives Harry a hug and a kiss. 'Haven't seen you in a bit.' She looks him up and down. 'Still growing, are you?'

'I hope not.' Harry hasn't grown since he was eighteen, but he's tall enough, even if he is verging on skinny.

'Hello, love.' Susan comes and gives Doris a peck on the cheek. She's changed her hair a little and doesn't look as tired as before.

Jim gives her a nod. 'Hello.'

'She's getting prettier by the day, isn't she,' says Harry. 'Just like you are, Dolly.' He winks at Dolores. But she's too thin, thinks Doris. And look at those pale eyebrows. And she's still as flat as a washboard.

'What you been up to?' Jim asks Harry.

'Oh, nothing much. Just work – you know.'

Jim nods, picking some wisps of tobacco off the table, but his eyes keep returning to settle curiously on Harry, like flies drawn to meat.

The other children are clamouring round Harry too now. 'Hang on, hang on,' he says, and setting Ruthie down, he pulls sweets from his pockets and hands them round. 'Chobble on these then. Although not you, little man,' he says to Reg, who's walking now and wanting the same as the others. 'You haven't got the teeth for those yet.'

Doris helps with clearing up a plate or two. She notes the drips of food slopped on the floor, the damp stains on the ceiling. She also notices the way Harry seems to belong in this house in a way she doesn't.

'Uncle Harry?' It's Michael. Dear God, Michael! 'I made a go-cart.'

'A go-cart!'

Michael nods. 'Out of the old pram.'

'He's good at making things,' says Susan. 'Maybe he'll end up at the Austin if he's lucky.'

So Michael likes to build things. Each of the children must have their own particular skills, their own little life, but Doris isn't curious; doesn't in fact want to know anything more about them.

'Want to see?' Michael asks Harry.

'Course. So long as I can have a ride.'

'You're too big!' grins Michael, but the younger ones all troop out with Harry.

Soon the table's cleared, and Doris touches the basket. 'Nan sent over some things.'

Susan comes to see. 'Oh, this'll fit you, Doll, won't it?' she says, holding up one of Doris' old jumpers.

Dolores takes it. 'It's so pretty!'

It's in a shade of baby blue, and it is pretty.

'The Duchess' hand-me-downs, is it?' says Jim. 'What else have you got in there? Your old pearls? Maybe a cameo brooch or two?'

Susan shoots him a look.

'Well, you're not going to deny your mother mollycoddles her, are you?'

Mollycoddles. The word makes her think of curdled milk, of coddled eggs.

He lights his pipe. 'How's things at Bill's anyhow? Not getting your hands too dirty, are you?'

Doris flushes, angry and embarrassed, hating Jim.

'It's nice of you to bring the things over,' says Susan.

'I'm going to try this on.' Still holding the jumper, Dolores grabs Doris' arm. 'Come on.' Upstairs in the bedroom she shares with Lilian and Ruthie, Dolores pulls off her brown cardigan and eases the jumper over her head. 'What do you think?'

Seeing Dolores in her jumper gives Doris a funny feeling, like looking into a trick mirror. 'It looks nice on you.' The baby blue does in fact suit Dolores' colouring.

Dolores fumbles around in a box in the corner till she finds a small square of cloth held tight on a frame. 'Look.' She hands it over. In the centre of a white square, the letter 'D' has been marked out and is half filled with stitched x's in pink, purple and yellow. 'It's going to be a hanky.'

'It's sweet.'

They sit down side by side on the bed. 'You can have it when it's done if you like.'

Doris looks up. 'But it's yours.'

'It could be yours too. D is for Dolores *and* Doris. Both of us are D. Palmer. Like two peas in a pod, en't we?'

Doris. Dolores. The same but not the same.

Dolores cocks her head to one side. 'Do you think Mum named us that way on purpose?'

'I don't know.' She doesn't like to think about it. *Dolores* sounds more elaborate. And foreign, which gives it a glamorous feel. '*Dolores* sounds like someone rich and famous – like an actress in the pictures.'

'Really?' Sitting there in Doris' jumper, Dolores looks pleased. And Doris smiles too, because she likes Dolores. At the same time, she's the tiniest bit jealous, although how can you both like someone and be jealous of them?

'Doris-Dolores-Doris-Dolores,' says Dolores. 'You do it too. Say it really fast, as fast as you can. Doris-Dolores—'

Doris tries, and they both say the names faster and faster until they blend into one: Dloris.

Dolores bursts out laughing. 'I wish you'd grown up here with us, don't you?'

No, Doris does not.

'I'll tell you a secret if you like,' says Dolores. 'But you have to tell me one back.'

'A secret?' Dolores keeps secrets? 'All right.'

Dolores smiles. 'I've got a sweetheart.'

'You do?'

'Don't look so surprised! I mean, I know I'm only fourteen, but we've known each other ever since the start of school. His name's Tom. Thomas Hobday.' From a small box labelled 'Treasures' under the bed, she takes out a cheap bottle of scent. 'He gave me this.'

Thomas Hobday isn't any better off than the Palmers then.

'And we're going to be married one day.' Dolores' face is all lit up and happy. You can be my bridesmaid.'

Doris forces a smile. 'All right.'

'That's my secret. Now it's your turn.'

Something did happen last week. When she was alone in the shop, a man with straggly hair and dirty clothes came in; and standing there in front of the meat pies, he'd opened his mouth wide and pointed into it, making the sort of sound a person might make if they couldn't speak. He must have been in the war – there were plenty like him around that had come back with something broken inside – but that hadn't stopped Doris from feeling scared and telling him to be off. She considers telling Dolores about this but decides against it. 'Promise you won't tell?' she says.

'Cross my heart and hope to die.'

'All right. Well then. Nan told me who she loves best in the whole world.' Doris stops, aghast at herself, but there's no choice now except to carry on. 'She said she feels bad because she ought to love everyone in the family the same, except she doesn't. It's me she loves best; that's what she told me.'

The lie hangs there between them like a dandelion seed that might blow in any direction. Then Dolores leans forward and kisses her on the cheek. 'I'm glad,' she says with bright eyes and that angelic smile. 'You deserve someone to love you best in the whole world.' And with that, Doris' fleeting sense of well-being turns to gall.

That evening in the privy, something terrible happens. When Doris, on the verge of tears, tells her, Nan turns away fast. 'About time too. I'll show you where the cloths are' is all she says, and leads the way upstairs to her bedroom. There she opens a drawer, and inside are two neat stacks of cloths, all cut to the same size and folded. She takes out one stack and hands it to Doris.

The cloths put Doris in mind of Reg's nappies, but she isn't altogether sure they relate to what's happened to her. 'Are these for cleaning myself with?'

'What? No, you silly girl. They're for putting *there*.' Nan's hand flutters vaguely. 'You know: between your legs.' Doris has never seen Nan so uncomfortable, yet she shows no alarm and doesn't question Doris, so this must be something that's meant to happen. She remembers now how some of the girls at school whispered about blood, complaining about stomach cramps and bother, but she hadn't had the foggiest what they were on about. Until now. This is what they were talking about – this bleeding. It must be.

Nan clears her throat. 'When they're dirty, put them in a bucket of cold water in the scullery.'

She nods. Again, like Reg's nappies.

'Don't let Harry see.'

She nods again.

'And don't tell anyone.'

'No.' Who would she tell? She hardly sees the girls from school any longer, and apart from them there's only Bill. Bill with his red-stained apron, his buckets of water to wash down the block, and sawdust spread on the floor to soak up grease and blood.

Nan shuts the drawer. 'You mustn't take a bath or wash your hair until it's over, mind.'

What? Nan telling her not to wash? Things are getting stranger and stranger. 'How long will it be?'

'A few days.'

'It's going to carry on like this for days?'

Nan gives a single nod.

'Mustn't I wash myself for that long then?' she asks, just to make sure.

'Wash your hands and face, of course – always be sure that any part of you people are going to see is clean – but nothing else. Is that clear?'

'Yes, Nan.'

Nan stops in the doorway. 'And stay away from boys.'

CHAPTER 17
Egg

Baghdad, 1940

She's standing in front of the dressing table mirror. 'I've gotten so fat.'

Leon clasps his hands over her stomach from behind. 'You are beautiful.'

Easy for him to say. Here he is, handsome as ever even in his pyjamas, and her with a belly like Father Christmas. 'I mean, just look at it!' Gone is her small waist; the inward curves have been reversed. 'You're not the one who has to put up with it.' Last night she'd lain watching him sleep, his body entirely his own.

'It will not be for much longer. The baby will come any day, *jan*.'

There's that *jan* again. But she's too tired to tell him off.

When he goes to get dressed, she turns sideways to see herself in profile and flattens down her nightdress. Good God, it's enormous! Round and terrifying and profoundly wrong, like the moon passing over the sun. Inside might be a boy or girl, complete or incomplete, there's no way of telling, not while it's still sealed beneath her flesh. She lays a hand on it. There's a ripple, then a sudden jab. It makes her feel queasy that it can be moving when she is standing perfectly still; that it already has a will of its own.

Easing herself onto the stool, she rubs some rouge into her cheek. 'Your mother's right, you know.'

Leon has a tie in each hand. 'My mother? My mother is right?'

'Yes.' A dab of rouge on the other cheek. 'She thinks you ought to leave that school and look after your father's business instead, doesn't she?' Smooth it over, rub it in. 'And I think she's right: you should give up teaching.'

Leon stands quite still. He decides on the green tie and hangs the other back up. 'I like teaching.'

'But you could put yourself to better use than that.' She watches him in the mirror. 'The oil companies need people who are good with numbers, and who can speak English.'

Leon turns up his collar and slings the tie around his neck. 'You want me to be a messenger between the British and the sheikhs?'

The British who control both king and government. And those bearded sheikhs in their long robes and headdresses, who remain beyond any sort of control. 'Well, why not?'

A shake of the head, an up-and-down of the eyebrows, and he proceeds to knot his tie – over, under, pull through, tighten. 'You know I will not do that.'

She sighs. She doesn't want to get into a political argument with him about the ins and outs of the British presence here. And perhaps he doesn't want to go to Basra or Mosul or Kirkuk or any of the other places they might send him. 'You could do as your mother wants then.'

He glances up. 'I don't want to work in trade – to sell carpets.'

His objections come as no surprise. 'You make it sound as if you'll be sitting cross-legged in the bazaar haggling with every Tom, Dick and Harry!'

'Well...' He shrugs as if she's right about that.

'Really darling. There are offices; it's an import export business, a respectable one. And it's not just carpets, is it? There are fabrics and antiques and... Anyway your brother seems to be making a pig's ear of it.' She turns herself round on the stool with a smile. 'And you'd be brilliant, I know you would.'

'Why are we discussing this? You should be resting. Relaxing.'

'I've done enough resting for a lifetime.' She reaches for a cigarette, lights up and inhales, enjoying that first rush of wellness. 'You've got a head for business, darling, *and* you're a marvel with numbers.'

'No. I tried to work with my brother but… no.'

Propping her cigarette in the ashtray, she heaves herself up. 'It might be different this time round. And we could do with the money.'

'Please,' he says, 'I do not want to talk about this.'

But something strange is happening. Something feels off. She looks down at the ghastly sack of a nightdress. Although she can no longer see her feet, she can sense enough to know that she's standing in a pool of water, and that the fabric of her nightdress is wet. 'Oh no,' she whispers. 'Oh no.' And it flashes into her mind's eye: Susan's front room, Michael with his cock out, an arc of piss.

Then Leon's beside her, holding her up. He leads her to the bed and sits her down. 'We have to go to the hospital.'

She nods. Yes, the hospital, they'll know what to do. They will do everything that needs to be done.

'I'll call Adnan.' Adnan is one of their neighbours and has a car.

'No, I can't. Not in his car. Not like this.'

'But we need a car, *jan*.'

Of course they must have a car. How else is she going to get to the hospital? Drag herself onto an *arabana* and clip-clop at snail's pace all the way there? 'I want to get changed first.'

'Is there pain?'

She shakes her head.

'I will help you.'

'No. No, I can manage.'

He cups one side of her face in his hand. 'It will be all right.'

Of course it will. She wasn't so sure at first, but now they'll have a son or a daughter of their own. A real family, at last.

Planting a kiss on her temple, Leon goes to arrange things.

There was no pain, but now one starts in the base of her belly, a tone of pain that she's never felt before. It's small though, nothing too bad, and she peels off her dress and underwear, throws them in a corner and finds some clean things to put on.

Adnan's already behind the wheel with the engine running when she and Leon come out. The drive to the hospital is unreal, the rest of the world far away. There is only here, inside the car, with Leon's hand around hers, a smear of dirt across the window, and the back of Adnan's head with its sticking-out ears. There is only now. Impossible to envisage that when she wakes up tomorrow, she will be a mother.

The hospital is unremittingly white. White tiled floors, white walls, nurses in white dresses and doctors in white coats, only their ties disrupting the brightness. While Leon registers her and makes an initial payment, she's taken to a private room – small, spare, clean – and made to lie down on the bed. The pain comes and goes, nothing too awful, nothing she can't tolerate.

There are two nurses, neither of whom speaks English. One presses around her belly as though she were a cow or a horse, then examines her down there while the other takes notes. Then they leave.

Looking out over the rooftops, quite suddenly she longs for clouds, ones that swell and gather and grow and change as if they were their own country. When she was in England she never thought about it, but now she misses the way they make you feel contained. Here there's only sprawling, empty blue.

A doctor comes in. In heavily accented English, he informs

her that it's still early; that it's likely to be many hours yet before the baby is born.

When Leon comes in, he has already spoken to the doctor. 'How are you feeling?'

'Not too bad. They've given me some tablets for the pain.'

They talk a little longer, then a nurse comes in and tells Leon that he has to leave.

'I will bring you some things from home. Your face cream, your hairbrush. I will be back soon.'

'Promise?'

He kisses her. 'I promise.'

As it gets dark, a nurse comes in with a plate of rice, vegetables and chicken, and a bag containing Doris' things from home.

'But where's my husband?' She looks past the woman and through the open door but can't see him. 'My husband.'

The nurse says something and shakes her head. It's too late, he can't visit now, that's what Doris gathers. The woman makes eating motions but Doris hasn't any appetite.

An hour later the pain begins again, stronger than before. She turns onto her side and curls up, gripping the bedclothes. Dear God, surely this can't be right? But instead the pain burgeons. It spreads outward like a dark pool until it's straining at her very edges. When they swam in the sea at Trieste, she'd stood in the shallows and been lifted up on the swell of each wave that came into shore, and this is what it feels like now: occasionally she's standing on solid ground, but just as soon as the sandy sea-bed takes form beneath her feet, she's lifted and carried away again.

Nurses come and go. They give her more painkillers that don't make the slightest bit of difference. She twists and squirms, trying to slip out of the pain's grasp, but it won't let her go; won't allow her to rest or sleep, or even just to be.

Night turns to day, but now Leon is not allowed to be in the room with her. To tell the truth she wouldn't want him to see her like this. When the pain comes, it wraps itself around her body and squeezes, testing to see what she can bear, trying to force out her insides, but nothing happens. The doctor says something about her hips being too narrow and the baby big and not in the right position. 'Get it out,' she gasps. 'Get it out.' Babies aren't meant to be so big and so hurtful.

She should never have come here, should never have married Leon or accepted this child to be placed inside her. What does she know about childbirth? Back home, women were 'in the family way' one minute and then there was a baby. What happened during the birth was anyone's guess. Certainly Nan never talked of it. Her friend Hilda had woken up one morning to find she had a baby brother. Another girl at school, Doris forgets her name, told them how she'd had to help deliver her mother's baby because the midwife hadn't arrived in time. But the thing was too little and died, so she'd done as she was told and put it in a soapbox and carried it to the churchyard, where she'd given the gravedigger a shilling to bury it along with a stranger in a public grave. Harry had told her where a baby made its exit from. That is the sum of what Doris knows about childbirth.

How can Susan have done this seven times? Doris clambers off the bed and onto the floor, as though the pain might remain put and be escaped that way, but is quickly hoisted back into bed by the nurses, their chatter meaningless in her ears. She sees Bill's shop window again, the red things in it, all moist and splayed and done with.

It's hot. The room feels like a Turkish bath. How she'd love some of the iced melon they sell in the streets. Or better yet, the sharp clarity of a winter morning; a splash of cold water on her face and frost stars on the window, and outside, solid puddles that turn white when you step on them. But there's none of that here and never has been, the sun won't allow it. Enormous and blurry-edged, it burns its way unforgivingly across the sky.

A second night comes, and now she knows that she will never be a mother. That's why she hasn't been able to imagine what it will be like to have a child; has never been able to picture herself fussing and chiding and feeding and cooing like other women do over their children. This, here, is all it will ever be – her locked into her pain, and the baby she can't imagine lodged inside her, refusing to be born. This is the end of her journey.

As night slowly dissolves into dawn, she begins to make terrible noises, noises she can't help. A doctor injects her with something that makes her feel groggy and sick. Then, looking down through a haze, she watches horrified as they put an enormous pair of metal tongs into her and pull out a dark sphere from between her legs, like a gigantic egg. Despicable, the way it is ripped from her. The way that even once it's out, they're still tangled together. She glimpses it, slick and raw as an internal organ; then it's cut free and she lies back, exhausted.

When a nurse touches her shoulder, she opens her eyes. It's here, wrapped up and squalling in a blanket, an alien, crinkled thing with features she doesn't recognise and black hair plastered over its head. Blood, she can feel it, is still flowing out of her, and the doctor is preparing needle and thread. She closes her eyes and turns away. She can't bear even to look at it.

CHAPTER 18
Giggleswick

Harborne, 1927

The train gives a lurch that makes her sit up – she's been dozing off again – and look out of the window. Through the smoke or steam, she's not sure which it is, she sees the first light of dawn.

Harry lights a cigarette. 'Bill's going to miss you today.'

The thought sends a delicious tingle down her spine. Here they are running away on this steaming clanking contraption, as though they're not their real selves. Doris' real self is still asleep back in Harborne, and when she wakes, will get dressed and arrive at the butcher's in time to take in the delivery of ice. 'He'll be all right. It's just one day.'

Even with additional services laid on especially, the train is still packed, but the other four passengers (three men, one woman) sharing this compartment with her and Harry are all asleep.

Harry tosses his match onto the floor. 'Well, I'm bored to death with work.'

'At least yours is respectable – working in a menswear shop, not handling dead animals all day long!' Now that the weather's warming up, the smell's worse too. But then, in winter the shop's so cold she has to wear layers and layers under her white coat and apron, and gets chilblains on her feet. But she doesn't tell Harry any of this. These days it seems there are more and more things they don't tell each other.

'It wasn't meant to be for long. I mean, I'm hardly going to become a master butcher, am I?'

'True.'

'And I'm sick of being surrounded by raw meat.'

Harry takes a drag on his cigarette. 'No good-looking chaps in this week then?'

She snorts. 'Not unless you count old Mr Fothergill. *A chop and two slices of tongue please*.'

When Harry laughs, she realises it's the first time she's heard him laugh in a long while. What's going on in his life? Not the getting up and having breakfast, then getting back home and eating dinner, but the in-between stuff. The real stuff. The friends he meets after work, or the places he goes on Saturday night when he stays out too late. The strolls he sometimes takes alone on a Sunday afternoon.

It was middle-of-the-night dark when she lit a candle to get dressed by in the small hours of this morning. The match had flared, and the candlewick had glowed then caught, settling into a flame. How different her bedroom was by candlelight – all those shadows and dark corners. Once dressed, she'd made her way downstairs, the lack of light concentrating her awareness of the house: the slight give of the carpet, the worn-smooth wood of the handrail, the cool orb of the doorknob.

Harry was waiting in the kitchen, where Nan had left a packet of sandwiches on the table for their trip because she didn't want them spending their money on 'overpriced rubbish.'

'What did you and Nan argue about yesterday?' she asks, keeping her voice low so as not to wake the travellers.

Harry flicks ash from his cigarette. 'Oh, nothing.'

The voices coming from downstairs yesterday evening had been sharp, jabbing. She couldn't make out any of it apart from that last bastion, 'What would your father say?'

'Does she want you to get married?' she asks, although the thought of Harry leaving Nursery Road and belonging to someone else makes her stomach fall away.

Harry takes a final drag of his cigarette before dropping the stub on the floor and grinding it beneath his shoe. 'Doesn't matter what she wants. I'm a grown man, she can't tell me what to do.' He holds up the pamphlet he's been leafing through. 'You should read this.'

He's changing the subject, of course. Another wall between them.

'It says here that more than three million people are expected to travel north. Imagine. Three million!'

She glances out of the window as if she might suddenly see crowds stampeding northwards. There are no people visible, but on the nearest road she sees the yellow headlamps of motorcars, all travelling in the same direction. 'They're not all going to Giggleswick, are they?'

'No, don't worry. Though there'll be a good lot of them there, I should think. It's the best place to see it. That's why the Astronomer Royal's setting up his things there.' Harry has told her how all the special instruments were assembled in Greenwich then transported to Giggleswick by Admiralty lorry.

'I wish we could have gone by Admiralty lorry too,' she says as the train grinds to a halt yet again.

'If this old boneshaker breaks down…' Harry frowns. 'If I miss it after all this.'

But a few moments later the train pulls away again. The conductor opens the compartment door, looks in at the sleeping passengers then gives her and Harry a nod. 'Don't forget, they're serving special cocktails in the buffet car.' And he closes the door and moves on.

'What d'you think?' Harry nods towards the poster above her head. 'After all, it's at a price that *cannot be eclipsed*.'

She rolls her eyes. 'It's not even breakfast time yet.' Besides, she's never drunk a cocktail before, or anything like it, as he very well knows. 'And I don't feel like it,' she adds.

He watches her for a while. 'Aren't you ever going to forgive me?'

'What? What do you mean? For what?'

'For not telling you about Susan.'

She rearranges her skirt. How lucky that the other people in here are asleep. 'Don't be daft, that was nearly two years ago.'

'Yes I know.' His face is tight, miserable.

If only things could be the way they were before she knew the Palmers existed, but none of that can be undone. 'I mean I could *say* yes; I could *say* that I forgive you…'

'So?' He leans forward, forearms on knees, towards her. 'Why don't you then?'

She takes a deep breath. 'All right then, I forgive you. There.'

Harry leans back again with a sort of smile. 'Why thank you, m' lady.'

Outside the station there are charabancs and bicycles, motorbikes and honking cars. Even with all the fuss in the papers – the scientific and not-so-scientific articles, the road maps and train timetables, weather forecasts and top tips, graphs and diagrams – there are still more people gathering than she'd expected. Perhaps everyone in England is here, because she's never seen so many people in one place. In towns lucky enough to lie in the so-called 'path of totality', hotels, cafés and picture palaces have been open all night. In town and village halls, special eclipse dances have been held; lectures, cricket matches and all-night jazz concerts. Heathenish behaviour, Nan calls it, clicking her tongue. Neither Harry nor Doris have gone to church with her for years, but Nan still relays the important bits: the fire and brimstone, the might of God's wrath and the end of days – which, according to the vicar, this eclipse might well herald.

Harry points at a signpost – 'Come on' – and before long they're trudging uphill away from the railway station.

The sun has risen at last, but the sky is cloudy. With the seams of her skirt straining, she climbs over a stone wall after

Harry to find herself in a field of sheep who look up curiously at them. A stile, another field, then a gate.

'Christ, this mud!' Harry, looking completely out of place in the countryside, raises his shoe to inspect it. 'So long as that's all it is, I suppose.' He glances at the sheep, their fleeces straggly with muck. 'Flaming June, eh?'

She laughs, but she's thinking of lamb shank and chops, of mutton scrag and the boned-out shoulder meat that has to be passed twice through the mincer.

'We'd have been better off on one of those ferries off the Isle of Man, dancing all night then watching it from the deck,' says Harry.

'Yes. Well, it'll have to be next time.'

Harry laughs. 'The next one's in 1999. You'll be… eighty-eight, and I'll be ninety-four – if we're going to be optimistic about it.' An old man and woman, standing at the other end of their lives gazing up at the sky.

Finally, they reach the spot, and she stops to make sense of the sight. Through early morning mist, she sees a stretch of land adorned with picnic blankets. People are dotted everywhere, chattering, pointing, waiting, all come here for one purpose. Amateur astronomers have brought their equipment, and journalists are carrying notepads, while other people are taking snapshots with cameras. From their various homes, all have travelled to converge in this one place where they're hoping for… what exactly? A thrill? A once-in-a-lifetime event?

'What time is it?' she asks Harry.

He checks his watch. 'Just gone six.'

Another twenty minutes or so then. Totality, as she now knows it's called, is to happen at six twenty-four. 'Will we see anything?'

He studies the sky. 'Looks like the clouds might be clearing,' he says hopefully. If they don't clear though, if in the end there's nothing to see, what a let-down that'll be.

She takes out two pairs of tinted spectacles from her

handbag and passes one of them to Harry. Everyone else has something similar – smoked glasses or pieces of coloured glass to protect their eyes when they look at the sun.

'The totality itself won't last long,' says Harry, 'but— ' Then he starts talking about the streaming corona and Baily's beads and the chromosphere, but the scientific details of it don't interest her. The sun's going to vanish, that's the thing surely, and she can't for the life of her imagine what that will feel like.

Birds are singing to welcome the dawn. Some children are chanting a rhyme, and there's laughter. She sees hats and coats, people in pairs or groups – friends, colleagues, couples, families – and on a neighbouring slope, cattle staring at all the fuss; at this new, peculiar sort of herd.

'Look, the clouds have cleared,' says Harry, and he's right. Soon enough it will happen, but until then there's only watching and waiting, here in this field in her mud-crusted shoes and splattered stockings.

From an astronomical party, a two-minute call gets passed on through the crowd, followed by a surge of whispering. 'Twenty seconds!' is called, and almost immediately it's as though twilight has fallen or the gas light been turned down. Through the sooted glasses she's holding up to her eyes, she watches the sun disappear behind the moon, as though someone's pushing a boulder across an opening, blocking an exit. Some people have brought dogs, and they all set up whining, the sound accompanying the motion of the moon. It grows darker and darker, and the colours drain quickly out of the landscape. Only a corner of the sun is left now, blinding against the blackness. Then, fast as a thought, darkness sweeps across the earth. Instinctively, people step back as the line speeds towards them, but there's no getting away from it. Then it's here, slipping and slithering among them like some cold, living thing.

All talk ceases. The birds stop singing, and there's an eerie and complete silence. Up in the sky, the moon is a flat black disc surrounded by a halo of red and yellow flames that flicker and pulse. The sun is jet black, but the horizon all around them is glowing faintly, as though other unseen suns are about to rise.

It's all wrong, all askew. And when she looks away, her blood runs cold. Because she's surrounded by an army of ghosts, colourless and entirely still, their faces upturned towards the same point, as if a door might suddenly open in the sky, or God's voice speak to them. But there is no door, no voice. The world and everything in it has been snuffed out in an instant. They – she, Harry and all these others – are dead, and this is the reckoning.

Harry's hand finds hers and closes around it. He steps closer, his shoulder against hers, and she knows that he's experiencing the same sick sense of dread. Then, amazingly, unbelievably, the boulder begins to slide along again, and a shard of light flares out with blinding brilliance. Colour leaches back into the world. The sky lightens, the clouds on the horizon glow and the hills turn green again. Birds start to sing, and just like that, the world is created anew.

There are whoops, there's chatter, and a general release of breath. The astronomers are fiddling with their lenses and equipment, their charts and cameras, trying to learn, to understand. There are smiles and laughter. Laughter! Didn't they see the sun up there, bristling and unlike itself? Didn't they understand that nature, without warning or discussion, can desert them? That there is no solidity or permanence to anything? She thinks of Pretty, who flew off and decided not to return, and feels that hollow loss again.

'You're still shivering,' says Harry, and rubs her arms.

'I'm all right.' But she's not all right. Because life is such a flimsy thing, and can pop like a bubble in sunlight, that's how fast it can happen. Eclipse. She might have known. Even the word has a thieving quality about it.

No sooner is it over than people begin to leave in their droves. The sight has been seen. They have got what they came for.

'Let's wait,' she says, 'or else we'll be trampled.' The truth is she needs time to recover. So they sit on a low stone wall and unwrap the sandwiches Nan made for them, relics from a previous life. There's a choice of potted meat or boiled egg, the yolk dusty and dry, but she doesn't care, barely even tastes the food in her mouth.

They don't talk about the eclipse itself but make comments instead on the view, the number of people, the village that must be quickly emptying again. Yet she can't shake off that shadow, the feeling that something terrible is going to happen. She doesn't know what or when, but it's coming.

Back on the train, she heads to the buffet car.

'Where are you going?' asks Harry.

She looks back over her shoulder with a smile. 'Don't you want a cocktail?'

The red grenadine and yellow lemon juice of the Eclipse Cocktail is startling, the taste sharp and sweet at the same time; unusual but not unpleasant.

'You make a lovely cocktail,' says Harry to the young man serving them. 'Chin-chin.' Then he turns to Doris and they clink glasses. 'Chin-chin, darling.'

CHAPTER 19

Doctor

Harborne, 1929

The soil is sprinkled with white. The wood of the deep beds is threaded with it. Frost has outlined the frills and veils of a Savoy cabbage, transforming it into a thing of extraordinary beauty. Doris has a fancy that this – a new frost and a tight, pinched quality to the air – is how the world was when it was newly created, before its crispness thawed away.

The allotment is busier than it used to be, and even on a January morning there's a man checking parsnip leaves for orange canker, and a woman pulling up leeks and shaking them free of soil. Doris always comes here on a Sunday. She likes the quiet of it; the silently growing plants, and how the habits of each one must be learned. Leeks are sluggish and slow to grow, swedes always thirsty. Kale is admirable, a survivor: it'll let you cut it away, then regenerate more leaves as fast as it can. Parsnips sweeten in a frost, and so do Brussels sprouts. The green marbles of them sparkle with frost as she twists them off the bottom of the plant, knowing that, like magic, the plant will grow upwards to produce new sprouts.

Jasper loves this weather. As soon as he's let out, he'll tread delicately around the garden, sniffing at things as though he's never smelled them before, or as if the scents are more clearly themselves. Perhaps they are. Did Stanley used to like the frost too? She can't think. All she can remember is how she wrapped him up in that silly swaddling cloth and how he never forgave her. Fancy, a cat holding a grudge! Then, years later, Nan had come down one morning to find him curled up in her chair, already stiffening. She had shed tears, Nan had.

Her breath whitening around her, Doris stands and gathers together the vegetables she's cut, twisted or disinterred – a few parsnips with long tail-threads that she's persuaded out of the hard earth, some fronds of kale and the sprouts – and hoists the basket so that it's resting against her hip. Will Harry still be in bed when she gets back? 'It's Sunday, let him sleep,' said Nan this morning, 'he hasn't been feeling well.'

Harry hardly ever comes here with her anyway. He hasn't got the knack for growing or tending to plants, nor even for digging. And he's been tired these last few days. Yesterday Doris noticed a sheen of sweat on his forehead. Still, it's gone ten o'clock and he'll be up now. He'll have breakfasted and will be reading a book or a newspaper, or fixing his bicycle, or getting his hair to lie exactly the way he likes it to.

When she opens the front door and steps inside, the air feels strange. Heeling off her shoes, she listens but hears nothing. Nan's not in the kitchen. 'Nan?' she calls, putting her basket down on the floor. But all is quiet. Nan is nowhere; has vanished. 'Harry?' But there's no answer.

Heart quickening, she goes up the stairs. Harry's bedroom door is ajar, and through the gap she sees a slice of him: one hand, and his chest rising and falling, rising and falling more quickly than it should.

'Harry?' She pushes open the door. The curtains are open but the air in the room is stuffy. 'Harry?'

He's lying on his back, still dressed in yesterday's clothes, except that his shirt is unbuttoned and his socks are halfway across the floor. The bedsheet is twisted around one arm and one leg, and his eyes are closed.

'Harry.' There's a tingling in her fingers. 'What's the matter?' She sinks to her knees beside him and takes hold of his hand. It's hot and clammy and limp as a dead thing. His neck and chest are flushed and damp.

With a moan, he tilts away from her as though the mattress were laid with hot coals, and his hand pulls away from hers.

Her throat constricts. What's wrong with him? She reaches to take his hand again then stops. It's upturned and there's something on his palm, a rash of some sort. She stands up and leans over him to look at the other hand. It's the same, the palm covered in blotchy red spots. Is it the measles? The pox? She draws his shirt open but there's nothing on his chest or stomach. Nothing on his face either, but glancing down the length of him, she sees the same rash on the soles of his feet.

She's never had or seen an illness like this before. Perhaps it's some tropical disease – leprosy or rabies. Through Harry's window is a similar view of the garden to the one she can see from her own room. The same frost-covered bushes, the same trees. And hidden among those trees, something that can creep up on you without you even noticing.

'Dot.' Harry's eyes are open.

'Harry!' She sits and takes his hand, not caring if what he has is infectious or not. 'Yes, darling, I'm here.' He's awake, at least he's awake, and that has to be a good thing. 'What is it, Harry? What's wrong?'

His eyes are unfocused. He wets his lips. 'Fetch me a cigarette.' His voice is hoarse.

'What? No! I'll be damned if you're going to lie here on your back, sick and smoking!'

He grimaces and closes his eyes. Groans. His face is damp with sweat.

'I'll get you something to drink.' His lips are dry and cracked. 'I won't be a minute, all right? All right, darling? I'll be right back.'

Downstairs there's still no Nan, and a sudden fury wells up in Doris. Where has she gone? How can she have deserted them like this?

She starts to fill the kettle. 'No, no, something cold,

stupid.' In the scullery she fills a glass with water. '*Does* he need something cold?' Now she doesn't know. She finds a clean cloth and fills a bowl with water.

Upstairs, Harry has sunk back into his fever. She says his name but he doesn't open his eyes or seem to hear her. Something is pulling him deep inside himself to a place she can't follow.

Dipping the cloth, she wipes his forehead and neck, and the details of him flash out at her: his stubble, the dark specks of it more densely packed beneath the ears and on the chin than on the cheeks; his eyelashes, thicker and longer than her own; the tiny crooked scar at the end of one eyebrow where he fell over in the schoolyard, or said he did.

'Stop it,' she pleads. 'Please!' But it's no good. He doesn't open his eyes or answer.

A sick dread washes over her. She can't lose Harry. Others might die of Spanish flu or be knocked over by buses, but not Harry. Harry who laughs and smokes. Whose hair curls up fifteen minutes after he's slicked it down with Brilliantine. Who polishes his shoes to an unnatural shine. Whose brown eyes are stuffed with life. For him to die is unthinkable, and she won't allow it.

She touches his hot, altered hand. 'Please don't take him,' she whispers to God or Science or whatever other force has blacked out the sun today. 'Not him. Anyone but him.'

Downstairs the front door opens. Doris raises her head. There are footsteps and voices, one of them Nan's. She gets up, her body light and insubstantial as she goes to look over the banister.

In the hall Nan is dropping her handbag, shrugging off her coat and pointing up the stairs. 'Where've you been?' Doris calls from her elevated position, her tone accusing. 'Harry's sick. He's sick and—'

But Nan is already surging up the stairs. Behind her is a tall thin man who gives Doris a nod.

'I know, love. Here's the doctor.'

Doris has never met him before, never even seen him. She'd remember such a humourless face.

Nan looks past her. 'How is he?'

'I… don't know.'

'In here, doctor,' says Nan, and Doris presses herself against the handrail as first Nan then the doctor with his Gladstone bag go past.

'Harry? Harry love?' There's an exchange of words in Harry's room, then a minute later Nan comes out again, closing the door behind her. 'He's having a look at him now.' Nan looks pale and dishevelled.

Doris follows her downstairs and into the kitchen. 'What's wrong with him? I came home and… and…'

'I don't know, love. But the doctor'll tell us. Even though I had a time finding someone to come on a Sunday.' She goes to the dresser, takes down the tea caddy where she keeps her housekeeping money and tips out the contents.

'Is that going to be enough?' There's hardly anything there.

Leaving the caddy on the table, Nan crosses over to the fireplace, puts her fingers to the bricks and eases one out.

Doris didn't know about any loose brick. She's never seen this hidey-hole. 'What's in there?' Nan draws out a small flat tin and blows a layer of brick-dust off it. Levering off the lid, she takes out a folded wad of banknotes. 'Well, you've got to save something for a rainy day, haven't you? Just as well too.'

Back at the table she silently counts through the one pound and ten bob notes, her lips moving. When she looks up again, her face is frightened. 'He'll know what to do.'

The moment the doctor comes back down, they fall on him. 'Well, doctor?'

But he only asks if he can wash his hands.

'Yes, of course.' Nan is edgy, anxious as she points him to the scullery.

Never has anyone taken longer about washing their hands.

The scullery tap is turned on and off, and on and off, and Doris hears the soap being dropped in its saucer several times. He'll wear it down to a nub if he carries on any longer, she thinks, but finally he comes out.

'What's the matter with him, doctor?' Nan leans towards the man, waiting for his answer. Her hands are clasped, fingers lost among each other.

The doctor looks from Nan to Doris and back again. 'Well,' he says slowly, 'I've made a thorough examination of the patient – your son, that is. At first his symptoms – fever, fatigue, probable pain in the joints – suggested influenza.'

Nan pales. 'Not… not the Spanish flu.'

'Oh no, no, that was done with ten years ago.'

Doris' shoulders soften.

'Like I say, that's what his symptoms *suggested*. But then of course there's the rash on his hands and feet. You noticed it?'

Nan nods.

'And that confirms the matter.'

Doris looks at Nan but Nan seems none the wiser.

'When young people are left to their own devices, Mrs Linnet…' The doctor raises his eyebrows and shrugs.

Nan looks confused. Doris can't think what he's talking about, but there's a tone to his voice. Disapproval. Disdain even.

'When I examined your son further, the source of the infection became clear.' The doctor's nose wrinkles as if he can smell something unpleasant. 'But perhaps it would be better if we didn't discuss this in front of, er…' He nods towards Doris.

It takes Nan a second. Then she lays a hand on Doris' arm. 'Go and see how he's doing, will you, love?'

'But why shouldn't I hear? I want to know what's wrong with him.'

But Nan is shepherding her out of the kitchen, a firm hand

on her back, and the next moment the door shuts between them.

Doris stands in the dim hall, surrounded by blank walls and closed doors. The doctor has started to talk again but she can't make out what he's saying. Taking the stairs two at a time, she goes up to see Harry.

His door is open and he's lying in bed, awake again. 'Hello.' She smiles.

Weakly he smiles back but says nothing. Although he still has his shirt on, he's wearing pyjama trousers now, and his slacks are on the floor.

She gathers them up and folds them onto the back of the chair. 'Feeling any better?' Except for the fact that he's conscious, he doesn't look good. He's still flushed, and his eyelids seem weighted.

'I feel like something the cat dragged in,' he croaks, trying to sit up.

She helps him, propping the pillow behind his back. 'Did he give you some medicine?'

Harry ignores the question. 'Be a love and fetch me my Woodbines, will you?'

This time she doesn't object, and finds his pack of cigarettes and matches. Woodbines. It makes her think of vines creeping around his lungs, tendrils bursting into flower. She strikes the match and holds it to the end of the cigarette in Harry's mouth. He sucks in his cheeks, then sighs out a cloud of smoke. 'Thank God you're here, Dotty.' And his head lolls back against the pillow.

'Tell me.' She sits next to him, bending to pick up the wet cloth off the floor. 'Tell me what he said.'

Harry drags on his cigarette. 'Do you know what syphilis is?'

She blinks the smoke from her eyes. Syphilis: she sees it written out, the curls and tails of its tightly-packed consonants. 'I've heard of it.' And she knows the sort of illness it is – that it's one of *those* illnesses, which you get from doing *that* – but nothing more.

'Well, that's what I've got.'

Will it kill you? she wants to ask. *Is it an illness that kills you?* It sounds as if it could; sounds like a venomous snake. She's trying to work out how to ask this question, how exactly to frame it, when a sound from downstairs provides her with the answer.

She stands up, her stomach collapsing inside her, but Harry hasn't heard. He's too busy leaning back, eyes closed, holding the smoke in his lungs, battling against the illness that's taking him over.

'I won't be a minute.'

Nan and the doctor have finished talking, and Nan is crying. She's taken out her handkerchief and is pinching her nose with it as the doctor slides the money she's just paid him into his wallet. The wallet goes into his pocket, then he does up the straps on his Gladstone and picks it up by its leather handle. How many times has he done this before, Doris wonders? Been called to someone's house, made a diagnosis and exited, leaving them in tears?

'Wait,' she says as he turns to leave. 'Wait. What's going to happen to Harry?'

The doctor turns round, surprised at first, then apparently amused. '*Happen* to him?'

'Is he going to…?' She swallows. She can't say it.

The doctor doesn't move. She tries to pierce through his expression and read what he's thinking but can't make anything out. At last he sniffs. 'He'll get better.' He puts on his hat. 'With the proper treatment of course.'

Something is dripping onto the floor. At first she thinks it's relief draining out of her, but no, of course it's only the cloth in her hand, the wet cloth that she's been holding onto and squeezing tight. She starts to laugh.

Nan stops dabbing her eyes and stares at Doris. The doctor's staring too. Because she's laughing, loud and open-mouthed.

She's laughing at the cloth in her hand and at the ten crescents of allotment soil trapped beneath her fingernails. At the knowledge that Harry is going to live. And the realisation that, in the two hours since she was pulling up parsnips, Death has walked into this house and left it again.

CHAPTER 20

Not Hovsep

Baghdad, 1940

He is a wondrous thing, like a new morning or a freshly-dug potato. Fine black hair is spun into a perfect whorl at his crown, and his ears are a work of art. The scent of him – milk, damp skin and something else that is particularly him – stirs incredulity in her, and his miniature fingers and toes, the feet (almost as wide as they are long) that fit in her hand. But sometimes she'll turn to him and all at once his body will look too small for his head, his arms and legs too short, and when he opens his mouth, that startle of red gums.

His moods are impossible to predict. He is happy. He is miserable. He is despairing. He is at peace. In the blink of an eye, one spills into the other. For no reason, a laugh can turn to tears, a smile become a scream. One second all is straightforward, the next it's the hardest and most impossible of all things.

Today is such a day. He was happy a moment ago but now he's purple-faced, crying as though the world were ending.

'What's the matter?' she says, picking him up. Oh, the soft, dense weight of him! How can he exist outside of her when his skin is so silky-new, the sort you might find beneath a scab; and when his every moment is fresh and unguarded because the world hasn't yet hardened him into self-consciousness? 'What is it?' She bounces him the way she's seen his grandmother do, but that only makes him cry harder, so hard that he's beside himself.

Frightened, she puts him back down, sits on the floor with him and pulls over his favourite toys – the tin car with wheels that go round, the coloured building blocks – but he won't even look at them.

'Are you hungry? Is that it?' But he can't be because he's only just had his milk. Leon's mother thinks that Doris ought to give him milk from her own breasts, but the very thought makes her feel ill. Every other day, a girl leads a cow along the streets, stopping at houses where there are babies and milking the cow on their doorstep. But the idea of Doris giving her baby milk straight out of an animal's udder is unthinkable, so she gives him evaporated milk out of a tin instead, mixed with sugar and water.

He's still crying. 'Oh, tell me what it is.' Should she be able to tell? Should she know instinctively? She could ask Adnan's wife what to do, but… no, that would show her up and have them feel sorry for Leon.

Graham's body is rigid, his hands fisted and his eyes squeezed shut as he lets out another piercing cry. His chubby arms pump up and down as if it ought to be clear, but it isn't, not to her. Splinters of pain stab at her: she's his mother, the only one he's got, she doesn't know how to look after him, and this fact will shape her son in ways she can't even imagine.

'All right. There, there.' Perhaps he's tired. Back onto her feet and she picks him up again, but he squirms and fights. 'It's all right,' she says, 'I'm here.' But he won't have it, and suddenly he flings himself backwards, spine arching, almost pitching out of her arms. 'No!' she screams, swearing and gripping onto him. 'What *are* you doing?' Her heart heaves, panic sparkling through her nerves.

When she looks up, the old woman is there, wide-eyed. Did she knock? Perhaps, but who'd have heard it in the din?

Leon's mother rushes gabbling across the room and extracts Graham from Doris' arms as if she's a danger to her own son. And although she hates to let him go, there's also relief in giving him over, there's no denying it. Immediately the old woman's tone turns soothing. She presses a hand to Graham's face, puts a finger into his mouth, and just like that, with his face still red from raging, he quietens and starts to bite and gnaw, his gums squeaking against the old woman's finger. And just like that, Doris sees Dolores with Reg; the way Dolores always knew exactly what to do.

Of all the moments for Leon to come home! But here he is in his suit and tie, looking tired, then surprised as he tries to jigsaw together the scene in front of him.

Seeing his father acts like an invisible switch, and Graham starts to howl again, and Leon goes straight to his son, shushing then kissing, and he and his mother talk as she dandles the baby. Doris hears Leon murmur Graham's name – although of course it's not 'Graham' he says because he can't say the name properly; around the middle it changes to something else. He and his mother would have named Graham after Leon's father, as is their tradition, except no son of hers was going to be called Hovsep.

Now she speaks over the old woman. 'He won't stop crying. He wouldn't even let me hold him.'

But when Leon looks at her, there's a new expression on his face. *It's me*, she wants to say, *remember? Why are you looking at me like that?*

The old woman carries Graham out of the room, and she and Leon are alone.

'My mother says you were shouting at him. Shouting.'

There's a lump in her throat, because it's all still fresh, right here in her sleep-addled head: Leon standing in the hospital room with his shirtsleeves rolled up and the baby cradled in his arms. The way he smiled down at Graham and made the sorts of noises people make at babies. How seeing it made her ache inside. Then, when they laid Graham on her breast, the unexpected bloom of a feeling that made her shrink away, and unravelled all sorts of thoughts in her head: did Susan ever feed her like this? No, it must have been Nan who fed her from a bottle, just as it was Nan who later taught her the word for sky and bird and sin.

Leon comes towards her. He looks softer now.

'No, don't.' He'll touch her and say comforting things, but she doesn't want him to. So she backs away and, before her tears surface, turns and leaves the room.

Still in his work clothes, Leon is in the armchair with Graham flushed and asleep on his shoulder. There's a plate of mashed banana on the table, and a clattering from the tiny kitchen.

'I'm going out.'

The hand that's been rubbing Graham's back stops as Leon takes in her makeup and high heels, her evening dress and the set of six gold bangles he gifted her for her birthday. He tries not to sound surprised. Tries but fails. 'Where are you going?'

'The Carters said they were meeting up with some others at the club. You remember, I told you about the club.' She adjusts the handbag strap on her forearm. 'They keep saying I should go, so… well, I'm going.'

Graham sighs in his sleep. How peaceful he looks collapsed on Leon's shoulder that way. Curious how she can feel the warm mass of him against her own shoulder and sense his small fingers at her neck.

'You keep saying I need friends,' she adds, as though he's objected. 'Well then. And you go to people's houses, don't you? You go and play cards and what have you.'

Leon remains still; moving might wake Graham. 'You could come with me.'

But they've had this conversation before, and she doesn't want to go with him; doesn't want to sit there not understanding a word and not know what to do. Instead she'll go to the club and talk about England and the latest news and try to comprehend how it could possibly be that the Germans are razing London to the ground. From the Carters, among others, she'll also receive a different version of Iraq to Leon's;

a version in which the British marched into a country where illiteracy was sky high and there wasn't a single road, and brought progress with them. Such talk makes her feel more important. It makes her feel better about herself.

A smell of frying onions is coming from the kitchen, a hiss as something's added to the pan. The old woman must be making a dish that Leon will enjoy for dinner.

'I can take you,' says Leon.

'No, it's not far.'

Perhaps he'll insist, she thinks. Or else tell her she mustn't think of going. Her a new mother and all, going out alone, and dressed to the nines. But whether or not he's thinking these things, Leon only nods. 'You have everything you need?'

She hesitates. A sensation has arrived that she doesn't know what to do with. Her love for Leon and Graham pulls at her like a magnet, and at the same time holds her at bay. She stands there, lost, as though the snake man in the *souk* has draped a snake around her neck then walked away.

'Have a good time, *jan*,' says Leon, and smiles a smile that doesn't quite reach his eyes.

CHAPTER 21
An Interview

Harborne, 1930

Harry's doing his exercises in the garden, squatting down and lunging forward, a manual open on the bench beside him. When he sees her, he gives a wave but doesn't stop. Nan has gone to The Back of Beyond with cough syrup – 'jollop' as the Palmers call it – for Reg, and a seed cake for everyone else, so they have the place to themselves.

Doris settles herself on the new bench.

'Any luck?' gasps Harry between one lunge and another.

She shakes her head and shrugs, as if it doesn't really matter. Of course it does matter, but at least Harry's outside and moving about. He's had to make a lot of hospital visits by way of getting better, but otherwise he spends too much time idling indoors, reading or just sitting staring into space. The other day she found him re-reading the letters Grandad sent from Catterick. At weekends he goes out. There are frequent quarrels between him and Nan; little ones about nothing, it seems. One time when he answered her back, Nan raised her hand to strike him – to strike her beloved boy! Then she checked herself, cheeks flaring as though she'd dabbed on rouge with a careless hand. Nan, who doesn't even own any rouge.

Out here the garden is prickling with spring. Buds are splitting out of dead-looking branches on the plum tree, and everywhere, pale, shiny new leaves are unfurling. Nan keeps the little patch at the front of the house pristine, weeding and looking after the sweet peas and Canterbury bells, and a row of hollyhocks that come up year after year. She even dons a pair of thick gloves and prunes the holly bush when it becomes too straggly. The back garden, though, must earn its keep, and there's a clothesline and a rubbish can, and the coal stored in the shed along with Harry's bicycle, Nan's mangle, a toolbox and a load of other rubbish that Grandad thought would come in handy one day. But in a corner of the garden, Doris has planted some annuals – snapdragons, verbena, phlox and asters – that are beginning to put out leaves, and will soon flower and draw bees and other insects.

Harry stops, leaning against his knees to catch his breath.

'Just what exactly are you trying to do to yourself?' she asks lightly, trying not to dwell on how sick and fragile he was not so long ago, because he's taken to doing this every day – not just squats and lunges, but press-ups, star-jumps, stretches and God knows what else.

'I've told you.' He reaches over to the bench for his cigarettes. 'I don't want a bourgeois belly, do I?'

This is what he says, but it's more than that. She has the sense that he's trying to form a shell around himself, laying it down in layers like varnish. Or armour. Yes, like armour.

'So.' He holds a flame to the cigarette gripped between his teeth. 'What happened? What did they say?'

'Oh, they were polite enough, but…' She points at his cigarettes. 'Can I have one?'

An eyebrow arches in surprise but he holds out the pack. 'Course.' He lights one for her, and she inhales just like she's seen him do a hundred times. 'Steady,' he laughs as she starts to cough. 'Don't breathe in so much, not at first anyway.'

Wiping her eyes, she nods and tries again, and this time round there's only a bit of coughing. And when that stops, it feels grown-up and elegant, what stars like Gracie Fields or Peggy Wood or Florence Desmond do.

'Now, how could they not want to employ you?' he asks.

'I mean, look at you.' And he waves a hand at her hair and makeup, her nails and shoes. And now, her cigarette.

'I did pick up a few things at the salon. Not that it's done me much good.' Unable to face another winter at Bill's, she'd left last November and found work in a beauty salon in Birmingham. It was further to travel of course, and she had no formal training, but the owner, Beryl, was willing to give her a chance: 'I expect you can learn on the job.' And there it was, Doris working in a place called a *salon*, a world away from the butcher's shop. In the salon there was electric lighting and hot and cold running water, a bank of reclining chairs and electric curling irons, and a row of helmet-like hairdryers. It was warm and clean with padded seats and shiny chrome fittings. 'Women come in here to feel beautiful and glamorous and thin,' said Beryl. 'Doesn't matter what they really look like, that's what you need to make 'em feel like.'

And she did try, hoarding pieces of information like treasure along the way: how to achieve a perfect line of kohl; how to blend rouge and outline lips; how to file and paint nails to match a lipstick. At the week's end she took discarded rouge and lipstick and eyeliner home and spent her day off experimenting with them in her bedroom.

Then there was hair. In the salon she watched long tresses fall to the floor, and learned how to create Marcel waves on a bob. And one day she looked on, terrified, as the permanent-wave machine was put into use and the octopus-like contraption suspended from the ceiling let down dozens of black wires to be attached to a woman's head. As though they were gorging on her, thought Doris. Still, the end result was astonishing.

All did not go well, however. The craze for pencil-thin eyebrows meant either plucking them to a narrow line, or else plucking them out entirely then pencilling in the desired shape. Beryl handed Doris a pair of tweezers and instructed her to pluck. This, she thought as she pulled out eyebrow hairs, was not so unlike Bill's: pain and unsightliness kept behind closed doors so that a more appealing end product could be displayed. But before Doris was halfway through plucking, the woman's eyes had started to water and she'd sat up. 'Not got the softest touch, has she?' she complained to Beryl, and another girl was quickly called to finish the job.

It was fair to say that Doris didn't have the knack of tending to other people. The final straw came when she scorched an old lady's fringe, and the smell of burnt hair sent the other customers packing.

'I'll do more practice,' she pleaded, preparing to get the wig and fake head out of the cupboard.

But Beryl was having none of it. 'There's some people are good at looking after others and some that aren't. And you're not, that's all.'

A Miss M. A. Bullows opened a prestigious new riding school in Metchely and Nan said she ought to try there – 'It would have suited your grandfather down to the ground' – but what interest did Doris have in horses? Then her old schoolfriend Hilda suggested the big telephone exchange in Birmingham city centre. There were no fringes to be burnt or eyebrows to be plucked there, and no horses either; and today she'd been interviewed for a position as a switchboard operator.

'Well?' Harry taps the end of ash off his cigarette. 'What did they say? Why wouldn't they take you?'

Taking another puff of her cigarette, she gazes at her toes, the blades of grass surrounding them and the grey flecks of cigarette ash. 'They checked everything: my height, my hearing, my eyesight.'

'All good?'

She nods. 'The man I had the interview with…' She saw him again, with that large moustache that bobbed up and down when he talked. 'He examined my hands and said they were quick enough.' Although how he could tell that from just holding them she couldn't guess. 'And he said my voice was good too – clear as a bell, he said, not too high- or low-pitched, and I don't speak too fast or too slow.'

'Right…'

'But he said I've got too much of an accent.'

'What a load of codswallop!' Harry stubs out his cigarette on the bench. 'Anyway, so what if you have? What's wrong with that? Not that you've got much of one.'

'They don't want voices with an accent or dialect.'

'Well, good luck finding that round here.'

'They get some of the girls to have elocution lessons before they hire them, he said. He told me the address of the place. And how much it costs.' She bumps the hard toes of her shoes together. 'If I had that much money to spare I wouldn't need a job, would I?'

A sparrow lands on the grass. It hops about, pecks at the grass then flies off again.

'I'll pay.'

Doris drops the cigarette, moving her foot out of the way just in time. 'What?'

'I said I'll pay. I've got enough saved. Anyway, you ought to be able to speak the King's English!'

She almost knocks him off balance with her hug.

He laughs. He's recovered from his illness all right, yet it's changed him. Not in any visible way maybe, but that doesn't stop her detecting it – hearing the different tone his laughter has taken on; its new, unhappy pitch. 'One of us at least should make something of their life.'

CHAPTER 22

Liquorice Lies

Harborne, 1930

As soon as the sweet shop door clunks shut behind her, she sees them: Dolores standing at the corner with two other girls, laughing the way small groups of girlfriends laugh. Before she can start walking the other way, the girls part and she's spotted. 'Doris!'

She shoves the Fry's Crunchie bar and the bag of aniseed balls into her pocket – she's too old to be seen buying sweets – and puts on a surprised expression. Dolores is smiling as she comes up – seems genuinely pleased to have run into her – and kisses her on the cheek. 'I haven't seen you for ages!'

'Yes I know. I've been busy – you know, with work.'

Dolores, however, does not take the bait. Instead she glances back down the road. 'I wish you'd met Joan and Irene. They're my best friends.'

Doris watches after them. The fat one waddles like a duck, and the other one has a face that'd fetch the skin off custard. No, she doesn't need friends, and especially not friends like those. 'You've had your hair cut,' she says.

Smiling, Dolores touches her hair as if to double check. 'That's right. I know I'm a bit late. I was about the last girl in England without bobbed hair.'

'It looks good.'

'Thank you. Not as pretty as yours. I wish I could get my hair to do that.' She nods at Doris' smooth bob, complete with a kissing curl flicked forward onto each cheek. 'But it just frizzed up the minute it was cut, and now I need half a dozen kirby grips to get it to stay.'

Poor Dolores. Yes, it'd probably take a whole tub of pomade to slick down that haystack. 'Although the windswept look's fashionable,' Doris says kindly.

'Is that what they're saying in the salon? Nan told us you were working in a salon.'

Doris lifts her chin. 'Actually I've a job in the telephone exchange now.'

'You do?'

'Yes. And I'm taking elocution lessons.'

Dolores blinks. 'You are?'

'Yes.' She doesn't tell Dolores about Harry paying for them, or about how every time she gets home from her class he greets her with a dramatic 'How now brown cow?' and every time she gives him a friendly shove or slap on the head in response.

'What's elocution?' asks Dolores.

Of course. She ought to have guessed that Dolores wouldn't know about such things. So she explains, casting it in the best light; something she's doing out of choice rather than necessity. She doesn't mention Mr Pope, who's taken to laying his hand on the girls' chests to gauge whether they're breathing correctly.

'You're ever so clever,' says Dolores.

She likes Dolores, she really does. Dolores starts to tell her about the children – who's done what and who's hurt themselves, and the diphtheria and scarlet fever that are going round the school. 'Reg'll be starting in September. I can't believe he's five already, can you?'

No, Doris can't believe it. Because it all still feels fresh: that awkward tea, Reg being passed between Susan and Dolores, Michael peeing all over her.

'I'm just going to pop into the shop and buy the little ones some sweets. Will you wait for me? Then we can walk part of the way back together.'

'Yes, all right.'

Doris watches through the window. Lemonade Crystals, a couple of everlasting strips and a bag of sticky sweets for a ha'penny an ounce. She sees Dolores being tempted by the caramel bars but putting them back after she counts out her money.

Doris knows what she ought to do. What she *ought* to do, because there's still plenty of money left in *her* purse, is go into the shop and buy a whole lot of things for her brothers and sisters. Instead she remains standing in the watery spring sunshine, waiting for Dolores to come back out.

'Was there candy floss at the fair?' Dolores asks almost before she's stepped out. 'Harry said you went to the fairground in Aston.'

'That's right. And he bought some floss for us both. We watched them spinning it round like thread.'

'I love the fair,' says Dolores as they start walking. 'Dad took us once when I was little. Are there still lots of rides?'

'Loads. There was a Caterpillar ride and a rifle range and a chairoplane and a Swirl. And the high striker of course.' A steady queue of men waiting, jackets off, to lift the hammer, hit the bell and prove themselves. She'd watched for a while, but maybe it was rigged because not one man managed it. 'There was a lion too, and a cow with six legs. And a fortune teller. And a mermaid,' she says sceptically. 'Although we didn't go in to see her. I went to see the World's Ugliest Woman instead.'

'Wait, I forgot to tell you!' And Dolores stops and snatches at Doris' sleeve. Then a hand is thrust up in front of Doris' face, and there on the third finger is a ring. 'Me and Tom got engaged.'

The hand hovers before Doris' eyes a moment longer.

'I know it's no great surprise,' says Dolores happily. 'I told you, didn't I. I told you we would. But still.'

'That's wonderful.' And she does feel happy for Dolores, even if Dolores *is* nearly two whole years her junior, and even though she herself has no boyfriend to speak of.

'He asked me on my birthday – that's ten days ago now. Said he'd been saving up for a year to buy it.' Dolores tips her hand this way and that to admire the ring. Silver, notes Doris, and that teeny weeny stone is no diamond. 'We've got to wait another year till I'm eighteen before we can get married though.'

They walk on, Dolores luminous beside her.

'Mum baked me a chocolate birthday cake with icing and candles. I wish you'd been there.'

Nan and Harry had gone to The Back of Beyond for the occasion, but Doris had refused to go with them. They'll all have sung Happy Birthday and given Dolores presents, and Susan will have hugged and kissed her. And now – now Dolores is to marry, and move seamlessly from one type of love to another, encased in it her entire life, like padding.

That's when wickedness washes over Doris. She stops short and puts her fingers to her lips – 'Oh' – as though she's just remembered.

'What is it?'

Doris doesn't speak. Wicked, that's what it is, yet it's dazzling, impossible to resist.

'You're not sick, are you?'

'Oh no, it's not that.'

'What then?'

With an effortful smile, she walks on. 'Nothing.' But Dolores is worried now.

'Doris? What's wrong? What is it?'

Again Doris stops. 'I… I can't tell you.'

'Why not? Is it a secret?'

Dolores and her stupid secrets! 'No, it's just… it's nothing really, just a silly thing. And I don't believe it either, you know.'

Dolores shakes her head. 'Believe what?'

'I shouldn't tell you. It's just a bit of nonsense is all.'

'Oh, please tell me.' A tiny fear sparks in Dolores' eyes. 'It's not about Tom, is it?'

'No. Well, not exactly.' She continues slowly. 'It was the fortune teller at the fair. You remember.'

'Yes.'

Across the road, a boy is struggling past on callipers, and for a moment Doris' attention veers off and she thanks her lucky stars that she never caught polio and isn't in any way disfigured.

'Doris?'

She draws her attention back. 'Well, I went and had my fortune read.' The lie tastes sharp as Lemonade Crystals, black as liquorice. There had really been a fortune teller at the fairground, or rather a middle-aged woman with hoop earrings and a scarf round her head who'd stood outside a tent examining people's palms. Doris hadn't liked the look of her and didn't want to give money to such a one.

Dolores grasps Doris' arm. She looks scared. 'What did she tell you? What was it?'

'She had a crystal ball, you know' – not true – 'and she told me all sorts of things; things she couldn't possibly have known. About Nan and Grandad and…' She flicks a look at Dolores then looks quickly away.

'Did she say anything about me?'

Doris doesn't answer.

'She did, didn't she?'

'She said I had a sister around my age. And she said…'

'What?' Dolores leans in. 'What did she say?'

'Well, she said there was going to be a marriage in the family, only… only the marriage wasn't going to happen.'

Dolores' eyes are wide and unblinking.

'I didn't think anything of it at the time, did I. I mean, I didn't know you'd gotten engaged.'

Releasing her breath, Dolores seems to shrink. With her other hand she covers the engagement ring, as though hiding it might solve everything. 'But why isn't it going to happen? Did she say?'

'No, there was nothing more than that. That was all.'

Dolores bows her head.

'But...' Regret stabs at Doris, and mixed in with it is fear that she will somehow be punished for telling such a horrid lie. 'But you can't go believing someone like that,' she says. 'It's just lies, isn't it? Just a lot of claptrap. That's all it is.'

CHAPTER 23

Letters

Baghdad, 1941

Last year Harry was called up for service, but then he broke his arm in a training accident and was medically discharged. Doris was glad. The moment she heard about the air raids on London, she telegrammed then wrote to him.

She got a telegram back: *All well. Love to all. Harry.* With her eyes closed, he was within touching distance, and behind him were stacked all their days spent growing up together.

A letter followed in which he asked after Leon and Graham (*Fancy you calling him that!*) and wondered how it could possibly be that he'd missed her growing a family. He wrote about the air raid shelters that had been put up in London streets, and the sandbags that had appeared around government buildings, hospitals and police stations; about the air raid sirens at night, the searchlights picking out the bombers and every window taped across in case it shattered. But then, in the very final paragraph, he told her that he was leaving London and heading back home.

Just for a while, just to please Mum. She can't bear it that I'm here and she doesn't know whether I'm dead or alive. And – I hardly like to tell you because I know you're going to wail – my arm has healed so I'm going to sign up again. Now don't worry, Dotty, because by the time that whole process is through, the war will probably be over and done with.

Anyway, just as well you're out of all this and steeped in domestic bliss.

All my love, Harry

A few weeks later Doris received a letter from Nan (addressed to 'D.' rather than 'Doris', she'd made that clear to Nan from the start) announcing that Harry had married and moved to Atherstone, twenty miles from Harborne.

Married. Doris had to sit down and read and re-read that word; couldn't understand, couldn't believe it. Yet it was there in black and white. *It was a whirlwind romance,* wrote Nan, *and took us all by surprise, I must say. But I couldn't be happier, for Elsie is a sweet girl.*

Elsie? Who the hell was Elsie? No one had ever mentioned her before. Oh Lord, Doris could just imagine her. Homely. Sisterly. A *sweet* girl. Oh, Harry.

But there was more, and worse. *He's had his medical examination, which of course he passed A1, and is to be posted to East Africa. They don't take into account that he's newly married, of course, so pray for him, Dot, just like I do.*

As for round here, all the university buildings are being used for the wounded, and all the schools and big houses around Harborne have been given over to the war effort too. Children are being labelled up like parcels and packed off on trains, which I'm glad enough about except that it's strange with hardly any around. Castle Bromwich has been badly hit since that's where the Spitfires are made, but then all the factories are being hit. The sky turned red when they blew up the big roads around the city, and the animals in Market Hall got out and ran about the streets, as terrified as everyone else. Can you imagine? Monkeys and such running loose on the streets of Birmingham! But I expect it's safe enough where you are.

Doris is writing a letter to Harry, which she'll enclose inside a letter to Nan. If he's left England already, Nan will know how to get it to him. Graham's asleep in their room, and on the sofa, Leon is half hidden behind his newspaper. He doesn't bother with the English press any longer, and reads only the Arabic papers. Afterwards he'll brood for hours.

Doris has covered all the preliminaries: the how are you and where are you, and how's married life. Now she moves on to Baghdad news. *As far as the war is concerned, we're quite out of things here, apart from the price of things going up in the markets. Not a bit like what you must be going through, darling,* she writes. *Hardly a month used to pass without a ruckus or demonstration about something or other. It used to be the Shia wanting representation in government, or else the Kurds wanting independence. But nowadays it's almost always about the Palestine problem – which is bound to be sorted out soon, don't you think?*

She glances up. 'You're grinding your teeth again, darling.'

The grinding stops. The mood here in Iraq has changed. Arab nationalism is on the rise, and tempers have flared over what's going on in Palestine. It astonishes her, what strong feelings people can have about something going on so far away. She knows that there have been uprisings in Palestine against British colonialism and British support for a Jewish homeland for several years now. The uprisings are led by peasants and farmers, and they are repressed. Cruelly, according to Leon. So cruelly that he blanches as he reads about it.

She doesn't want details, but she knows this much about her husband: he sails through life thinking the best of people. So finding out that they're not as good as he believed does, of course, come as a great shock.

I wonder how much you hear about what goes on here. Perhaps you know it already, but perhaps you don't so I shall tell you. There's been a lot of hoo-ha about the Iraqis wanting to govern themselves fully – without us having a say in it, that is, because it seems we can do no right in this part of the world. Anyway, on the 1st of April, as though it were a joke, some army generals overthrew the government. It was quite a thing, with people crowding onto the streets to watch soldiers ride past in open trucks. We saw it from our rooftop.

Well, with the pro-British government gone, it was a tense wait to see who would arrive here first, the British or the Germans. The generals were hoping it would be the Germans – they'd rather side with them, you see, if only to be rid of us – but thank goodness it was the British who arrived first. They raced across the desert from Egypt and Palestine, guided by Bedouins – yes, riding camels and wearing long robes! Out there where it's so hot you daren't touch metal with your bare hands. Is it that hot where you are, I wonder?

She thinks of Harborne with its damp evening air, its Ovaltine posters pasted to brick walls, its *seasons*.

Anyway, things boiled over the very next day when the mob broke out against the Baghdadi Jews. It was ghastly.

She hears again the shrill voices in the street, the sound of running feet and cries of '*qutal el yehud!*' She knows only a few words of Arabic, but *qutul* is one. It means to kill. And she knows what *yehud* means too: Jews. When she'd opened the front door to see what was going on, Adnan's wife was at their window waving for her to go back inside, and gesturing to lock the door and all the windows. But Leon wasn't home, and in the next hour Doris went to hell and back not knowing what was going on and imagining the worst – for her and Graham, yes, but mostly for Leon. What would she do if anything were to happen to him? How would she be able to go on? She'd sat and stood and paced and chewed her nails. Prayed, even. And wished to heaven there was some whisky in the house.

At some point she'd put Graham in his cot and gone up onto the roof terrace. There were cries of 'Allah! Allah!' but she didn't know if it was the attackers shouting or other Muslims pleading with God to make this stop. Black smoke rose into the desert sky. In the distance children were being passed across rooftops, and once she saw a young woman leaping from roof to roof, jumping gaps, with men in pursuit.

Afterwards, the calling of names in the streets – names

of the dead or lost – until she couldn't stand it any more and covered her ears.

Finally, Leon had arrived home, his tie loose and a sheen of sweat on his face. Out there, knives and killing and mayhem, the entire world gone stark raving mad. She'd touched his shoulders, his face and hair, as if that were the only foolproof way to confirm that he was really all right.

But don't worry, darling, because we're all fine. And you are too I hope. We'll soon be moving away from the old part of the city though. I shall let Nan have the address as soon as I know it. Leon's getting a new job, you know, so we'll be able to have a bigger house in a safer district. I'll be able to tell you more next time, but for now, I miss you very much.

Always your

D x

Leon, of course, has agreed to no such thing, but the need for them to move is a pressure in her gut now. And to move, they'll need more money, so Leon will have to stop teaching and take up the reins of the family business. That's all there is to it. Yes, he may like his job, but he needs to think of her and Graham.

Graham has woken up. Leon puts down his newspaper, goes to fetch him and comes back in with Graham in his arms. Graham blinks, his cheeks still pink with sleep, and Leon peppers him with kisses. She'll convince him to do what she wants. Once she sets her mind to something, she rarely fails.

CHAPTER 24
Malaise

Harborne, 1930

This is the entire world: a ridged landscape of sheet and pillow in shades of white and grey, a corner of blue coverlet, a patch of wall. If she raises her eyes there are curtains too, faded where the sun has shone in. Outside, small white clouds scud across the sky, appearing on the left-hand side of her window and disappearing on the right, but she – her head, and below it a leaden body that moves only to breathe in and out – lies immovable on the bed.

Wrinkled lines on the cotton sheet. Lines. Lines connecting people in different parts of the country, bodiless voices traversing miles in no time at all. Voices making appointments, conveying good news and bad, whispering of love or raised in argument. No roads or trains, buses, cars or bicycles are involved. The voices dart away like swallows, knowing that they'll quickly arrive at their destination.

Sitting on a high stool, Doris is a conductor. From the minute she puts on the headphones, disembodied voices come flying at her, each on a different mission. Obeying the flashing of tiny lightbulbs, she takes a call, finds the recipient on the switchboard, connects through, rings them and waits for someone to pick up. If there are lots of lightbulbs flashing at the same time, though, it becomes a pantomime with too many plugs to pull out and plug in. The wires remind her of the permanent-wave machine in Beryl's beauty salon, except now it's her that's the octopus.

How grateful she is to Harry, how eternally grateful that he put up the money for elocution lessons. How elated she'd been to get the job, ready to burst out of her skin with pride. But the miserable day-to-day reality of it… Still, she'd rather die than have him know how she feels; than let him think her ungrateful and his money gone to waste.

'What number please?' then 'Hold the line please,' over and over again. Each time she hopes the voice she hears will be Harry's, but knows it won't be. And always, the effort it takes to dress neatly and sit up straight, to be polite and unruffled, and keep her eyes on her work and not chat with the other girls. Their supervisor is constantly breathing down their necks, reminding them not to yawn or blow their noses, to transfer calls faster and never sound tired. 'You girls are *always* to be compliant, *always* to behave and sound feminine and keen to please. For God's sake never be sharp with a caller; the gentlemen get enough of that at home, I should think. And remember, bring the smile into your voice.' So among the multitude of voices she hears her own, dialect-free, sounding happy and capable, until finally at the end of the day she can pull the headphones off her aching head. Her brain buzzes with the echo of wordless chatter, but around this hive of voices, the world is a dull, heavy, colourless thing.

A knock on the door and Nan comes in. Doris doesn't need to look round to know this. She's familiar with Nan's tread and scent, the sound of her clothes moving against themselves.

'You can't sleep the whole weekend away,' says Nan's voice.

Why not? she thinks, but can't summon the energy to say the words out loud.

She hears Nan bend to gather up yesterday's discarded clothes from the floor and put the dropped hairbrush back in its place. 'That boy called round again. Jack Morgan.'

Silence.

'And I don't see why I should keep on having to send him on his way. What's wrong with him?'

He's got no backbone, that's what's wrong with him, Nan only has to look at him standing there tongue-tied and shifting from one foot to the other to realise that. Anyway, hasn't Nan learnt her lesson about matchmaking? Doris had come home one day to find guests – Nan's friend Clarice and Clarice's daughter Maggie – in the parlour with Harry and Nan, the four of them awkwardly trying to make chit-chat, and a desperate look in Harry's eyes. But Nan was only thinking, so what if Maggie had hair on her upper lip and perspired more than a normal body? She was a nice girl.

A hand is pressed to Doris' back, and from far away, the thought comes to Doris that she likes this sensation – its warmth, and the firmness behind it. 'What is it, love? What's wrong?' asks Nan, even though she must know. 'Are you sick? Shall I bring you a hot water bottle?'

Silence.

The scene drifts in and out of Doris' mind. A cloudy June day and she and Harry in the Lyon's tearoom. They've ordered cake and he's admired her new cloche hat with its upturned rim and velvet bow. They've finished their cigarettes and stubbed them out, and she has paused to admire the neat pink and yellow squares of her Battenburg cake before cutting into it.

At first she'd thought something had hit her on the head or walloped her the stomach, but looking up, nothing had changed. There was Harry facing her, and the clatter of the tearoom, and behind the counter, the waitress still making eyes at him.

'What do you mean, London?' she blurted at last. 'What do you mean, Harry?'

He blathered on about finding better work and standing on his own two feet, but it didn't wash. London. The London pavements were thick with blackguards, and life rolled and crashed heedless through the streets, didn't he know that?

A sudden urge had come over her then to wrestle him to the ground and pin him there until such an absurd notion as moving to London passed away.

'Do you know how they treat it?' Harry's eyes were lowered.

'What?'

'Syphilis. Do you know how they treat it?'

All those hospital visits that he never spoke about, not a word. 'No.'

'They inject you with arsenic.'

'No. No, that can't be right. That's a poison! I'm sure I've got that right. It is, isn't it? A poison?'

'Nonetheless.' He doesn't look up. 'That's what they injected me with.'

The room wavered around her. The smell of marzipan was sickly in her nostrils.

Harry picked up his fork and brought it down slowly onto his vanilla slice, exerting just enough pressure so the pastry layers cracked. The muscles in his jaw rippled. 'The doctor said I was a deviant. *Arse*-nic, he said. *Arse*-nic.'

The sun flashed out from behind a cloud, bright as a knife blade, then retreated again. Doris was conscious of the tightness of her ribs around her lungs. 'How… how dare he? I'll show him deviant!' She would go to the hospital. She'd find that doctor and— 'Wait. Is that the real reason you're going? Because of what he said?'

For a moment Harry didn't speak. 'And then there's Mum. People gossip, you know.' Laying down his fork, he reached over to put his hand on Doris' and finally met her eye. 'You do know what I'm talking about, don't you? Don't you, Dotty?'

Oh, Harry. Darling Harry. She shrugged. 'You don't take to girls.' She'd always understood this about him. That in this respect he wasn't like other men, and that made her love him all the more.

His face relaxed. 'I knew you understood.'

She'd looked down at his hand covering hers, at their

half-drunk cups of tea and uneaten cakes, and was almost able to hear her heart shatter into pieces. Out on the street, passers-by were picking up their pace, sensing the coming rain. How lucky, she remembers thinking, how lucky Harry was to be able to up and leave just like that, without having to wait for someone to marry him first.

'Well?' Nan's still there. 'Did you hear me, love? Why don't you write to him?'

Write? But she *has* written, Nan knows that. It's been three months since Harry climbed onto a train and his body sped away from her all the way to London, and since then she's written six letters. She's told him all about life in Nursery Road and what Nan's been up to. She's mentioned Susan and the children even though she's only seen them once. And of course she's told him all about her new job: how she takes the bus every morning to the central exchange in Newhall Street, Birmingham, and how flustered she was with all those plugs and wires on her first day. She's told him about callers who are rude, and about others who flirt brazenly with her just because she isn't there in the room with them. '*Sometimes*,' she wrote, '*I'll take ages to put their call through, or I'll cross their wires*.' Because how strange it must be, how disconcerting, to suddenly find yourself the wrong person, in the wrong story.

Having heard not a word back from Harry, she asked in her third letter whether she might be able to visit him. She could sleep on the floor, she wrote, or stay in a B&B for a night or two so long as it wasn't overly expensive.

Then a letter arrived. It was addressed to both her and Nan, and she could barely wait for Nan to come downstairs before ripping it open. Inside was a single page, and not half of it covered.

Dear Mum and Dot,

I hope you're both well. I am. You can hardly tell it's autumn in London, there's so little greenery. Except for the parks, that is, where the trees are beginning to shed their leaves. I smelled a bonfire yesterday that made me think of the allotment. Do you still go there, Dot?

I've found work in a legal office in Holborn, which is lucky given the levels of unemployment. I do their accounts for them. The flat I'm living in is small – there's not enough space for visitors, I'm sorry to say – but big enough for me.

I'll sign off now. Love to you both.

Ever your

Harry.

There was no mention of her staying in a B&B. How many times has she read and re-read the wretched thing, tried to peer through the lines and catch a mood, a suggestion of happiness or regret? But she has detected nothing. The words are detached and aloof, like an article you might glance at in a magazine. He's in London, a place she can't envisage, meeting people who are strangers to her, seeing and hearing things that remain invisible to her, and all of these things are changing him into someone who'll no longer be her Harry.

She gasps. Arms are tunnelling beneath her, one on either side. Nan's woollen cardy is scratchy, her brooch hard. This is the way she used to hoist Doris up when she was a little girl and sick in bed. That's impossible now though, can't Nan see that? She's too big, and heavy as stone.

But Nan doesn't hoist her up the bed or even try to sit her up. She simply remains that way, bent over and clasping Doris' body against her own so that Doris can't untangle who needs what: whether she needs looking after or whether Nan simply needs a body to hold on to.

Gently she's laid down again, sinking back into the warm place she's made on the mattress. and Nan strokes her hair. 'Why don't you get dressed and come downstairs, eh, love? I'll make you something to eat. Anything you fancy.'

'I'm not hungry.' She's never hungry these days, only tired; tired even though when night comes, she can't sleep.

Nan lets out her breath. 'What's one to do?' she murmurs, then leaves again, closing the door behind her.

For hours Doris lies listening to the sounds of the house: Nan moving about downstairs, the clank of the pipes, the whistle of the kettle, the front door opening and closing. Finally, when she can't ignore the need for a cigarette any longer, she heaves herself up with a monumental effort, then sits for an eternity acclimatising to this new angle of things.

Her cigarettes and matches are on the bedside table. Placing a cigarette between her lips, she lights it and inhales, then releases the smoke from her lungs. In her lap the pack of Woodbines with its orange, brown and black design brings him back. So does the smell of the smoke, the action of lifting the cigarette to her lips again and again.

When she's done, she opens the bedside drawer and takes out her address book. It falls open at the correct page, and of course she doesn't need to look at the address because she knows it off by heart. Still, there it is in Harry's handwriting. As if by magic, she sees his hand gripping the pen and moving along the page, leaving behind it these very marks like a track of tiny footprints. Before he left, he'd written it formally and with care in her rather empty little book: his name followed by the address of a London boarding house.

'G?' It had sat there, fat and startling, between his first name and surname: *Harry G. Linnet*. 'What's the G for?'

'For my middle name, silly.'

'You've got a middle name?'

'Of course, didn't you know?'

She shook her head. Had he always had one? How on earth could she not know such a thing? Was it because she had no middle name herself that she'd assumed he didn't have one either?

'It's Graham.'

For no particular reason, she'd laughed. *But that's someone else's name*, she wanted to say, as though he were a child, *not yours. Your name's Harry. Harry, not Graham.*

'What?' He smiled. 'Doesn't it suit me?'

She bit her lip. 'No. Maybe. I'm just not used to it, that's all.' She'd brushed it off yet it had unsettled her; that you can be familiar with a person your entire life and not even know their name.

She touches the words in her address book – the small blob on the first stroke of the H where the ink flowed too fast from the pen, and the curls and lines after it. Write to him, Nan said, and she'd like to. She wants to tell him about the caller yesterday who had a pipe in his mouth the whole time he spoke to her, she could hear it click against his teeth the way Grandad's used to. And about the romance that one of the other girls has struck up with a mere voice, although she hasn't yet decided whether to meet him in person or not.

Yes, she'd like to write to Harry, but in three months he's only written a miserable half-page that she and Nan have had to share out between them. 'No.' She shuts the little book with a snap. 'I shan't. If you want to hear from me again, you'd better pick up your pen and write about more than just the weather – hadn't you, Harry *G.* Linnet?' And she falls back down onto the bed, closes her eyes and curves her body in on itself.

CHAPTER 25

Aisha

Baghdad, 1943

When she opens her eyes, morning sun is slanting into the room and onto the bed. She moves her feet and hands, stretches her legs and neck and back. Her body is heavy with sleep and warm with sun. The two windows letting in the light are large to match the large room, the large house and large garden.

'It is what you want, no?' Leon had asked when they first came to look at it.

'Yes. Oh, darling, this is exactly what I was thinking of!' Here on the west bank of the Tigris where the houses are big and modern, with gardens – *gardens!* – that wrap around them. Where she can have a proper kitchen, and a bathroom with a proper toilet in it, for God's sake.

Leon had stood in the living room and gazed out at the garden, then past that at the road and the houses obscuring the river that flowed between him and his old life. 'Then we buy it.'

'Really? But— '

He'd turned to her. 'So we buy it.'

'Just like that?'

He'd nodded and clicked his fingers. 'Yes, just like that. If,' he repeated, 'it is what you want. Whatever you want, *jan*.'

It was most certainly what she wanted, especially after the two days of violence and mayhem that they'd witnessed.

Softly so as not to wake him, she turns a little and watches him sleeping. What is he dreaming of in there? She wishes she could be with him, but of course she can't step into his dreams any more than she can travel with him to the other places he now goes to – Kirkuk and Mosul and Basra and Erbil, and beyond that to Persia. Because having taken over from his brother, Leon is now the primary agent for the import export business, and is doing better than even she could have foreseen. He's expanded their trade and now imports all sorts of luxury goods: tea and coffee, furs and bolts of silk – *real* silk – to be made into bespoke dresses for well-to-do women like her. And gold. Gold that's melted and worked in Baghdad then exported again. Cargo from abroad gets unloaded in Basra and is brought upstream on sailed boats. Leon knows all the ins and outs of selling it too, knows the holy days of every religion and sect and when is a good or bad time to do business with each. He spends evenings working on orders and bills, calculating for future stock and checking that which has already been sold. When he looks up sometimes, his gaze is still intent and sunk in numbers. Yet he seems made for such work, even if it means he's away for days – sometimes weeks – at a time.

Today he'll leave again, and his body and voice and smile and reasonableness will all go with him. This hand resting on the pillow, with its short, neat nails and particular knuckles, each fingertip swirled with a tiny maze of prints, will no longer be here. At times, like now, she thinks she can't bear it; that she won't let him leave, because she hates it when people leave. And why should she be without him? Why should he miss the things Graham is learning to do: turning the pages of a book, walking backwards around the garden, catching a ball, or not catching a ball and collapsing in a heap of furious tears. But Leon isn't here to witness most of these things.

Leon stirs in his sleep. He mustn't go, and yet he must, because that's the pay-off: their own large, comfortable house, well away from his mother, where Doris can run things as she pleases. Also, there'll be a reunion to look forward to when he returns. He'll hold out his arms for her and she'll lock herself against his body as if they've found each other all over again. *Whatever you want.*

Taking a deep breath, Leon opens his eyes, blinks, focuses, then smiles. 'Good morning.'

She smiles back. 'Why, good morning.'

When he's dressed, she re-knots his tie for him. 'That's better.' She brushes a speck of lint off the shoulder of his jacket. 'You could do with a new suit. Why don't you buy yourself one while you're away?'

He turns to find his wallet. 'Yes, perhaps.'

Perhaps he'll buy himself a new suit. And perhaps he'll go and never come back and she'll be left here all alone. She goes to the window. Stop it, she tells herself, stop thinking such thoughts. The earlier blue of the sky is changing to grey. There may be rain, only light of course, and not lasting more than ten or twenty minutes, but still rain. She imagines it turning the desert to mud, his car wheels sinking, preventing him from going forward, or coming back to her and Graham for that matter, stranding him in the middle of nowhere.

'Her people,' Leon says, 'are still in the desert where she left them.'

'What do you mean, left them?' asks Doris.

'Nobody knows why she came to the city. It is not a thing you ask.' Leon considers. 'Perhaps someone died, or she was not happy.' In any case, he explains, she has no allegiances now, but she's clever, and has already picked up some English. 'She will work hard and help you in the house. This way, when I am not here, you will not be alone.'

Doris doesn't question it. Why not have a live-in servant rather than a girl who just drops in for an hour or two now and then to cook and clean? Or perhaps she doesn't question it because she knows precisely when Leon decided on the matter. It was a Thursday because he'd been to one of those *kahwas* after work, a sort of café where music's always blaring – some woman singing in Arabic, or else someone playing the bloody *oud* – and men smoke *nargils* and drink tea from thin glasses, or Turkish coffee from tiny cups, and play endless games of backgammon. The kind of place where you find all sorts of riff-raff. But when Leon arrived home that evening to a bawling child, an inedible dinner and a shirt she'd just scorched with the iron, she saw it roll in on him like a giant wave: even if he had to pay handsomely for it, they had to get help.

And here's that help now in the form of Aisha the Bedouin serving up a tray of tea to Doris and Leon's visiting mother. Black stars, dots and symmetrical patterns are tattooed on her chin, on her cheeks and in the centre of her forehead. Perhaps they're a protection against evil spirits, or they may be Bedouin symbols or runes, Doris hasn't a clue. She doesn't know either whether the girl might have more beneath all her cloaks. Either way she's even more outlandish than the farmers' wives who go door to door decked with bangles on their ankles and rings in their noses, carrying containers of yoghurt stacked into towers on their heads.

Aisha is quiet, with watchful eyes and two glossy black plaits that hang down from under her headscarf. She moves through a clean house where everything is shipshape and orderly, and sunlight gleams on spotless windows. This, thinks Doris as she pours tea for the old woman, is how it ought to have been from the very start. And how pleasing it is to have Leon's mother see the house to advantage like this.

Settled on the old woman's lap, Graham's attention is fixed on a little cloth doll she's brought for him. He turns it over, touching its face and hair, and plucking at its dress. The old woman probably made it herself, cutting out the tiny clothes from scraps of material and stitching them carefully together. The little shoes too, and the frilly hat. Then she'll have stitched on a face and snipped lengths of black wool to make hair.

'Boys aren't meant to play with dolls, you know,' says Doris. Wasn't that what once earned Harry a hiding from Grandad?

The old woman seems surprised that Doris has spoken but

doesn't understand a word of it. Graham taps the doll's hat with a forefinger, looks up at his grandmother and makes a noise. It's only when the old woman smiles and repeats the sound back to him that Doris realises with a shock that the noise isn't just gibberish, but a word in one of their languages.

Good God, her child speaking a foreign language! How long has this been going on? Without Leon here to identify such sounds as words, who knows? She grips one of her hands with the other and squeezes. She'd thought Graham was being slow to speak. But now, how can she make him understand that he has to speak English and not this other language, when he has no concept of what a language even is?

Well, something must be done about it. She'll make an effort to speak even more to him; she'll have the radio on more often, and ask Leon to only use English around Graham. Yes, that should do it, until he can go to school and learn things properly.

'Aisha!' she calls, and the girl appears. 'Would you bring something to eat?' She touches her thumb and first two fingers to her mouth.

The girl retreats and returns with a plate of biscuits. Doris holds one out to Graham. 'Here you go, darling,' she says with a smile. 'They're your favourite.' He'll come to her now. Now he'll come.

Graham looks at the biscuit then goes back to tinkering with his doll, sucking now on the frilly hat.

Doris swallows, and not knowing what to do with the damned biscuit, takes a bite. In her mouth it crumbles into sand-like grains, sweet and at the same time salty.

Before Aisha leaves the room, the old woman asks her something. They talk, slowly because the old woman can only speak a little Arabic, and it strikes Doris that all three of them are strangers in Baghdad.

The rest of the biscuit disintegrates in Doris' mouth. She wants to get up, wants to leave. 'What are you talking about?' she asks Aisha.

They fall silent, and Aisha turns to her. 'She ask… what Mister Leon eat?'

'What he eats?'

Aisha nods. 'She say he like *dolma*. And *borek*. She say you make.'

Ha! If they think that she's going to spend her days in the kitchen folding vine leaves and pastry into tiny parcels, then they can think again. 'Tell her I've better things to do. And tell her it's none of her business.'

Did they know this, Leon and his mother? Did they consider that Aisha could translate while he was away?

Graham is no longer on the old woman's lap. He's laying the doll on a cushion and dragging the cushion along the floor.

The old woman puts a hand on her chest. 'Leon.'

Her son, she means. There, where her heart is. A part of her. Protected and nourished inside her body, and then, after she pushed him out (easily, no doubt, painlessly), she continued to protect and nourish him. She'll have fed him from her breasts like an animal, and been familiar with the sound and smell and movement of him from the start. She'll have understood his first words, and responded to them.

Doris stands up and looks directly at the old woman. 'Well, he's mine now. They both are. Leon's my husband, and Graham's my son.'

Leon's mother looks small sitting there in her son's armchair.

'You've always hated me, haven't you? Right from the very beginning.' Dear God, those awful days. The heat, the endless visitors, that burnt bloody fish.

She turns away and goes to the window, where she turns on the wireless and lights a cigarette. Behind her she hears Aisha leave the room, but she carries on smoking and looking out at the bleached, desiccated garden. The wireless is tuned to the BBC World Service, and it's a relief to hear real English being spoken, but then the programme ends and the Greenwich Mean Time pips begin, counting down to a new hour.

CHAPTER 26

Shadow

Baghdad, 1944

To look at, the letter is just like any other she's received from Nan. King George's head is on the stamps, and it's been opened, read and re-sealed by first a British and later a Baghdadi censor. But Doris has not got very far through reading it before her fingers slacken and it floats, swinging, to the floor.

It's there now, lying on the cool hall tiles, only a short distance from where she herself is sprawled, stretched out face down on the floor. Inside, though, she's still falling, waiting to come to rest.

Graham's playing in the garden, she saw him there a minute ago, and Aisha's upstairs changing bedding, but here in the hall there's no movement, no sound except the bang-bang-bang of her heart against the tiles, insisting that she's still alive.

She cannot absorb it. It's lodged somewhere behind her eyes, or in her throat, or else in the deep pit that's opened out in the centre of her. She cannot absorb it because it's not true.

Squeezing her eyes shut, she sees Nan sitting dazed but quite upright in the parlour, a letter scrunched up in her hand.

'Nan?' Treading softly, she goes in. She knows something's not right because she's just dragged a saucepan of eggs that's boiled dry off the hob.

Nan doesn't move. 'It's William. He's gone.'

'Gone?' Have they sent him to Europe after all like a proper soldier?

But that's not what Nan means. 'He's dead, Doris. Your grandad.'

Doris doesn't understand. What does Nan mean, dead? Dead like the rosemary bush that got waterlogged and turned brown? Like the spider Nan hit with the bristly end of the broom, leaving behind only one leg? Has Grandad been drowned or squashed? 'Isn't he coming home?'

She shouldn't have asked because Nan starts to twitch and make loud gulping noises. That's when she notices the letter clutched in Nan's fist, the words crashed in on themselves. The letter's been typed out on a typewriter, folded and sealed in an envelope, then sent over hills and across rivers, through towns and cities to land on Nan and Grandad's doormat. Nan's doormat now.

On the mantel is a photograph of Doris and Harry when she was a year old, him proud in a stiff collar and buttoned-up jacket, and her stood on a chair beside him, her black hair as messy as though she were out in a gale. 'Nan, where's Harry?' But Nan only shakes her head.

Doris opens the front door and goes to look up and down the street. There's a girl watching over two small children, the milkman doing his rounds and the sad-looking publican's wife walking her two sad-looking hounds, but no Harry.

Her heart's racing as she re-enters number 45. Nan's still in her chair, only now she's bent forward with her face in her hands. 'It says he caught the Spanish flu. There were too many of them, all crammed together like sardines.'

Doris stares at Grandad's empty armchair as though he might reappear in it. She stares at the pattern of curling leaves and thistles for so long that it stops resembling leaves and thistles and becomes coastlines and islands, a map of where Grandad might have gone. Flu that travels all the way from Spain. Buses that come at you so fast you don't see them.

A noise makes her look up and there's Harry standing in

the doorway, his face flushed and his clothes sweated through. He's been running. Perhaps he's run a hundred miles because his chest is heaving and all the blood's risen to the surface of his skin. He stands opening and closing his hands like a puppet whose strings are being pulled. 'Harry,' she whispers, her heart lifting, because he's not dead but alive. More alive than he's ever looked.

Was he dead before Doris found the letter opener? Before she slit the envelope along its top and slid out the single sheet of paper inside? Of course he was, and yet it's the tiny procession of black shapes on the paper that killed him, and in the same instant felled her too. And now she's down and will never get up.

She wants to force time backwards; push so hard that the moon will roll back off the sun.

He's dead. He's dead. He's dead. Those are the words her heart's thumping out. She'd walk barefoot a hundred times around the globe if it would change that fact, but it wouldn't. Nothing will. She has managed to hold the war at arm's length for so long – the pictures in the newspapers of London blasted to smithereens and children playing on mountains of rubble; the news on the radio and announcements between comedy programmes; campaigns won and lost; and camps, not only prisoner-of-war camps but a rumour of others, the thought of which fills her with something beyond horror. She's held all of this at arm's length but now it has entered her house, leapt into her hand and cut her down.

But he can't be dead, he can't be. In the same way that birds are still there at night even though you can't see them, he must be somewhere too.

'All right. You are going to be all right.' Leon's home from work. He's raising her off the sofa because she's drunk – outrageously drunk. At some point she crawled into the living room, where she mixed herself one martini after another until the room began to soften and her thoughts melt.

With a firm arm around her waist, Leon leads her out of the living room and across the hall. The letter, she notes, is no longer on the floor but must have flapped away somewhere else.

'Gone.' The word slips and slides around her mouth.

'Yes,' says Leon, pausing at the bottom of the stairs. 'I am so sorry, *jan*.'

A fresh burst of pain. 'I… I always told him… the truth.'

'Of course. Of course you did.'

'And *he*… he told me the truth too.' They'd always been honest with one another. But what need is there for truth any longer?

Her feet stumble over a step. It's dark out; Graham can't be playing in the garden.

The bedroom springs into being as Leon turns on the light. Here it is, neat and cool and empty just as it was this morning. The bed flows towards her and Leon eases her onto it.

'Don't leave me,' she slurs.

Leaning her forwards against him, he unbuttons the back of her dress. Her feet, she sees, are already bare. Where did she leave her shoes? Or did they walk off by themselves? Leon's shoes are still right there on his feet. He crouches down, easing her dress over her hips and down her legs.

'I love you,' she says, but the words are blurred by the nightdress he's unrolling over her head.

He pulls the bedclothes to one side, and after she lies down, covers her over. But she wants to stand back up – yes, stand up and untuck his shirt and slip her hands up onto the comforting warmth of his back. That's what she wants to do, except her body seems disconnected from what her brain wants.

'Don't go,' she says, but it comes out as a moan.

'Sleep, *jan*, sleep.' And Leon switches off the light and pulls the door to.

Days turn into a week, and one week becomes two, and then three. And still she can't get up or shake the life back into her mind. One day tears arrive. They rack her body and turn her wild, and when they stop she's exhausted. Then they come again.

She refuses to open the curtains and the room acquires a thick, subterranean feel; there's a slant to it, a subtle bend in its straight lines, as if it's being crushed by some enormous weight. But she ignores that. Instead she focuses on Harry. Harry dressed up in her bonnet and pinafore, prancing around the room and stopping to declare, 'Why, *hello* darling, how *charming* to see you!' Harry dancing the Tiger Rag. Harry lying in bed burning with fever – 'Be a love and pass me a cigarette, will you, Dot?'

The doctor's been several times, but each time she's sent him away. Leon has pleaded and begged. Aisha has carried up one dish of food after another, but it's pointless. Martinis and cigarettes, that's all she wants. That and to be left alone.

Here's Harry handling Pretty the pigeon, doing press-ups in the garden, reciting Homer. Occasionally she thinks of Nan, and a different variety of tears spring to her eyes. Poor Nan opening the door to the telegraph boy – angels of death, people call them, she's heard – and turning back to a house suddenly emptier than it was a moment ago.

She pushes herself up into a sitting position – she ought to telephone Nan – but then she slides back down the bed and closes her eyes and buries her cheek into the pillow. Outside, the faraway noises of the world continue: traffic, the clip-clop and bells of an *arabana*, loud Arabic music from a wireless, children shrieking in play. Dully, she calculates that she hasn't had a monthly since February, and that this probably means—

She presses her face deeper into the pillow.

CHAPTER 27

The Club

Baghdad, 1947

'You remind me of one of those Persian cats, Dolores.' Sara Elmwood turns to her husband. 'Doesn't she, Bernard?'

A waiter passes with a tray of dishes – Jacob's crackers, salmon, slices of ham. A band's playing English songs, to which some couples are dancing. Balloons and streamers are strung up and people are wearing paper party hats. Doris was wearing one too until a short while ago, when she decided that it detracted from her look.

'I don't know what you mean,' says Bernard. Doris doesn't know what Sara means either, although she can't imagine a woman like that purposely trying to offend.

'Oh, you know, the ones with long hair that are fed and groomed and treated like queens.'

'Ah,' says her husband, 'I see.' Bernard, overweight with round glasses and a weak chin, is some sort of expert in oil extraction. Perched on his too-large head, a small pointed yellow hat looks comical.

Doris laughs. 'Me a cat! And a Persian one at that!' Laughing again, she thinks of Stanley wrapped up like a mummy; his accusing meows. No, she doesn't like cats. In the final month of her pregnancy with Lynette, as she lay beached on her bed, huge and waterlogged, she'd watched scorpions move across the ceiling, throwing frightful shadows. When she first moved here, Leon taught her to always check her slippers before putting her feet into them. To look under furniture and take care near woodpiles. Lying watching them, she thought they looked fearless and strangely beautiful. And the sting in their tail? Why, that was nothing more than an insurance against their own pain.

'Well, treated like a queen wouldn't be far off though, eh?' says Bernard, looking at her get-up.

A delicious warmth spreads through Doris. Yes, she is treated like a queen. Look at her new black velvet strapless dress, the diamond dress clips and earrings she sketched out on a piece of paper and sent as an order to the jeweller. 'Oh, I don't know.' She looks at Sara. 'What was it they said about the Queen's dress? Embroidered with seed pearls and crystals?'

'Yes, that's right.' Sara smiles, her hat slipping. 'It sounded perfect, didn't it? Just like a fairytale.'

The royal wedding of Princess Elizabeth and Philip Mountbatten took place in Westminster Abbey this morning, with two thousand guests, and people crowded down either side of The Mall to see the Irish state coach drawn by two greys. Sara is familiar with the layout of London, being, like most of the others here, a southerner. Each time Doris is introduced to someone, she wonders whether she might hear a Midlands accent but she never does. At the same time, she hopes that none of them can detect the shadow of her own old accent, like a hint of tarnish on silver.

She and Sara discuss the dress – the ivory silk tulle train, the almost ethereal quality of the whole as described in the broadcast, the work it must have taken to tailor such a thing and how beautiful the princess must have looked. Scarcely two years since the end of the war, and with bread still being rationed, England was desperate for a sight like this one.

'She chose him herself,' says Doris. 'They say she accepted him without so much as asking her father's permission.'

'Although he's poor by comparison, of course,' says Bernard. 'And a foreigner.'

Sara leans confidentially towards Doris. 'His sisters weren't invited. All four of them married to Germans, you know.'

'Really.' Doris scans around the club, searching for Leon. It's the first time he's been here, and the place is crammed. He doesn't know any of these people – they aren't his set – but he could hardly refuse, the occasion being what it is. Anyway she'd persuaded him; although when they arrived she thought it might have been for nothing.

He'd stopped short at the entrance, staring at the sign on the wall: *Foreigners Not Allowed*. 'Foreigners?' he'd said.

'Oh, don't worry, darling, it doesn't mean you. You're accompanied by a member.'

He'd given a strange laugh. 'But who are the foreigners here?'

'Don't, darling.' She'd linked her arm through his. 'Let's have fun tonight. Please.'

Bernard peers into his empty glass – 'I'll fetch us some more drinks' – and he heads to the bar, his hat bobbing up and down.

Ah, she can see Leon talking to someone on the other side of the room. But the conversation has ended and now he's standing alone, turning his glass round in his hands. He'd rather be at home with Graham and Lynette; she can see that.

Lynette, the apple of Leon's eye. In Doris' belly, she'd lain so still that there were times Doris thought she couldn't possibly be alive. When the time came, she was born easily, with as little bother as a birth could give. And she was not dead. Her birth set the pattern too for the years since, for she was an easy baby: cried little, rarely fussed and had a smile for everyone who looked her way.

Bernard returns with champagne, and the conversation turns to politics and the protests that have been taking place in Baghdad against the partition of Palestine.

'We'll be heading out of there before long,' Bernard says with certainty, 'and that'll be the end of another mandate. They can fight it out among themselves.' His moustache brushes against the rim of his glass as he takes a sip of champagne. 'Just like this country. Our mandate here ended in '32, and here they are, Kurds, Sunnis, Shi'as and what have you, all fighting one another.'

Sara looks worried. 'They like us less and less.'

But Doris isn't going to worry about anti-British sentiment. She glances across at Leon and the woman he's started speaking to; assesses the woman's figure and face, how attractive she is. Not very, is the conclusion.

As Bernard lights a fresh cigarette for her, he makes a joke and she laughs, then laughs again louder, and just as she hoped, Leon looks over. What does he see, she wonders? Not the poor creature she was when he first met her, blinking rain from her lashes, fingers clasped around a paper bag of sweets. Nor the shadow of herself that she became for months after Harry died, a woman who didn't want to bathe or wash her hair, whose nails Leon had to clip as though she were a child. Who, when she finally got out of bed and drew back the curtains, found that the flowers in the garden had budded, bloomed and died back again; that in the house, the carpets that had been rolled up and stored for the summer months had been unrolled and laid out again.

She sips her champagne. No, Leon will never see that Doris again. What he must see from now on is the woman she is tonight. Thirty-six but passing for thirty. Slim and poised in a beautiful dress, her hair arranged in careful waves and curls. This woman glints with diamonds and confidence. Extended from her right hand is an ivory cigarette-holder, from the end of which a cigarette releases curlicues of smoke. Her lips and nails are painted a bold shade of red, her large eyes are rimmed with kohl and her eyebrows pencilled into two perfect arches. This is the woman Leon must see.

And yet… it was that scrap of a girl standing in the rain that Leon fell in love with, wasn't it?

She looks around. The local gossips prattle, no doubt,

about the way she parades down the streets as though the city belonged to her, swinging her hips and wearing sunglasses, high heels and skirts with slits in them, her shirts open to the breastbone. She never touches their food, they must remark, and no dog cares to bite her nor any cat to scratch her. But she doesn't care what they whisper, because all of it is as much as to say that she's a woman who possesses her own life entirely, and is strong enough to keep hold of it. She must remain strong too, if she's to withstand the horrors that life hurls her way.

She wishes Leon would come over – the woman he was talking to has moved away and he's standing alone again, after all.

'And did you ever go to see the Babylonian ruins like you said you would?' asks Sara.

Doris takes a drag of her cigarette, leaving a trace of red on the ivory mouthpiece. 'I drove out there the other week.' She drives now, and has a car of her own. Unusual, of course, for a woman, especially out here.

Sara's eyebrows rise. 'Not by yourself!'

'Yes of course. Leo was away.' Leo is what she calls Leon when they're not alone. 'Why shouldn't I go by myself? I wanted to see them; what's left of them anyway.' Years before the war, apparently, the British had snaffled a large number of artefacts, while the Germans took down the Gate of Babylon piece by tiny piece, transported it in barrels down the Euphrates and shipped it off to Germany. They took an entire ceremonial avenue this way too.

'But a woman!' says Bernard. 'And an Englishwoman at that. In the desert all alone.'

'Oh, rot.' She's sick of shaking heads. 'Why that writer woman Agatha Christie's been accompanying her husband to Iraq on digs for years.'

'Yes, but she doesn't go by herself,' says Sara. 'Weren't you scared?'

'Of what exactly?' There's nothing left to be scared of.

'It's not easy driving in the desert,' says Sara admiringly. 'I don't know another woman who's done it.'

'I'm a good driver.'

They're discussing the ruins when Leon finally comes over.

'Ah.' Bernard assumes a different expression and tone of voice. 'Hello again.'

Leon nods in greeting. Even though she was the one who talked him into coming, now that he's standing next to her, she feels uncomfortable, on edge.

'We were just talking about your wife's trip to the ruins of Babylon,' says Bernard.

'Yes,' says Sara, 'how wonderful to do as you want and go where you like!'

Leon smiles at Doris. 'She has always been independent.'

Watching him talk to Sara, she thinks about how especially handsome he looks in his suit and bow tie. And Sara, with her bony shoulders and that puce dress sagging round her hips, is no threat, of course. Leon says it's a gift, the way she focuses on other women's faults.

'Leo's been travelling all over the place. Damascus, Beirut, Istanbul – all the well-to-do cities. And Europe too, oh yes. Italy, Spain, Switzerland. I should start travelling with you, shouldn't I, darling? Just think what a lovely time we'd have.'

Leon kisses her cheek without comment – discussing their personal lives in public isn't something he likes to do – and he and Bernard prepare to go to the bar for another round of drinks.

'Another champagne please, darling,' says Doris. Yes, things have turned out well since Leon took over his father's business. Their house is filled with hand-woven rugs, engraved silverware, and enamelled plates and bowls from Persia. Hers is now a life of massages and Turkish baths, of perfume in cut-glass bottles and the latest fashion in clothes. She lays out various outfits on her bed, matching this blouse with that skirt, this jacket with that dress, a new necklace with both.

Ignoring the sensation that she's gazing down at a woman who has dissolved into air.

Leon and Bernard return from the bar.

'Whisky?' says Doris, looking in surprise at Leon's glass.

'They didn't have *arak*.'

'Ugh, that nasty local stuff, I should hope not! Why not have champagne like the rest of us? Tonight's a night for champagne.'

Leon sips his whisky. 'This is fine.'

Putting down her glass, she fits a fresh cigarette into her holder. 'Do you want one, darling?'

Leon shakes his head.

'You used to smoke, remember?' Years ago, to keep her company. Does he remember?

Bernard clears his throat. 'There'll be fireworks in a bit,' he says to Leon, and checks his watch. 'Any minute now I should think. I hope they get it right this time. A fellow had his hand blown off one New Year's Eve. Shocking mess. They've no idea how to work such things, you see.'

Leon drinks down the rest of his whisky.

'Oh, cheer up, darling,' she whispers. 'It is a party, after all.'

The music stops, and begins again with 'God Save the King'. Everyone joins in, their jollity given way to something altogether different. Everyone apart from Leon, that is.

When they're done, he fetches Doris' stole. The Elmwoods are already heading out to the garden to watch the display. He settles the stole around her shoulders, a forefinger lingering to touch one of the creature's glass eyes – tenderly, she notes with surprise, as though it could still feel.

'Aren't you coming to watch?' she asks when he doesn't follow.

'No. I want another drink.'

'But darling.' Everyone's gathered on the lawn now. 'The fireworks have started.'

CHAPTER 28

Drowning

Baghdad, 1949

One morning when she's out by herself, she comes across a commotion by the river, a clot of people and noise. A woman has been fished out of the Tigris, her long dress and headscarves heavy with water. Now she lies sprawled on her stomach, arms thrown above her head. One of her shoes is missing, and the sole of her bare foot, Doris sees, is hard and cracked. She touches a man on the shoulder – an *effendi* in a Western suit – and he turns round. 'Who is she?' she asks.

He understands English and shrugs with his mouth. 'A woman.'

'But what happened?'

'We do not know.'

They turn her over, for she's dead of course, but Doris doesn't want to see her face. She turns and walks quickly away, but questions unwind in her head. How did the woman come to be in the river? Did she slip? Was she thrown in? Perhaps she jumped in herself. If she did jump, what would drive a woman to that?

She turns away, pushing to get through the people, bypassing donkeys and water buffalo that have been led down to the water's edge to drink. In the marketplace, with the smell of the Tigris still in her nostrils, she glimpses cakes and ribbons, pears and hanging scarves, hears the cry of *'turshi!'* from the pickle-seller. Somewhere, someone's hammering metal, a repetitive ringing clang. She passes a street barber with a razor in his hand and his client's throat naked and exposed, and a desperation builds in her, a hunger to embrace her children and press them close enough to feel their little hearts beating in their chests. The feeling swells. Graham. Lynette. Leon. The thought of them fills her with a fierce happiness. This – her children, her family – is the apex of her life, this moment with its sunlight bright as blades and its scent of hot metal and pomegranates. Nothing before or after will ever exceed it.

Graham's schoolbag is on the floor in the hall. 'Hello?' she calls. He and Lynette are in the kitchen with Aisha, she can hear them. 'I'm home.'

The ice truck has been round this morning. The man in his leather apron has carried a huge block of it into the kitchen, and now, with the icebox freshly stocked again, Aisha has made the children fruit sherbet. On the table are flatbread sandwiches next to slices of cucumber and tomato. 'There you are,' she says, coming in. 'My little darlings.'

The children look surprised, as does Aisha. Doris doesn't usually come into the kitchen to find them, or call them her little darlings. But today's no ordinary day. Today something has shifted. In one of those instants of clarity, a screen has been pulled aside.

'Mmm, that looks delicious,' she says as Graham takes a sip of sherbet.

He holds out his glass. 'Do you want some?'

'What? Oh no,' she laughs, suddenly happy. Her child, offering her his drink. 'Do you want to go and see the date men?' That's something the children would enjoy. The city's surrounded by date palms as a protection against desert storms, and in these groves, barefoot men with their *dishdasha* robes tucked in clamber up the trees using a wide leather belt that loops around the trunk. They hack down the dates, while below, other men thrash the branches against the ground, sending the fruit flying off.

Graham shakes his head. 'No, thank you.'

She bends and slips an arm around him, but he tenses beneath her fingers, his small shoulders drawing closer together. She retracts her arm.

'Lynette,' she says, crouching down and smiling at the little girl with the green bow in her hair. 'Come here, darling.' And she holds out her arms. She wants to feel the frills of that dress against her cheek, sniff the dark hair, close her eyes and absorb her daughter.

But Lynette steps back, and with her eyes still fixed on Doris, the little hand feels for Aisha's dress. When she has hold of it, she leans against the maid the way Doris has seen dogs lean against their owner's legs.

The raw, loving softness inside her alters, and by the time she has stood up, the children have reverted to what they were before: Graham the embodiment of her physical pain, Lynette the embodiment of her grief for Harry. And reinstated in her chest is the knowledge that loving a thing must, sooner or later, tear your heart to pieces.

Aisha says something to them in Arabic – Doris recognises the word for 'mother' – but neither of them moves. Aisha lays an encouraging hand on Lynette's head but Lynette just tucks her chin in and watches Doris from beneath thick black lashes.

It's four o'clock, and standing in the shade of a eucalyptus tree, Doris waits by the convent gates for the bell to signal the end of the school day. As soon as it starts clanging, the nuns and girls file out. Each nun has on a white habit with a black apron, and a headdress that makes Doris think of a bird with white, outstretched wings. With their crosses and rosaries and not a plucked eyebrow or speck of makeup between them, the nuns are their own breed. The little girls, in white summer uniform and shoes, are quiet and subdued. Too quiet, some might say, too subdued, but a convent education is the best one for a girl in Baghdad.

What would the nuns make of the enormous doll Leon

brought back for Lynette from his last trip to Seville, with its ruffled dress and curling hair? Although Lynette doesn't seem to know how to play with it. Sometimes she'll pretend to give it food or put it to sleep, and when it 'cries' she tells it to go to its room immediately.

One of the nuns comes forward, her habit swirling, to unlock the large metal gates. It takes some doing to drag them open, and then the girls pass out one by one – '*Au revoir ma soeur.*' '*Au revoir ma soeur.*' '*Au revoir ma soeur.*' – to whichever parent, maid, chauffeur or errand boy has been sent to fetch them. Are these the girls whose houses Lynette goes to for birthday parties? Should Doris recognise them?

Still inside the gates, Lynette stops dead.

Doris smiles and extends a hand. 'Come along, darling.'

The nun follows Lynette's gaze, and her eyes rake down to Doris' feet and back up again. Small lines appear around her mouth. '*Ta mère*?' she asks Lynette.

Lynette nods.

'*Vas-y alors*.'

For several moments nothing happens. Then a slow '*Au revoir ma soeur.*'

'There you are,' says Doris cheerily.

'Where's Aisha?'

'She's not here.'

Lynette looks around. 'But where is she?'

Leon's eyes open wide. He hasn't been in the house five minutes. 'What?' His voice is balanced between astonishment and anger. 'But why?'

Doris drops the last of the nuts and dried fruit into the batter. 'She got too big for her boots, that's why. Anyway I never liked her. That way she had of looking at me as if… well, as if she knew everything there was to know about me.' It had discomfited her. 'And all those tattoos.' As she stirs, the raisins and walnuts sink into the cake mixture, travelling round the bowl in a slow vortex.

Leon shakes his head, bewildered. 'But did she do something? Did something happen?'

All afternoon Doris has been thinking about Aisha. Aisha who swept the floors and ceilings with a bundle of dried palm leaves, and ground spices in a stone mortar, making a sound like the sea. She's been thinking of the strange tunes she hummed that seem to have no beginning or end. Her habit of picking Lynette up and patting her on the behind, and how Graham followed her around the house like a dog while she talked to him, even though he rarely said anything himself. The way she had a man come and write down everything she wanted from the market, then return with a couple of boys in tow to carry the stuff. How easily she moved around the kitchen, opening and closing cupboards, laying out ingredients then tidying them away again. In the heat of the day, Lynette would sometimes fan her while she cooked. Then for lunch there might be okra and saffron rice, or chicken with nuts, and in the evening Aisha would sprinkle water on the floors to cool the house. She knew that putting *sassafras* in the children's hair would prevent lice, and told them stories about tents and camels and sandstorms and gazelles. Doris has been thinking about how she came across her standing on the roof terrace with an armful of dried laundry held to her chest, completely still and attentive, as though she could hear the desert.

Now, steeling herself, she says it: 'She's been taking things.'

'Taking things?' repeats Leon.

'You know – food, money. That necklace that went missing the other day.'

Leon's mouth falls open. Whenever things are mislaid, they always turn up again behind a sofa or in a box of toys or under one of the children's beds. 'But she has worked for us for a long time. Are you sure?'

'Of course I am. Anyway it's done now.'

'But where did she go?'

'How should I know? Back where she came from, I

expect.' She sees Aisha standing quite still, the way she stood when Doris told her she was to leave, only now she's standing alone in the middle of the desert.

Leon says nothing.

Tipping the bowl over, she watches the thick batter fall slowly into the cake tin. 'You're behaving as though she's one of the family.'

It's cool in the garden with evening drawing on. She kneels by the flower bed, turning the soil over with a trowel. The manure she's had put in hasn't made much difference; the soil's still fine and powdery, and turns to mud when she waters it. There's no escaping the fact that, Tigris or no, they're living in a desert. The seeds and cuttings she had imported have died, but a few of the hardier plants and some of the roses aren't looking too bad. As a rule of thumb the plants that live here are lean and robust. They survive rather than flourish.

Swallows flicker across the sky. They travel great distances, people say. Perhaps, before coming here, they were in England. If they were, what do they make of the blazing heat and relentless glare of Baghdad? Why would they swap swaying trees and pastel-coloured sunsets for this?

In all the years she's been here, she's never once returned to visit Nan. Nan, Grandad, Harry: it's as though they're away someplace, like Leon when he travels for work, and will be back before long. And what about Doris Palmer of 45 Nursery Road? How can that Doris possibly be the person she is now? Thinking of it gives her a strange, asymmetric feeling, like a hand missing a finger or an eye trimmed of its lashes.

She gazes down at the sparse flower bed. It's late May but no daffodil or crocus shoots have pushed out of the earth; no primroses either. There'll be no tall rows of blue delphiniums, no bees slipping in and out of foxgloves, no lilacs leaking their scent into the evening or robin watching for worms.

Beyond the garden wall, there have been more strikes and demonstrations, by students, postal workers, railway workers, oil workers and the general poor, all wanting more money, yes, but most of all wanting the obliteration of the 1930 Anglo-Iraqi Treaty: an end to British interests, British influence, everything British out here in fact. Oil workers marched two hundred and fifty kilometres across the desert to Baghdad to make the point. Others walked through machine gun fire on Ma'mun Bridge, with only one schoolgirl arriving unhurt on the other side. One girl standing alone, alone in a desert.

What sort of society forbids people the right to protest? Back home, in England, such a notion would be simply inconceivable. She stabs her trowel into the earth, digs deeper but can't find what she's looking for. The Harborne allotment comes into her mind, the peace she used to find when she had her hands in the earth. This soil though will never be dark and crumbly, full of leaf skeletons and minuscule wriggling things. What wouldn't she give for a changeable sky, for clouds and wind and rain – all the different sorts of it, even the icy sort. Rain drumming on the roof and trickling down windows. The give of wet earth underfoot. Dripping leaves. Moss. Shade that's blurry-edged and not sliced sharp as a razor. Dark afternoons and rooks cawing in an oak tree. The crack and hiss of a wood fire. Crumpets and cricket and tea – the proper sort, not what you get here, which has driven her to coffee. In the hall, a stack of Harry's books and the smell of apples baking or a suet pudding steaming in the pot.

She wishes her children could know and love all these things. She glances at the house. In the kitchen the light is on. Leon's giving the children some supper, for neither of them liked Nan's fruitcake; they couldn't taste the comfort in it, the proof of love which she once tasted.

Going back inside right now to face them is unthinkable. Sending Aisha away has made Doris a villain, but she'll work out how to forge a connection with them. Not today though. Once they've all gone up to bed, she'll go in and light a cigarette, mix a martini and smooth away the day's edges. Tomorrow she can think what to do.

CHAPTER 29

Chalk

Harborne, 1931

The knocking won't stop. It's insistent, urgent. Why on earth doesn't Nan answer the door? She should have been back from church an hour ago. And who can possibly persist in making such a din? It's enough to wake the dead.

These are the thoughts that slide through Doris' head as she lies in bed watching the late morning light leak in through the gaps around her curtains. She turns over and shuts her eyes, pulls the bedclothes over her head. 'Go away.'

But the knocking doesn't stop.

Growling, she throws off the covers and sits up. It's Sunday: she shouldn't have to get up, shouldn't have to do anything at all. She ought to be able to lie here all day if she wants to – which she does – because tomorrow it'll be back to work and the endless, cheery 'What number please? Hold the line please.'

As she passes the kitchen, she sees that the milk bottle has been left uncovered on the counter. Well, if the milk's turned it won't be her fault, and Nan'll just have to make scones with it. Strange though for Nan to forget something like that.

When she opens the door, she thinks for an instant that she must still be asleep and dreaming because Michael's there, hand raised to knock again. She blinks. Michael, here outside Nan's house, where in all these years he's never once been. Nor have any of them for that matter; it's always been Nan and her and Harry who've made the visits. That's the way it began and for some reason that's the way it continued.

She stands there, not knowing what to say. Isn't he going to say anything? What does he want? Why has he come here? She's completely unprepared for this. Clearing her throat, she lifts her head a little higher. She's not a child any longer, whereas he's a lad of fourteen with a face full of acne. The world runs on different tracks now.

'Hello,' she says coolly.

Michael looks strange. 'You've got to come.'

'What do you mean? Come where?' Can't he see she's still in her dressing gown? What time is it anyway?

'Granma says.' Michael's hands are restless. 'You've got to come over.'

Doris is awake now. 'Is Nan at yours?'

He nods. 'Since yesterday.'

Nan had gone out in the evening, Doris remembers that, but then she'd fallen asleep. Hasn't Nan been home all night then?

Michael glances at her bare feet. 'I'll wait for you to get ready.'

Her heart gives a great leap. 'Nothing's happened to Nan, has it?'

His lip twitches. 'No. Not Nan.'

Michael's pace slows as they reach The Back of Beyond. She looks from him to the house. The door's ajar but he's loitering, reluctant to go in.

All right then. All right. Slowly, she goes up the step and pushes the door open.

It's quiet inside, and still. Almost on tiptoe, she steps into the hall. There's no one here, she thinks. They've all gone out.

'She's in there.' Michael is behind her, pointing to the closed parlour door.

For a moment she thinks he means Nan, but then she understands. But it can't be. The Palmers have got their wires crossed, that's what, the way you do in the telephone exchange.

The wooden panels of the parlour door are so still they seem to be moving. Doris has never seen a dead body before. When Mr Pearce, a neighbour, passed away, she refused to go round like everyone else to pay her respects. The mere thought had made her stomach twist and tumble, just as it's doing now. She thinks of the hole in the bread the other morning; the way Nan had snatched the slice from her hand before she was able to take a bite. But that's just one of Nan's superstitions – isn't it?

Michael's waiting for her to go into the parlour. Michael, the parlour. But there's no malice in his face now, no evil intent. Should she go in?

The sound of a chair scraping across the kitchen floor makes her start. She walks on to the kitchen but stops in the doorway, unable to make sense of what she's seeing. Susan is seated on a chair in the middle of the kitchen. Her knees are spread wide, and Ruthie's kneeling between them. Susan's head is bent, her face close to Ruthie's crown, and with her fingers she's parting her daughter's hair. 'I'm sure it's lice. Lil's been scratching, and if one of you've got it then all of you have.'

Nan's standing on one side of her. On the other, Reg and Lilian are lined up waiting their turn. The girls' eyes are puffy with crying, and Reg is sucking his thumb and looking bewildered.

Nan lays a hand on Susan's shoulder. 'They don't have lice, love. Susan. Susan!'

But Susan carries on, parting Ruthie's thick hair over and over again.

'Susan.' Nan bends down. 'Stop, love. Please stop.'

The front door clicks shut – Michael's left, gone back outside – and Nan looks up and sees Doris. Susan finishes with Ruthie and pulls Reg to her. Kneeling between his mother's legs, Reg starts to sob, and Doris wonders whether he understands what's happened. Then Nan's coming towards her, taking her by the shoulders, steering her out of the kitchen.

'But what's she doing?' says Doris.

'She'll be all right.' Nan's voice is thick with distress. 'Women lose children all the time. All the time.'

It feels like a dream. The morning's been whisked away, like a hand that was being held over your eyes, and what's revealed is happening somewhere else, in some parallel universe. Last spring Reg had a cough that Dolores caught. Reg got better, but Dolores couldn't shake it. By Christmas she'd lost weight, and when she coughed it seemed to wear her out. In the New Year she was sent to West Heath Sanatorium for tuberculosis patients on the other side of Bournville, but was so homesick that two weeks later they sent her back.

Overnight, Nan has aged. Her face is worn and her hands are shaking like an old woman's. 'We've got to prepare things.'

'Prepare?'

'There'll be visitors soon, come to see her. Friends. Neighbours. Someone'll have to open the door and show them in.' Nan stops outside the parlour door to gather herself. 'The midwife came last night and laid her out.' As well as assisting at births, midwives do this task too, and Doris wonders if the midwife last night was the same one who brought Dolores into the world.

Nan opens the parlour door and steps in – softly, as if there's someone asleep inside. Doris follows. Part of her wants to run away, but the other part of her is curious.

Inside, the curtains are pulled closed, and the darkness has a grainy, silt-like texture. But when Nan draws the curtains, Doris sees her. A door has been taken off its hinges and laid across two chairs, and on it, Dolores is lying perfectly still. Yet as daylight pours in, it seems to Doris that what she's looking at is a sculpture made of wax or clay; that although this looks like her, the real Dolores must be upstairs playing with Reg, or in the yard turning the mangle, or perhaps gone out for a walk with her friends. The one place she would never be found is lying on a door in the parlour.

Nan throws open the window. 'There. You must always open a window to let out the soul.' She lays the two framed photographs face down and covers the mirror with the cloth off the table.

Doris creeps closer. Dolores is wearing her best dress, and a penny's balanced over each eye. A prayerbook has been wedged beneath her chin – to stop her mouth from falling open, Doris supposes. Her hands are on her chest, and strips of muslin have been wound round her wrists to hold them together, and round her ankles. Her hair is combed and there's cotton wool plugging up her nostrils.

Doris touches a white mark on the door near Dolores' head, and it comes off on her fingers. Chalk. There's another mark next to Dolores' feet.

'Jim measured her out,' says Nan, but her voice breaks and she covers her mouth. Her face puckers and twitches, and it takes her several long moments to regain control. 'Jim and Bobby've gone to the undertakers for the casket. They ought to be back soon. *If* he doesn't come back via the pub, that is.' Gazing down at Dolores, her tone sweetens. 'That daft woman didn't brush your hair properly, did she, my angel?' She smooths Dolores' hair and adjusts a hairpin with a little metal daisy on it above her ear. 'There, you're all clean and neat now. Spotless enough to meet the Lamb of God.' Nan's face crumples again and tears slip down her cheeks.

Doris kneads her hands together. A heaviness, large and white and muffled, drags at her chest.

The front door opens and Nan quickly wipes her face and stands up straight. Jim is back. When he comes in, his face is ashen and there are dark rings beneath his eyes. 'Carpenter says he'll bring it round by midday,' he tells Nan. 'Bobby's helping him.' Doris can see that he's trying not to look at Dolores. He tips his head towards the kitchen. 'I'll go tell her.'

But whatever he tells Susan sets her off because she starts

wailing as though she's been scalded, filling the house from floorboards to rafters with her grief. Nan hurries to her, and a short while later she and Jim lead Susan out of the kitchen. 'Come on, love,' Nan says. 'Come and lie down.' And they shepherd her up the stairs.

Doris is left alone in the parlour. Or rather not alone. She doesn't move, and neither does her sister. The absolute stillness of Dolores is unnerving. Up close like this, her skin looks white and silken, like the membrane on raw meat. How would it feel to the touch, Doris wonders? It takes a good while to make up her mind to it, but then she reaches up and tentatively puts a finger to Dolores' jaw. It's chilly and smooth, like white pudding. Quickly she draws back her finger. For some unfathomable reason she recalls the pigeon that Harry kept that summer when they were little. The flapping and kerfuffle as soon as the hatch was opened, then the way it gained height and sped across the sky until neither she nor Harry could see it any longer. The emptiness of the cage it left behind.

'Dolores?' she whispers, and for an instant she thinks Dolores will sit up, catching the falling pennies with a laugh. *Doris-Dolores-Doris-Dolores-Doris-Dolores. Two peas in a pod, en't we?*

But she doesn't get up. It's not a game.

Doris sways, suddenly unsteady. In this room, her heart is the only one still pumping blood. She is warm and Dolores is cold as stone. Air is flowing in and out of her lungs while... Dolores' poor lungs! She, Doris, has a lifetime before her and a thousand choices more to make, but Dolores has none. Here lies her sister in the last dress she'll ever wear, the world closed off to her.

Mixed in with her sorrow is a new awareness of her future and a gladness that she is still alive. There are spots on Dolores forehead, and more on the side of her nose. On one of her tied-together hands is a graze. It looks recent, and Doris imagines the flinch Dolores gave when she received it; how perhaps she held it up to her mouth for an instant to soothe it. The warmth of her mouth against the scrape, and when she took it away again, the dampness left behind on her skin.

'You're the kindest one,' she murmurs, looking at the pennies and the prayerbook and the metal daisy hairpin. 'Of all of them, you're the kindest one.' And she blots her tears with her sleeve.

The next day goes by in a haze. A neighbour comes to take in the washing. Another brings a meal. The coffin arrives and is set out in the parlour with Dolores inside it. Then visitors come – neighbours and their children, and Dolores' friends – asking to see her. Some cry, handkerchiefs pressed to their faces, others talk to her or touch her, and the rest stand beside her in silence. The two friends Doris saw her with outside the sweet shop come too, distraught and red-eyed. Dolores' fiancé, Thomas Hobday, arrives too, and cap in hand, sits white-faced and motionless beside her for two solid hours, thinking perhaps of their not-to-be wedding day and their unborn children. All of this is normal, Doris tells herself, it's what usually happens when someone dies, and yet it feels staged, like a play that must soon come to an end.

A telegram's been sent to London, and Harry arrives with a black armband on his coat sleeve. His hair's cut in a different way and he's wearing a new suit, but he's here and she can scarcely believe it. Her Harry.

He kneels next to the coffin and when he lifts his face, he's crying. 'Poor Dolly,' he says. 'Poor, poor Dolly.' And the sight of him sobbing so openly appals her. Two years back it was her kneeling beside him. That awful doctor. Her desperation. The wet cloth dripping water onto Nan's floor. *Not him. Anyone but him.*

His tears fall in dots onto the floorboards, and guilt swirls around her heart. How was she to know? She couldn't possibly have foreseen that it would be Dolores who'd be chosen instead of him.

The following day they all stand in the churchyard. Spring is making the birds sing and flowers push up out of the earth. The coffin is hefted off the back of the undertaker's carriage and they all gasp as it tilts (Dolores will be sliding inside it, her cheek pressing against the wooden side) but then it's righted again. Words are spoken by the vicar but she doesn't know what it is he says, what anyone could possibly say in the face of such a thing. Susan, Jim, Nan and Harry, the children. She stares steadily at her feet, which seem far away, too far away to be her own.

And then the box is being lowered into the ruptured earth and there's wailing – 'She never deserved it, she was a good girl' – and fresh tears. The other siblings each throw in a flower, but Doris stands apart, like a passerby who's stopped to observe this scene. And as the first clods of earth thud onto the coffin, she thinks of the presents she saw in the bottom of Susan's wardrobe, all ready for Dolores' eighteenth birthday; the vanity set with 'DP' engraved on the backs of the mirror, the comb and all the brushes.

Afterwards there are endless cups of tea, and Harry smoking and smoking in the paved back yard.

She sees him to the train station where, in spite of a blue sky, an icy wind whips along the platform. Sitting on the bench beside him, she pulls her coat up around her neck, and curls and uncurls her frozen toes. 'You don't write,' she says. The train will be here soon so there's no point beating about the bush. 'Why don't you write?'

He shrugs. 'Don't know, it's just… my life now… it's difficult to write down such things.'

'Well, try. I don't care what you write about.' Don't beg, for *God's* sake. 'Only it'd be nice to hear from you. Once in a while – you know.'

He gives a tight smile. 'All right. All right Dot, that's me told off.'

She turns to him. 'You are happy, aren't you? Living in London?'

'Happy?'

She nods, chin scraping against her coat collar.

For a long time he doesn't speak. Then he unbuttons his coat and reaches into a breast pocket. He draws out his wallet and opens it, takes out a photograph from one of the pockets and hands it to her.

It's a picture of him and another man. They're standing side by side and the man has an arm around Harry's shoulders. He's a little older, with fair hair, and not as handsome as Harry, but handsome enough. Two smiling young men standing side by side, in a park probably, because there are trees. 'Is this… is this why you don't write?' Here, on this icy-cold platform, a photograph, an announcement right here in her hands.

Harry's watching her, tense, waiting to see what she'll say.

'Very dishy.'

His burst of laughter is like the release of a pressure he's been holding inside him. It takes her aback, it's such a long time since she heard anyone laugh. He leans over and kisses her hard on the cheek, sending a thrill of happiness through her.

'You are happy then,' she says.

'Is that all it takes to be happy?'

'I don't know. Isn't it?'

As he takes the picture back from her, he turns serious again. 'Are you going to tell Mum?'

A gust of wind makes her shrink into her clothes. 'Do you want me to?'

A moment passes. 'Can't say that I really care. I'll be miles from here; you're the one who'll pay for it.'

'In that case let me think.' She puts her hand to her chin and pretends to consider. 'No, no I don't believe I will tell her.' Nan probably already knows, or at least guesses, even if she'd never admit it to herself.

Harry puts the wallet back in his pocket. Impossible to

think that a moment ago he was laughing. He speaks in a low voice. 'The names they call us, Dot – you wouldn't believe it. The other day someone spat at me.'

She flinches.

'We weren't even doing anything. Just talking, laughing.' He frowns. 'How can they even tell?'

Down on the track, the rails begin to thrum, and with a shuddering breath Harry stands up.

'You mustn't mind,' she says, standing and putting a hand on his shoulder. 'You mustn't care. You're better than the lot of them.'

He gives her hair a friendly tug. 'It won't always be this way, you know. Me leaving and you staying here.'

The train has pulled in and is slowing, the brake blocks grinding painfully against the wheels. Unbearable. Simply unbearable.

That night she dreams that she and Dolores are both laid out side by side in Susan's parlour, their life's business cut short, and wakes up with a start.

CHAPTER 30

Buttons

Harborne, 1933

There's a man between her legs. Systematically, her back is being pressed against the hard edge of the dresser, making whatever's inside it quake and rattle. Even though his face is close to hers, the man isn't looking at Doris but through her, as though at things that were invisible up until now. In spite of his pretences, it's his first time too, that's clear enough.

She feels the breath leaving and entering her body, passing dry across her lips. How can you be this close to someone and yet not close at all, no more than strangers? That red-tinged hair, the nick beneath his ear which he must have got while shaving. He was more attractive an hour ago when he was stood at the far end of the room and the air was smoky.

There was beer and wine from the off, and later on when gin was doled out, the music and laughter grew raucous. Someone burned toast in the kitchen, but even with the windows propped open, it stayed stuffy. The Victrola never stopped though. Nor did the dancing. Doris danced with her friend Gladys, and then with two men. She didn't know either of them, but the way they held her made a pleasant heat form in her chest. Then couples started to wander off in search of somewhere quieter, picking out their coats from the pile just inside the front door.

At eleven o'clock, when the party began to slow down,

Gladys said she was going home. But Doris wasn't ready to leave. 'I think I'll stay a little longer.'

Gladys' eyebrows lifted a fraction. 'All right.' She smiled. 'Ta-ra then, see you Monday.'

Then someone vomited out of the window and the rest of the partygoers cleared off. Holding her cigarette off to one side, Doris was pretending to search for her coat when he came up. 'Lost something?' He was the owner of the flat, which was impressive in its way; the one who'd handed out glasses and poured the first drinks. Not bad looking either, in spite of the slicked red hair and the ghosts of spots.

'Oh – yes, my coat,' she said. 'I can't think where I put it.' Even though it was October and cold, she'd decided against a coat. A coat would have ruined her silhouette.

Together they searched for it in every room in the flat – living room, kitchen, bedroom, then back to the hall again. The last of the guests were clattering down the stairs, giggling and laughing.

'It'll turn up,' he said.

She took a drag of her cigarette. 'What'll we do? Wait?'

He gave a nervous laugh. 'For a coat? What, like waiting for a bus?'

She shrugged.

Closing the front door, he cleared his throat. 'Have another drink?'

'No thanks.'

He looked a little put out.

'I don't want a drink.' A curl of smoke rose slowly from her cigarette. Without unlocking her eyes from his, she pinched the fabric of her dress where it sat snug against her thigh and hitched it up just a fraction. 'Not a drink.'

Then before she knew it, he was kissing her, his hands on her shoulders, her neck, her breasts, her behind. And she was kissing him back. Or at least trying to.

Nan would call that wicked – would call *her* wicked – but she's welcome to call things what she likes. These last years the world has faded like a handkerchief hung out too long in the sun, and before Doris fades along with it, she must focus on laughter and music, and the rising feeling in her belly and the tingle in her breasts. What goes on within the contours of her skin is all there is, so she must fill it with as much pleasure as she can, else on the final day of her life she'll find that she hasn't experienced a damned thing. She thinks of that day two years ago in the churchyard, of the coffin being lowered into the open ground. Being good doesn't pay. It doesn't pay at all. So yes, why not? Put on a dress that clings too close and reveals too much, drink wine and then gin; smoke all you want, draw a man in between your legs and try to enjoy it.

The music has finished playing but the record's still spinning, the needle swerving and hissing against its surface. The boy groans. The cigarette she dropped has burned a tiny circle in the carpet near his left foot, but she doesn't care and nor does he.

The boy's thrusts pick up pace. Somewhere in the neighbourhood a dog is barking. A faint smell of burnt toast still hangs in the air. Is this what all the fuss is about? She's heard stories – oh, lots of stories – but none of them suggested that it would be like this. This is painful, awkward, ungainly. The boy (she can't help thinking of him as a boy rather than a man) has ripped the seam of her dress too, which makes her dislike him. He's breathing hard, with his mouth open, and still not looking where he should be looking: at her.

But it doesn't last long, which is a mercy.

She pushes him away, releasing herself; tugs the skirt of her dress back down and the neckline back up. The boy is smiling inanely and looking pleased with himself. She glances round for her shoes. Her back hurts from being pressed against the dresser.

What she wants is to light a cigarette, sit down and listen to another song, only she doesn't want to do it with him in the room. Perhaps she ought to say something, but she can't remember his name. Did he even tell it her? She knows she didn't tell him hers. So she says nothing, just smiles and, leaving him to button up his flies, heads to the bathroom.

How lucky he is to have a toilet in the flat, not like the outdoor privy at number 45. She cleans herself up then peers into the small mirror above the wash basin. But she looks no different, except that she's a little pale and her lipstick's almost gone.

'I can see you home if you like,' he offers when she comes back out.

'No, you're all right.' The thought of the cool night air is appealing, as is the thought of being alone.

Stifling a yawn, the boy doesn't offer again, and she puts on her shoes, finds her handbag and leaves.

She turns the key in the lock. Her makeup feels sticky and she wants to wash it off, take off these blasted shoes and pour a glass of water. As she opens the door, Jasper tries to slip out. Stanley liked nothing better than to sit in front of the fire in winter but Jasper's an altogether different cat, intent on the business of hunting and mating. 'Go on then.'

But inside the house, a light's on in the parlour and another on the landing. Surely Nan isn't up waiting for her. For God's sake, can she have no privacy?

The parlour door's open so there's nothing for it. Standing tall, she sashays down the hall and stops in the doorway. The fire's died out in the grate but Nan's still sitting in Grandad's old armchair. For years now she's been earning money doing piecework, or finishing work done by hand. Her sewing basket's out, her glasses are perched on the end of her nose and there's a stack of clothes beside her. She's been threading a needle but has stopped, the thread held up in her left hand, and in her right the needle, like a splinter.

When she claps eyes on Doris, Nan inhales sharply. Standing in the doorway, Doris must present a full-length portrait, and sure enough Nan's eyes travel down over the amethyst-coloured dress and silk stockings in Daring Nude;

they settle a moment on the strappy high heels, then sweep back up to the neckline and the hair that took her two hours to curl, set and pin. Without a word being uttered, Doris knows what Nan is thinking. *Street walker*.

The needle and thread are lowered and Nan's face twitches. 'What in God's name do you think you're wearing?'

Doris lengthens her neck. How glad she is that at this moment she's able to look down at Nan. 'Why, a dress. Shoes. *Clothes*.'

Nan pushes herself to her feet. 'How could you? How could you have gone out dressed like that? Look at you!'

Doris' heart picks up pace. 'What do you want me to wear, a corset and bustle?'

Harry would have smoothed things over. Rubbing Nan's shoulder, he'd have said, 'Oh, Mum, she looks fine. More than fine, she looks gorgeous. She's young, remember?' And Nan would have sniffed and muttered, but then her mood would have settled. That's what would have happened if Harry were here, but he isn't, and Nan is all morals and starch and suet puddings.

'Reeking of perfume, and with that rubbish on your face. Dis-*grace*-ful!' And Nan turns away as though she can't bear to look at her a moment longer. As far as Nan's concerned, visible makeup spells the end of days and the fall of mankind.

'I'm twenty-two, I'm allowed to wear makeup.' One thing is for certain: nothing glows and burns between Nan's hips, and never did. She'd never in a hundred years have done what Doris did tonight. At least, it must have been different back in her day.

'Not in my house you're not,' says Nan, swinging back round. 'Where've you been?'

'Nowhere,' says Doris, feigning calmness.

Nan comes up – comes up so close that her face is large in front of Doris'. 'Where. Have. You. Been.' The words are hot, like the wrath of God.

'I went out with a friend.'

'What friend?'

'Gladys. From work.'

Nan lets out a long breath. 'And where did you go?'

'Just to a party, that's all.' Why shouldn't she? Young people go to parties; that's what they do.

The suspicion in Nan's eyes solidifies into certainty. 'You've been with a man, haven't you?'

'No,' laughs Doris. 'I haven't been with anyone.' Good God, is it visible? Is there some evidence of what she's done? Some subtle change that Nan has detected?

'Who is he?'

Doris can smell that particular smell that is Nan: tea leaves and soap, the cod liver oil she takes for her aching joints and the whisky she takes for other, nameless pains.

'Don't think I don't know what you've been doing, Doris Palmer!' Nan's eyes are desperate. 'And then what'll happen, eh?' Her voice wobbles, the words losing their hard edges. 'Look what happened to your mother.'

The needle and thread are still grasped in Nan's fingers, and for a moment Doris thinks that she will stitch her closed; sew shut her eyes and ears and mouth and you-know-what. Then the thread'll be bitten off – snap!

But of course Nan does nothing of the sort. Instead she covers her face with one hand, a blue thread dangling down like a strange tear. When she uncovers her face she looks defeated. But any soft feelings in Doris have cooled and set hard. 'I'm not my mother. I'm nothing like her.' She almost doesn't say it but then she does: 'And I'm nothing like you either.'

In her bedroom the air quivers. She kicks off her shoes – these stupid, stupid shoes that have made her feet hurt – then peels off her dress, struggling out of it like an old skin. How pretty the shop windows looked the day she went out to buy these clothes, with their displays of coloured scarves, long strings of beads and fashionable hats and dresses. But such things, it seems, aren't for people like her, they're for other sorts of women – women who spend entire mornings in beauty parlours, then later, when it gets dark, dine out in candle-lit restaurants. Lives like theirs are sealed behind glass. They belong to someone else. That's why, when she finally got up the courage to go into one of the shops, she came out clutching her purchases to her like a thief.

Now her dress is lying empty on the floor. Gone is the fun and music and sex of the evening, and here she is once more, sitting on her bed in this room with its shabby wallpaper and worn-out rug, her old doll Maud with the painted mouth and eyelashes staring at her from the shelf. Maud, prim and neat just the way Nan would like Doris to be.

The room is suddenly too small, the room of a child. If she stays here any longer, she'll burst out of it, joists shattering and the door flying off its hinges. But where else is there for her to go?

It's late when she gets up. Her head's throbbing and her mouth is dry. Pulling on her dressing gown and jamming her feet into her slippers, she shuffles downstairs for some water. The house is silent. Nan will have gone to the shops as she always does on a Saturday.

Stepping into the kitchen, Doris stops, blinking against the sunlight, and stares at the objects on the kitchen table. At first she can't identify them. They're familiar, yet entirely out of their context.

The next moment it falls into place and she understands. Nan went to bed late. She stayed up to put her sewing things away, folding pieces of fabric corner to corner and hem to hem, stabbing needles back into the pin-cushion, winding up bobbins and hatching her plan. Then this morning she got up early. As soon as she woke she made up the stove, and once the fire was going she crept into Doris' room and picked her things up off the floor – the floor that, now she thinks of it, was bare. Carrying the clothes downstairs, Nan would have examined each item. She'd have seen a pair of too-sheer stockings and a dress that in her mind was only half a dress, if that. She'd have noted the bias cut, and knowing clothes as she does, would have understood that that particular cut causes the fabric to hug a figure and emphasise its curves. Nor would she have missed the section along the hip where the seams had been forced apart. Nan would have worked out the reason why too, for what Nan can't tell from examining a dress isn't worth knowing. Frayed hems tell a story. Waistbands are taken in or let out for a specific reason, while skirts lined in silk point to a full purse. So yes, as clear as if she'd been there, Nan will have read the haste with which the skirt was yanked up, and how the spreading of Doris' legs and the thoughtlessness of some unknown man had placed such a stress on this particular seam that the threads could no longer hold together.

With Doris asleep upstairs and the fire in the stove burning nicely, Nan had carried the clothes across the kitchen and carefully, deliberately, fed them into the flames. The stockings that cost Doris sixpence in Woolworth's. And the dress that ought to belong to a street walker and not to Anne Elizabeth Linnet's granddaughter.

One concession though. Nan saved the buttons – of course she did. Waste not, want not. And here are those buttons in a heap on the kitchen table, while over there in the glowing stove lie the cinders of Doris' evening. Trying to get maximum use out of the fuel, Nan made herself a pot of tea too by the looks of it, and perhaps even sat here watching the despicable things burn, as though that would cauterise the wickedness out of Doris' soul.

CHAPTER 31

Family

Baghdad, 1954

Lynette gathers the things onto the tray – teacup, knife, plate, cut crystal ashtray. The edge of her fringe moves in the breeze from the electric fan. A thick head of glossy black hair, inherited from Leon's side apparently. 'Would you like anything else, Mummy?'

Doris brushes crumbs off the coverlet. 'No darling, I'm not terribly hungry. A woman's got to watch her figure, you know. A moment on the lips, a lifetime on the hips. But a coffee would be nice.'

Lynette picks up the tray. Wedging it against her left side, she positions the crutch beneath her right armpit and makes her way slowly back out of the living room.

After a week of being ill, Doris' strength is starting to return and she's taken over the sofa. Now that the fever's gone and her stomach is settling, this is a far more practical place to be. Here she has everything she needs within reach: magazines, newspapers, cigarettes, radio. It's cooler too, and it means Lynette doesn't have to struggle up and down the stairs.

Doris can hear her in the kitchen emptying out the ashtray and putting things away. She doesn't do everything of course, she's not a servant. A woman comes to do the laundry and ironing, and another to clean and cook, but Lynette has learned to do most things. At ten, she can already keep the house running and cook simple meals. Although Doris hasn't been up to cooked food this week. Instead, Lynette's brought her nuts in little enamelled bowls, biscuits, slices of cheese with watermelon and European-type bread from the department store on Al-Rashid Street.

Lynette hobbles back in with a coffee, the cup rattling on its saucer.

'Ooh, mind you don't drop it.'

The cup is set down on the little table beside Doris.

'Thank you, darling. How's your foot today?' Two weeks ago, Lynette was rushing down the stairs to greet Leon. She'd taken the last two steps at a jump but landed badly: a sudden twist, a crack and a horrible yell of pain.

'It's fine.'

That's the way things always are with Lynette: fine. Her room's always tidy, her dress always neat, her fringe a straight dark line. Even with a broken ankle she still manages just as well, as though she's used a crutch all her life. What a beautiful baby she was with her rosy cheeks and eyes the colour of wet rock. Lying in her cot, she'd explore her own fingers and toes, her knees and stomach, laughing at her own cleverness. Doris would sit and watch her, enchanted. But the nuns have done a good job. She's the epitome of acquiescence and good behaviour.

When Lynette comes back in to collect the coffee cup and wipe down the table, Doris wishes she could pull her over and hold her close, as though they were the mother and daughter she'd once imagined they would be, rather than this. But she doesn't. She can't.

'I was reading,' says Lynette. 'And I read that a linnet is a bird.'

'Yes. Yes that's right.' She's heard of it, although she can't think what it looks like.

Lynette goes to the window and looks up, as though she might see one. 'Am I named after a bird?'

Doris laughs. 'No darling, you weren't named after a bird.'

Although she may as well have been, she's that timid. 'It's just a pretty name, that's all.' She reaches for the bottle of nail varnish she bought in Madrid. They've done so much travelling these last few years accompanying Leon on his trips that it's a relief to be at home for a while. 'Would you mind, darling?' She holds out the bottle. She's already done her fingernails. 'It's always hard to do my toes.'

Lynette perches on the end of the sofa and bends over Doris' feet.

'When you're older, you can wear nail varnish too.' They'll be closer then perhaps, more like friends.

Lynette doesn't reply. Doris studies her: the pigtails, the tongue poking out in concentration, the awkward leg in its plaster cast. Poor leg.

'You ought to wear brighter colours, you know. They'd suit you better.' The dress Lynette has on was a gift from his mother; Doris would never have bought anything in that colour. That particular shade of baby blue.

The nail varnish brush twitches and Lynette rubs at a stray mark of varnish on Doris' toe.

Doris tuts – 'Here' – and passes Lynette a tissue.

'They're done,' says Lynette soon after, and screws the cap back onto the bottle.

Doris angles her feet to see. 'Thank you, darling, that's wonderful.'

Lynette smiles. How strange, that similarity to Dolores. The same streak of selflessness. Black hair of course, but the same lips. When she smiles, it's like seeing a ghost.

Doris turns her face towards the electric fan. 'It's so hot.' The ceiling fan's on too.

'Will you sleep on the roof with us tonight?'

It's what people do here in the hot months. Beds are kept on roof terraces throughout the summer. Fifty degrees in the daytime, dropping to thirty at night, still hotter than is fit for a civilised person. Summer is an endless glare of days, of no breeze, of blue sky unbroken by a single thread of cloud.

Then all at once it's winter and the dust turns to mud. But by January that's all over, and after a short spring, summer begins again. Out there, animals are succumbing to the heat, horses, donkeys and cows lying dead in fields (or what passes for fields around here). She tries to imagine Harborne in such heat, how terrible that would be.

'Will you, Mummy? It's nice up there. Cool. And there are thousands and thousands of stars. Daddy tells us all about them. He says that even though we can see them, they're not there any longer. He says that we're looking into the past.' She pauses. 'Mummy? What's wrong?'

'Nothing, darling.'

The two fans whirr, round and round.

'In the morning the doves start to coo and wake us up.' This is said in a way that's meant to tempt Doris to join them.

'I'd be eaten alive.' Drifts of insects swarm around the porch light each evening as if from nowhere, and they'll do the same around the lamp on the roof. And what with the muezzins calling, neighbours chatting across rooftops, cocks crowing through the night and the infernal dust... From up there the entire city is the colour of dust, like sandcastles on a beach, except for the domes of the mosques standing out in blue and gold. 'No, not today.' She'll have a bath instead. Then, with the place to herself, she'll wander around naked, leaving footprints that'll quickly evaporate behind her. 'Is Graham still out?'

'He's gone to Fareed's house.'

'That boy with the funny eye?'

Lynette nods. 'But he said he'd be back before Daddy.'

Doris goes into the hall, treading on soft rug then cool tiles then soft rug again. The nail polish on her toes is dry. Graham's sitting at the piano hammering out scales and arpeggios. It makes her think of being indoors on a blustery day while on the other side of the glass, trees fling themselves one way then the other, leaves breaking free to fly away on the shape of the wind. 'Goodness, darling, what a racket.'

He stops mid-arpeggio.

She shouldn't have said that. She ought to praise him. 'Although you do need to practise.'

The piano stool scrapes back across the tiles and Graham heads for the stairs. A few moments later his bedroom door clicks shut.

Leon would have praised him. 'I wish,' he'd said the day they'd bought the piano, 'that I could have learned to make music. But my parents didn't think about that.' And standing at the instrument, he'd pressed down a key and waited until the note died away before lifting his finger again. Doris hasn't a musical bone in her body, so Graham must have inherited this interest from Leon's side. Because that's how it works, isn't it? Inheritance.

She's still searching for her cigarettes when Leon gets home. The children have heard the front door too because they're there before her. Coming down the stairs, she stops to watch. Leon is bending down to hug them, one with each arm. A kiss for Lynette, then a tickle on her cheek with the end of her own pigtail. 'How is your ankle, *jan*?'

'It's getting better. It feels a lot better today.'

'That's excellent!' He ruffles Graham's hair. 'And how about you? Did you have a good day?'

Graham is like a different boy now. He chatters on about Fareed's house as though it weren't a mere hovel, and tells Leon how he and the other children played. 'Then Fareed's mother gave us bread and jam and said that I'm a wonderful boy.'

'You are a wonderful boy,' agrees Leon.

'You should come next time,' Graham says to Lynette. 'His mother wouldn't mind.'

'Maybe *I* should come,' says Leon, and the children laugh.

'We went down to the river and watched the men fishing with nets and— ' But Doris doesn't know what happened next because Graham shifts into Arabic, and suddenly the three of them are simply making noises, and she's marooned on her own little island.

When Graham stops talking, Leon finally hangs up his hat. When he turns back, Lynette bursts into giggles.

'What?' he asks. 'What is it?'

On his head is Lynette's sun hat.

'Daddy,' scolds Lynette, and there it is, that look of adoration she always elicits in Leon.

From virtually the first moment she met him, Doris guessed that Leon, who's so gentle and caring, would make a good father. Except there's only so much love to go around, isn't there? And here she is being sidelined.

She waits for him to see her on the stairs, glamorous as Bette Davis in *All About Eve*, but he doesn't look so she descends. 'Hello, love.'

All three look round at once. Leon takes off Lynette's hat and hangs it up. 'Hello.' He gives her a smile.

Doris reaches up to kiss him, but at the same time there's a crash, a metallic clatter that makes her jump.

Lynette bends to pick up her crutch.

'Butterfingers,' snaps Doris, still startled, and when she looks at Leon, the air between them has altered.

'Has something happened?' Leon looks past her into the hall as she closes the door: at Lynette going slowly up the stairs, and Graham running a finger lightly, silently over the piano keys. 'Are the children all right?'

'Of course they're all right. Really, darling.'

The lines on his forehead clear, and he goes to the drinks cabinet.

'Let me do that. You relax. What would you like? Whisky?'

Leon takes off his jacket and loosens his tie. There are damp patches beneath his arms. He tells her he'd like some *arak*, and with a sigh she pours a finger of the stuff into a small glass and adds water. Instantly the clear liquid turns an opaque white. It makes her feel like a witch brewing a potion.

'Here you go, darling.' She mixes herself a martini.

'What did you want to talk about?'

She crosses to the sofa but is too restless to sit down. 'It's Graham.'

Leon leans forward, listening.

'He's reached a difficult age.' Another sip of martini that slides bright and glowing down her throat. 'He's starting to run wild.'

'What do you mean?'

'I mean he's falling in with the wrong sort. He's always out. I can't keep track of where he is. Goodness only knows what he gets up to.' She sees Graham, hairline gleaming, skin aglow and clothes dusty. He eats goodness knows what from the market, then gets his hair cut by a barber who's also a dentist.

Leon sits back. 'He's a boy. What does it matter if he goes out with his friends? If he drinks Coca Cola and listens to Elvis Presley?'

She peers into her glass. 'He ought to go to boarding school. A good one. In England.'

Leon leans forward again, elbows on knees, and she knows that she's in for an argument.

'Lots of people do it. The Elmwoods have sent their son back home to boarding school. The Wilsons have sent both of theirs.'

'Yes, but we are not like that.' He tips the last of the *arak* into his mouth and puts the glass down on the table. 'I will not send my son abroad.' There's certainty in his voice. This is not a thing he'll agree to.

'But it would do him a world of good being among English boys. And the education he'd get… well, it's second to none.' Harry had loved school more than anything; all that maths and science that had meant nothing to her. After it was decided he couldn't go any longer, Doris would hear him through the wall at night, sobbing. Why shouldn't her son have what Harry wasn't able to?

'I will not send my son to another country,' says Leon. 'He is at a good school here.'

'You went all the way to England to get an education, didn't you?'

He doesn't answer at once. 'Because there was no university in Baghdad. And the Iraqi government paid for students to study in England.' He smiles bitterly. 'They thought it would help to modernise the country.'

'Either way, you got a good education. Well, don't you want Graham to have one too?'

'That was different. I was already a man.'

'But darling…' She puts a hand on the back of the sofa. 'You make it sound as if I want to send him to jail! Well, it's not jail, it's England. I'm English and so is he.'

'He has lived here all his life.'

'So? He'll love it.' Harry's smile, his stacks of books.

'It would be a shock – such a shock, don't you see? For a boy like him to be away from Baghdad, without his family or his friends.' He shakes his head. 'I cannot do it.'

She goes to the window. Flowers are wilting in the beds, and the new lawn still refuses to take. Graham's drifting away, not physically maybe but in other ways: his sun-darkened skin, the languages he speaks, his taste for Arabic food from the stalls in the *souk*. Behind her she hears Leon go the drinks cabinet. The clink of a bottleneck against glass, the splash of liquid as he pours a second drink.

'All right,' she says. 'So you want him to stay here where the situation's so unstable, and going from bad to worse.'

Leon remains silent.

'You said yourself that people are humiliated by what's going on in the Arab world.' British control in Iraq is slipping, and the nationalists are more popular than ever. She swirls the martini around in her glass, watching the way the sun flashes and sparkles off it. 'If things were to blow up again… my

God.' She gulps down the rest of her drink. 'Graham's always gadding about, and you know as well as I do that they hate us – the English, I mean. If anything were to happen to him…'

For a long time, Leon doesn't speak. When he does, the words come out quietly. 'Do you want to move back to England? Is this what you are telling me?'

The question catches her by surprise. Her, move back to England? The idea floats into view – trunks and suitcases packed and transported, along with her, back to the place where she was born.

When she turns round, Leon is still at the drinks cabinet but the glass in front of him is empty again. 'Do you want to leave, Dolores? Leave Baghdad? And me?'

His words skitter through her, and in their wake a rush of blood, a thumping of heart, a tingle on the back of her neck. She puts down her glass, strides to him and takes his hands tightly in hers. 'How could you even think such a thing? I'll never leave you.' Doesn't he know this? That without him, she wouldn't want to continue?

With a shock she notices how tired he looks; creases on his forehead and small lines around his eyes that didn't used to be there. There's grey in his dark hair.

'Baghdad has changed, that is true. Life is not the same as it was.' Freeing his hands, he pushes his fingers through his hair, mumbling about recession and inflation and people going hungry. About unrest and nationalism. 'I have to think,' he says.

His words are sweeping her along in their current with a swiftness that's frightening. 'I'm not saying we should leave Baghdad, darling. I don't want to leave.' Needing the time to think, she refills her drink. Her red nails against the glass look distant, like an advert in a magazine. She's sown doubt in Leon and senses an advantage. Lynette is safe with the nuns, and needn't go to school for much longer anyway. But Graham… 'Wouldn't it be best for him, darling? Some sort of stability. There's always some trouble going on here. Some protest or march or tribal to-do. And we could… well, why not buy a house in England? – we can afford it – and that way we could visit and Graham wouldn't be alone.' A second property. Five minutes ago none of this had occurred to her, but now that it's in her head, the idea seems perfect, a flawless egg that has been there all along, just waiting to hatch.

Leon sinks into his chair like a sack of flour. Evening sun slants into the room. The curtain is swaying in the breeze from the fans, a barely-there, lulling motion. 'Are you happy?'

The question shocks her. 'Whatever do you mean?'

'It is good to ask sometimes. To know these things – important things that we never ask.'

'Of course I'm happy.' She goes and kisses him. His lips feel cool against hers. 'Of course I am, why wouldn't I be?' The gold bangles slide up and down her arm as she smooths her hair. 'We both are, aren't we?' Her pulse thuds in her ears. This honesty, come out of nowhere, is new territory, and loaded with danger.

'I am not sure.' The sunlight fragments, cut up by curtains, tables, chairs. It lies around the room in bits and pieces.

She wants to ask what he means – what on God's earth he could mean by such a statement – but doesn't want to be pulled down this new, dark path. She forces a little laugh. 'Look at us. We have everything we need, don't we?' She waves her hands around the room with all its finery.

'Yes. We have a house and two beautiful, healthy children and enough money to live a good life.' He's proceeding with care. 'But sometimes we do not… feel like a family.'

Suddenly unsteady, she sits down in the chair beside his. Family. Does he want a family like the Palmers, crammed around the kitchen table, with laundry strung from the rafters? 'I haven't been well, you know that. It's difficult to be a family when you're ill.' The weave of her skirt appears magnified, an endless in and out, a horribly neat entanglement. Oh, why on earth did she ever start this conversation? This, here, wasn't what she intended. And now this talk of family has needled a raw spot at the very centre of her. She looks up. 'What a load of balderdash! We're a family same as any other.' She gathers her defences. 'Can I help it if you're not here half the time?'

'I try to be here as much as I can. I work to give you the things you all want.'

'I know. I know that darling. Let's not argue, please. I hate it when we argue.' Dropping onto her knees, she brings his hands to her lips and kisses them. 'I love you.'

His mouth turns up a little at the corners. 'I love you too.'

She sees them then, fallen off the table and half hidden by the tassels skirting the sofa: the cigarettes she's been searching for. 'Say you'll consider it then. Starting school in England. Buying a house there too, somewhere nearby. It'll be good for us all. A sort of fresh beginning.'

CHAPTER 32

Rex

Baghdad, 1954

Leon's bought a Christmas tree which, in her absence, they've decorated. It's not a fir of course, but it is tall, and so smothered with tinsel and baubles that you can't see what's underneath anyway. She'll rehang the decorations tomorrow; it'll have to stay there till after the Armenian Christmas on the sixth of January, so it may as well look its best.

'Have you told him?' Leon asks.

She's taken off her makeup and, sitting at the dressing table, is rubbing Pond's cream onto her face. 'No, not yet.' Neither of the children know why she went to England: that she's been visiting boarding schools – and has decided on one. She has even registered Graham, in fact, and paid a healthy deposit in order to do so.

'What is it like?' Leon asks, not for the first time, and again she tells him the things the headmaster told her about the schedule of the day, mealtimes, the strict rules needed to maintain the reputation of such a place. She tells Leon how fine the building looked and how smart the boys were in their uniforms, how polite and respectful.

Sitting on the bed in his pyjamas, Leon listens attentively. He doesn't look happy, but then, he was never going to be happy about it. As it happened, a fortnight after she broached the idea of boarding school, he and Graham got caught up in yet another of the protest marches for 'unity' and an end to

Western influence. As usual, the police came down hard on the protesters, and Graham had seen too much. That's when Leon finally gave in, and now it's been decided: boarding school in England, as well as a second house.

She dips her fingers into the pot for more cream. 'He won't start till next half term of course, not until the end of next month.' She's still trying to come to terms with the rest of the trip. Initially there had been nerves because it had been such a long time – sixteen years in fact – since she was there. Next came exhilaration, and after that, shock. Overcoats, gloves, scarves and umbrellas. Everyone speaking English. Trains and buses, pubs and hotels. There had been stacks of fir trees in the markets and a giant Norwegian fir in Trafalgar Square, its fairy lights fuzzy-edged pinpricks in the fog. Regent Street was hung with large, lit-up angels. And the smell. She'd never considered that England had a smell, but it did, something of wind and leaves and wet pavements.

But there had been another side to being back in England. She couldn't believe the prices of things for a start. There were more people than she remembered too. London boomed with traffic, and there were obscenities scrawled on walls. On the pavements, sleet settled as slush, and chain smokers huddled in doorways with their collars turned up. One afternoon a drunkard had staggered into her as he lurched out of a pub, paper streamers dangling from his head. These are the things she tries to blot out.

She'd wanted to see Nan and wrote to tell her she'd be in England, but added that there was no time to travel up to Harborne. *Leon and the children will never forgive me if I'm not back in time for Christmas!* The truth was rather different. The truth was that she couldn't bear the thought of being back in Harborne with its memories of Harry, where she'd once been forced to make visits to the Palmers, and where Dolores had died. 'I'll be back soon enough though,' she wrote, 'to look for a house. Yes really, we're going to buy a house in England!' It would have to be a beautiful house, and nowhere near Harborne. The southern counties, she's thinking, or perhaps

Scotland. 'And as soon as I've found somewhere, you're to come and stay.'

With a last look out at the night, Leon draws the curtains.

'I'll tell him tomorrow,' she says.

'No.' Leon's eyes meet hers in the mirror. 'Not before Christmas. After Christmas, I will tell him. I will explain.'

On the fifth of January she wakes up alone. The bedside clock tells her that it's nearly eleven o'clock, late even by her standards, and when she goes downstairs she finds that the others had breakfast hours ago.

'Where's Daddy?' she asks Lynette, who's already preparing lunch.

'He went out.'

'Oh.' Leon's offices are closed for the Armenian Christmas. 'Did he say where?'

Lynette shakes her head.

Half an hour later, Graham comes thundering down the stairs. 'Daddy's home. Come and see, Lynette, come and see what he's got!'

The children surge into the garden, and Doris follows.

'Oh, Daddy, it's so sweet!'

'Can we keep it? Can we, please?'

'Yes, of course.' A black mongrel with floppy ears is wriggling in Leon's arms. 'It is for you both. A Christmas present.'

The dog quivers as it's set down and wags its tail uncertainly, and the children collapse onto the grass beside it.

'Leon?'

He looks up, still smiling. 'Hello, *jan*.'

'What's going on? The children have already had their presents.' When she was in London, she went to Hamley's specially. 'And we never give presents for the Armenian Christmas.' Tomorrow they'll go to his church for the Blessing of Water, then to his mother's for the meal. The old woman will have been preparing for days.

Leon bends to pet the dog. 'He will be good for them.'

Graham looks up. 'Is he a boy? What shall we call him?' He and Lynette start making suggestions. Fluffy. Nero. Honey. Fred. 'What about Rex?' says Graham at last.

Leon smiles. 'Yes, Rex is the perfect name.'

Doris fishes in her dressing gown pocket for her cigarettes and strikes a match. 'You might have asked me. Bringing home a dog! It's not one of those street dogs, is it? The creature's probably ridden with fleas.'

'He's not a street dog,' says Leon.

'Where on earth did you get him from then?'

'A man I know. Does it matter? He is a nice dog.'

'We can buy him a basket,' says Lynette. 'One like they have in books.'

'And he'll have to have a bowl for food and another for water,' says Graham, stroking Rex's head. 'Won't you?'

'You should have gotten a proper breed at least – a spaniel or an Alsatian. A poodle.'

'But look at him, Mummy, he's so lovely,' says Lynette.

Rex starts to wander around with his nose to the ground, and the children follow, calling him as if he already knew his name.

Doris flicks ash into the patchy grass. 'Why didn't you tell me?'

Leon looks happy watching them. 'I wanted it to be a surprise.'

But he doesn't fool her. When Graham was little and had to have a tooth taken out, Leon insisted on going with him to the dentist's, and sat next to Graham blowing bubbles and exclaiming at their size, their oily colours, the way they floated, to distract Graham from the pain that was about to come. 'You mean you did it to make Graham feel better before you tell him.'

Leon stops smiling.

Will Graham be so upset? She glances over, suddenly worried, to where he and Lynette are trying to shepherd Rex back.

'Where's he going to sleep? He can sleep in my room.'

'No, mine.'

'I'm sure he's not house trained,' says Doris. The end of her cigarette glows as she draws it in, the thin paper crisping. 'He can stay in the garden.'

Lynette's face drops.

'He'll be happier out here, darling, in the fresh air.' She points to the awning under which the children used to keep their toys. 'We can put his food and water over there.'

Lynette kneels down and puts her arms around the dog. 'But it's cold, and he'll be lonely.'

'He'll be fine. He's an animal. Animals don't belong indoors.' And clear as day, she sees Stanley settled on the kitchen chair, eyeing her.

Two evenings later, Leon decides to tell Graham. 'I cannot leave it any longer. He should know.' And he goes upstairs, his tread slower than usual.

Doris turns up the radio and tries to concentrate on what's playing. It must be some sort of comedy because there's laughter, but for the life of her she can't make out a thing. All she can hear, from upstairs, is Graham's voice. Whether he's speaking in English, Arabic or Armenian she can't tell, but his tone is clear enough. Protesting, argumentative, unhappy.

It turns to pleading.

She makes herself a drink. Two. Lynette comes downstairs. 'What's happening, Mummy? What's wrong with Graham?'

'Nothing, darling. He and Daddy are just having a chat, that's all. Go back to bed.'

After that no one comes down. Doors open and close, and the house grows quiet.

Doris remains in the living room. If she went upstairs she might run into Graham or Leon, so she flicks through a newspaper. Later she gets out a deck of cards and plays solitaire, listens to the radio again and eats a few dates. When she finally puts her head out of the living room door, the quality of silence tells her that everyone has gone to bed.

She stretches out on the sofa and closes her eyes – she'll

sleep here – but when two o'clock in the morning comes and goes, she gets up again, goes into the kitchen and makes coffee, a strong one to spite her insomnia. The only other sound, apart from the water coming to a boil, is the dog whining softly outside.

The next morning she's woken by the sound of hammering. When she pulls back the curtain, she sees Leon in the garden with tools spread out at his feet. The gate's been hanging lopsided on its hinges for months, and the dog has already escaped once through the gap underneath. Now Rex is standing next to Leon, sniffing the tools and watching him work.

She goes out, intending to kiss Leon good morning (because it's still morning, just), but when he looks round the expression on his face doesn't invite kissing.

'Good morning,' she says instead.

There's a spanner in his hand. 'Good morning.'

Rex jumps up at her, his tail wagging. 'No,' she says firmly, and he returns to stand against Leon's legs.

Leon bends to give him a pat. 'You know,' he says, 'one of my first memories is of dogs.'

'Dogs! But they don't like dogs over here.'

He doesn't look at her. 'I remember the sound of popping. It continued for days, never stopping.'

What on earth is he talking about?

'When I was older, I found out what it was. The British military police had just arrived in Baghdad and they were shooting all the dogs. Thousands of them. A city full of sick and starving dogs.'

She doesn't like the turn this conversation has taken. 'I wish you'd stop talking in riddles. What do you mean?'

'Was it kind or was it cruel? I do not know. Sometimes it is difficult to tell. But not always.'

A deep breath. 'Are you saying I'm cruel, is that it?'

He doesn't respond.

It's cold, and she pulls her dressing gown close around

her. 'Is it fixed now?' she asks, even though she can see that it isn't.

'Not yet. I am not sure I can fix it. I am not sure it is possible.'

Leon, the fixer of broken things. 'Oh. Well, we can always get someone in to look at it.'

'Whatever you want,' he says, but swaps the spanner for a hammer and holds the gate straight. The fig tree has lost every last one of its leaves, but the myrtle bush growing right up against the gate is still green. She fancies she can catch a hint of fragrance coming off it, even now in January when the bridal blooms, white with a mass of gold-flecked stamens, are long gone.

'How did Graham…?' She chews her lip. 'I mean, is he all right?'

Without looking at her, Leon nods once.

'Good, I'm glad.' Relieved, she reaches a hand towards his cheek but he leans away. A tiny movement, no more than an inch, but it's like a knife going in under her ribs. A muezzin begins to wail. The gate's hanging at a strange angle, almost entirely off one hinge. She withdraws her hand, and before she loses control of her face, turns on her heel and heads back into the house.

In the kitchen she leans on the counter taking deep breaths. Then, mechanically, she slices a lemon in half, squeezes the juice into a glass and adds hot water. This is how she always starts the day. It quells the appetite, and the sharpness first thing is oddly pleasing. There's no pleasure in it today though.

Perched on a high stool, she watches Leon from the window. She wants to go back out. She wants to cross the garden and turn him around, then, with her hands on his shoulders, raise herself up onto her toes and kiss him. His hands will go to her waist and he'll kiss her back, and they'll remember their real selves. It would be that easy. Wouldn't it?

'I miss you,' she murmurs as Leon hammers the gate. Although it looks as if he's trying to destroy rather than mend the blasted thing.

CHAPTER 33

Parade

Harborne, 1937

She's wearing a new shade of lipstick, Pink Berry, and has plucked her eyebrows fine. They're far nicer than those of the woman standing next to her, which is pleasing, given the amount of pain it caused her to get them to look this way. All around, people are jostling for the best view, but she isn't budging. Sports events started early in the school field, stopped when the rain got too heavy, then started up again when it held off. Dances were performed to much clapping, and the Coronation Queen was crowned (although Doris didn't think she was prettier than anyone else).

Now the parade is beginning. A bicycle parade passes, then a fancy dress parade followed by a marching band, then a large float with 'God Save the King' emblazoned on the side, surrounded by the names of all the Commonwealth countries. The spectators ooh and aah and clap and cheer. And eat – she sees a toffee apple, a Mars bar, a sandwich dropped and abandoned on the ground. The town hall's doing a roaring trade in tea and cake, while others have set out wares in baskets or on tray tables on the pavement. The pubs are serving special Coronation ale, which some men have clearly already drunk too much of.

What a contrast this is to all those miserable pictures of hunger marches these last five years protesting the Means Test, the cut in the dole and an incompetent government.

The Midlands is lucky though, she knows that. The heavy industries of Scotland, Wales and the north-east have ground to a halt, but here where factories like Bournville's or Austin depend on electricity and not coal… well, everyone in the world seems to be driving an Austin 7 and eating chocolate.

There are paper flags and bunting. A man hauls a boy onto his shoulders for a better view. An elderly woman clutches a pair of binoculars she doesn't need, and right at the front, someone's dog cowers as each part of the procession appears, then once it's passed, stands and barks after it, its body lifting a little off the ground with each bark.

Tipping back her head, Doris looks up at the sky, an unrelenting grey stuffed with cloud. It's going to start to rain soon, she can feel it, and she hasn't brought an umbrella. Not that there'd be enough space among all these people to open it even if she had. Later on there's going to be a whist drive, and dancing in the evening after the King's speech – although whether he'll manage to get it out before midnight is anyone's guess. It's quite bad, they say, his stammer. That other flighty one, Edward, has taken off with Mrs Simpson and is soon to be married. The scandal of it! And the allure, the adventure.

It's starting to rain, of course it is, a fine mist of drizzle swarming downwards. If she stays, she'll be soaked before long. The parade's almost done, and soon its bubble of noise will have shifted further down the road, but as it is the chatter and music and barking of that blasted dog has given her a thumping headache. Perhaps, like Nan, she ought to have gone to Susan's for the street party, but she couldn't face it; can rarely face visiting The Back of Beyond at all any more.

Turning to leave, she steps on something. A shoe. And inside it, a foot. A man's foot.

'Oh, I'm so sorry,' she says, removing her foot from his and looking up.

For an instant the person she's looking at is part and parcel of this day with its extraordinary floats and curious sights. Because he isn't what she expected to see. What she expected was a man like any other, and he isn't that. His hair is black, his skin darker than what she's used to, his features attractive. Then there's the style of him – nothing fancy, but immaculate. The cut of his suit, his tie neatly knotted, and cufflinks for goodness' sake!

'I never saw something like this before,' he says.

It takes a moment, and his hand raised towards the procession, for her to realise what he's talking about. 'No,' she says. 'No, nor did I.'

He's carrying nothing, isn't clapping or cheering, just watching everything around him. As a Union Jack approaches, a little girl in a party hat squeezes past to get to the front of the crowd, but as she passes, her hat is knocked to the ground. Without hesitating, the man picks it up. The girl stops to look up at him, but he doesn't say anything, simply places the hat back onto her head, and she continues on her way.

The gesture, insignificant as it is, causes something to click in Doris' chest, and suddenly she wants to know this man. Catching his eye, she smiles what she hopes is her most charming smile.

He smiles back. A layer of drizzle has settled on his shoulders and hair. Drops of it are clinging to her eyelashes too. This blasted rain. Her hair! Her makeup! Annoyance flares in her mind like a klaxon.

A paper flag flaps near her face, making her flinch, and him look over again.

'Pity,' she says. 'It's literally raining on our parade.' She smiles, ready to laugh, but realises that he doesn't understand the reference. 'It's a saying, you know. Don't rain on my parade: don't spoil a good time.'

'Ah,' he gives a single, slow nod. 'I understand.'

She can't place his accent, but it makes her feel good to have the upper hand this way – automatically, just because he's a foreigner, someone else from someplace else.

'But it is stopping now,' he says, glancing upwards.

'Yes.' He's right. The drizzle, miraculously, is clearing.

'Does it always rain here? Even in spring?'

'Not always, but… well yes, yes it does.'

They laugh, and he's even more good-looking when he laughs, like a dark Errol Flynn. But it's not only that. He's forbidden, like stealing into someone else's garden or flirting with your best friend's boyfriend. And then there's this: here he is, an outsider, and yet he has such an air of sedateness about him, such a calm solidity. And how can that be? How is he not uncomfortably out of place?

The crowd has started to move, to disperse or follow the parade along. The dog, no longer barking, has located the abandoned sandwich and is making lunges towards it, half-throttling himself with each attempt.

'There are some more things happening up that way in a bit.' Pointing up the road, she notices a little hole in her glove. 'A Punch and Judy show, and I think a magician.' Quickly, she slips off her gloves.

He hesitates. 'You are going there?'

'I was planning to, yes.'

A burst of laughter makes them look round. Two young women are chatting together nearby. They're not ugly either, Doris notes. Reaching into her pocket, she pulls out a crumpled paper bag. 'Humbug?'

'Excuse me?'

She opens the bag and holds it out. 'They're sweets. They're called humbugs.'

'Hum-bugs.' The word makes him smile.

'Here, try one.' She takes one, and so does he.

'We do not have sweets like this where I come from,' he says in his funny accent.

'Oh? And where's that? Where do you come from?' She manoeuvres the humbug into her cheek as she waits for the answer.

'Iraq. Baghdad.'

Oh! Oh. She's heard the name on the wireless – something to do with British airbases or the like. In any case it's somewhere far away, beyond Europe. Still, no one need know. She'll tell her friend Gladys about this, of course. Poor Gladys who's had a tooth pulled and is resting at home trying to ignore the pain. Doris is already thinking of the words she'll use – how *chic* this man is, how dapper and polite. Possibly she'll embellish a little and say that he missed the best part of the celebrations because he couldn't take his eyes off her. She'll describe her green dress, the one that shows off her waist, and the new hat she bought at Baxter's, and the way she has her hair pinned at the sides. But she'll leave out the part about the rain. And she might leave out the part about Iraq too.

Jostled by people pushing past, the man manages to hold out his hand. 'I'm Leon.'

His hand is large and warm around hers, and makes her wonder immediately what he's like in bed. But he's waiting for her name.

'Oh. I'm…' *Doris Palmer! Doris Palmer! Got no mother and got no father!* Harry who left her. Susan who gave her away. Doris is not who she wants to be. 'I'm Dolores.'

In her mouth, the humbug has dissolved in a way that's left a sharp edge on one side, and smiling at Leon – Leon with his dark eyes and raindrops scattered on his pomaded hair like diamonds – she suddenly tastes blood.

CHAPTER 34
Knobbly Feet

Harborne, 1937

It's been exactly a week. They made no plans to meet again. She'd waited for him to say something, but perhaps he'd felt as awkward as she had. Either way, they said goodbye and parted with nothing further arranged, and now it's been seven days – the longest seven days she can remember ever living – so why is she still waiting?

Because she told him, didn't she. That's why. When he asked, she told him where she worked, and her eyes have been glued to the door ever since.

Please let him come. Let him appear on the other side of that glass, and when his eyes find her, let him smile, push the door open and step back into her life. It's been a week after all, seven days, and there's a momentousness to that number: not too soon after meeting, nor too late. So it'll be today. Today is the day he'll come. She might have known it would be exactly a week. Not wanting to seem too keen, he'll have waited it out thinking about her – about Coronation Day and the undeniable something between them.

Is this what it feels like to go fishing? To throw out a line and sit and wait, and wait and wait, not knowing if anything will ever happen. She thinks of a thin line trailing along streets and across roads, up staircases and through doorways to wherever he might be. He's a student at the university so she knows that's where he'll be; and if she wanted to, she could find him, but she won't be the chaser. If he wants her, let *him* come and find *her*.

She runs her fingers over her hair to make sure it's in place. Any minute now he might come in, and she must look the part: be striking and attractive enough for him not to regret making the journey. This isn't like the telephone exchange, where she sat invisible at the centre of a web of wires and no one she spoke to could see her. She's glad to have left that job. 'Concentrate on what you're doing!' the manager would bark if you so much as turned your face away from the switchboard. 'You're not paid to look around.' And she's stopped getting a headache from having those blasted headphones clamped to her head morning, noon and night.

'Times are changing,' she said to Nan. 'Automatic exchanges are taking over and I'll be out of a job soon anyway.'

Surprisingly, Nan hadn't been upset. 'Yes, a job in a shop. You'll see more people that way.' And Doris knew what she meant, because hanging in the air between them was the silent fact that by the time Nan was Doris' age, she was already married and a mother, and the bulk of her life's work was complete.

And men do come into the shoe shop, but they're either too old or too ugly, or else have knobbly feet or ones that stink to high heaven. And then there's the way that some of them look at her when she kneels to fit their shoes, a gaze that makes her skin crawl.

The day drags on, and she carries shoes out and puts them away again; brings out more and puts those back away too. 'Open-toed? Square-toed? Contrast stitching is in fashion now.' 'Those? Ah yes, they're very sturdy, Madam.' She smiles – 'How they suit you!' – and talks about buckles and heels, slippers and brogues, arch supports and the practicalities of tan calf versus white kangaroo suede till her teeth ache.

It's a quarter to four. She brushes herself down. He'll come before four, she feels it in her bones. Because if he doesn't come today perhaps he shan't come at all, and that's unthinkable.

He'll be the next customer. All right, the one after that then. Her heart picks up pace. He'll be the first person to come in after four o'clock.

Five o'clock comes and she's deflated, confused, unhappy. Then angry. How dare he? Well, stuff him then! He's had his chances – yes, he's had a million chances to come and find her. She's too good for him, that's all. That's what you get with foreigners; and him not only a foreigner but one from some godforsaken place in the middle of a desert! Well, he can go and rot.

It's Saturday afternoon. The shop was busy earlier but now there's a lull. Gladys is serving a woman with a little boy. It's an agreement between them that Gladys serves the children. Whenever you try to fit their shoes, they fuss and squirm, and they seem always to have snotty noses. In return, Doris has agreed that she'll serve the older customers with their misshapen, difficult feet.

Gladys is measuring the boy's foot right now, trying to sit it in the Brannock's device, but he's starting to snivel. Both she and Gladys hope that Mr Cruickshank will get one of the new 'pedoscopes' that measure the feet using x-rays. It'll be fun to see the toe-bones wriggling around inside the shoes, as well as being proof to the mothers that there's plenty of growing room in them.

The little bell above the door rings, and when she looks up, there he is. Him. Leon.

Her entire body lifts, ready to float away. Because he has come, he's here, and everything has changed in an instant.

He takes off his hat. 'Hello.'

She's suddenly too busy breathing to speak. 'Hello,' she manages.

'I wanted to come here and today… today there are no lectures.'

She nods. Smiles. How strange that there's no trace of anger or upset left anywhere in her.

'I remembered you said you work here.' He looks around. Gladys has looked up, and is reading the situation between this man and Doris. She'll know that this is him, the man Doris met at the parade, although Doris only mentioned it lightly, pretending it meant nothing. Still, Gladys will see in an instant how things lie.

'Yes, I do.' Doris glances down at the large ledger on the counter. 'I... was just doing the accounts.' She can't possibly admit that her job is to grovel at people's feet! Leon must never see or even imagine her that way. Silently, she prays that no other customer will come in. Not now. Not while he's here.

'Ah,' he beams, 'so you are good with numbers.'

She nods, hoping he won't put her to the test. 'I'm glad you came.' In the mirrors set down near the floor, she sees the lower half of his legs reflected from different angles.

There are footsteps, and Mr Cruickshank appears from the back room. He adjusts his glasses and looks round the shop. He looks at Doris, at Leon, then back at Doris. 'What are you doing there?'

Her heart sinks. Picking at the corner of the ledger, she calculates what best to say. What will get her out of this situation? *I'm just serving this gentleman, Mr Cruickshank?* Or would Gladys' get-out phrase of *Just making sure everything's spick and span* work? But no, neither of these will do right now. She clears her throat. 'I'm just checking the stock, Mr Cruickshank.'

Mr Cruickshank frowns and compresses his lips.

'That is, this gentleman had some questions and... I was just answering them,' she says. *Please don't ask what questions. Please.*

Mr Cruickshank looks at Leon now, staring quite brazenly and with a sudden hardness that she's never noticed before.

The bell above the door rings again, shrill and unwelcome. Another customer, an elderly man. Oh God – no, no she can't, she just can't go and serve him. She ought to, of course, that's the agreement, and anyway Gladys is still putting shoes back away into their boxes. The mother is trying to persuade her son that the last pair of shoes he tried on are perfect, but the little brat's saying he doesn't like them. There's a stamped foot. Soon there'll be tears.

Mr Cruickshank gives Doris a stiff nod. 'Carry on then.' And throwing Leon a rather dirty look, he turns to go back to his desk off the stock room.

Doris isn't sure what to say. Is Leon offended? Is he wishing he'd never come here, never met her? She pulls a face. 'He's a bit strange,' she whispers confidentially.

The new customer raises a hand to catch her attention. 'Excuse me. Miss?'

She bends over the ledger, her face turning warm. She'll die, she'll simply expire on the spot if Leon sees her crouching down in front of that old man and tending to his feet.

'Miss? I'd like to try on some—'

'How can I help you, sir?' It's Gladys – oh, thank heaven Gladys has stepped up to him, while behind her the mother, empty-handed, is hurrying her boy out of the shop.

Leon looks at the shoeboxes scattered across the floor. 'I should leave. You are busy.'

'Wait,' she says. 'Please.' He's about to slip out of the shop and vanish again. 'I finish work at five.'

They look at one another and the moment stretches, a step not yet taken. Then Leon smiles. He smiles that smile she remembers from Coronation Day, and the universe is an exquisite place again.

CHAPTER 35

Rage

Baghdad, 1955

Leon is away, so Lynette has stayed with the old woman these few days. So has the dog. Now Doris is driving them both back home. 'How has school been?'

Lynette's face is blank. 'Fine.'

How many times Graham had exclaimed at the sight of grass – 'Such a lot of it!' 'It's everywhere, just everywhere!' – on the train from London to the school. Then he'd sink away into himself again. And how small he seemed standing in the dormitory with his suitcase set down beside him; somehow smaller than he really was.

'And your grandmother. Was she bearable?'

Lynette doesn't answer so Doris asks no more questions. The rest of the way home, the silence is broken only by Rex panting and moving from one side to the other in the back of the car. Doris thinks of Graham taking hold of her hand as she turned to leave and holding on tight. 'I don't want to stay.' How for a moment she thought she would cancel all the plans and bring him back home.

She runs up the stairs. 'Lynette?' The house has been deathly quiet since dinner – until this noise. 'Darling, are you all right?' It's a noise that makes her think Rex must have found his way into the house, gone upstairs and, in a moment of madness, attacked her daughter.

She flings open Lynette's door. She expects to see Rex, to see blood.

But there's no dog and no blood. Lynette swings round. Her hair is loose and messy, and it's snowing, flakes whirling around the room and settling on her dark head; on the bed, the floor.

Doris can't make sense of it. 'What's all this?'

Lynette is breathing hard. Her cheeks are red, her eyes sparkling. The bedspread has been pulled off her bed, and the pillow has been eviscerated.

'Lynette.' Something has happened and her daughter's gone berserk.

Lynette's chest is rising and falling. 'You send them all away. All of them. Aisha. Daddy. And now Graham!'

Doris blinks. This is not her daughter. This is someone else inside her daughter's skin.

'You don't care about anyone!' screams Lynette, and for a moment Doris thinks that Lynette might spring forward and bite her.

She gathers herself together. 'H-how dare you!'

And Lynette doesn't spring forward snapping and snarling. Instead she says something, quite clearly, quite distinctly, in Arabic. Guttural words filled with hate.

Doris walks forward two steps and slaps her hard. This, from her own child! She can only imagine what she said.

Lynette holds her cheek. Tears spring to her eyes, spill onto her cheeks.

Doris has done the wrong thing – again – but this time she hasn't a clue what the right thing to do would be. Other mothers might know, but all she knows is how shaken she is that this girl, her once sublime little baby, is able to wound her so deeply. 'I won't stand for it, do you hear? I won't!' She waves a hand round at the room. 'Now tidy up this mess.'

The next morning Lynette is up early and has already made breakfast. They eat in silence. Doris doesn't look at her daughter. She'll go out shopping, that's what she'll do, and buy herself some new clothes; or get the seamstress to make her up a dress from a picture in Vogue; maybe get her hair done. They can show her how to plump it up, because it's growing thinner. What she won't do is think about what happened yesterday evening. She refuses to do that, to feel that pain again. When Leon gets back later today, his presence will break the ice.

But after breakfast she begins to wonder whether she might have dreamt it all. It's so unlikely, after all, so utterly out of character for her daughter to have behaved that way. There's no sign of anything amiss in Lynette's room either. But when Doris goes to empty her ashtray into the bin and lifts up the lid, a waft of feathers rises up like snow.

Doris can see that Lynette is holding back tears as Leon hugs her hello. Outside, the dog is still running around. He went crazy the moment he saw Leon. Never in her life has Doris seen such a welcome. Who'd have thought that Rex could jump so high or that his tail could wag so fast? And the frenzied dashing round in circles, the joyful whining, the scratching of nails on verandah tiles. For several minutes it seemed that the animal might explode out of sheer love.

There was no such display, she thinks, when she returned from her travels.

For the rest of the day, the dog attaches himself like a burr to Leon. Whenever Leon is outside, Rex follows him, and when Leon comes inside, Rex stands waiting by the door. And when Leon pets or talks to Rex, the dog looks up, tongue out and mouth open in what she can only understand as a smile. Neither she nor Lynette say anything about the pillow or the words or the slap.

'Oh no, not already, Daddy,' wails Lynette, her shoulders sagging.

Leon has just announced that he'll have to leave again soon for Damascus, then Beirut.

Doris is aware of her heart beating. To be left alone with

Lynette again, and so soon. 'But you've only just got back, darling. Can't it wait?'

'It is only for a few days; then I will be home for a long time.' He's establishing new business connections, setting up contracts and trying to ensure future work abroad in case they have to leave Iraq. That's why he's working so hard and is away so often, she knows that, but on another level it makes no difference. She can still hear Lynette's voice: *You send them all away*.

She could go with him – Beirut is always fun – but she doesn't want to go to Damascus again, and she's still tired from her own trip.

Without Graham, and with Leon gone again, the house feels empty. Lynette is subdued, and the dog goes into a decline. He lies watching the gate, and each time footsteps approach, raises his head then sinks back down again, disappointed. Once he lies so still she thinks he's dead, but when she goes out to check, he looks up at her without lifting his head so that the whites of his eyes show.

She straightens up. 'Wretched thing.'

It's not you, those sad eyes seem to say. *It's not you I want*. Lynette's eyes say the same thing.

CHAPTER 36

Choices

Harborne, 1937

Without warning, the world has swung into clearer focus. Outlines are more crisp, colours more bright, scents sharper. Everything, from the waft of Bovril to the blare of a car horn, contains its own intense particularity. And inside her chest, her heart has become mobile, rising and arcing like a pendulum.

The hours before she and Leon meet are especially thrilling, when the blood's thrumming around her body and her stomach hitching at the thought of him. She allows herself to savour it, like chocolate melting in her mouth; and in her mind, she navigates the streets that keep them apart – walks along them, runs down them at full tilt. Because it's her he wants.

'Where are you going all dolled up?' Nan asks.

Doris has on a new dress and a good hour's been spent putting Marcel waves in her hair. 'Just to the pictures with Gladys.'

Nan tuts her disapproval and carries on lining the pudding basin. The silent pictures were a modern evil that Nan hoped would quickly lose their charm, but instead things have gone the other way. Nor is what Doris said altogether a lie because she and Leon do go to the cinema. Inside they sit side by side in the dark, and although her eyes remain fixed on the projected images moving and talking on the screen, she hardly sees or hears any of it. Every atom of her is focused on the hand enclosing hers, absorbing the details of its curved fingers, its thumb, the pressure each of these exerts. She waits, hoping he'll do more than just hold her hand, but he doesn't.

'Shall we go for ice cream?' she says afterwards.

'It is too cold for ice cream!'

She laughs, dropping her cigarette and grinding it out beneath her toe. 'It's never too cold for ice cream.'

One day they go to the Hippodrome. Another they drink tea and eat cake. She introduces him to steak and kidney pie, trifle, fried-egg rolls, Horlicks, currant bread and butter. She shows him what galoshes are and teaches him a few choice phrases, and it's as though she's teaching a child.

Other girls look at him curiously but also with undeniable interest, their faces announcing that *they'd* like to get to know him. And she's glad – glad that she's done better than them and has something they want. *They'd* like to be walking arm in arm with him but it's her who's snared him.

Nearly two weeks after he comes to the shoe shop, they kiss. Properly kiss, with his full lips against her own, and the click of her teeth against his.

They walk in Cannon Hill Park and stop to listen to the bands play, the music drifting across the grass towards them. They point at billboard advertisements and visit the City Museum and Art Gallery. They watch a single policeman directing hordes of traffic – cars, horse and carts, buses and vans plastered with posters. In the Bull Ring market an Italian woman's selling violets, and Leon buys Doris a bunch. She will press them, she tells herself, preserve them forever, a line sent whirring back through time and space from wherever she is to this moment.

He talks about the Spanish Civil War and the four thousand Basque refugee children who've arrived at Southampton. 'It is too terrible,' he says, 'to be a child arriving in a strange land without your parents.' He talks about the way Germany has taken over the Rhineland again, and how Hitler and Mussolini have promised to support one another. Then – and she's on safer ground here – they talk about the marriage of the Duke of Windsor and Mrs Simpson at a château in France. She's seen photographs so she knows all about the dress (blue crepe with a buttoned bodice), the halo-shaped hat trailing a long veil, the enormous diamond and sapphire brooch. She's studied the adoring way the Duke is looking at his new wife in all the pictures, has read about the noticeable trembling of his hands as he placed the ring on her finger. An American divorcee, a scandalous thing; yet they look happier than anyone else.

In the Botanical Gardens Leon tries to teach her to whistle with her fingers in her mouth. It's so unexpected, this sound that comes out of him, that she wants to learn how to do it too.

'Fold the tip of your tongue back,' he says. 'Yes, like that. Now blow.'

She puffs out air but no whistle. 'I can't do it,' she laughs.

It takes a good five minutes of trying, but then she startles a pigeon with a sharp whistle.

'Hey! I knew you could do it!' beams Leon.

'I can. I really can!' He's taught her how to do something new with her body.

'Let's do it together, at the same time,' he says.

'All right.' And they let out an ear-splitting screech that turns heads and makes them huddle together laughing.

'Tell me,' says Leon later, as they walk with his arm linked through hers. 'I want to know about your family. Your parents.'

She doesn't break her stride but carries on past the azaleas, a thousand flares of orange and purple. High up in the blue June sky, puffy clouds are racing along so that it seems the Earth is spinning at great speed. And now, here, is a choice. She could tell him the whole truth and lay herself bare. She could, but if she did she'd be opening a can of worms. Leon would learn that from the start, she wasn't wanted by her parents; and that even now, they still don't want her. Knowing this will undoubtedly affect how he sees her. He might decide against the whole thing. At best she'll be tarnished in his eyes.

‘They’re dead.’

He slows, shocked, and takes hold of her elbow so that she’s forced to stop too. ‘Both of them?’

‘Yes.’

His face is filled with distress. ‘I’m sorry. So sorry.’

It surprises her, this upset on her behalf. ‘It was a long time ago, I don’t remember it,’ she says, as if that will somehow make it matter less.

He makes sympathetic noises and looks at her with such compassion that she feels guilty. But he doesn’t move off the topic. Instead he asks how her parents died; and she tells him what Nan told her all those years ago: that they were knocked over by a bus. What does it matter what she tells him anyway, so long as it’s not the truth?

He takes this in. ‘And brothers? Sisters?’

She shakes her head. ‘I’m an only child.’ She smooths over the past, like icing a cake, obliterating all imperfections. ‘I don’t have any brothers or sisters.’

They walk on in silence, and it seems to her that each flower and leaf they pass is stilled and listening, taking note of her lies. And she thinks of The Back of Beyond, and how when she met the Palmers, she lost her family for a second time.

‘Who do you live with then?’ Leon asks before she can change the subject.

It’s a relief to tell him something that’s true. ‘My grandmother.’ And she’s mentioned Nan to him before. ‘I’ve always lived with her – and my uncle. Although… well he is my uncle, but he’s only six years older than I am.’

‘Ah. So he is more a brother than an uncle.’

‘Yes, that’s it.’ He sits in a category, shining and untouchable, that’s all his own. ‘His name’s Harry.’ Saying his name gives her a sudden pang of longing for him. ‘He’s moved to London though, so now it’s only me and Nan.’

As they step onto the lawn, they’re walking close together. How neat this place is, with its octagonal bandstand and looping paths and every blade of grass cut to precisely the same length. Its order soothes her. Here there are no anomalies.

'What about you?' she asks.

'My family, you mean?'

'Yes.'

He takes a moment. 'My parents are Armenian.'

This means nothing to her. 'What's that?'

He seems surprised. 'It's a country. Although now it has become part of the Soviet Union.'

Such faraway places; nothing she knows anything about. 'But now they're in Iraq?'

'They escaped the genocide…' (Another word she doesn't know. How is it that he knows English words that she's never heard before? She'll have to remember to look it up in Harry's dictionary.) '… and went to Iraq. My father, he died two years ago.'

'I'm sorry.'

For a while they walk in silence, then Leon continues. 'We did not get on so well, not at the end. My mother says we are the same – our characters – but I cannot see it. I could never please him. I tried, but…' He shrugs. 'My mother and my brother are still in Baghdad. He is a year younger than me.'

This brings up the subject of their ages, and with a shock she learns that Leon is twenty-three, which is three years younger than her. So when he asks, she lies. It's only a white lie, and what else is she to do, have him think that she's too old for him? So she shaves six years off her real age and tells him she's twenty. She looks young for her age, everyone always says so. Quickly she changes the subject. 'And what will you do once you've finished at the university?'

'I have one year more. My father wanted me to take over his business. 'What use is an education when you have a family business to run?' That is what he used to say. My mother agrees with him, but I am not suited to trading.'

His mother. What sort of a woman is she, Doris wonders briefly, but can't imagine such a figure. What she can see is that in spite of his family's wishes, Leon came here, and she admires him for it: a man who refuses to be pushed around. A man with some backbone. 'What *are* you going to do then?'

'I would like to teach.'

'A teacher!' She almost laughs out loud. He's top of his year and looked up to by the other students, why on earth would he want to be a teacher for goodness' sake?

'I like children.'

Good Lord.

'And money is not so important to me.'

'But isn't it nice to have nice things? To have an easy life?'

He laughs. 'I will have a job, and enough money, that is all I need.' He turns to look at her. 'And you? Do you like your job?'

In the shoe shop? Is he joking? 'Oh, I don't mind it,' she says. 'It's all right.' Compared to Bill's or the telephone exchange maybe. But if she had the choice, she'd never do another day's work of any sort in her life.

CHAPTER 37

Potted Shrimp

Harborne, 1937

Leon goes home for the summer holidays. Not down the road to Dudley, nor even as far as Nottingham, but over land and sea to a place she can't even imagine. All summer she thinks of him going about his daily business somewhere far, far away, and when she does, it sets up a quivering in her lungs. She thinks of him kissing her, and prays to God he's thinking about that too.

Then, just as summer's drawing to a close, like a miracle he's back, handsome as ever, smiling and calling her Dolores with that lilt he puts into it.

But Nan has got wind of it. 'Who's this man then?' she asks with a knowing smile over breakfast one September morning.

Doris almost chokes on her tea. 'Man?' Has Nan read it in Doris' happy face? In the frequency with which she lapses into daydreams? Or the bother she takes about her clothes these days?

'I hope he's a good sort.'

Doris takes a deep breath. It seems pointless to enter into an argument about his existence. She's old enough now for any man on the horizon to be a welcome sight. 'He is.' And she's overwhelmed all over again by Leon's good qualities. 'He's clever. And kind.' Not to mention sexy, she adds to herself. And gentle, funny, thoughtful.

'Who's his family? What sort of people are they?'

'Oh, he comes from a good family.' How else is she to answer? His father's dead, his brother distant. But he talks about his mother. He told Doris how she used to look after him when he was a little boy and sick in bed; the treats she used to prepare for him so that he'd eat. There were times though when she'd shut herself away for days. He could hear her weeping, and knew that the past was biting at her heels. 'He's perfectly polite.' She builds a defensive wall around Leon. 'He's got excellent manners.'

'Well,' – a final long scrape of butter onto Nan's toast – 'make sure they stay that way.'

It takes Doris a second to understand. 'Nan!'

Nan hacks the top off a soft-boiled egg. 'Why don't you ask him round?'

'What, here?'

'Of course here, where else would you invite him round to?'

Doris starts to stutter out an excuse.

'Ask him round to dinner perhaps,' says Nan. 'I could get in some potted shrimp.'

'Shrimp?' As if shrimps congealed in a pot of butter could impress a man like Leon.

Nan's head snaps up. 'He's not Catholic, is he?'

'No, he's not a Catholic.'

'You're not Catholic, are you?'

They're sitting in a café. It's cold out and the windows have steamed up. In front of them are two mugs of tea, a plate of fried eggs and bacon for Leon, and bread and kippers for her.

He stops eating. 'Not exactly. Armenia has its own church, the Armenian Apostolic Church.'

Oh. 'And that's Christian, is it?'

'Yes. Why do you ask?'

'No reason.' They've never talked about religion before. It's not high on her list of priorities.

'What about you?' Leon gathers the last of the fried egg onto his fork. 'Are you a Christian?'

'I suppose so.'

'You are not sure?'

'I am, only…' When she and Harry were children Nan took them to church, didn't she? All those torturous hours must count for something. 'I am a Christian.'

Leon laughs.

'Was it good to be back – you know, in Baghdad?'

'Of course. It is my home.'

His home. And when he finishes his studies, he'll leave and go back there. She knows this, although she tries not to think about it. 'Tell me about Baghdad; what it's like.'

'What do you think it is like?'

Is he testing her? 'I don't know.'

'But what do you think?'

'Do they wear long robes and ride camels?'

Again, he laughs, but this time it's a sharp, humourless sound. 'Of course. And live in tents and kidnap Western women.'

She bridles. 'Well, how in God's name should I know?' She thinks of Rudolph Valentino as *The Sheikh* keeping Agnes Ayres prisoner in his camp – although of course at the end of the film it turns out he's not an Arab at all and so the two can live happily ever after.

Leon takes a deep breath. 'There are streets with cars and horses and carriages just like here. Shops, schools, trees. It was the British who created the country – decided Iraq's borders I mean. Did you know this?'

She shakes her head.

'Then they brought us a king. And not an Iraqi, but a Hashemite prince…'

She doesn't ask.

'… and when he was crowned, they played "God Save the King".'

Briefly she's caught, not knowing whether to be apologetic or delighted.

Leon sighs. 'But yes, many things are also different there. The houses, for instance. And the clothes.' He indicates outside. 'And the weather!'

She looks at the dismal grey street. 'I'm surprised you left.'

A little smile. 'Well, it is also not easy being there. My family. Families are never easy.'

He can say that again.

'And mine… you see, for Armenians, what happened to our people is always there. It is as if we are always carrying a heavy weight. And I wanted to get away from that. To breathe, and be with people who do not have a terrible past.'

She feels the blood drain from her face. If he wants someone with no past then he's barking up the wrong tree.

He's looking at her. 'You are not like the women I know.'

Shakily, she lays down her knife and fork. 'Oh? What women do you mean?' How many women does he know? How pretty are they? Are they younger than her?

'Back in Iraq.' He stops to think. 'Or even here. The other students.'

She blinks. 'There are women studying mathematics?' This had never occurred to her.

'Yes, a few.'

She feels depleted. Is that something she could have done? Although she was never any good with numbers at school. A clatter of cutlery in the kitchen and an order is called out. She refocuses on the matter at hand. 'How am I different?' She leans forward, elbows on the table (never mind, Nan can't see).

'Well, you are strong. You know what you think about everything.'

She beams.

'But that is not really who you are.'

'What?' Alarm in her every nerve. 'It's not?'

'The first time I saw you – you remember that day?'

She nods. How could she forget? That was the day it all began. Her love. Her lies.

'You looked cold, and it was raining, and your hat was crooked. You looked like someone who is lost.'

She sits back. 'Oh. So I struck you as a pathetic figure. Is that how you see me?'

Carefully Leon puts down his cutlery. 'No, I do not mean that.'

'I looked like someone to feel sorry for, you said so.'

He shakes his head.

'What then?'

Two tables away, a man looks up from his paper, eyes enlarged by thick reading glasses.

'I was trying to explain – that you are confident, but that there is another side. A side you do not show. That anyway is how I see you.'

She takes deep breaths. She can just see herself standing all alone in the rain with her crooked hat and dripping hair.

'Are you angry?'

She's not sure whether she's angry, but she's *some*thing. Yes, she's certainly something.

Leon reaches for her hand. 'Do not be angry with me.'

Her innards soften like wax held to a flame.

'Please. I missed you when I was away. So much.'

A cow-eyed girl standing alone in the rain with her bag of humbugs. Uneducated. Pitiable. She must wipe that image out of both their minds. 'Then kiss me.'

'What?'

'You heard.'

He glances around as though she mustn't realise where they are and she watches him weigh up his options. He's a rational man. He'll consider what's socially acceptable, then he'll consider the possible consequences of acting and not acting.

Another bellow from the kitchen: 'Meat pie and spuds!'

Her cheeks are burning. He's going to refuse. She's made a fool of herself.

But Leon gives a sudden, soft laugh. Raising himself off his chair, he leans across the table, over what's left of the bacon, kippers and tea, and puts his lips to hers.

She cups his head and draws him closer. Beneath her fingertips she can feel his hair and skull, the nape of his neck, and they kiss, their lips greasy and their mouths delicious, as unchristian a kiss as there ever was. Let everyone see that she's no miserable little orphan but a desirable woman. And yes, a woman utterly unlike the others he knows.

She can't put them off meeting forever, but she has it all planned: it's to be a 'Leon – Nan, Nan – Leon'-type transaction at the front door when he picks her up this evening, and there's the job done. This way there'll be no chance of Nan mentioning Doris' real age or, God forbid, the Palmers and The Back of Beyond.

Even though Doris is expecting him, it's somehow still a shock to see Leon on the doorstep of number 45. They smile nervously at each other. He's clutching a box of chocolates for Nan. He's explained before that where he comes from, it's unheard of to visit somebody's house empty-handed.

'Hello,' Nan calls, and comes to examine this man Doris has been keeping so quiet about. Doris sees the tiniest of shock waves pass over her face.

Leon takes off his hat. 'Hello, Mrs Palmer.'

'Mrs Linnet,' corrects Nan.

'Oh.' A moment's silence. 'Excuse me. Mrs Linnet.'

Lord, thinks Doris, not two seconds and it's going wrong already. Why didn't she think of telling Leon about Nan's surname? What she has told him, offhand, is that Nan often calls her Doris – 'a sort of nickname, yes exactly' – or even Dot, and please not to call her Dolores in front of Nan because Nan doesn't like it.

Leon hands Nan the chocolates as though he were her

suitor in some bygone era, and Nan accepts them with a tight smile. Doris reaches for her coat.

'Come in and have a cup of tea. Doris, take his hat and coat.'

'Tea?' Doris blinks, but Leon has stepped inside and is already shouldering off his coat.

In the parlour, the cushions have been rearranged and Nan's set out a tea tray with the best china and a Dundee cake studded with almonds, all of it only fit to prolong things. Oh, why did Doris spend so long upstairs preening instead of keeping an eye on Nan?

They each sit at a distance from the other and Nan pours, her face twitching in and out of a polite smile. 'And where do you hail from?'

Leon glances at Doris and she flushes. Yes, she knows, she ought to have told Nan herself, only she couldn't bring herself to. And now she must rely on Nan's good manners!

'I come from Baghdad.' Leon adjusts his thighs on the chair. 'In Iraq.'

Nan's eyebrows rise a little higher. 'Oh. Really.' She lowers her head over the teapot. 'And I expect you'll be going back there at some point?'

He hesitates, then recovers himself. 'Yes,' he says. 'In July, when I graduate.'

'Of course. I see.'

Doris slices cake – small pieces, all the quicker to eat – and hands it round. She doesn't want any herself. Nor tea. She only wants to put on her coat and haul Leon out of there.

'Cold weather we've been having,' observes Nan, as if such a thing were peculiar for February. 'Not what you're used to, I suppose, not in… Bagh-dad.'

This, thinks Doris, must be the first time Nan has spoken that word in her life. Leon talks a little about the weather in Baghdad, the hot days and cool nights. He explains how in order to keep cool, men wear *keffiyehs* and women *abayas*, although some wear Western clothes. He tells Nan that a river runs through the city, and fishermen's boats called *quffas*, round like bowls, travel up and down it all day.

Silence.

Leon glances around the room. 'You have a beautiful house, Mrs Linnet.'

'Yes, well we like it, don't we, Dot? We like it here in Harborne.'

Doris perches on the very edge of her chair, her tea cooling on the occasional table, her plate of uneaten cake balanced on her knee.

'I've lived here ever since I was married, you know. And Dot – well, she's lived here her entire life. Practically her entire life anyway.'

Except for those first months, Nan means, when Susan was arriving at the decision that she didn't want her daughter.

'She came here to live with her grandfather and me when she was only a tot. Did she tell you?'

'Er, yes,' says Leon. 'Yes of course.'

Nan looks taken aback. She hadn't expected that. Gripping her fork, Doris tries to relax her face. Does Leon suspect that something's off? Perhaps he's sensed it, like an error far back in one of his calculations. But when she looks at him, nothing seems amiss.

'She told me her uncle also lives here?' says Leon.

'That's right,' Doris chimes in, clutching at this lifeline. 'Yes, Harry.'

'Only he's in London now,' says Nan.

With a trembling hand, Doris spears a piece of cake onto her fork, but it doesn't hold together long enough to reach her mouth. 'Leon's studying mathematics at the university.'

'Oh?' says Nan. 'Harry ought to have gone to university, he'd have been a great success. But there you are; he's making something of himself in London.'

Leon nods. 'I am sure.'

'We're a good family, you know. Doris has a good family here – not riff-raff like some people you'd meet.'

A good family? Is that what she calls them? Putting down her plate, Doris gets to her feet. This has gone on long enough. In another second Nan might blurt out some horrid truth that'll send Leon scarpering. Something about Dolores, or the Palmers, or how Doris was given away like an unwanted pair of shoes. At any moment the rotten truth might spill out. 'We'd better go,' she says to Leon with a smile. 'We don't want to be late.' Although there's still another two hours before they need to be at the dance hall. The band won't even have set up.

Nan looks at the clock. 'Surely you don't need to leave yet? He's only just arrived.'

But Doris insists. 'It's later than I thought.' And silently she vows that Nan and Leon must never meet again.

CHAPTER 38

Snow

Harborne, 1938

All winter she's been waiting for a morning when she'll open her curtains to find a world turned white and muffled and crisp. Today exactly that happened, and now she's heading east in the direction of Balsall Heath towards the spot where she and Leon have arranged to meet. Her boots compact the snow, making it squeak. Dirt and rubbish have been blotted out, and lampposts, cars, rooftops and trees are all hooded in sparkling white.

There he is, she can see him at the far end of the street at their meeting place. Her heart swells, and with a smile she crosses the deserted road, raising an arm ready to wave as soon as he looks this way. Children are shouting and laughing somewhere. Her breath streams out, miraculously visible in front of her. Buttoned into her bottle-green coat, she steps across pristine snow, leaving her own particular set of prints behind her. She's walking on water, she thinks suddenly. Yes, that's what she's doing, walking on water towards Leon.

The impact knocks her off balance. The child lets out a cry as they collide, and falls over in the snow. The two children he was running after don't stop, and are soon gone. The boy sits up blinking, a brown bobble hat askew on his head.

'Stupid boy! Can't you look where you're going?'

'S-sorry. I slipped.'

She glances down at her clothes. 'Just look what you've

done! Barging into people like that!' In his fall, he's snagged one of her woollen stockings and left a rip in it. She's spattered with snow too. But worse than either of these things is the fact that he has knocked her buoyant mood clean out of her.

The boy's face crumples.

'Oh, for goodness' sake, what are you crying about?' Because, with his eyes squeezed shut and his mouth hanging open, the boy is blubbing. The front of his coat and trousers are covered in snow where he went sprawling; but she wants him gone now because Leon has seen them and is coming over, and this is not the rendezvous she'd envisaged.

She bends over to help the boy up and sets him on his feet. 'There. Now off you go.' And when he doesn't move, she gives him a discreet shove: 'Go on! Hop it!'

Startled out of his misery, the boy wipes his nose on his sleeve and jogs off after his friends.

'Hello,' calls Leon.

Oh, how she wishes she hadn't dealt so harshly with that boy. What must Leon think of her? Leon who is always so kind, so caring and considerate. She goes to meet him. It's good to be close to him, it's always good, but inside she's quaking. Just now he glimpsed a part of her character that he's never been exposed to before, and there will be shock. And disappointment. Disappointment in her. *Who is this woman?* he'll be thinking. *Shouting at that child. Shoving him away like that. No, she is not at all the woman I thought she was.*

As soon as he reaches her, he'll say something. He'll look uncomfortable saying it because he's a gentleman, but he'll say it anyway. He'll say that he was wrong – about her, about them – and that he wants nothing more to do with her. He'll say something along the lines of 'better to nip it in the bud, before things get too serious.' Except he won't say nip it in the bud because he doesn't know expressions like that.

But when Leon gets to her, he doesn't look angry, or disappointed.

'Hello,' she says.

He gives her a kiss.

'Oh.' She reassesses the situation. 'Oh.'

He touches her cheek, fingers brushing the hair poking out from beneath her hat, and she laughs. He's not disappointed with her at all! In his culture, telling a child off and showing it the error of its ways must be something that's respected. In any case he's seen this other side of her and it has made no difference. He loves her regardless!

She smiles up at him. Around them, the world has been cast fresh and new, and she feels proud, as if the snow is somehow her doing. 'Isn't it lovely?'

'It is.' He looks at her with a sudden tenderness. 'Beautiful.' And she wonders what she's done to deserve this.

'You're cold,' she says, shivering at the touch on her face. Leon's wearing a hat and scarf but his hands are bare. 'Haven't you got any gloves?'

'Yes, but I wanted to feel the snow.' He bends to scoop some up and holds it, shimmering and glinting in his cupped palm like a handful of crushed diamonds.

She laughs. Has he never gathered snow in his hands before? It's all wonderful, so wonderful. 'I'm glad you got to see it.' Then, glancing up at the sky, 'Looks as though we're going to get some more too.'

A woman trudges past with empty shopping bags, trailed by her girl, who stops to push snow off a picket fence, a postbox, a window ledge. But Leon's attention is still on the snow softening in his hand. A day of unexpected marvels for him as well as for her. He prods it, then tilts his hand so it slides to the ground.

'That's not what you do with a handful of snow,' she says.

'No?'

'No.' Now it's her turn to gather some. She packs and shapes it between her mittens then steps back, smiling.

The snowball lands in the centre of his chest, leaving a dusty circle of white. And suddenly they're playing like children, her squealing and exclaiming, him dodging and crouching, both scooping and throwing and laughing.

When it starts to snow again, he stops to look up. She looks up too, and all at once they're inside a snow globe, trapped in the whirl and spin of it, dizzied by the trajectory of one, two, a thousand snowflakes, and she's filled with a tingling, magnetic happiness. Never mind the slushy wetness trickling down the back of her neck, or her numb hands and wet hair. The universe presses bright against her face: this wondrous world, and she and Leon the most wondrous things in it.

They've gone back to the room where he boards. Although it was his suggestion, it was her who shivered and said she was cold and wet (which she was), while thinking the whole time how close by he lived.

He feeds a couple of coins into a meter on the wall – *clunk, clunk* – and an electric heater glows into life. She hands him her coat and he hangs it off the back of a chair next to the heater. The mittens and hat she's taken off are wet too. So are the ends of her hair. Her collar's damp, and snow has slid into her boots and melted there. All in all, she feels small and tight and frozen.

She tries to draw her attention away from her body to the room around her. His room. How long she's wondered about this space, and the conditions under which she might see it. Has he thought about that too? And was there an ulterior motive, in spite of the circumstances, to his asking her here today? She starts to blush. Is it the same as asking a girl to a hotel room? But he isn't from round here, she reminds herself. He operates by different rules; thinks differently to other men. Although when all's said and done he's still a man. And just because his morals are high doesn't mean the thought of *that* hasn't entered his head. But no, given the state of her, what else could he do but invite her to come back here and get warm? Still, it feels as if something has changed. There's a new softness in his voice, a new affection in his eyes.

The room has two windows looking out onto the street. A metal-framed bed – the one he lies in each night – sits against one wall, and there's a chair, a small desk with a lamp on it, and a dresser and wardrobe made of some flimsy, pale wood. The rug is worn threadbare in places, and the damp stain he told her about has loosened the wallpaper on one wall. This room's different to hers – emptier, sparser. And it's where he goes to sleep and wakes up each day. She wonders what his morning routine is. She'd like to watch him as he shaves, carefully and with practised skill. She'd like to watch him pull on a crisp shirt, do up its buttons, construct a tie around his neck then sit down to lace his feet into polished shoes.

She goes to have a look at the pile of books on his desk, but the titles of the books are meaningless to her, and so is the writing on a sheet of paper lying on the desk. Leon has jotted down some words in what must be Arabic or Armenian, and there are numbers and figures that might be mathematical signs or foreign letters, she can't tell. A distance widens between them. These are things she knows nothing about, books she'll never read and wouldn't understand if she did.

A framed photograph stands in the corner of the desk. She tries not to be too obvious or eager as she looks. Is it a woman? Some sweetheart from another time and place? But it's neither of these things. The picture shows Leon with an older man who, judging by the resemblance between them, must be his father. It's a studio shot, the two men standing on a patterned rug, not touching or smiling but looking straight ahead at the photographer. 'You look like him.'

He comes over. 'Yes. My father. We did not always see eye to eye. But this…' He touches the frame in a way that tells her this picture is a prized possession. '… this was a good day.'

His honesty touches her. How wonderful not to have any pretensions. She takes his hand and gives it a squeeze. 'I'm sorry. He'd be proud of you now though.' A temptation arises, like a door being prised open, to confess something about herself too. To reveal more of herself, just as she had done out there in the snow. 'I—' she begins, then stops. How to say it? 'What I told you in the park…'

'In the park?'

'We were talking about our families, remember?' That day with the clouds whirling above them and the grass a stinging green. 'You told me about your family. And I… I told you about my parents.' She swallows. 'How they were killed. Do you remember?'

'Of course I remember.' And now it's him who's squeezing her hand.

'Although that's not exactly… what I mean is…' She takes a deep breath. 'It's difficult. Difficult to say.'

'I know.' His voice is heavy with sympathy. Then his brow crinkles. 'You are shivering.' He turns the chair round to face the electric fire and makes her sit down.

She wraps her arms around herself. 'I'm meant to be used to the cold.' Her boots are out in the hall, and her feet are frozen. She puts one on top of the other and starts to chafe them, but Leon kneels in front of her and takes her right foot in both his hands – his large hands that are somehow already warm – and rubs until she can feel her toes again. Then he does the same with the left foot. His warmth against her is delicious, luxurious. Thank God he never saw her kneeling in front of anyone in the shop. Although here he is kneeling at *her* feet without hesitation or shame. And it thrills her to have him there; not fitting her for shoes but drawing the blood tingling back into her toes.

She smiles – 'Thank you' – then glances towards the desk again, at the picture of him with his father. She was going to tell him, truly she was, but just as quickly as it opened, that door has closed. 'What you're studying looks difficult,' she says instead.

'It is not so difficult.' He says this without pride, as a mere fact.

'That's because you're clever.'

'So are you.'

She laughs. She knows she's not that, but is happy for him

to think so. He thinks well of her, always. Thank heaven she didn't get as far as telling him the truth just now. What a fool she was to even contemplate it!

'And you are kind,' he says. 'Warm-hearted.'

She must look surprised because he says, 'You are. Truly.' He takes her hand in his and passes his thumb over the top of each knuckle, then up and down each finger; turns her hand over and circles the palm with his thumb, slowly, attentively, until she's ready to weep, because nobody has ever touched her this way. She pulls him an inch or two closer, and he leans up then and kisses her. Their lips move against one another's, exploring, opening, sending shivers along her body that have nothing to do with being cold.

When they stop kissing, he looks at her as though she's freshly precious. She touches his cheek. Beneath her fingers is a dark shoreline of closely-shaven bristles that, given half a chance, will sprout into a thick, full beard. It gives her a strange sensation to know that there's something pulsing and growing just here beneath his face.

'You are loving.' He kisses her again, and his hands move to her knees, up her thighs to her waist. Hers are on his shoulders, in his hair, her fingers tunnelling into its thickness to reach his scalp. Thank God – oh, thank God she didn't tell him.

Surely now it'll happen. She wants more, and he must too, mustn't he? But she holds herself back as she's done all these months because she doesn't want to give a bad impression. She must pretend that she, like him, has never done this before. Because this isn't like those few encounters she's had – trivial, throwaway things – this is different, and it must seem as though it's his decision.

Her face is warm. 'Always try on the shoe before you buy it' is their motto in the shop. And she will, here and now; she will try on the shoe.

Leon's breath is urgent, his lips warm against her throat. 'We should stop,' he says.

'Yes. We should.'

CHAPTER 39

A Dog's Dinner

Baghdad, 1955

Graham returns for the summer holidays. Leon goes to collect him from the airport, and asks the woman who cooks for them to make Graham's favourite meal, a casserole of ground beef and aubergines in tomato sauce served with rice. For herself Doris sets out cheese, fruit and some crackers. 'Breakfast like a king, lunch like a prince and dine like a pauper' is what Nan always used to say.

As soon as she hears the engine she hurries out onto the verandah. The car's pulling in. She's spent the whole morning baking a welcome home cake – twice, because the first batter curdled, and Graham deserves nothing less than perfect. When it had cooled in the afternoon, she iced it white all over and piped his name across the top in blue icing, her heart swelling with love as she worked.

The engine cuts. The passenger-side door opens and a boy gets out. The boy's taller than Graham and far thinner – and yet it is Graham. When he sees Doris his mouth twitches – a smile? a grimace? – but he says nothing.

The netted verandah door crashes open and Lynette charges out, but at the bottom of the steps she pulls up short as though the ground has fallen away in front of her.

Doris gathers herself. She clears her throat and goes forward. 'Hello, darling.' She makes herself smile. 'Look at you! How you've grown!' And she kisses the boy who used to be Graham.

Leon has got out of the car. He's hauling a suitcase from the car boot (the same suitcase; *that* hasn't changed) and she sees that he's struggling not to cry. When their eyes meet, the look in them makes dark wings start beating in her chest.

They dine in a silence broken only by the occasional cheery-toned comment or question from her, and a 'yes' or a 'no' from Graham. After dinner, Graham and Lynette go up to their rooms.

Leon takes off his glasses. There's a splash of tomato sauce on the tablecloth in front of him. He hates tomato sauce, has always hated it, but requested and ate that aubergine dish for Graham's sake. Afterwards, they cut the cake, severing Graham's name into pieces, but nobody had much appetite for it. Served on bone china plates with gilt edges, the slices were tasted, nibbled at a little, then abandoned. Now, with his glasses laid on the tablecloth and a hand placed flat on either side of his dessert plate, Leon stares down the table at the remains of the meal. For a moment she wonders what he sees without his glasses, how blurred the plates and cutlery must appear, the icing and coloured wedges of cake.

She goes to the living room to find her cigarettes – takes one out, sets the end on fire and inhales, wanting the smoke to cloud over the image of her husband sitting lost at the head of an empty table.

Today Graham says that he'll feed Rex.

'All right,' she says, a little surprised.

He carries a chair out into the garden, then takes out Rex's bowl of food and positions it directly in front of the chair. 'Leave,' he tells Rex. He has been teaching Rex the 'leave' command all week, and the dog has learned quickly. From the kitchen window she watches Graham turn the chair round and sit astride it back to front, resting his arms along the top rail.

Rex approaches his food, but before his nose can touch it, Graham commands 'Leave!'

Rex starts back. He turns around a couple of times, whining, then creeps up to the bowl again. But again the order comes: 'Leave it!'

Saliva drips from Rex's jowls onto the paving stones, evaporates in the sun and is replaced by more drips. Flies circle and settle on the food. Now and then Rex sidles up to the bowl, but is still not allowed to touch it.

Footsteps clatter down the stairs and Lynette appears in the living room, where Doris is trying to finish a painting she's been working on, although in reality she can't focus on anything but what's going on outside. 'Mummy! Do you see what he's doing?' Her chest is heaving. 'Graham's stopping Rex from—'

'Yes.' Doris wipes her brush on a rag stiff with old paint. 'I know.'

Lynette absorbs this information. Her nose wrinkles; she dislikes the bright, heady smell of turpentine. 'Aren't you going to stop him?' She waits. '*I'm* going to stop him then.' And she starts for the door.

Dropping her brush, Doris takes hold of Lynette's shoulder. 'No you're not.'

Lynette's head snaps round. 'Why not?' She's flushed with injustice.

But Doris can't put it into words. She only knows that they mustn't interfere; that no one must push Graham off his path again, even if what he's doing is cruel. And that the entire thing's the end result of a botched job – a job she has herself botched. 'You're not to go outside. Leave him alone.'

Lynette swallows audibly. 'But… why is he doing that? How could he be so mean?'

But Doris doesn't know the answer to that. Perhaps he's thinking of school, although what particularly she doesn't wish to know.

'Why don't you do something?' There are tears in Lynette's voice.

She imagines going outside then, striding across the garden to Graham and telling him to stop, to go inside and let the poor dog eat, it's been over an hour now. But somewhere inside her is a tiny seed of fear: fear of her son and what he might do, because she's no longer certain of his limitations. If Leon were here and not at work, he would make Graham stop. Yes, certainly Leon would. But as it is…

'Please, Mummy,' pleads Lynette, straining towards the door.

But Doris tightens her grip. 'No. He's… only teaching Rex to do what he's told. And you're not to mention a word about it to Daddy, is that understood?'

Biting her lip, Lynette pulls away and runs upstairs, slamming her bedroom door shut. It's almost an hour later before Graham finally stands, stretches, reaching his hands to the sky, and points to the bowl of food. 'Take it,' he says, and picking up the chair, he limps back into the house.

CHAPTER 40

14th July

Baghdad, 1958

She doesn't know how long the phone has been ringing. Graham, is her first thought. Or Leon. But when she gets downstairs and picks it up, it's Sara Elmwood. At this hour. Barely six in the morning.

'Sara? What is it? What's happened?'

The silly woman's in an absolute panic, can hardly get her words out. 'The army. The government. They've attacked it. Attacked the palace.'

'What? What on earth are you talking about?'

Sara starts crying. There's a shuffling sound and Bernard Elmwood's voice comes on. 'Dolores?'

'Yes. What's happened? I couldn't make head or tail of— '

'There's been a coup.'

'A coup?'

'Didn't you hear the gunshots?'

'Yes, but that's nothing unusual.'

'Well, they've taken over the government.'

She can't believe it. 'Are you sure? Are you sure it's not just another rally?' Violence keeps breaking out between the religious groups. On religious holidays, the Shia get fired up and it all ends in the usual demonstrations. Or else the ruling Sunnis taunt them about something and it kicks off. That's been par for the course these last years.

'The palace is under siege, and they're saying…' Bernard

pauses. She can hear Sara whimpering in the background. 'Well, let's just say I wouldn't want to be in the king's shoes right now.'

'You don't mean…?'

'I shouldn't be surprised. You know what these Arabs are like.'

Nineteen forty-one. The mob gone crazy. The butchering of Jews, and of Muslims who tried to protect them. The horror that rippled through the city afterwards. For her, the realisation that she could have lost Leon that day. Then in forty-eight, that uprising they now call the *wathba*. Protestors machine-gunned on the bridge. Bodies in the water. The Tigris turning red.

She can't believe it. Doesn't want to. 'No, it'll blow over, surely.'

'Perhaps. But I doubt it.'

Dear God. 'What should we do? What about the embassy?'

He cuts her off: 'No. That's the last place you should go. They'll attack that soon, if they haven't already. All hell's breaking loose out there.'

The Baghdad mob. It's happening again, only this time their anger is against the royals, and the Brits who put them there in the first place.

'You could try the airport,' says Bernard.

'Is that what you're going to do?'

'Not sure. We'll hang on a while longer just to make sure. See what happens. But then… probably, yes.' There's a quaver in his voice. Fear. Bernard afraid. Unimaginable before this moment. He clears his throat. 'Anyway, we wanted to let you know, what with, er…' – he searches for the name – 'your husband being away. And what with you having children.'

Child, she thinks. Only one here, thank God. How right she was to send Graham away.

Bernard's duty to another British citizen done, he wishes her well and she hangs up.

As though the thought has made her materialise, Lynette is standing at the top of the stairs in her nightdress. God only knows how long she's been there. 'What have I told you about eavesdropping?' Doris' nerves are stretched taut, and the words come out harshly.

'I wasn't eavesdropping.'

Doris goes into the living room to find her cigarettes. She lights one and inhales deeply. Her hands are fluttering.

Lynette follows her. 'Was that Daddy?'

'No.' Leon is in Basra. Basra with its canals and villas, the so-called Venice of the East. That's what he has to contend with, and not this mayhem. Basra! Leon may as well not bloody exist.

She looks around at her rooms, her things. And yet how can they be hers if a mob might simply charge in when they felt like it?

Lynette is waiting for her to say something.

'There's trouble, trouble going on in the city.'

'Trouble?'

'The army's overthrown the government,' she says, not knowing if Lynette will comprehend what this means. Bad news; a girl in her nightdress. It brings to mind another awful day: an early morning knock on the door, and herself still in her nightdress. Dolores lying on a door, the extent of her marked out in chalk. A catastrophe too vast to be contained within the parameters of just one day.

Lynette turns on the radio. It's tuned to the Arabic station Leon was listening to before he left. The man's voice coming out of it is ranting, angry, and also victorious, she senses that without understanding a word.

For several minutes, as Doris finishes her cigarette and considers what to do, Lynette sits close to the radio, listening.

Doris crushes her spent cigarette in the ashtray. When she looks up, there's a strange expression on Lynette's face.

'Well?' says Doris. The man on the radio is still ranting.

'He says... he says *today is a day to kill and be killed*.'

They stare at each other. 'Turn it off.' Doris steps across and fumbles with the knob until she finds the World Service.

She wants to hear a calm English voice. A voice with some perspective, some sanity. Bernard and the man on the radio must have it wrong, and order will soon be restored. It must.

Over the next twenty minutes the World Service broadcasts that a group of Iraqi army officers have staged a coup and overthrown the monarchy. They have proclaimed the liberation of the Iraqi people from a monarchy put in place by the powers of imperialism. Iraq is now a republic that will uphold ties with other Arab countries, they say.

Then comes the news that King Faisal and a number of other members of the royal family have been assassinated. That the prime minister has gone into hiding, and Abdul-Karim Qasim, one of the two instigators of the coup, has declared himself Iraq's new prime minister and commander-in-chief.

She turns off the radio. Without her noticing, Lynette has left the room.

Bernard telephones again. Then, shortly afterwards, Leon calls. 'Are you all right? Is Lynette with you?'

'Yes, we're all right.' But she's not all right. She's already had a martini to steady her nerves. Then a coffee. Then another martini.

'Nobody knew. I didn't think… did not imagine…' He breaks off. She pictures him raking his fingers through his hair, his eyes still puffy with sleep.

'They're rioting, running mad. Gangs of them tearing things down, setting fire to things, looting. Bernard just told me. And there's no police. There's no one to stop them.' Is this what life is – an endless swing from war to peace and back again?

'My God.' She can hear Leon breathing. A momentary worry about his blood pressure. 'I didn't know, *jan*. Or I would never have left you and Lynette. Lynette,' he says again.

A memory flashes into her head then: Leon with Lynette in his arms, even though she was really too big to be carried, her dress puffed up over his elbows. When Doris and Leon first moved here, it was Doris he carried over the threshold. But now there is no longer any room in his arms. Who, she wonders – what a moment to wonder! – who does he love more, her or Lynette?

She pushes the thought to one side. 'They're finding families with connections to the monarchy, even just well-to-do families, and attacking them. Killing them maybe.'

'All right, *jan*, all right. Now listen.'

'But I don't understand. I don't understand how this can be happening. How can they just wake up one morning and not want a monarchy any more?'

'Dolores…'

'But *how*?'

'Because they are hungry. The poor. You don't see them but they are there. Poor and hungry.'

'Rubbish. Baghdad has never seen a better decade.'

'*Jan*, listen. I have spoken to some people, and the airport is still open. Go to the airport—'

'That's what the Elmwoods are doing.'

'Yes. Go to the airport. There will be flights.' He mutters something to himself in Armenian. 'God willing there will still be flights. I have contacts. I will make more calls.'

'But I don't want to go to the airport.'

'Let me speak to them and then I will phone you back.'

'No, I don't want to go,' she says again, but he's not listening.

'Take only what you need. Never mind everything else.' He pauses. 'Dolores?'

But all at once she's furious with him. Furious that he's not here and she is. That he didn't know better, didn't see this coming. That he brought her, an Englishwoman, to this place where they hate, and have always hated, the English. And now he's gone off and left her here like a sitting duck!

'Go and pack.'

'I'm not going to the airport!'

There's silence at the other end of the line.

'They'll be fools if they haven't taken over the airport. They must have by now, and I'm not going to waltz right into their arms.'

'There is no choice.'

'There's the embassy.'

'The embassy has been set on fire,' says Leon quietly.

She's appalled. The United Kingdom is a force for good; ever since she came out here, this has been the solid core of her belief. Her religion, one might say. Look what her country's done for this patch of desert. It has brought paved streets and cars, bridges and trains, planes, ships and dockyards, medicines and vaccines, department stores so you don't have to haggle in the marketplace, cinemas and horse racing and tennis. Plumbing, for God's sake. Toilets you can sit on. They'd say that the British installed a dummy king and filched their oil. That they made a mess of Palestine. All your fault, that's what they'd say.

'Don't they *want* to be civilised?' she bursts out. 'They', because no matter what he might say, Leon is not one of them. Not with his Armenian heritage and being married to an Englishwoman. He's an outsider here, just like her.

She bumps her suitcase down the stairs. She has packed clothes and toiletries, and in a separate bag is her jewellery box and their passports. Lynette's small case is already in the hall, and she is standing beside it. She is dressed and has even plaited her hair – a plait above each ear, looped up and tied with white ribbon.

'Where are we going?' she asks.

'To England.'

'How long for?'

'Only a couple of weeks until things have calmed down.'

Lynette nods.

'We'd better pack some food,' Doris says, and they go into the kitchen and pack fruit and bread and cheese and dates, which at least keep well. They fill bottles with water.

Just as they finish putting everything in the car – suitcases in the boot, jewellery under the loose passenger seat and the food on the back seat – another car pulls up.

'Adnan!' Their old neighbour. 'I'm so glad to see you!'

When he gets out of his car, Adnan's face is grey. 'Miss Dolores. Miss Lynette.' He looks at the suitcases in the open boot, the bags of food on the back seat. 'You are leaving.' He sounds relieved. 'I will take you to the airport.'

'What?'

'I will drive you.'

'Don't be absurd. What's the point of that? Anyway, we're not going to the airport.'

He looks at the packed car then back at her. 'Where, then? Where are you going, Miss Dolores?'

'To Iran.' Persia, as she still thinks of it. The nearest border.

Adnan is shaking his head. 'No, it is not safe.' He waves his arm back towards the city. 'There is *thawra*. There are men destroying. It is too dangerous.' He glances over Doris' shoulder at Lynette.

'I'll take back ways.' Although she'll have to cross the river and get to the other side of the city, they both know that.

A thought pops into her head. 'Did…?' she begins, then stops. She was about to ask whether Leon sent him; called and asked him to come here and accompany her to the airport. Possibly. Very likely, in fact. But she doesn't ask. She would rather believe that Adnan has come just because he likes her.

'Miss Dolores,' Adnan pleads.

'We'll be fine.'

He must realise that it's pointless trying to dissuade her because he opens his car door and reaches in. 'Take this.' He hands her a long black headscarf.

'Thank you, Adnan.'

He gives a slight bow. '*Allah ma'kun*.' God go with you.

He remains standing by the gate as they drive away. Away from her house and all her things – her plates and silver, her shoes and paintings, all the things she's not able to take.

'Mummy!'

'What? What is it?'

'Mummy, stop!'

'Whatever for?'

'Rex. We forgot Rex!'

'For goodness' sake.'

'But Mummy.'

'Adnan will look after him. He'll take care of him till we get back.'

Lynette is kneeling on the passenger seat looking back. 'But… he doesn't even like dogs.'

They drive in silence. Doris has put on the headscarf. She hopes it's clean. It's only ten o'clock but already hot, too hot to be in a car, and certainly too hot to be wearing a headscarf, but she keeps it on. She drives towards the bridge. It's been damaged, she doesn't know how, but men are still crowding to walk across, and there are cars moving along it. When she turns onto it, she sees cars with foreigners inside; the scared faces of children peering from back windows. One of the cars has got bullet-holes along its side. As she drives across, the air stirs, a suggestion of breeze as they pass over the water. And the smell of the river.

On the other side, there are people everywhere. She turns right towards the *Shorjah*. Looting has begun in Al-Rashid Street. Shop windows are being smashed and goods carried out and packed onto trucks. There's smoke in the air. Someone calls to her to stop but she ignores them. She tells Lynette to get down, and as she drives on, the sound of crashing and smashing recedes.

As she moves from the north end of Al-Rashid Street to the south end, she looks across to the copper market. Knives are being toted, and this time she instructs Lynette to get down and cover herself with the blanket that's in the back. Two dead men are being dragged along the street on the end of ropes. Further along, as the road joins the Tigris again, rioters are swarming around the luxury Baghdad Hotel that caters to wealthy foreigners. She doesn't stop.

Queen Alia Square is a solid mass of black-haired men. She's never seen so many people in one place before. There are tanks and the canvas tops of military vans visible above the sea of heads. More placards. People cheering from windows and rooftops. She turns off and heads east, out of the city.

Lynette is staring out of the window. Doris has never been to this part of Baghdad before, not in all the years she's lived here. And why would she? These outskirts are squalid, the houses not houses at all but hovels made of mud, with sacking held down by sticks where a roof should be. What do these people do in winter? In the sweltering heat of summer? Disease must be rife. There are barefoot children running around, boys in long dirty shirts and girls with tangled hair. A bicycle with a twisted wheel leans against one of the shacks. In a doorway stand two older girls in black *abayas*. Who are these people? She's read about dams that have been built along both rivers; an English engineer called Haigh has drawn up plans to drain the southern marshes. Are these Marsh Arabs who have migrated north, or are they only poor Baghdadis?

'God almighty,' she says and drives on, crawling along one miserable road after another. Unpaved dirt roads. There's no electricity or plumbing here either, she can see that plainly enough; can smell it even more plainly. She winds up her window and tells Lynette to do the same. But even through closed windows she can hear men calling excitedly to one another, and the unbearable high-pitched trilling sound that Arab women make in celebration. News of what's happening has reached here too, then.

The road widens and the hovels grow few and far between. She's nearly out of the city when two men waving their arms run in front of the car and she's forced to brake. One of them has a rifle. They're shouting at her in Arabic but she doesn't know what they're saying. The older man, the one with the gun, is wearing trousers and an old jacket over his shirt, and has a *keffiyeh* wrapped and knotted around his head. The other man is young and bare-headed, wearing a long *dishdasha* that was, once upon a time, white. He runs over, flings open the car door and – shouting – gestures to her to get out.

She turns off the engine and gets out. The boy (for he can't be more than twenty years old) is wearing flip-flops and his feet are filthy. He goes to the passenger side and makes Lynette get out too. She runs round the car and Doris draws her close. They stand with their bodies pressed against each other, their backs to the car.

There's an exchange between the two men and the young one opens the boot. He pulls out the suitcases and drops them onto the ground.

'*Iftahun*,' orders Keffiyeh man. Doris knows what that means – 'open them' – but the younger one doesn't need prompting; he has already opened her suitcase and is rummaging through her clothes.

'What do you want?' she asks, even though it's perfectly obvious what they're after. Money, jewellery, anything they can sell. And even with a gun being waved about, she wants to yell at the boy to stop, because he's flinging her things out into the road; her shirts and underwear and beautiful silk dresses falling into the dust. But she bites her tongue and he carries on until he's satisfied there's nothing of value there. Not to him anyway. The shameful Western clothes of an infidel woman are of no use to him.

Keffiyeh man goes over and opens Lynette's small suitcase. The barrel of his rifle noses among her things, and when he pushes the clothes to one side, there at the bottom of the suitcase is paper: Graham's sheet music. The man snarls something, she's not sure to whom. The hands gripping the rifle are broad and rough.

The younger one pushes past her, leans into the car and grabs her handbag off the driver's seat. Opening it, he tips it upside down so all its contents fall out. Her purse. Her compact. Cigarettes. He picks up the purse and pokes inside, removes the money and pockets it. Then he tosses the purse to the ground. There is more money – most, in fact – in the bag with her jewellery, but he's not to know that.

He checks the back seat and finds the bags of food. She sees him eat a date and take a bite from a loaf of bread. Still chewing, he takes out the bags, goes round to the passenger side of the car and checks the glove compartment – *Don't try to lift the seat. Don't* – but emerges empty-handed.

Lynette is standing with her arms at her side. She looks as calm as if she were at school, lining up for an inspection by the nuns.

Keffiyeh man says something to her. She answers in Arabic and he looks at her, intently, as if he's trying to work her out. She sounds just like one of them, thinks Doris. Her daughter, like one of them.

The younger man speaks now, a stream of Arabic as he jabs a finger at her and Lynette. He wants to kill them, thinks Doris. He's found nothing in the car and now he wants them dead. They might be killed out here, in this godforsaken place where no one will ever find them.

She steps to the open car door. 'Take my jewellery,' she says. 'The lot of it.' She reaches into the car but both men start screaming at her.

'Mummy!'

She turns back again, her hands held open. 'I was just going to— ' But her words are lost in all their noise. What did they think? That she was going to get in and drive off without her daughter? Is that what they think of foreigners?

'Mummy.' Is that what Lynette thought too?

The younger man has dropped the bags of food and is trying to grab the rifle from Keffiyeh man. They tussle for a few moments before Keffiyeh man elbows the other off.

Drawing up her cuff, Doris undoes her watch – its strap woven from golden filaments finer than hair so that it twists and moves like a living thing – then fumbles beneath the headscarf and unhooks her earrings. 'Here.' She holds out watch and earrings in a shaky hand. 'Take them.'

The boy marches over, snatches them from her and retreats again.

But it's not enough. Keffiyeh man cocks the rifle.

We're going to die, thinks Doris. We're going to be murdered by these slum creatures. Because today is a day to kill and be killed. Then they'll take the car then and sell it – sell it because they can't afford to put petrol in it.

Lynette hasn't moved. Her calmness is unnerving. '*Allahu-akbar*,' she says now as Keffiyeh man points the rifle at them. '*Allahu-akbar*.'

Doris screams and grabs Lynette, hunching over her as a shot is fired. Her eyes are shut, but she hears the gun being cocked again and there's a second blast. Then a third.

With her arms pincered around her daughter, Doris' heart is like a hammer in her chest.

There are no more shots. The air rings as the gunfire dies away. And within the circle of her arms, Lynette is motionless. Lynette, who just like this city, can flip from placid to raging in an instant (*You don't care about anyone! You send them all away.*) Who stands calm as you like in the face of death.

Doris does not – cannot – open her eyes. Lynette is dead. That is the dark tunnel that stretches forward, endless, from here. Lynette is gone, and Doris' heart will break, and Leon will never forgive her.

But when she opens her eyes, Lynette is not dead. She is limp and pale, and the men are gone.

'Lynette? Darling?' She checks her over but there's no sign of injury. She keeps hold of her, propping her up against the car until the colour starts to come back to her cheeks. 'Are you all right?'

A little nod.

'Thank God.' Doris is shaking. 'Thank God.'

She helps Lynette into the back seat, gathers up their things and closes the boot. Then she gets in and starts the engine, puts the car into gear and pulls away, accelerating fast to get away from this horrible, horrible place.

She grips the wheel hard to stop her hands from shaking. A cigarette, she needs a cigarette. She tips the whole box out onto the seat next to her, takes one and lights it. Inhales composure back into her body. The bullets were fired into the air. Into the air, and not into them. All the while she keeps glancing at Lynette in the rear-view mirror. Lynette's face is slack. She looks in shock.

They pass out of the city into the open. Doris is already thinking ahead. England. Home: she wants to go home. When they get to Tehran, she can organise how to get there – a flight, a train, by car, or a combination of all three.

'What did that man say to you?' Doris asks through the smoke.

It takes Lynette a few moments to locate her voice. 'He asked me where I come from.'

'And what did you say?'

In the rear-view mirror, Lynette meets her eyes. 'I said I come from here. That Baghdad is my home.'

CHAPTER 41
45 Nursery Road

Harborne, 1958

She opens her compact, its round mirror cracked, and there's her eye, her nose, part of her mouth. On the day the compact was tipped out of her bag, she and Lynette had driven fast out of Baghdad, leaving the Tigris behind them, or else she might have tried to toss the compact into its waters, for according to Nan's pecking order of superstitions, a broken mirror brings the very worst of luck. Seven years of bad luck, in fact, unless you immediately gather up the pieces and throw them into flowing water. But Doris had already had enough bad luck by then, and she likes this compact.

Afterwards she learned more of what had happened on that day. When the prime minister allowed part of the Iraqi army, together with their ammunition, to move through Baghdad, Qasim had seized his chance. The royals were executed, and the body of the prince regent – what was left of it – strung up outside the Ministry of Defence for days. The prime minister had tried to sneak out of the city dressed as a woman, but was recognised by a grocer. He was shot, buried, dug up again and his body mutilated. Looting, violence, destruction. In the weeks that followed, a string of show trials and executions. A republic was declared. Now, they said, there will be peace.

But the city was broken, and there was no going back. Leon arranged for their house to be sold, and their furniture and other belongings to be crated up and shipped to England to furnish her new house with.

On the long drive to Tehran, Doris had tried to reconcile the city of champagne and horse races with the Baghdad of bloodshed and madness she'd just witnessed. Two entirely different faces. *Doris-Dolores-Doris-Dolores*. By the time they'd reached the border, she and Lynette had already slipped back into their previous roles, those seconds of physical closeness followed by the opening up of grief only a memory now in her body, like the place where a thorn has just been pulled out.

The train lurches, making her look up. There are houses and buildings again. They're drawing near Harborne.

Leon had offered – 'Do you want me to come with you?' – but she'd said no, and so he's somewhere in Europe instead. Spain. Or is it Portugal? Lynette is with him. Graham's boarding school is a hundred-odd miles south of where she is now. They're all so far away from one another that the strings, she suddenly thinks, may snap.

Lynette, in all probability, will be looking miserable and complaining that she misses Graham or that she misses Rex or that she wants to go home. There's no news of the dog. Such a pantomime over a dog! Even if Adnan is looking after him, Doris isn't convinced that it will make a difference. Whenever Leon went away, Rex would pine and go off his food. But she doesn't want to think about that. Such dumb devotion unsettles her.

The train slows, brakes screeching, and they come to a standstill. She walks from the railway station. How many years has she imagined lying in the grass in Cannon Hill Park while a brass band played in the bandstand or children splashed in the paddling pool, and further out, a game of cricket was being played on the pitch? But her heels click along new pavements. There are houses and shops and road signs that didn't used to be here, and the row of chestnut trees has been cut down, wiped away as though it never existed.

Her mind resists, clinging like a burr to what it once knew, a Harborne that remains suspended in time and is even now hiding somewhere: at the end of this road perhaps, or around that corner.

As she nears Nursery Road, her pace slows. This is the corner where Harry fell and broke his little finger, and there's the tree they used to collect conkers from, its roots still bulging. Mrs Johnson was found wandering up and down this stretch of road in her slippers, having forgotten yet again where she lived, and Harry had linked arms with the old woman and led her, chatting the whole way, back to her front door.

Nursery Road, when she reaches it, is more drab than she remembers, its houses smaller and more squat. It doesn't really look this way, and yet there it is. She stops outside number 45. The yew has been hacked down and pulled up and replaced by a picket fence. Behind that, in the front garden, weeds have sprung up among the remains of last year's soft and winter-rotten plants. The paint on the window ledge is flaking off and the doorstep's unscrubbed. Resisting the urge to knock, she fits the key she's kept all these years into the lock. Turns it. Slowly pushes open the door.

How can a space smell empty? Yet it does. Empty and unlived in. Exactly where it always was is the coat rack, bare now as a winter tree. There's the same old stair carpet, and the handrail that Doris' and Nan's and Grandad's and Harry's hands passed over a thousand times. All is the same and yet not the same. It's like walking through a distorting mirror.

She shuts the door behind her, and for an instant is convinced that she'll find Nan in the kitchen making suet pudding and Harry polishing his shoes ready for school in the morning. Nan will look up, her hands dusted with flour. 'There you are, Dot. You ought to have been home half an hour ago.'

A frantic feeling scrabbles up her throat, but she presses it back down. *I didn't know how to reach you*, Susan's letter had said. *I found this address among Mum's things but I don't know if you are still in Baghdad and if this will ever get to you*. By the time the letter arrived in Baghdad, the city was in mayhem. It had been forwarded, but by then Doris had already missed the funeral. She hadn't even known that Nan was ill. Pleurisy, Susan said in the letter, then complications. Something about sepsis. And that Nan had left the house to her, Doris, rather than to Susan.

Doris looks into the parlour. The mantelpiece is thick with dust. There's no furniture in the room and the pictures have been taken down, leaving pale rectangles where the floral wallpaper is still crisp and bright.

She stands at the bottom of the stairs. Up there is her bedroom, and Harry's, and Nan's. Harry's door, she can just see the corner of it, is still closed. A dead man's room. And now Nan's gone too, and Doris' love for the two of them is left chasing its own tail, for she'll never love anyone the same way, nor will anyone else ever love her in the same way. Unequivocally. In spite of.

She goes through to the kitchen. That too is as bare as a kitchen can be. She walks across the dirty floor to where the table used to be, and the dresser. There are signs of mice – in Nan's kitchen! mice! – and a leak has turned an upper corner of the wall green.

How long did Nan live like this, and why didn't she tell Doris? If she had, Doris would have sent money, would have come herself. But Nan was never one to ask for help, and chances are this was more than just lack of money. It was a surrender. Doris shivers, huddling into her coat. Thank God. Thank God she has Leon.

Poor Leon. How devastated he'd been at what happened in Baghdad. His home taken away just like that. His mother had gone to stay with relatives far from the capital (let them put up with her!) and he had to abandon his Baghdad business.

She gazes around at the kitchen. *I miss you*, she thinks, picturing Harry, and suddenly she remembers and runs her fingers along the brickwork of the fireplace. Not this one, nor this one. This one. Just as she once saw Nan do, she eases out the loose brick. Susan may have cleared the house ready for selling, but Susan didn't know about this hidey-hole.

Bending to peer inside, she extracts a small tin, inside of which are one pound and three shillings, a daguerreotype and a letter. The daguerreotype is small, a studio portrait of Nan and her sister as little girls. Doris has never seen it before but she recognises Nan from other pictures, and knows this must be the sister that died at a young age. Dressed in best frocks and with ribbons in their hair, the two sit crushed together in a single chair, holding hands and looking utterly serious. Nan never spoke of her sister. Did Doris really know Nan? Did Grandad? Or Harry? Each of them existed within their own life, and concealed what they wanted to from the others. The house is the only one that truly knew them – that held them in its pockets, that saw the way they examined themselves in the mirror, heard the conversations they had behind closed doors, and watched them as they lay dreaming in bed. The house, present all along, had been privy to every major and minor incident in their lives.

The letter in the tin box, its paper discoloured and spotted with age, has no envelope. Doris unfolds it.

My dearest Anne,

How are you all, love? Here I am still at Catterick, but better off where I am than getting on those trains. Lads set off from here to all sorts of places – the Far East, India and other countries I've scarcely heard of. The Prisoners of War keep coming too. There are thousands of them here now. They have put some to work building roads around the camp, for the place was only ever meant to be temporary. The horses keep arriving too, by their thousands. I see to them, but having to send them off again, knowing what will become of them, is enough to make a man weep. That and the smell. You cannot imagine the smell, Annie.

But that's enough of that. Did I tell you that Catterick was called Richmond Camp but they had to change it because the

Post Office kept confusing it with another Richmond down south? When I get back I shall go fishing, and sink my line in and sit there with only the sound of the water, and under it those crafty beggars avoiding my bait. That's all I want. That and to see you, Annie, and Harry, and Doris too of course.

Love to you all. Ever your

William

Staring at his name, Doris has a vague impression of a moustache, and a smell of animals and leather. All the rest is gone. She puts the things back into the hole and replaces the brick. She won't take them. This is where they belong, in this house where Nan and Grandad lived and breathed and were perhaps sometimes happy.

She looks out at the back garden that's gone to rack and ruin. She remembers a day when she and Harry left Nan at the sink scrubbing the Sunday roast tin and complaining about the quality of the soap, the brush, the tin itself, and went out into the drizzle to huddle in the shelter between the plum tree and the shed and smoke, young and with the rest of their lives ahead of them. The plum tree's bigger than it was and is leaning over, its branches on one side resting on the ground. It's in full flower, a traitor in frills. And beyond it, past the brambles and uncut grass, is the place where she once believed Awd Goggie lived. What would he see if he was watching her now? A slight woman with thinning dark hair and too-large eyes dressed in a burnt orange two-piece suit, the skirt narrow, the jacket loosely cut, with outsize buttons and a fur collar. On the other side of the dirty glass, her figure would appear blurred. Perhaps he'd mistake her for a ghost.

It's started to rain, and she puts up the umbrella she brought with her, locks the door and walks away without looking back. Number 45 is nothing more than an empty brick box now. And there are things that you have to close the door on. Like your son's face when he comes home for the holidays, thin beyond recognition. Like what happened in that slum on the outskirts of Baghdad. Like Dolores lying still as still can be in the parlour at the Back of Beyond. And Harry. Yes, there are doors you have to close just so you can carry on.

A wind has sprung up that's playing havoc with her hair, but she struggles on with the umbrella to the end of the road and then downhill, away from the green and the pub, past the row of terraced cottages and on until she reaches The Back of Beyond.

'Here's The Duchess now,' she hears Jim say, except Jim isn't here. The house has a new facade. It has net curtains, and cat shit in the tiny gravelled front garden where the rose bush used to be. Susan's children left home years ago, and she and Jim moved to be closer to his new job. They're all of them gone, Palmers and Linnets both.

Oh, why did she come back? She didn't tell Susan or Harry's widow or anyone else that she was coming. It was a last chance to see the old place, that was all; to try to locate something – an intangible, elusive something that she left behind in Harborne. But she found nothing. There's nothing to find.

At some point on the way back to the railway station, her umbrella blows inside out and she gives up and takes it down, its spokes sticking out at strange angles like broken bones. Soon her face is wet, and her hair flattened against her scalp. Rain slips in through the gap between her neck and her bedraggled fur collar and slides down her back. Most of the people she passes are wearing a Mackintosh. Why didn't she think to bring one? Or at least a hat. She'd thought an umbrella would be enough.

Ignoring the looks people are giving her, she bows her head against the wind and watches her smart shoes walk along the pavement, a little spray of water kicked up with each step. The Harborne she knows is a make-believe that never existed, and suddenly she wishes that when the Luftwaffe was flying overhead, they'd dropped a thousand bombs on it.

CHAPTER 42

Breaking into Pieces

Beirut, 1965

The water turns off. She's been waiting for Leon to come out of the shower.

As soon as the bathroom door opens, she holds it up between thumb and forefinger. 'You coward!'

A towel is wrapped around Leon's waist, and his hair is wet. He reaches to the dressing table for his glasses. Yes, let him see that she knows, that she has proof now of what's gone wrong between them.

Half an hour ago he came in as usual and they talked about exactly nothing. He asked what she'd done this morning. Had she taken a walk on the promenade? Leon does a lot of business here in Beirut, so they usually rent the same apartment not far from the beach, and even this late in the year, the weather's still warm; the climate in Beirut is wonderful. 'What time is Lynette due back?' he asked her. 'Is there wine in the fridge? Has the man been to deliver the gas bottle?'

She wanted to scream. *Why don't you put your arms around me? Why don't you kiss me?* But he'd done neither of these things. Instead he took off his shoes and placed them side by side, perfectly aligned. Then he took off his jacket and tie, unbuttoned his shirt and went in for a shower. He looked well, she thought, better than he had in a while: brown, rounded, robust. Lately he was more like his old self, laughing, cracking jokes with Lynette, leaving food out for the neighbourhood cats.

She heard the shower turn on and the splash of water like rain. When his shirt slipped off the chair, she picked it up to put in the laundry basket. Before doing so though, she pressed it to her face and inhaled. Soap, warm cloves, figs, sweat. Then, without thinking, she slipped her hand into the pocket of the jacket hanging on the chair. Empty. A single side-step and she slipped her hand into the other pocket, which was also empty – except for, nestled against the seam, something barely there, something as hard and narrow as a needle.

Hooking it with her nail, she drew it out to see. It wasn't a needle. The piece of wire was copper-coloured and turned back on itself. One side was crimped, and each of its two ends was tipped with a tiny tear-shaped drop of plastic. A kirby grip.

She doesn't wear kirby grips.

A single hairpin and the universe had come crashing down, stars clanging, constellations smashed into shards.

Now Leon's black-rimmed spectacles are on, and he's standing naked from the waist up, taking it in: her, the hairpin between her fingers, and what this means.

'You stinking bloody coward!' she says again. Coward because he's turned to another woman, because he's deceived her. 'You're a liar just like the rest of them.' Like Nan and Grandad, Susan and Harry.

The hairpin drops to the floor and she launches herself at him, all teeth and nails. He grabs her wrists as they come down but she catches him on the cheek, knocking his glasses askew.

'Dolores!' He tries to hold her off.

Wherever she touches him, his skin is damp. He yelps as she kicks him in the shin.

Beneath this Leon with his greying hair and lined face, she still sees the younger one – the fresh-faced, black-haired man, handsome as the devil, who divined the way straight to her heart.

Her stockinged feet slip on the floor. 'How could you?' She tries to free her hands, to get them close enough to hurt him. 'We stood in a church and said our vows!' She's shaking with rage. 'I almost died giving birth to your son!'

And everything else they've been through. Facing down Nan. Travelling across Europe all the way to Baghdad. The heat. His mother. Dancing. Lying with her hand on his hot chest, his heart taking its time to slow down.

He doesn't deny it, that's the thing. He can't, she knows that, because it's true. But if he'd only argue! If he'd only say that there's been a mistake, some idiotic misunderstanding. Crossed wires. *You'll laugh when I explain. Just let me explain*. But he says none of these things. On the contrary, he loosens his grip on her. Releasing her wrists, he lets his arms drop to his sides as though he's taken the decision to allow her to tear him to shreds, a just punishment for what he's done.

She batters his chest. 'You pig! I hate you! I *hate* you!'

He doesn't react, only flinches at the harder blows.

'Who is she?' Young, that's what she'll be, not on the wane like Doris. Not begun the slide into old age – because the six-year lie about her age has caught up with Doris now.

Leon remains mute.

Enraged, she slaps his arm hard, then goes in to bite him on the shoulder, leaving a red ring of teeth-marks.

That's when he comes alive again, and at last – at last! – puts his arms around her: all the way around, the way she's seen him do with Lynette. It catches her by surprise until, as he brings her into him and holds her firmly against his body, she realises that this isn't affection so much as defence.

It scarcely matters. She struggles and fights till her muscles turn to jelly. Then, slowly, the arms around her soften as well and the two of them stand propped up against each other, their raspy breathing the only sound in the room.

When did I lose you? she thinks. Because you're not an

Edward or Edwin or Whatever-His-Name-Was in Baghdad. Or the bellboy in that hotel in Rome. No. You, Leon, wouldn't have a fling. You wouldn't have meaningless sex. So when did it happen then? When did I lose you?

Slumped there with her cheek wet against his bitten shoulder, she unwinds their relationship, retreading the path of their life together. Was it when she fired Aisha, or sent Graham to boarding school, or scolded Lynette for… oh, for a thousand things? Or did it go even further back than that? Was he still hers when they arrived in Baghdad? She tries to think. When did he stop following her with his eyes, or feeling for her hand if they were standing near each other? When did he stop kissing her neck? Stop calling her *jan*? She can't think. Maybe it wasn't any one particular day, but rather a gradual change, imperceptible, like the appearance of a wrinkle.

A fly's crawling along the windowsill. Start, stop, start, stop. It flies at the glass and falls back, then tries again, not understanding how it can be that this is not the way out.

'I went to Birmingham,' says Leon

For a few moments she stops breathing. 'What?'

'One time when I went to visit Graham, I travelled to Birmingham. To Harborne.' The words form slowly. 'I went to see your grandmother.'

She doesn't move, but pressed up against him this way, Leon must be able to feel the quickening of her heart.

He shifts and braces himself as if he's about to pick up something heavy. 'She told me. About your mother. And your sister.'

She detaches herself from him. Steps back. It's all there in his face: he knows everything, every last shred of it.

It's as though, stripped of clothes and with his body scrubbed clean, he can finally be honest. 'You stole her name.' It sounds so matter-of-fact when he says it. She stole her sister's name, in much the same way as you might take a handkerchief.

'When?' Her voice is strangled. 'When did you see her?' Nan's been dead nine years!

He looks tired now. 'Does it matter? A long time ago.'

Nine years? Ten? Even longer ago? All this time, he's known. And Nan never told her, never wrote of any visit. Was she ashamed of her role in the whole thing? Or was she just ashamed of the lies Doris told? Lies, lies, always lies.

She gazes at Leon, trying to see into his thoughts. Part of her expects him to start ranting and shouting as though he'd just now found it out. 'Didn't it matter?' she whispers. 'About my family? My name?'

He bends down towards her as though explaining things to a child. 'Of course it mattered. All these years I did not know the truth about my own wife. Not even her name.'

How is it then that she can't recall a change in him at any point that would have suggested he'd found it out? Unless... unless after all it hadn't surprised him that she'd lied, or that she wasn't who she said she was. Because that lie is woven into the very cells of her; is part and parcel of who she is. In that sense, it is no longer a lie.

'Why, Dolores? Why did you do it?'

What should she say? *Because I wanted you to see me differently. I wanted to possess her softness, her capability, her serenity. Nan's angel. The girl everybody loved.* But she says none of this. It's not what she wants to talk about right now. 'Is that why you...?' She bites her lip hard, unable to finish the sentence. 'How long has it been going on?'

'A while.'

'How long?' she asks, louder.

'Two years. Nearly three.'

It takes some moments to absorb this. 'You mean whenever you had business here.' Leon's way of working has had to change. He doesn't have an office or warehouses any longer, but now arranges the movement and sale of goods between traders in different countries. To do this he travels extensively, and she and Lynette go with him, or sometimes follow at a slower pace. They stay in various cities for days or weeks or even months at a time. Like nomads. Like Bedouin. 'Did you have business? Or did you come here just to see her?'

He rubs his forehead, the skin moving beneath his fingers.

'Well?'

He shakes his head. 'I do not want to talk about her.'

Her hands ball into fists. 'Well, *I* want to talk about her.'

'She is not relevant.'

Doris has never felt less like laughing, yet she laughs. 'Not *relevant!*'

'No. It is not her that is the problem. It is us.' He goes to the dresser, drops his towel and takes out clean underwear. He puts the underwear on, then puts on his trousers and pulls on a clean shirt. 'Our whole marriage' – fitting one button after another into its slit – 'has been based on lies. You not telling me the truth, and me not seeing what was in front of my eyes.'

'Wait, what do you mean, not seeing? What's that got to do with my name, for heaven's sake?'

He stops buttoning and looks up. 'Do you remember that day in the snow?'

'What snow?'

'In Harborne. That day it snowed.'

He doesn't need to elaborate any further. It's one of those days that glitters in the memory, easily found, jewel-coloured and busy with detail. She and Leon are still young, still laughing, still newly in love. And that elated feeling inside her, mimicking the dancing snowflakes.

'Do you remember the child?'

She doesn't answer. What is he talking about?

'A little boy. He had fallen. He fell – do you remember?'

She remembers. That's right... yes that's right, some clumsy child had run smack bang into her and she'd told him off. 'Yes,' she says, and she has the sudden feeling, inexplicable, that something is wrong – like fitting the wrong key into a lock, or taking a cake out of the oven that's about to sink in the middle.

'You remember it.'

'Yes, I remember,' she snaps. 'He ran into me, what of it? What on earth's that got to do with anything?' She's affronted. Fancy that being the thing he remembers! That and not how gloriously happy they were that day. How that was the day they first slept together.

'Were you angry?' he asks quietly. 'When the boy ran into you.'

A noose is tightening. 'I... I don't know. Why?'

'Were you?'

'I said I don't know! How am I supposed to remember that?'

He doesn't take his eyes from her. 'Try.'

She swallows. Thinks. 'All right then, yes. He ripped my stockings. He covered me in snow, I remember that.'

Leon's shoulders sag.

'But darling, what does it matter now whether I was angry or not all those years ago? What in heaven's name does it matter?' She raises her hands to her temples. She doesn't understand what's going on.

Leon's head lolls forward. His voice has shrunk. 'I thought you were comforting him. Helping him.' Outside, a dustbin truck is doing its rounds. A rev then a pause, followed by the clatter of metal bins. 'I saw you holding a child and I thought it was kindness. I thought... I thought it was love of children. But it was not that.'

There's a tightness in her chest.

'I saw it wrong. It was not that at all.' His voice catches. He raises his head again. 'Maybe that was only what I wanted to believe. And I imagined how it would all happen after that – how we would be happy and you would love being a mother and...' He trails off, a hundred unfulfilled possibilities filling the room.

'Wait, what are you saying? Are you saying that your love for me was based on a trick of the eyes?' The words *trompe l'œil* pop into her head. A blanket of snow, tricksy light, a mesh of falling flakes. *Got you*, they seem to say. *Got you*.

'I look at it again now, all these years later, and I can see how it really was. But I fell in love with you. In that moment I saw a nurturing, compassionate woman helping a little boy who had fallen. You were amazing, that is what I thought. Like a diamond. Like a star.'

She can scarcely breathe for the lump in her throat, the howling in her head. 'But it was a big misunderstanding?' Like receiving a present that when you open it isn't what you expected; nor in fact what you wanted. Still, you ought to have known from the shape of the damned thing! From its weight, the feel of it in your hands. 'And now you don't love me any more, is that what you're saying?' She can't comprehend it. That their life together has hinged around a single moment in the snow.

He turns away and finishes doing up his shirt.

She remembers it all now. How she thought that Leon had seen her – really seen her, all sides of her – that day, and still found her worth loving. Were they both mistaken then? Him, for thinking her anger was compassion, and her for believing that he'd seen what she was and loved her in spite of it. Dear God, was their entire relationship founded on a misunderstanding?

'Answer the bloody question!' she yells, although she'd do anything for him not to answer, not to say it. Her head is spinning. The snow, that child. That was the moment Leon fell in love with her, and also the moment he fell out of love with her. How can they be the same moment? 'You should have run back to your mother and let her choose a nice Armenian girl for you. Yes, that's what you should have done. A nice girl to cook and clean and smile and squeeze out one child after another without a word of complaint.'

He turns back round to face her. 'I did not see how things really were. Who you really were. I should have seen, and that is my fault not yours.'

‘Oh, you’re pathetic!’ Yes, pathetic in shouldering the guilt when she’s the one who deserves all the blame. And cunning too, because it gives her no option to retaliate.

He’s putting on his socks and shoes now. ‘It is over, Dolores. We both know that. It was over long ago.’

Was it already doomed on that snowy afternoon, before it had even begun? Out in the Beirut street, someone’s laughing. Another person joins in. Life is carrying on, except that it’s not. She hears Grandad’s voice, clear as a bell: *It’s all breaking into pieces, Dot. The whole world is breaking into pieces.*

Leon picks up his watch from the dressing table, winds it and puts it on, arm held against his stomach as he does up the black leather strap. He picks up his jacket.

‘Where are you going?’ She follows him into the living room. The light has changed, afternoon moving towards evening. ‘Are you going to meet *her*?’

He puts on his jacket.

‘Well? Are you?’ She crosses the space between them. ‘Don’t,’ she pleads, taking hold of his arm. ‘Don’t go.’

He grabs her with such force that for a moment she doesn’t believe it’s Leon. His fingers press painfully into her flesh. ‘I have lost too many years. Too many, do you understand?’ He lets go of her with a jolt.

There’s a frantic knocking against her ribs. ‘But I love you.’

They stand looking at one another. Then he shakes his head. ‘I do not understand your love.’ The syllables pierce her body like little knives.

She wants to close the space between them, dig her nails into him and cling on like a raptor to its prey, but instead she goes to the coffee table and tips a cigarette out of its pack. She flicks open the lid of a silver lighter and lights the cigarette. Inhaling sharply, she holds the smoke in her lungs, then lets it cloud out into the room. ‘All right, suit yourself.’ Head up, she thinks. Stomach in. ‘Go if you like.’

As soon as the door closes, she mashes out the cigarette and brings both hands up to her face; holds her features together. When she takes her hands away again, she sees a bottle of her perfume on the sofa. She picks it up and hurls it at the front door. It misses and hits the wall instead, shattering and leaving a splash of wetness and, a moment later, the scent of her – only too strong, heady, almost overpowering.

She drops onto the sofa and a cavity opens up in her chest, vast and black. On the shelf beside her is a framed photograph of her and Leon, the very first picture they ever had taken together. It had been a drizzly day in Birmingham city centre and the photographer, ginger-haired with a big moustache, had seated her in a chair and placed Leon behind her with one hand on her shoulder. And oh, Leon is so painfully young, so very beautiful. And so serious! It makes her want to laugh because he's never looked so severe in his entire life. And herself – dark lipstick, and her chin tipped down so her eyes look especially large beneath the cloche hat. She's wearing a woollen coat with cloth-covered buttons done up to the neck. She can still remember how, even through her coat, the weight of Leon's hand made her tingle.

She gets up. 'Wait!' she calls at the closed door, as if Leon might still be standing on the other side of it. She finds her shoes and opens the door. 'Wait!'

CHAPTER 43

I've Got My Love to Keep Me Warm

Harborne, 1938

They've come outside to catch their breath. According to Nan, dancehalls are places designed to encourage drunkenness and ruin girls. This one's the sort of place that makes your skull ring. Where after a few drinks, nerves ebb away and sparks begin to fly between men and women. Where, as the evening wears on, faces turn pink and shiny with exercise, and there's a thick smell of sweat and perfume.

She and Leon have danced all evening, moving in time, with his hand on the small of her back. They danced to 'Minnie the Moocher' and 'Puttin' on the Ritz'. They danced to 'Nice Work if You Can Get It' and Noël Coward's 'Some Day I'll Find You', and she felt the way Leon moved, and kept imagining the body beneath his suit. All in all, she knows everything she needs to about him: that he moves well, that he's a good man and that he will put her above everything.

Standing under a lamppost, they light cigarettes. For six nights a month – four before a full moon and two after – the lamps remain unlit, but the full moon has waned so the lamplighters have been round and left a line of stars down the street. Out here the music's fainter. Leon hums along (he can't hear a tune without humming along to it), but when she starts to shiver he props his cigarette in his mouth, slips off his jacket and wraps it around her shoulders. She huddles into the warmth it still contains of him.

‘Soon we will freeze,’ he says, hunching his shoulders. ‘They will find us out here like statues, with the cigarettes still in our hands.’

She laughs. ‘Why do you smoke if you don’t like it?’

Leon shrugs. ‘To keep you company.’ And the end of his cigarette glows orange as he takes another drag.

She inhales the sharp night air. ‘They say there’s going to be a war. That it can’t be avoided any longer.’ Vaguely, she remembers the last war; recalls Nan sitting in the parlour with a letter crushed in her hand, and later, returning soldiers walking down the street like scarecrows. But she won’t think about that. What’s the point? She drops her cigarette to the ground. ‘But you’ll probably be gone by then – back home I mean.’ Only a few short months and Leon will graduate, pack his bags and leave.

He’s a slower smoker than her. ‘We could leave together.’

Her stomach hitches sideways. Does he mean…? Oh God. But she mustn’t assume, perhaps she’s got it wrong.

‘Together?’

He extinguishes his cigarette butt against the lamppost and turns to her. ‘Marry me, Dolores, that is what I mean.’

How many times has this moment played itself out in her mind? Granted, Leon isn’t on his knees; he isn’t flushed or nervous, nor is he making plans to remain in England. He’s standing quite quietly, looking down at her and waiting.

‘You mean, go to Baghdad with you?’ This she’s tried to imagine too, but never with any success.

Leon replies with a single nod.

Even if she can’t imagine it, why shouldn’t she go? Does she enjoy getting dressed as fast as she can every morning in a race with the cold? Or eating a breakfast of cooling porridge? Does she enjoy being an exile in her own family, and seeing blazing out of that entire tribe an undying love for someone dead? A love that ought to belong to her. Here she is hemmed in like a penny trapped in the lining of an overcoat.

And she loves Leon. Although ‘love’ is a silly, insufficient word. There *is* no word for what she feels: that she wants to be with him, near him always. That she's astounded, shaken out of her orbit because he also wants to be with her – unlike Susan; or Nan and Harry who had no choice in the matter. If she marries Leon, he'll always be there to look after her, to keep her fed and housed and loved. Always. That is the contract he's offering.

If she says no, she'll go back home to suet pastry and boiled tongue, to the wireless on a Saturday evening, and Nan who never laughs any more. In the garden of 45 Nursery Road, the plum tree will grow fresh leaves every spring and shed them again every autumn, and she, Doris, will grow old and end up alone like poor Miss Ibbs. If she says no, all she'll have left of Leon will be memories, static and unchanging.

'Dolores?' He takes her face in his hands as though he's keeping her from drowning.

'Yes,' she says. 'Yes.'

CHAPTER 44

Mirror

Beirut, 1965

Outside their building she looks left and right. Two suited men in white *keffiyehs* go by, deep in conversation. A scooter buzzes past, the girl's hair flapping around her shoulders, her miniskirt showing tanned, shapely legs. Then it's quiet again.

Beyond this peaceful residential street, Beirut is the envy of the Middle East. A cosmopolitan city, its seafront is strung with five-star hotels where bikini-clad women sun themselves beside pools. Sparrows twitter in the tall pines and shoe-shine boys rest beneath striped shop awnings. Trams trundle past Parliament Square market, and in nearby Hamra Street, university students smoke and quarrel in cafes. Domed mosques bulge out of the skyline, while roadside shrines to this or that saint overflow with flowers. Later, as the sea walls begin to glow in the evening sun, there are cocktails at the Hotel St. George; and at nightfall the city will light up with music and restaurants, nightclubs and casinos.

She pictures it on a map, this tiny country crushed so tight between its neighbours that its land has heaved and folded into mountains that rear up past the snow line. Skiing and sunbathing: no wonder the people here are always cheery. What do they know about suffering?

A bell jangles. The door of a little shop nearby opens and closes, and her heart leaps as Leon comes out, but he doesn't see her and heads the other way. What did he go in there for? He sometimes buys nougat, which he likes. Or perhaps it was something for *her*. That woman. Chocolate or a pack of cigarettes, the brand she prefers above others.

But what does it matter? What does it matter? She starts after him.

Leon turns a corner and walks down the next street, away from the sea. She follows. He passes a bookshop, a grocer's with a mound of oranges outside and a group of men in fezzes drinking coffee and smoking *nargils*. Then he crosses Clemenceau Avenue and carries on towards Sanayeh Garden. She knows it well, a square of trees and grass and flower beds with benches along the paths and old men playing backgammon in the shade.

Leon heads towards the large fountain in the centre. It's a pleasant evening, the sky clear and the air warm. Doris is stuck on a path behind a woman with three young children, and when she manages to get past them, Leon has already reached the fountain, walked round it to the far side, and is no longer alone. In front of him is a woman.

Doris would know Leon any which way, whether seen from above or below, from the side or, as now, from behind. Instantly she'd recognise the lie of his hair, the turn of his ear, the angle of his shoulders and set of his arms. She'd recognise them because he's hers. The woman, on the other hand, is one she's never clapped eyes on before. She's about Doris' height, but plumper and fairer. Younger too, in her early or mid-forties perhaps. Keeping them in her sights, Doris assesses the woman's qualities: her backside (large), her legs (not bad), her hair (honey-blonde and thick, held up in a French twist), her clothes (pencil skirt and matching jacket, beige with red piping) and shoes (light brown heels).

Arm in arm, this woman and Leon set off, and Doris follows. You can tell plenty about two people from behind, it turns out. You can tell that they've known each other a long time, and that they're comfortable in each other's company. You can tell that they like being close to each other. In the way they touch one another and tilt their head towards the other as they talk, you can sense affection. You can tell that your husband is smiling – yes, smiling, even after the scene you and he have just had – at this fat-rumped woman. Because there's no denying she's fat – or plump at any rate. Fleshy. And after all these years of Doris watching what she ate.

They've stopped outside a restaurant. Are they considering having dinner? Or maybe only drinks. She waits for them to go in but Leon says something, his hand on the woman's elbow, and they carry on walking.

As she follows, Doris realises that she hasn't got her handbag with her, only the key to the apartment grasped warm in her palm. She follows them until they stop outside the front door of an apartment building. They go in, and the door clangs shut behind them. A minute or two later, the lights in the second-floor apartment turn on.

It's dark by the time she gets back to the flat, and there's nobody there. Leon's with that woman, and Lynette is out with a young man she's met – an Arab, as if that'll be allowed to go anywhere. Aglow in a white dress, her black hair heavy and glossy, he picked her up earlier to go dancing, and she won't be back till late. Doris turns on the light and kicks off her shoes. She stands in the living room for a time, then goes into the kitchen and turns on the light there, as if that might reveal something new. Into the bedroom next, where she sits heavily on the bed. Hauling up her legs, she lies down. She's tired, so tired. She slides Leon's pyjamas out from under his pillow and presses them to her face. Don't think about what they might be doing. Don't. And don't think about the days he left early or came back late. Or the trips he made to Beirut without you.

She turns over. Does that slut know Leon's body? Has she touched his bare skin? Run her hands over his shoulders and down his arms? Touched his hip-bones? Woven her fingers between his? And what about him? Does he marvel at skin that hasn't yet begun to wrinkle? Does he lift that honey-coloured hair in his hand and enjoy its weight? Does he compare their eyes, their legs, their breasts? He must, surely, and one must come out the winner, because there's always a winner.

She wonders what they talk about. Assuming of course that they talk at all and don't just go at it like animals. Does he tell that woman things he doesn't tell Doris? Things he thinks and feels and hopes and dreams. Has he told her about Graham and Lynette? About Doris? Is that what they talk about? No, he wouldn't. He wouldn't.

She turns over again. Perhaps they listen to music together, the woman reaching for the dial on the radio. It'll fizz and crackle, then snag on a tune she likes. Then they'll lie back on the sofa, his arms around her, to listen. He'll hum along the way he always used to, and she'll place her hand on his chest and feel the thrum of his voice.

But Leon belongs to Doris! All the way from the soles of his feet to the crown of his head, he's hers. Didn't he stand in a chapel and proclaim it? Sitting up, she flings his pyjamas to the floor, stands and stamps and kicks at them until they get tangled round her ankles.

She gulps in deep breaths. There's nothing of his left on the dresser so she flings the wardrobe door open. Inside, inhabiting a small fraction of space in comparison to her own clothes, his shirts hang quivering on their hangers, cool and clean; two pairs of trousers and a jacket. An impersonal lot. Below them though, pushed into a corner, is a pair of shoes whose leather has been warped and shaped by his feet, the bottoms worn down in just those places where his gait exerts most pressure.

She goes to the kitchen and returns with a large pair of scissors. Sits on the bed with a shoe in her lap like a dog. First the laces. They fall off easily enough, but the rest is too robust; requires a knife, the serrated one from the kitchen.

It's slower than she'd have liked, but hacking and sawing first one shoe then the other finally does the job, and when it's done there's something absurdly satisfyingly about the sight of them, all tattered and ruined. He can't put his feet into them now, can he? Can't walk in them. Can't walk away.

She pours herself a whisky from the drinks cabinet. She doesn't like whisky but that's part of the appeal: she doesn't want anything pleasant. She winces as she swallows it down, then pours a second, but nothing changes. In the fruit bowl is a single overripe banana flecked with brown. She can smell it. She looks down at her hand on the counter, its painted nails; looks at her feet, the big toe beginning to bend inwards from years of wearing heels. Leon doesn't want such toes. Can they be unbent, she wonders absently, or are they beyond repair like his shoes?

I do not understand your love.

She pours more whisky and empties the glass. Her throat burns. Is her love really so alien? She pictures a small stunted thing that bites whenever it's approached. 'Damn you,' she says to Nan and Susan. 'Why couldn't you have taught me what to do?' Because there's a knack to loving that it was their duty to teach her, like how to roll pastry or starch a collar. They never did though. Many things were never said or done.

The light in the bathroom hurts her eyes. The bath is still wet from Leon's shower. A touch unsteadily, she positions herself in front of the mirror. The light is so harsh, so unflattering. But she must look.

Her eyebrows are the first things she notices, balanced on her face like a pair of displaced brackets. In her youth she plucked them so fiercely that at some point they stopped growing back and now have to be pencilled in each morning. Beneath them are her cow's eyes. Beneath those, lips that are too thin. And then there's her hair. Her poor hair! Once upon a time Leon said nice things about her hair, but that was before it began to fall out and clog the drain. She started to wear hairpieces, which was the fashion, attached by an Alice band or clipped on as a bun or a ponytail. That was before things got worse.

She undoes the metal clips behind her ears and drags off her wig. Dropping it on the floor, she takes off the grip band. Her hair is thin and has been flattened against her head by the weight of the wig, but even so her scalp is visible all over. She looks at the shaggy thing on the floor, tinted red but too stiff and thick to look real. When she looks in the mirror again, the sight makes her want to weep. This is what she's become, and Leon knows it because she can't sleep with her wig on. Her dress, white with a large geometric print in pink and mustard, the makeup and jewellery, clothes and handbags, perfume and poses have all been fake. This is what she really is.

She senses it first, a soft-edged presence at her shoulder, and then she's there, clear as day, reflected in the mirror behind Doris. Dolores. Her skin is still fresh, her hair still glossy and her blue eyes full of sympathy.

Dolores has been alive in Doris' mind for so many years that she isn't entirely surprised to see her. 'You'd have made him happy, wouldn't you?' she says. 'He'd never have left you.' Dolores is the sort of woman you'd want as your wife. And if you were a child, the sort of woman you'd want as your mother.

She wipes her eyes, dragging mascara across her face. Dolores is still there, watching her.

'If only I could have been more like you.' She turns to look Dolores in the face then, but when she does, the bathroom's empty. 'Dolores?'

White tiles. A water-specked bathtub. She turns back to look in the mirror, but there's only herself.

CHAPTER 45

Facts

Beirut, 1965

She doesn't understand, not really. She understands the facts, of course, but that's not the same thing at all.

She understands that it was night-time: this is one of the facts. It was late. Or early, depending how you look at it. Leon left the woman's flat, leaving her asleep in bed, and walked out into the cool Mediterranean night air. He didn't take a taxi. Perhaps he couldn't find one, or maybe he was enjoying the feel of the fresh air against his face, his throat. In any case he started to walk. Another fact: he was heading in the direction of their apartment – his and Doris'. And it was somewhere between one apartment and the other that it happened.

He undid the top button of his shirt, she imagines. But it didn't help. A woman walking past with her husband gave him a strange look, perhaps. Then, half a minute or so later, he crashed to the pavement.

Lying there, he must have heard laughter and music coming from nearby Phoenicia Street with its bars and nightclubs. As the blurred circles of street lamps and car headlights floated and bobbed around him, he may have been confused about what was happening. Or it could be that he only heard, for an instant, his mother's voice calling him in to dinner the way she used to when he was a boy.

It's early. The new day is just beginning to bleach the sky, and there's a flush of pink on the horizon. Her wig is back on, but she's wearing no makeup and has a crashing headache.

A doctor with the thickest eyelashes she's ever seen on a man takes her into an empty room at the end of the corridor and closes the door.

'Your husband had a heart attack,' he says gently in good English.

She can hear her own heart beating in her ears. Her head is throbbing. 'Where?' she asks, as if it mattered, and he tells her that too.

She swallows. 'Was he alone?'

'Yes.'

Standing, because she declined to sit down when he offered her a chair, she sways. He brings the chair over and positions it so that when her knees give – which they do – it's there to catch her. Like a game of trust. Falling backwards into waiting arms – only there are no arms, just a hard plastic chair.

In a daze, she waits for more. For the doctor to tell her how they resuscitated Leon; how he's now hooked up to monitors but resting comfortably; how she'll be able to see him soon.

'Where is he?'

The doctor frowns. 'I am afraid…' He shakes his head – slowly, as if in here no fast movements are permitted – and the air turns thin and pinched, like it was when she was skiing high up in the Swiss mountains.

'What do you mean?'

When he says the words, the room pitches and tilts.

'No. You're wrong. It can't be him. He… he didn't have a heart condition.' Perfectly healthy men don't just keel over for no good reason.

Nevertheless, that's what has happened, he says. He adds that he's sorry, as though it were his doing.

She shakes her head. 'But…' Her hands are shaking too. Her handbag has slipped to the floor. 'I don't understand.'

There's a sink in the corner of the room and he fetches her a glass of water. Do they keep glasses in here, she wonders, for exactly this sort of situation? She takes the glass, even though she isn't thirsty. How can water possibly help?

She can't think, her thoughts are all jumbled up. This doctor's telling her that her husband is dead, and yet only a few hours ago Leon was standing in their bedroom with a towel wrapped round him, still wet from the shower. He was putting on his glasses and telling her he didn't understand her sort of love. 'Are you sure?' she asks. 'Are you sure that the man is my husband?'

The doctor is certain. Saying that he'll be right back, he leaves the room. When he returns, he has Leon's keys and wallet. 'These are your husband's?'

Her throat contracts. He takes the glass of water away and hands over Leon's things, along with a small navy velvet box, the sort a ring might be kept in.

'This…?'

'It was in his pocket.'

Another blow. He must have bought it for that woman. Spent his money on jewellery for *her*, the one responsible for all of this.

Doris can't open it. And yet… She blinks, trying to understand. If this was intended for that woman, and Leon spent the evening and night in her flat, then why hadn't he already given it to her? She fingers the box. Surely it can't be for herself? Over the years, Leon has bought her enough jewellery, God knows, but now… *It is over, Dolores. It was over long ago.*

Her dress has cradled around the wallet and keys in her lap. Slowly, she raises the box's lid. As suspected, it is jewellery, but not a ring. Inside the box is a pair of earrings. And she has seen these earrings before.

It takes her a few seconds to place them. A shop window three days ago. Lynette touching Leon's arm – 'Aren't they beautiful?' This addressed to Leon, because he's the only one she talks to. Doris usually finds things out indirectly.

Who will Lynette talk to now, Doris wonders? Nobody

perhaps; and then all the things she'd have told Leon will gather like grain in a silo, heavy and pressing against her sides.

'We did everything we could,' says the doctor.

'Was Leon… was he already dead when the ambulance got there?'

It takes a moment for the doctor to reply. 'No. But by the time he reached the hospital.'

She looks up. 'Didn't the ambulance men help him?' Her voice is choked. 'Couldn't they have done something?'

'He needed to be in a hospital, and…' The doctor looks away.

'And what? Did they take too long to get there?' They were asleep perhaps. Do ambulance men sleep at night? 'Is that it?' She's getting angry. As if that will change anything.

'They left as soon as the phone call came. But yes,' he concedes, 'that was some time after your husband suffered the heart attack.'

'I don't understand.'

The doctor doesn't meet her eye. He says something she can't quite catch.

'What's that? What did you say?'

He clears his throat. 'The people who saw him, they did not realise. They thought… they thought that he was intoxicated.'

Intoxicated! They thought Leon was lying drunk in the street? She imagines strangers veering around him, giving him a wide berth, disgusted at such a thing.

Although she's no longer looking at him, she hears the doctor breathe out. 'I am sorry.'

CHAPTER 46

Cemetery

Beirut, 1965

Sitting in the cemetery, Doris tells Leon everything that's happened, just as though they were catching up at the end of a day spent apart. The weather has turned and it's overcast. There's no one else here. All around her is white marble: marble graves, marble headstones, marble crosses. Attached to the top of some of the graves are little box-like shelters where a lit candle can be placed. This may be an Armenian custom, she's not sure, because this, the Armenian cemetery, is where Leon has been buried. She'd insisted on it, and after much wrangling (and a not insubstantial donation to the church), had succeeded. It's what he would have wanted. Probably.

'And Lynette,' she says aloud. Dear God, Lynette. Telling her had been a ghastly job. *He's dead. Daddy's dead.* By then the word had lost its meaning; Doris might as well have been saying 'He's hungry' or 'He's asleep' or 'He's over there.' As soon as the words were spoken, though, the colour drained out of Lynette's face, and she was so utterly still, and remained that way for so long, that Doris thought perhaps the words had turned her to stone. Those particular words, she is well aware, carry the power of armies.

Lynette stood like a pillar of salt. The tears and screaming and vomiting came afterwards.

It was easier to tell Graham, over the telephone where she couldn't see his face; easier not to know how he looked or what he did after he hung up. He has finished university and started a job in London, but flew out for the funeral.

She tells Leon about that too: about his funeral. How the priest droned on and on. Then the prayers and songs, not a word of which she could understand. She tells him how Lynette refused to go into the church or see the body. That standing outside the church with her black hair and a black dress on, she looked pale as pale can be, except for her red, swollen eyes.

'I left her outside, I had to.' She wipes the top of the headstone, even though there's no dirt on it. 'She misses you so much. Already. So much.'

Back in the apartment, the perfume Doris hurled at the wall has left a smell that can't be got rid of.

'Were you on your way home?' she whispers, her hand still on the headstone. 'Did you realise that after all it was me you loved?' And then, his poor heart. She sees Leon's deep chest again, its rough covering of hair, the warm olive skin.

She has travelled from one end of her life to the other only to find herself in a graveyard again. And yet this couldn't be more different. Underfoot and all around, everything is hard stone. Here there's nothing to signal the arrival of spring, or of autumn; no grass or yew tree, no mud or scurrying blackbird.

'I won't leave you, you know.' She sees their house in England – its large rooms, the French windows opening onto a garden on the very banks of the Thames, complete with weeping willows and a landing stage. It's already furnished with their things from Baghdad, as well as new furniture which she's bought, but apart from the occasional visit, it's been sitting empty all these years. On first returning to England, she had expected a sort of contentment, the kind you associate, in stories at least, with homecoming. She had expected to settle there. That, after all, is what she'd wanted. But England had moved on without her. She was a pear on an apple tree, a goose in a duck pond. 'Anyway, there's nobody left over there.' Lebanon, this strange little country that's neither East nor West, can supply her with everything she needs, and so she will stay here, close to Leon.

Although there are a few headstones engraved in Arabic, the majority here are, like Leon's, engraved with Armenian letters. As the first fat drops of rain begin to fall, Doris stands in front of the square of stone that her husband has now become and gazes at the black, inscrutable marks. 'I forgive you,' she says.

And then she tells him her plan. Because she knows, doesn't she, where the fat-rumped woman lives. And there's not a thing now that Leon can do to stop her.

CHAPTER 47

Not from Round Here

Harborne, 1938

'Are you out of your mind?' They're in the garden, where Nan is unpegging laundry. Above them the sky is a metallic grey.

Stay calm, she tells herself. Remain gracious. 'I've thought it through,' she says, 'and that's that.'

A sudden gust, and Nan's enveloped in a half-hung sheet. She yanks it off the line and stuffs it unfolded into the basket, its edges catching the mud. Nan never treats clean linen this way. 'You will do no such thing, Doris Palmer.'

The one time that Doris went along with Bill to the slaughterhouse and waited outside, she saw, in the gloom of the warehouse, a lamb running for the open door then tipping forward as it was caught by the tail. Its legs continued to make running motions as it was hauled back inside into the dark. This is what it feels like now: that Nan is trying to hold her fast and keep her from running forward into her life.

But Nan shan't stop her. 'I certainly will marry him if I want to. And I do want to.' Leon. He warms every part of her, inside and out, like a sun.

'But he's not an Englishman! Nor a Scot, or a Welshman, or even an Irishman! He's not even white!'

She swallows; shivers because she's come out here without her coat. 'Of course he is. Of course he's white.' Isn't he?

Nan's eyes are glittering. Is this what an announcement

of marriage does? 'He's a foreigner! You don't know what they're like.'

For a moment Doris has a sense of something repeating itself, but like gossamer the idea floats away before she can catch hold of it. 'I know what Leon's like,' she says, but Nan isn't listening.

'What will people say?'

It's Doris' turn to be angry. 'I couldn't give a hoot!' Nan's values are straight out of the ark.

'You don't know what you're letting yourself in for, my girl.' Nan waves the peg in her hand at Doris as she speaks. 'People like that are... are feckless!'

Feckless is a word Doris has never heard Nan use before. It catches her by surprise.

'Good-for-nothings.' The peg in Nan's hand stabs the air. 'He knows he's onto a good thing, that's what – marrying into a respectable English family.'

Doris laughs out loud, she can't help it. 'Respectable? Oh please! Let's not talk about respectable.'

Nan gives an indignant sniff, then her expression changes. She gives Doris a once-over. 'You're not in trouble, are you?'

'Trouble?' Leon's cold room, the heat of their naked bodies pressed together. Nan has never discussed sex, as though not discussing it might prevent it from ever happening. 'No!'

Nan lets out her held breath. 'Well then.' There follows a tirade. Words fly around the garden, combative yet low enough so the neighbours can't hear. How could Doris do this? A foreigner from God only knows where. And exactly how long has it been going on anyway? Doris is certainly a dark horse, keeping it to herself all this time, that's for sure. And what would Grandad say?

Again, Doris laughs, releasing the tightness that's been building in her during Nan's speech. She has scarcely any memory left of Grandad. A voice singing in the bathtub, a pair of freckled arms, someone who made Harry cry. He's almost evaporated now, faded into nothing. Her laugh curls out into the winter air then falls away.

'You're to call it off, do you hear me?'

'You can't tell me who I can and can't marry.'

'But… he's going back to his own country anyway, he said so.' Tossing the peg into the basket, Nan takes hold of Doris' hand in her own cold one. 'You're sure you're not in trouble?'

The wind has picked up again. Doris' ears and nose are numb. 'Like Susan, you mean?'

Nan's eyes widen, and Doris can see that her words have found their mark. And here it is again, the feeling that this scene has been played out before. And it has. Didn't Susan find herself unmarried and pregnant? Call a spade a spade.

Doris yanks her hand out of Nan's. 'Why didn't Mum want to keep me? Why did she give me to you?'

Nan stammers, lost for a moment. 'J-Jim wouldn't have it, that's why. We… we ought to be grateful he married her at all – that's what your grandfather used to say.'

Doris hardens herself. 'Because my real father wouldn't, you mean.'

Nan winces.

'Well?'

'We never met him. He wasn't from round here.'

The skin on the back of Doris' neck tingles. 'Not from…?'

'And then he went and cleared off, didn't he.'

Doris feels dizzy. 'Where to? Where did he go?'

'Hm! Back where he came from, I expect. Susan would never breathe a word about him.'

She stands there, ice-cold, and tries to understand. He may have been from anywhere, then, her father; may not even have been English. And he left her, abandoned her before she'd even arrived in the world.

'Doris?' Nan grabs hold of Doris' arm, as though she were about to fly away. She does want to fly away, just like Harry did, and get away from all this. And she will. She'll escape from these box-like houses, this women's prison of rolled-up sleeves and tied aprons, of pots and chopping boards and potatoes growing eyes in the pantry. She'll remove herself from her family's lies and pain, because if she stays she'll end up bitter like Nan, or sunk into unhappiness like Susan. She'll go anywhere rather than risk becoming that. And how could it possibly turn out any worse?

'You won't do anything stupid, will you, Dot? You won't do anything rash?'

CHAPTER 48
Wicked

Beirut, 1965

She dislodges the spent cigarette from its holder, lets it drop to the ground and grinds it beneath her shoe. Around her feet, the pavement is littered with cigarette butts. A shape moves in the window of the second-floor apartment across the street. In the forty-five minutes she's been standing here, this is the third time she's seen movement, and now that the final cigarette has been smoked, there's no longer any reason to delay.

On a rooftop, laundry flaps like a distress signal as she steps into the road and crosses over, her heels tap-tapping. The tiled lobby of the apartment building is dim and cool. There's an elevator but she takes the stairs. Up, round, up again, and there it is. Beside the doormat stands a potted plant – a rubber plant, she notes, tall as her shoulder, but the soil is bone dry. It's crying out for water, only the water would have to be poured slowly, drop by drop, giving it time to sink in and loosen the parched soil. If she had a watering can…

She almost laughs aloud at the thought.

She reaches into her handbag (cream leather, short handles, a snap clasp) and feels around inside. When she finds it, her hand closes around the gun. The little thing is cool and solid, with a weight to it. A lady's gun, the man in the shop told her. Or did he say pistol? Is there a difference? It was the sort of shop that sells guns for hunting songbirds and such, but in a country like this you can buy anything, and the man had asked no questions. There's no second-guessing Englishwomen, he must have thought, but it was all money to him. Briefly, he'd instructed her in how to use the thing.

How on earth has she ended up here? Throw a lucky man into the sea and he'll come up with a fish in his mouth – that's what they say here. But her luck began and ended before she was born. She closes her eyes. Through the open window on the landing, she can smell the sea. Is she capable of killing a person?

She opens her eyes. Above the doorbell is a strip of paper with a name printed on it. *Pilar Morales*, it says. It's time. Leaving the gun in her bag, Doris presses the doorbell. A moment later she presses it again and holds it down. It sounds like a little scream.

The door opens and she releases the bell. It's her – the woman, Pilar – her face alarmed. She looks at Doris, then at the hand still hovering near the doorbell. It's clear that she doesn't know who Doris is. 'Yes?'

Her eyes are green, and she has a rather flat, wide face with soft features. The corners of the mouth are turned up, suggesting good will, a readiness to give the benefit of the doubt to this stranger who's caused such a disturbance in her apartment. On the walls behind her are colourful paintings, a soft sage-green scarf spilling off a coat stand.

'Can I help you?' Her English has a Spanish accent. She does not, then, speak Arabic.

'Help me?' Doris' mouth twitches. 'It's rather late for that, wouldn't you say?'

The woman blinks.

'My husband. He was *my* husband!' Elbowing the woman out of the way, she goes in.

'What are you doing?'

Doris swings round to face her, and several long moments pass during which neither of them moves.

At last, the woman closes the door. She's turned pale. 'I...' she begins, but then her mouth closes and no more comes out.

Doris takes the measure of her. She has on a simple brown dress, belted at the waist. Her feet are bare, her hair loosely pinned up. In her ears are small gold earrings. She wears no rings, and her face is clean, like those paintings of saints you see in galleries. 'I wanted to see,' she says, 'what sort of woman you were.'

The other shakes her head. 'No, it wasn't like that. We did not mean to— '

'Didn't mean to!' There doesn't seem to be enough space in her lungs for air. 'If it hadn't been for you, he wouldn't have been wandering through the city in the middle of the night. None of this would have happened if it hadn't been for you.' This woman, this weak and spineless thief, has killed him.

'Please.' Both hands rise, patting the air in a conciliatory gesture, and the woman indicates towards a sofa and a couple of armchairs. A tasteful arrangement, Doris acknowledges at the very back of her mind. 'We can sit down. Please.'

Did Leon lie on this sofa with his head in her lap? Did she stroke his hair and allow him to rest, here in this apartment with its bright rugs and underwater quiet? Was this his sanctuary?

'I can make tea,' says the woman uncertainly. 'Or coffee. Or... maybe something to eat.'

Does Doris look as if she needs feeding? Probably. She wants to laugh. Yes of course, this woman is a feeder, a provider of sustenance. She exudes warmth, and men tumble into it like flies into honey. Doris' gaze slides down to the bare feet on the rug. The woman has a groundedness, a connection to her surroundings that Doris will never have. 'Do you have children?' ask Doris.

They're still standing. 'No. No children.'

Ironic. She ought to have, because she's one of *those* women. 'Well, I do,' says Doris.

The Spaniard nods.

'He told you?'

'Yes.'

A deep breath. 'Did he tell you about me?'

The woman walks around Doris, warily, like a lion tamer. 'Yes.'

Through one of the windows, Doris sees the straight line of the sea, a darker blue than the sky. It's hard to get the words out: 'What did he say about me?'

The woman's eyes flick to Doris' face. She speaks slowly, each word balancing on its own weight. 'He told me how glamorous you are. How stylish.'

Is this appeasement? She can't tell. God only knows what Leon really said about her. Perhaps, together, they laughed at Doris. Well, she thinks, it's easily solved.

She opens her handbag, takes out the gun and points it at the Spaniard. It wobbles a little. The handbag drops to the floor, both hands being needed for this job.

The Spaniard yelps. Her eyes widen and remain wide open. Doris can see her breathing now, the rise and fall of her chest.

'What are you doing?'

The pistol quivers as though it's not small but rather a heavy object. 'What does it look like?'

How has she ended up here? From Birmingham to Baghdad, and now Beirut. This is where her life has steered her: here to this apartment, this moment. She recalls a school experiment Harry once told her about: chemicals dripped into each other, and then… froth, smoke, bang!

During the warm sleepless hours of the night, she's gone over and over this scene. How she'll get this woman – this woman who all but killed Leon – to take off her clothes, every last stitch. She'll watch her fumble with the zip, unlatch buttons, shuffle the dress over her fat behind or hoist it up past her chest and over her head. If she resists, Doris will wave the gun a little, like using a crop to encourage a horse. The underwear will come off too, oh yes, so that by the end this woman will be standing here stark naked. Doris will sneer at the dense thighs, the flabby belly and hanging breasts, then, with another wave of the gun, she'll make her turn around to show off her mottled buttocks and rounded shoulders.

She's considered the next part too. How the woman will tremble and shake with terror. The tiny movement of the gun's barrel as she aims it.

The bullet shall hit the Spaniard clean in the chest. Her eyes will fly open in surprise, and in pain. Blood will spurt out and spill over her breasts and stomach. Then, with a groan, she'll crumple onto the floor, or perhaps crash down across the sofa, and lie there staining the upholstery.

And that'll be that. The end of Pilar Morales.

For some unknown reason she thinks of Dolores' young body laid out on the door in the front room of The Back of Beyond. She thinks of Awd Goggie, and how her wickedness has now reached its peak.

Her arm jerks. Then it sags and falls to her side. The little gun-or-perhaps-pistol slips to the floor, landing with a soft sound on the rug. The woman lets out an exclamation in Spanish. She's still standing there, fully clothed and alive. Through the rectangle of window, the sea's still there too, and the Beirut skyline.

The Spaniard closes her eyes, her lips moving in what might be a prayer. When she opens them again she's calmer. 'What do you want?'

The question catches Doris by surprise. A minute ago she'd wanted to hurt this woman, to debase her, both in retribution and in order to feel better.

The woman asks it again, more gently: 'What do you want?'

But Doris doesn't know the answer. What is there left to want? A lump rises in her throat. 'Why did he leave in the middle of the night?'

The Spaniard shakes her head. 'I don't know. I have thought about this, but I don't know. I was asleep.'

'He was on his way back to our apartment.'

'Yes. Perhaps.'

'He was on his way back to me.'

The woman says nothing. How can she confirm or deny

what happened in the middle of the night when she was fast asleep? The truth is, neither of them will ever know.

Laughter unravels inside Doris. It spirals upwards and outwards, grows stronger and louder.

The shock on the Spaniard's face turns to bafflement, then to pity. She pads over and wraps her arms around Doris. And Doris sobs in the woman's arms. Because in the seconds it took the Spaniard to walk those three steps, Doris' laughter became tears.

Pilar's shoulder is soft and her embrace solid. Making little noises, she moves her hands back and forth over Doris' back. And the motion, the sounds, the solidity make Doris wish that it had been Pilar who'd brought up Graham and Lynette, and not her.

They move to the sofa and sit in silence. Time passes. Minutes, hours perhaps. When Doris was a little girl, young as spawn, she once stood beneath the plum tree in the garden of number 45 and, with her head tilted back, started to spin. It had been raining, and a hundred tiny suns sparkled among the wet leaves. With her skirt lifting up, she spun faster and faster, weaving the little suns into cobwebby circles. Beyond her fingertips, the house and garden blurred like a painting wiped over with a cloth, and her body and mind unhitched themselves from gravity until the only thing left was her breath. This is what it feels like again now.

In a low voice, Pilar begins to speak of Leon. Perhaps it's only because she's stuck for something to say, but she starts to tell Doris about her husband, as though relating the life of a man neither of them had ever met. He was born in Baghdad in nineteen fourteen, she begins, and goes on from there, walking through his life. When she reaches that part of it, she says 'And then he met you.'

Pilar holds up her hand. 'The first time he saw you, you were trying to hide a hole in your glove.' Her fingers curl into her palm.

The hole in her glove; Doris remembers it now. In spite

of her efforts, Leon had noticed it. But far from putting him off, it had endeared her to him. Something in the core of her aches. He hadn't wanted a perfect, glamorous woman at all, but someone with vulnerabilities. If only she'd realised.

'You were beautiful, that's what he said. Beautiful and young. Like a little girl dressed for a party.'

A dusting of face powder. Lipstick. Scent. A new hat. How young she'd been. 'I was someone else then. So was he.' The coronation parade for a new king. 'But then everything changed.' The same king years afterwards, weighed down by war and worry, suffocated by lungs that could no longer breathe and veins that could no longer carry blood around his body.

She had pointed up the road towards the place where a Punch and Judy show was going to play out, and that road had brought them both here, to this woman's flat. Was it all fated to end this way? How far, Doris wonders, would she have to go back to identify where her life was first set on its track? The images come to her in bits and pieces: Graham's red, outraged face when he was born; Leon standing on the verandah of their first house, a constellation cupped in his hands; Nan finally letting out the truth, tomatoes tumbling across the table.

But by that point her life was already hurtling full throttle towards its destination, so she must go even further back – to Susan disowning her, to Susan falling pregnant. Was Doris' life already scuppered at the moment of her conception? Perhaps. So then the shape of Nan's life must be taken into account, and that of Nan's mother, and so on and on. She sees it now, how a brokenness has been handed down from mother to daughter for generations, passed on like a poisonous gift. That is the secret that Awd Goggie, concealed in dark foliage, has always known.

And now she's here in Beirut, on this woman's sofa. Pilar is kind, that's the thing. Here Leon must have felt seen and heard again. Could breathe again. In these surroundings, he must have confronted his failure to see the person Doris really was, and his failure to stand up for his children. The entire thing, he probably concluded, had been well and truly bungled.

'Your name is Pilar, isn't it?'

The woman nods. 'And you are Dolores.'

Dolores. So Leon didn't tell her quite everything.

'It means pain,' says Pilar.

'What does?'

'Your name. In Spanish it means pain. *El dolor*. And *dolores* – that means many pains.'

It's dark outside.

'Where will you go?' asks Pilar. 'Will you go back home, to England?'

But home, Doris has come to understand, is not a tangible place. Leon and the children used to lie on the roof watching stars, yet among the entire scatter of cold rocks flung across space, this is the only living planet, a delicate bubble of blue and green that might pop at any moment. And there is no single place on it that she can call home.

She shifts, preparing to get up.

'What will you do?' asks Pilar.

'Do?' If only she could remain in this moment and never budge. But such things aren't possible. This afternoon has been nothing but a lull, a respite, a hiatus.

If you take a right at the end of Al-Rashid Street, the road narrows. Here, in the coolest part of the day, you'll see families strolling or setting up picnics by the river. Get on a boat downstream, though, and you can find somewhere quieter: groves of palms, orchards, birdsong. But that way of life doesn't exist any longer.

Still, she has a choice. She can go and live in her house by the Thames with all her fine things ranged in it – brass ornaments, enamelled plates, Persian rugs, a baby grand piano for heaven's sake – things she hasn't the slightest use for. There she'll sit and watch the garden slump into winter and reawaken in spring. She'll grow old the way others do, with knobbly hands and feet, and dine on toast and tinned sardines, their little parcels of flesh filled with tiny bones.

Or she can remain here in Beirut, accepting Lynette's entanglement, and see what comes. She could stop smoking and wearing green eyeshadow and speaking her mind. She could muster up the courage to tell her children she loves them. She could take up yoga and learn French (easy to do here in a francophone country), and somehow manage to grow young again.

She has a choice – doesn't she? – and she will decide. But not today. Not yet.

She struggles to her feet. She is no longer Leon's wife. She's not his anything. Right now she's nobody's anything. Nobody's bastard child or unwanted baby, nobody's daughter or granddaughter or niece, nobody's sister or mother, nobody's duty or responsibility. Nobody's cross to bear.

'Dolores? What will you do?'

Spring will come, she knows that. It'll start the way it always does, as a pulsing throb deep beneath the earth. Then one morning, out of nowhere, a green haze will have appeared on the trees; and after that it'll be everywhere, green things pushing out of the allotment soil in a way that never ceases to astonish her. But today spring is an impossibility.

Snow has fallen all night, settling flake on flake, layer on layer, and today the world's a new place, sparkling and glinting in white. Not a single hard edge is left, only soft curves and piles of feathery snow. Imperfections have been covered over, all mistakes made good. Doris' skin is tingling cold, her breath clouding out of her mouth like smoke, and every fibre of her is utterly alive. And there he is – Leon, waving and coming towards her. He's smiling. Her Leon. His lips and particular arrangement of teeth. His warm hands. The way he walks, and the timbre of his voice. The air is thin and bright and wonderful, carrying the call and laughter of children. Carrying love towards her. Heart aflutter, she smiles and waves, and sets off towards him. A white new world has been created just for them, and everything is possible.

Acknowledgements

My deep thanks to Anna Owen and Katherine Davey for their unwavering support and faith, and to Sam Owen for hospitality and gentle encouragement from the sidelines. I'd also like to thank the Royal Literary Fund for supporting writers, myself among them. To my editor, Ross Dickinson, for his insightful reading, excellent suggestions, tact and enthusiasm, and the rest of the brilliant team at the Book Social, thanks are hardly enough.

Among the books I consulted as part of my research, the following were particularly helpful: *Baghdad: City of Peace, City of Blood* by Justin Marozzi (Penguin Books, 2014), and the memoirs *Once Upon a Time in Baghdad: The Two Golden Decades, the 1940s and 1950s* by Margo Kirtikar (Xlibris, 2011), and *Memories of Eden: A Journey Through Jewish Baghdad* by Violette Shamash (Forum Books, 2008). Any factual errors are entirely my own. I'm also indebted to David Davidson for information about the postal service between the UK and Iraq in the 1940s. And last but not least, Matt, Bronnie and Alice, thank you.